# LIMULUS

by
PAUL J. CUCCOLO

PublishAmerica
Baltimore

© 2005 by Paul Cuccolo.

All rights reserved. No part of this book may be reproduced, stored in a retrieval system or transmitted in any form or by any means without the prior written permission of the publishers, except by a reviewer who may quote brief passages in a review to be printed in a newspaper, magazine or journal.

First printing

At the specific preference of the author, PublishAmerica allowed this work to remain exactly as the author intended, verbatim, without editorial input.

ISBN: 1-4137-7464-4
PUBLISHED BY PUBLISHAMERICA, LLLP
www.publishamerica.com
Baltimore

Printed in the United States of America

*This book is dedicated to Christopher, Trevor, Morgan, Jackson, and Sophia, with the full measure of a grandfather's love.*

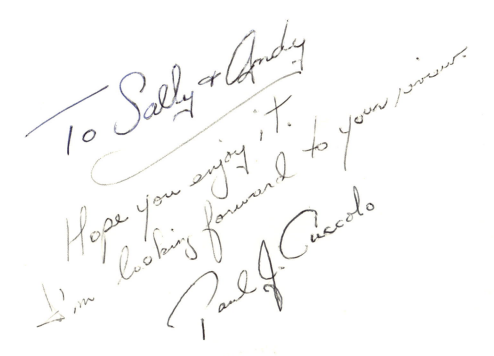

## ACKNOWLEDGMENTS

This book could not have been completed or published without the ccouragement, support and technical assistance of family and friends.

I am especially grateful to my son-in-law, Nathan Blattau, and my cousin, Tim Cuccolo, for their creative and technical expertise, which they unerringly and happily provided, often under the most pressing of circumstances.

For their inspiration and encouragement I thank my very dear friends, Connie Wychulis, Marcy Holteen and Sharon Rushton.

And to my wife, Barbara, whose patience, loyalty and devotion lifted my spirit in the darkest hours, I give my eternal love.

# CHAPTER 1

Frank Costa leaned hard against the weathered oaken door and pushed his way into the outer foyer, a small but welcome haven from the snow and biting winds he had fought from the supermarket to his apartment on Avenue C in Brooklyn. He shook and stomped the snow from his clothing and boots before opening a second door and stepping into a hallway filled with distant music and a medley of culinary aromas. He stood for a moment, catching his breath, luxuriating in the comforting warmth of steam heat hissing from archaically scrolled radiators. The tune was faint but undeniably Count Basie's "A Train." He searched for clues to the food, inhaling deeply, smiling as he matched scents with the favored dishes of his neighbors.

*Joe's having liver with onions and mushrooms and Mattie's cooking a gumbo. John will stuff himself and be up all night. He'll never learn.*

As he made his way to the second floor, he wondered how often he had climbed the warped, creaking stairs, noting how they had seemed to multiply and grow steeper over time. More than forty years had passed since the day he moved into the two-story, eight-unit brownstone in Brooklyn's Canarsie section, then home to a mix of Jewish and Italian families. In time they had all moved out, or died, as his wife had many years before, leaving him the token white.

He was friendly with all the residents and their children and he moved comfortably among them. There had been some incidents in the past, but none too serious, and he hadn't been exposed to anything his neighbors hadn't endured as well. It was just the way things were in the big city, so he accepted occasional episodes as part of life, exactly as everyone else seemed to. Besides, there were terrorists to worry about now.

At the top of the stairs he paused to chat with Mattie Turner, the bubbly long time resident and housewife who never missed an opportunity to spread neighborly cheer.

"Why, Frank," she cried, "I'm so happy to see you. How are you? Isn't this weather just terrible?" she rattled on. "I was just making my way over to Louella's to talk to her about the fund-raiser at church. You'll be coming, of course. Those poor people need every cent they can get."

"Wouldn't miss it for the world, Mattie, and if I can help setting things up or tending a booth, you just let me know."

"Well thank you, Frank, I know I can always count on you, but I do want you to take it easy this year. I'm worried about you. You're not getting any younger and you just push yourself too much. We'll have some of your boys there to lend a hand and you just let them do the heavy work, you hear?"

Frank Costa knew better than to argue with Mattie Turner, so he simply smiled, nodded his head and wished her a good evening.

Her laughing voice followed him around the corner to the door of the left-front apartment. He shifted the bags of groceries, cradling them in his left arm, while his right hand explored the pocket of a well-worn jacket. He flipped a dozen or so keys until his fingers pinched the right one. Even before the door was fully open he felt the rush of cold air from across the room and scolded himself for leaving the window cracked.

Once inside, he turned to close the door and caught the movement of something dark, maybe a shadow, from the corner of his eye. He thought to focus on it but a sudden shock invaded his body, sending waves of chilling energy from his skull to the very tips of his fingers and toes. For just the briefest second he wondered what was happening.

Lieutenant Albert Wilson gazed through frosted windows as wintry gusts battered the aging glass. Two stories below, street lamps and the lights of an occasional car illuminated hunched and faceless forms gingerly sliding across crystal-covered sidewalks. The chaotic stereo of urban life that was Manhattan's Thirty-Fourth Street had given way to the muted tones of a winter's eve. Wilson stared at it aimlessly, his mind occupied by more pressing thoughts.

The newsstands that sentineled each corner were boarded and none of the usual vendors hawking food or clothing could be found. New York City was in the third day of its worst winter storm in a decade, and though the effort had been applauded, most observers agreed that the Department of Sanitation had lost the battle. Plows and bucket loaders kept the main avenues open but most side streets had been cleaned too infrequently to prevent accumulation on all but a few. Only the relentless trudging of diehard commuters kept the snow from piling on the sidewalks. In its place were treacherous planks of ice that pedestrians found unnavigable, preferring to brave the terror of slush-filled streets. Those who could afford to stay home did so, leaving Manhattan a lifeless shadow of its normally tumultuous self.

But Wilson and every other New Yorker knew that more than the storm had emptied the city. The bombings of the Holland Tunnel and a mid-town subway, coupled with the release of an unknown, highly lethal bacterium in a crowded Radio City Music Hall had raised the stakes in an increasingly deadly game, the outcome of which was at best uncertain. Questions about the identity and location of the terrorists, where they would strike next, or how they could be stopped went unanswered. While the public remained convinced that al Quaida was behind it and that there was more to come, federal and city officials preached life as usual. Even those who bought into it did so cautiously.

The police force tried to stay focused, dealing with the usual spate of violent crimes, for while the attention of most was centered squarely on the terrorists, the criminal element assumed the advantage, going about their business with cool efficiency. Catching bin Laden's disciples was the feds' job, but it seemed no more daunting than what the NYPD faced.

"Damn, how I'd like to be home right now," Wilson mumbled to himself, turning from the window and refocusing on the scattered paperwork cluttering his desk.

He had chosen to stay in the city when the storm was announced rather than risk the drive to his home in White Plains, a one-hour excursion even in the best of weather. Common sense and dedication to duty made the decision easier, for it was a matter of record that Al Wilson had never missed a day of work during his twenty-four years of service. Duty, whether to his family, friends, or station was a matter of principle to which he made no concession.

Orphaned at ten and raised by grandparents, Albert Wilson was in every respect a self-made man. Awarded a football scholarship to college, he studied hard, achieved better than average grades and still managed to work enough hours to buy his own clothes and provide his own spending money.

After graduating, he returned to Brooklyn with a degree in Social Studies, maturity beyond his years and a self-assurance that hard work in whatever field he chose would be rewarded.

The father of a neighborhood friend had encouraged him to consider a career with the police force, but it was the pride in his grandparents' eyes that sealed the decision, and Albert Wilson became one of New York City's finest.

Following a three-year courtship, he married Camille Slaton, sister of a fellow officer and secretary to the Principal of a high school in the Bronx. Three children, two boys and a girl, followed in the next five years, and despite the pressures of the job, the uncertainty of the future and the routine tribulations of raising teenagers, Albert Wilson had to be satisfied with what he had accomplished.

He smiled as he pictured his family seated around the dining room table, devouring the pork roast Camille had promised. Surely she remembered the applesauce. Pork roast was nothing without her cinnamon flavored homemade applesauce, and no feast was complete without hot gravy, homemade biscuits, salad, mashed potatoes and a vegetable or two. He indulged himself with visions of asparagus smothered in melted cheese, carrot spears generously coated with brown sugar and molasses, and his all-time favorite, green bean casserole with onions and mushrooms awash in a cream sauce. Albert Wilson's appetite was as endless as the love for his family. Aside from work and an occasional sporting event, thoughts such as these occupied his mind and he freely admitted that life's other distractions held little interest for him.

He was interrupted by a knock on the door.

His administrative aid, Emilio Fernandez, a portly twenty-year veteran, entered and placed two neatly tied packets, each three or more inches thick on his boss's desk.

"Here you are, Lieutenant," he sighed with relief. "On top you got all the precincts' stats; on the bottom you got the forms for the annual evaluations. Anything else you need before I leave?"

"No, I don't think so, and uh, thanks Emilio. I know this is a pain in the ass. Couldn't do my job without you. I mean it." Wilson looked up from the stacks, smiled and gave a reassuring nod. Fernandez stiffened with pride, said good night and left.

Wilson glanced at the paperwork, shook his head in resignation and stood to stretch his arms and arch his back. His weight had gradually crept over two-fifty, surpassing that of his beefiest college days, and even on a six-foot, three-inch frame, the disproportion on his hips and stomach had begun to stress his back, which ached in varying degrees from morning to night. A solid exercise program and sensible diet were in order and he knew it, but a rigorous work schedule had provided the excuse to avoid both. His eating habits were suicidal...six or more cups of coffee every morning to wash down half as many deep-fried doughnuts...thick, spicy deli sandwiches for lunch…and six or more hours later, a sumptuous feast at home, just before retiring.

*Someday I'm going to have to do something about it,* he concluded, as he did after every reflection.

He circled the desk and pulled the black leather overcoat from the corner tree, a 40th birthday present from Camille. Four years of hard wear and the coat was still as good as new, testament to the tailor's skill and the endurance of good English leather, for its owner gave it neither special treatment nor respite from rain and cold. From early October through late March, the only certainty in the Police Headquarters on Manhattan's 34th Street was that a knee length black leather coat would arrive by 8:00 AM, warmly concealing the expanding form of Lieutenant Albert Wilson.

He threw on the coat and a woolen watch cap, nestled the paperwork beneath his arm and headed out through the squad room, nodding as he did to four of the second shift detectives sitting at their desks typing reports and phoning for leads.

At the head of the stairs two bundled detectives emerged from the men's room, appearing none too happy that they would shortly abandon their cozy quarters for something close to a wind-chill factor of minus twenty. Wilson figured nothing less than a major felony would drag them outside on a night like this.

"What's up?" he asked.

"We got a call on another mugging over on Canal near Third. Sounds like the same pair that hit the last two nights. This time it got out of hand…a coupla' shots…a DOA."

Ben Zimmerman and Carmine Pecora were two of the older, more experienced detectives in his command. Zimmerman was about five-eight, didn't weigh more than one-fifty and was an exercise fanatic. His partner was tall, and like his boss, had trouble keeping his weight under two-fifty, though his taste for expensively styled, well-tailored suits masked his obesity well.

Wilson wished them good luck and headed to the bottom of the stairs where he took a minute to talk to Patrolman Matt Flannery, a ruddy-faced, native New Yorker, with whom he had attended the Academy. For reasons known only to the stocky Irishman, he had never sought promotion, though Wilson and a score of other senior officers had tried to convince him that he could serve the City and the Department more productively by leading and teaching, encouraging him to take the sergeant's test, which he doggedly refused.

"I'm satisfied with the way things are now. I still have my parents. I'm home with them every night. And with the world like it is, I'm not sure they'd feel very safe without me. Besides, a lot of other guys want it more and would probably do a better job," he had told them repeatedly.

Maybe he was right. He had enough money and nobody needed the headaches of supervision at any level. More importantly, there were too few experienced cops patrolling the streets, and they were needed a lot more there than behind some desks shuffling papers.

They reminded each other to drive carefully and gave the traditional "thumbs up" before Wilson made his way through the crowded lobby to the exit foyer.

As he pulled open the heavy outer door, he tucked his chin, pulled the packets closer to his chest, leaned into the elements and headed up the street and around the corner to the parking garage. His black unmarked LeSabre, standard issue for senior supervisors, sat in its assigned space. He hit the button on the keychain, unlocking the doors. Deftly maneuvering the packets, he opened the back door and deposited them side-by-side on the seat. He started the engine, buckled himself in, checked all the mirrors and waited for the car to warm up. It would take an hour and a half to make the trip and it was already 7:30. He hadn't been home for three days and he was famished, unable to resist obsessing over the treats he was certain his wife had prepared especially for him. But a devilish smile made its way across his broad, still handsome face as he debated about which he would have first, Camille or the pork roast.

# CHAPTER 2

The ride home was long and tiring, but thankfully, uneventful. Every driver seemed too cautious or too reckless, testing his patience, draining his energy. By the time the car pulled to a stop at the top of the driveway, Wilson's head and back both ached. The only thing he wanted now was the roast dinner, to be followed by a relaxing soak in a steaming bath and a long winter's nap. Intimacy would have to wait.

As he had hoped, the meal was something special, particularly the stuffed mushrooms parmesan from a recipe in an Italian cookbook, a gift from Frank Costa. In it Camille had also discovered stuffed eggplant and sautéed calamari, delicacies she promised to prepare that weekend.

The bath did wonders for his headache but little to disguise the pain in his lower back. So without a hint of regret, he kissed his wife goodnight and drifted off to a much needed, well deserved sleep.

He awoke to a tug at his shoulder. "Al, come on, wake up. It's Larry Kennedy. He has to speak to you," Camille said, barely disguising the concern in her voice.

Wilson fought through a stupor, forcing his eyes open as he rolled left towards his wife. With his vision only reluctantly coming into focus he abandoned an effort to read the nightstand clock.

"What time is it?"

"Five-thirty. Now here, take the phone."

He fumbled it, finally managing to position the receiver on his ear. Closing his eyes and settling his head back on the pillow, he yawned.

"Larry, this better be damned important."

"I'm afraid it is. I got some bad news, Al."

Sergeant Larry Kennedy, a twenty-six year veteran of the force, was Wilson's senior detective on the third shift.

"Frank Costa was murdered. I got a call from Bobby Avent over in Brooklyn. It happened late last evening or early this morning." Hesitating, he added, "He was beaten to death, Al."

Wilson's eyes closed tightly. Camille watched her husband take a deep breath. She resisted the urge to ask why.

"Did they tell you anything else?"

"No, but Bobby said to give him a call. He seemed...I don't know...reluctant to talk to me. Maybe he was just busy. I'm probably paranoid when it comes to him."

There had been a time when the two had clashed over disciplinary action Kennedy had meted out to a uniformed black officer who had appealed it through the Black Officers Association of which Avent was a representative. Though more than five years had passed, the comments and accusations each had directed at the other left scars that would not easily heal.

"Okay, Larry, I'll call him. Does Dan know?"

"No, I don't think so. Avent hasn't filed the report yet and I've only called you."

"Alright. Don't try to contact Dan. It's my job to tell him. And if you haven't told anyone except me, keep it that way until I talk to you."

"Okay, Skipper. I'll wait for your call."

He handed his wife the phone, shut his eyes and took a deep breath.

"Dan Costa's father was murdered."

"Oh no, Al," she said, while recalling images of generous deeds and selfless devotion for which Frank Costa was famous.

Wilson sat on the edge of the bed and dialed Avent's number at the Brooklyn precinct.

"It's Al, Bobby."

"It's not a good day, big guy."

"No, it sure ain't. What can you tell me?"

"We got a call around three this morning from one of Mr. Costa's neighbors, an Arthur Turner, who was returning home from work when he noticed that the old man's door was open. He went in and found him lying in a pool of blood. He called it in right away and then sat down to wait for us. Two uniforms got there just before Joe DeLorenzo and Calvin Washington. They're the ones that called me."

"I don't guess there's anything you've learned that's going to make this easy, is there?" Wilson asked.

"No, in fact I was just headed there when you called. My shift's over but

I think I'll stay on it. I'll call you as soon as I get some background. You going into the office?"

"It was going to be a day off," he replied, adding, "but I think I might take a ride out there. Do you mind?"

"Hell no, man, you know you're welcome anytime. And I'll take all the help I can get, 'cause if Joe D. is right, some kids did this. The place was torn up a little and quite a few things are missing according to the friend that called it in. It all sounds like two, three young guys…druggies…maybe a street gang, the kind that are hard to crack."

Canarsie in Brooklyn had become a difficult precinct in which to solve felonies. Gangs committed much of the crime, and since so many of the teenage boys belonged to gangs, the suspect list could be impossibly long. On top of that, some neighborhoods in Canarsie and the police who were charged with protecting them had become alienated amidst counter charges of indifference, bigotry and lack of cooperation. Barely one in three felonies resulted in arrest and only half of those in conviction. To successfully investigate and prosecute without witnesses was difficult at best, and all too frequently in places like Canarsie, witnesses were harder to find than criminals.

While her husband shaved, Camille Slaton scrambled a couple of eggs with bacon, brewed coffee and buttered some toast for him before returning to bed. He was already dressed.

"I'll probably be home late this afternoon unless I can help bring this to a quick close. I might as well stop by the office. No point in using up a vacation day."

Camille offered a weak smile. "He really was a good man, Al. Why does it always seem to happen to the good ones?"

"Because there's more of them, Honey. The bad guys get it too, sooner or later."

He bent over and kissed her on the forehead. "Love ya'."

He walked out with his wife's eyes trailing him admiringly. "Please drive carefully, Al. I'm starting to get used to you."

An hour and a half later Wilson pulled the Buick up alongside a Brooklyn blue and white at 1420 Avenue C in Canarsie. Two uniformed officers stood at the bottom of the stoop dissuading a hoard of curious neighbors. He approached them, flashing his gold shield.

"Al Wilson, Manhattan Homicide."

"Second floor front, Lieutenant."

Wilson climbed the worn brownstone steps to the large double doors. He wiped his feet on the foyer mat before entering the inner hall. The old wooden stairs creaked beneath his weight. As he reached the top, he saw two uniformed officers, Bobby Avent and an attractive, well-dressed young woman gathered in the hallway.

Avent saw him and motioned him forward.

"Sorry for your loss, Al. I know you were close to him."

"It's a big loss for a lot of people, Bobby," he said softly. "The old man was a friend to anybody that needed one. He was good and kind, and there aren't a whole hell of a lot like him to go around." There was no mistaking the respect in his voice.

"What have you got?"

"This is Marilyn Kyme," Avent replied. "She's with the Coroner's office. Marilyn, this is Lieutenant Wilson from Manhattan, a friend of the victim's."

A stunning woman in her late twenties with long, raven hair parted in the middle looked up at Wilson through what he thought were the prettiest green eyes he had ever seen. He was aware that he was staring at her, but her eyes captivated him.

"The Lieutenant and I have spoken before…on the phone" she added, redirecting his attention and prompting a smile, though he couldn't recall ever having spoken to her.

"It appears the victim died from at least two blows to the top and back of his head," she stated matter-of-factly. "He's been dead for a while, twelve hours or so I would think. I'll know for sure when I get him back to the lab."

"Are you going to have to do a full autopsy?" Wilson asked.

"If you want to know all the details…which blow killed him, the direction it came from, how many objects?"

"I know his son. He'll probably want a Catholic burial, a viewing…all that."

"I won't open the skull unless I have to, or unless Fiore orders it."

Wilson knew Chief Pathologist Dante Fiore well and had done him some favors in the past. He would call him later.

He excused himself and entered the apartment. Frank Costa's body, partially covered with a white sheet, lay on a gurney, the top and back of his head covered with blood, his still thick, gray hair barely discernible in the reddened mass. A pool of dry blood was on the carpeted floor to the right, just three feet or so from the door. Al Wilson swallowed hard as he looked at the contorted muscles in his friend's face, reflecting the trauma of death's moment. He reached down, touched the old man's hands gently and pulled the sheet up over his face.

He looked about the small parlor, recalling his visits, regretting that he had not done so more often. Dan Costa and he had been in Brooklyn back in October for an inter-borough conference and had stopped in for a glass of wine at the end of the day. Some of Frank Costa's friends on Staten Island still pressed grapes and made wine of a quality comparable to most commercial labels. Mr. Costa had been given enough to offer Al a bottle. He was that way with everything…his time, his money, whatever possessions he had…he shared them all and he had done so all his life.

When his wife died, Frank Costa kept his job as a motor transit repairman, but poured all his energy into organizations and activities for kids. He started Saint Anthony's Boxing Club under the auspices of the P.A.L., coached basketball at the C.Y.O. and the local Y.M.C.A., and upon retiring, dedicated another twenty hours a week to raising money for the Fresh Air Fund for underprivileged city kids. No one did more; not the bureaucrats who got paid to run the programs, not the black activists, not even the minority charities.

Wilson studied a photograph displayed alongside an inexpensive print of the Holy Family. The picture had been taken twelve years earlier at Quantico, Virginia, just about a year before Rose Costa lost a long and painful battle with cancer. The strikingly handsome, newly commissioned Lieutenant in the United States Marine Corp stood between his parents whose pride beamed from the aging black and white.

*Please, God, welcome home Frank Costa. He's earned it.*

Wilson entered the kitchen, drawn by aromas reflecting the victim's Italian heritage. He nodded to a forensics officer dusting for prints.

From under the wall-mounted cabinets a string of garlic cloves dangled alongside a three-pound ball of wax-coated provolone. Boxes of spaghetti, cans of tomato sauce and assorted spice containers overflowed the shelves of a makeshift pantry that had once housed a water heater. More religious pictures and family photos gave the room a warm, comfortable air. Only some dishes scattered on a counter-top that the killers had displaced during their search for cash appeared out of place.

He walked to the two small bedrooms and bath in the rear where open drawers and strewn clothing were drawing the interest of another forensics tech. A shelf mounted plaster copy of the "Pieta" and a crucifix surveyed Mr. Costa's room from a wall above the bed. The smaller room, the one that had been his son's, housed records and memorabilia too numerous to display. These lay scattered and broken.

The absence of any blood outside the parlor suggested the murder had taken place there and that none of the assailants had been injured, if in fact more than one had been involved.

"Al, unless you want to take another look, I'm going to have the body removed," Avent called out from the parlor.

"It's your case, Bobby. I would be interested in hearing about your findings, Marilyn. Here's my card. You're not obligated to call, of course, but I would be very grateful."

"No problem, Lieutenant, I'll be happy to let you know whatever we find. I'll just advise Dr. Fiore if you don't mind. I'm sure he'll give it his okay."

Wilson smiled. "Thank you, and say hello to Dante for me. By the way, you didn't happen to notice any other marks on the body, did you? Any sign of a struggle?"

"No, but my examination was cursory. There certainly weren't any other injuries of significance, no torn clothing, nothing obvious under the fingernails. But we'll know better when we're able to examine the body in detail."

Kyme turned to a uniformed officer and an ambulance driver, whispered a few instructions and left

Shortly afterward, a second man dressed in whites arrived to help his partner roll the gurney out the door and down the stairs. Al Wilson watched from the parlor window as they loaded the body into the Coroner's wagon. Thirty or more people of assorted age and race, some leaning on each other, fighting back tears, gathered on the sidewalk.

"I want whoever did this, Bobby. I want them as much as I've ever wanted any perps." He turned to face Avent. "If there's anything I can do, you call me...anytime. Okay?"

Avent nodded, but he was relieved that Wilson had no official jurisdiction in the case. As much as he admired and respected him, Avent coveted the independence his own supervisor permitted him. At this point his ego couldn't handle a more demanding superior. Despite what he had told Wilson on the phone earlier, he intended to direct the investigation as he saw fit and without unwarranted meddling from higher up, much less from an official from a different borough. They were still facing each other when two plain-clothes detectives entered from the outer hall. Wilson recognized the young white officer as Joe DeLorenzo, whom he had seen with Dan Costa and their dates at a few social functions. He recalled that the two had been neighborhood chums, high school buddies, and had even gone through the Police Academy together. DeLorenzo's reputation was one of an intelligent, skilled detective, well known and highly respected. Only Costa, the youngest Detective Sergeant in the history of the Department, had been promoted faster.

The older black detective with him was Calvin Washington, a twenty year veteran with whom Wilson had briefly served during his uniformed days. By reputation Washington was a quiet, dedicated officer who followed orders and the manual to a tee. Some mistook his reticence for indifference or occasional ineptitude, an opinion to which both Avent and DeLorenzo took strong objection. Avent was admittedly protective of black officers' reputations, but in Washington's case, his support was totally justified and more than seconded by DeLorenzo, his partner for the last four years.

Both detectives approached Wilson and shook his hand.

"Sorry we have to meet again on an occasion like this," Washington said.

"It's been a few years, hasn't it?" Turning to DeLorenzo, Wilson said, "I'm aware of how close you were, Sergeant, and I'm sorry for your loss."

The young detective had a tired look on his face. He acknowledged the condolence with a slight nod and turned towards Avent.

"So far we have very little, Lieutenant. A second floor neighbor, a Mrs. Turner, spoke to the deceased a little before 5:00 PM yesterday as he returned home with some groceries. She says on Thursdays he spent the morning and most of the afternoon and evening at St. Anthony's, cleaning the church, coaching basketball and boxing, before coming home to eat. Then he would go back around 6:30. Calvin called St. Anthony's. Mr. Costa left there a little after four but never returned. The priest in charge, Father Boland, says he called here last night at nine and again at eleven but got no answer. He said he thought it was odd and was getting ready to call again when Calvin rang."

"Funny he didn't try to call earlier this morning," Avent commented.

"Morning masses," the sergeant reminded him.

Avent nodded.

DeLorenzo continued, flipping the white lined pages of a pocket size notepad.

"A Miz Louella Melvin lives in the opposite side front apartment. She claims there was a lot of noise in the apartment around midnight, but the guy on the first floor directly beneath the deceased claims he was up with stomach problems until after 2:00 AM and he's sure he didn't hear anything." He paused briefly before adding, "Calvin and I think Miz Melvin may be a bit senile. We kind of discount her story."

"Unless the guy on the first floor is involved," Al Wilson interjected.

Joe DeLorenzo shook his head. "Mr. Costa told me a couple of times how fond he was of Mr. Gadsden and that they were good company for each other. Mr. Gadsden was one of his best friends. Besides, he's seventy if he's a day. The m.o. sure seems like a B&E gone sour; you know, some druggies looking for cash."

Satisfied, Avent motioned to him to continue.

"Mr. Arthur Turner was returning home at 2:45 AM from his job with an office cleaning service in the city when he noticed the door to Mr. Costa's apartment was slightly open. Turner lives with his wife and son in the apartment to the opposite rear of Mr. Costa's. He claims that he pushed the door open and saw the head of the deceased lying in a pool of blood. He says he went immediately to his apartment and called 911. The timing jives with dispatch records."

"How do you make this Turner guy?" Avent asked.

The sergeant deferred to Washington.

He started slowly, deliberately. "I don't make him for the crime, certainly not the homicide, but I kind of get this feeling that he's uneasy over more than just the murder of someone living in his apartment building. He didn't look us in the eye the way everyone else did. I mean, he was really sad, but at the same time deep in thought, if you know what I mean?"

He was about to elaborate when his partner interrupted. "I'm not a psychologist, but Turner's demeanor was definitely different from the other neighbors. Like Calvin says, there's something on his mind and we intend to dig deeper, but we wanted to get to everyone who lives here as quick as possible, so we didn't spend as much time with him as we intend to."

Both senior officers seemed satisfied and no one spoke for half a minute or so as they glanced at each other and around the room.

"Who lives in the other apartments in this building?" Avent finally asked.

DeLorenzo flipped a page. "First floor on the other side is a single, middle-aged woman, a Miz...." and he hesitated as he searched his notes. "Ah, here it is, a Miz Feathers, Tonee Feathers." His partner smiled broadly.

Avent wasn't amused. "You got something you want to tell us, Calvin?"

Washington suppressed most of the grin. "Miz Feathers is an exotic dancer, or so she claims. She's all woman, maybe forty, no more. Good lookin' too. Whether she dances upright or in the horizontal might be up for debate, but she's no killer. Besides, she and a man returned to her apartment this morning after the murder was called in and just after Joe and I arrived."

"What else," Avent asked, dismissing suspicions about the plentiful Miz Feathers.

"Downstairs, besides Gadsden and Feathers, there's a couple in their late sixties, John and Mavis Clevens, very nice people. There's a spinster named Pratt, a former teacher, harmless as hell. And on this floor in the rear, another couple in their late thirties, early forties, Lewis and Felicia Giles. They have two teenage daughters, the only youngsters in the complex besides the Turner boy. Everybody seems really nice, good folks, certainly nobody we'd make for the murder."

"And nobody heard anything around five in the afternoon?" Wilson asked. "I mean, a man gets his head bashed in, hits the floor, probably hard, and nobody in the whole damn building hears it?"

No one commented so he continued. "And if it did happen late afternoon, no one saw anybody leave? These guys carried out a twenty-five inch TV and a tape player that I know of, probably a lot more other stuff, and no one saw anything?" Wilson recalled what he had seen during his October visit, and he was sure of the TV and player, though he couldn't remember anything else.

"We talked to some people who gathered in the street," DeLorenzo said, "people that knew Mr. Costa. None of them reported anything suspicious and no one thought he was having trouble with anybody in the neighborhood. In fact, Mr. Gadsden, who was probably closest to Mr. Costa…they used to play checkers and knock-rummy together…he said things have been pretty quiet for the past two months, since the tunnel bombing. He claims that after that things really calmed down; no muggings, no violence to speak of, at least not around the building. So this just might be what it seems, a random B&E, money for drugs that the poor man just happened to walk in on."

It was a long time before anyone said anything. Wilson broke the silence.

"I have to go call Dan." His eyes searched those of the three other officers. "I leave this investigation in your very capable hands."

He walked to the door, stopped and turned towards the windows. To no one in particular he added, "But if this were my case, I'd work very hard to prove that Mr. Turner doesn't know more than he's told you, because I don't believe that's true. I believe he does know something and that it probably involves someone he knows well." Then, turning his eyes towards them, he concluded, "Good day, gentlemen, and good luck."

He walked down the hall to the top of the stairs, stopped again and walked back to the Turners' apartment door. From there he looked at the door to

Frank Costa's apartment. He squinted, breathed deeply once and headed down the stairs into the cold morning air. A dozen or so people were still milling about, talking quietly, looking up at the windows on the second floor where three detectives privately considered the observations of a very respected senior officer.

As Wilson approached his car, an older gentleman reached out and touched his arm. The man wore a long, heavy coat and woolen cap, but looked cold and tired, his eyes red, face drawn. He pointed to the gold shield hanging from a chain around Wilson's neck.

"Are you in charge, sir?"

"No, I'm from a Manhattan precinct, but I knew Mr. Costa, the deceased."

"Yes, so did I. He was a good man. He didn't deserve this."

Wilson nodded, patted the man's arm in some abstract, reassuring way and headed towards the Buick.

"Sir, you see to it that they catch whoever did this," the man called out. "It's not right that someone like him should go out that way. We got to start putting these killers where they belong. It's time we start doing the right thing."

As Wilson closed the door and searched for the seat belt he wondered if the old man was simply pleading his dead friend's case, or echoing the cry of a city that just wanted to live in a less violent world.

# CHAPTER 3

It was almost noon by the time Wilson arrived at the 34th Street Precinct. Larry Kennedy followed him into his office.

"Shut the door, Larry. Have you told anyone yet?"

"No, and I don't think it's gotten out of Canarsie. No one called me asking any questions."

"Good, let's keep it that way until I get a hold of Dan."

Though he was an exercise fanatic into weightlifting, yoga and health food, Kennedy looked older, thanks in part to a baldpate, stocky frame and dedication to the job. He took the investigation and solving of every case personnally, as though the sole responsibility for law and order rested on his shoulders. Privately, Al Wilson worried that someday it would break him, while wishing that he had ten more like him. Kennedy remained standing in front of the desk while Wilson picked up the phone and punched in some numbers. Their eyes met but neither spoke.

"I'm looking for a Sergeant Dan Costa. He's staying at your hotel."

Dan had been sent to Washington, DC for a four-day seminar on the role of municipal law enforcement in the fight against terrorists. Even though he was arguably New York City's best homicide detective, he was also thought to have the most potential of any law enforcement official in the city, and at every opportunity was being exposed to the kind of professional seminars and round-tables that senior personnel needed to attend.

A minute or so passed before Kennedy heard Wilson say, "Alright, please take this message to him, 'Urgent that you call Al Wilson.' Thank you."

"Dan's at the seminar luncheon. They're bringing him my message, so I guess it's okay to tell your people. But Larry," he added quickly, "some of the guys are going to want to make calls, volunteer some of their time. Tell them I think we ought to let the Brooklyn guys handle it their way. I've already told

Avent we're at his disposal, so let's not be too pushy or nosy, if you know what I mean."

Kennedy seemed reluctant, but Wilson knew that whether he agreed with his decision or not, Larry Kennedy would do as he was ordered and without comment. He was a good cop and a loyal subordinate.

Wilson glanced at his watch; 12:30. Normally, he would be approaching one of the five neighborhood restaurants or delis he had selected for his midday meals. If the weather were inclement, he would call the desk sergeant who organized phone orders for the eat-ins. Neither option appealed to him today. He would simply wait for Dan's call and convey the news as compassionately as possible.

Al Wilson and Dan Costa had met seven years earlier and had become devoted friends. Costa's star was hitched to Wilson's wagon, and though some black officers resented it, they privately admitted that Dan deserved his promotions and could more than stand on his own.

Costa had been a uniformed officer for just two years when he was promoted to detective and assigned to Wilson's Manhattan South Division near New York University's main campus. Almost immediately he distinguished himself and Wilson was quick to recognize his talent. When chosen to head the largest squad, the one on Thirty-Fourth Street, Wilson saw to it that Dan Costa was transferred with him. After two years Costa took and passed the Sergeant's exam, allowing his mentor to place him in a supervisory roll on the day shift, further enhancing his career opportunities despite his relatively young age. Now, three years later, he had done nothing to diminish the esteem in which he was held, not only by superiors, but by every law enforcement officer with whom he came in contact. Honest, dedicated, loyal, intelligent...these were the words his peers used to describe him, and though some privately resented his promotions, none could question his qualifications.

The phone rang. Wilson hesitated, dreading the task he faced. Finally, he took it, half hoping that the voice would not be his friend's.

"Al Wilson."

"Hey, Boss. What's up?"

"Hello, Dan, where are you?"

Costa laughed. "Where am I? Where did you send me?"

"Yeah, I know. I meant are you alone, in your room?" and his voice trailed off, exposing his mood and the job he faced.

"Al, what is it? What's happened?"

"Dan, I wish like hell I didn't have to tell you this, but your dad was killed late yesterday afternoon, the victim of what looks like an assault and burglary."

Wilson hesitated, waiting for his friend to say something, but he heard nothing.

"I'm just so damn sorry. I don't know what to say," he mumbled without really choosing the words or wondering if Dan was listening.

Again seconds passed before Wilson asked, "Dan, are you alright? Can you hear me?"

His friend responded softly, "Yeah. Yeah, Al, I hear you. I'm just having trouble believing it."

"I'm sure I don't know exactly how you feel right now, but I remember when my mom died, how much it hurt, how confusing it all was, and I just want you to know that whatever you need or want me to do, all you have to do is tell me."

"Thanks. Can you tell me anything else? Did he suffer?"

"He was struck in the head from behind and apparently died instantly. There's no indication he ever saw his assailant, but I'm waiting for Fiore to call me. One of his assistants was at the scene and promised to advise us A.S.A.P."

"It was at his apartment?"

"Yeah. The place was ransacked, not real bad, but enough to suspect a burglary. The TV and tape player are missing. Avent would like to have you make a list of anything else that might be missing."

"Who did he put on it?"

"Joe D and Calvin Washington. They both want you to know they'll get whoever did it, and Joe said to tell you he'll make sure the charges stick."

"They think there's more than one perp?"

"They seem to think so; so does Avent. He was there all day and sends his regrets. When you figure out your schedule, maybe you should give him a call to let him know when you can take an inventory."

"I'll call Joe D. I'll catch the four o'clock commuter to La Guardia and meet him there tonight. I'll see you in the office tomorrow morning."

"You don't have to come in in the morning. I think you should take some time off, don't you?"

"I'd rather come in. I'll need the work to keep my mind off everything."

"You're probably right," Wilson said without conviction. "Okay, I'll see you in the morning, unless you want me to meet you tonight at your dad's. I really don't mind."

"Thanks for the offer, Al, but you get on home to the family. I'll see you in the morning," and he hung up.

Wilson held the phone, staring at it as if something more should be said, finally snapping out of it when he heard the dial tone. As he glanced up, he saw the faces of the dayshift's detectives staring at him through the paneled glass that separated the squad bay from his office. He walked to the door, opened it and announced that Dan had been told, that he would be in tomorrow and that any leads or scuttlebutt concerning the case should be forwarded to Detectives DeLorenzo and Washington in Brooklyn.

"Because of race related problems in Canarsie and Mr. Costa's reputation, there will be more emotions surrounding this case than are needed, so let's not add to them. Our help has been offered, and if and when it's accepted, we can pitch in. Otherwise, we will relay information as I have directed, and that, gentlemen, is an order."

In a less commanding tone he added a final thought.

"Some of you have lost loved ones, but none tragically that I can recall. Dan Costa has lost a wife and a father in less than three years, both tragically, one might say unfairly. Let's try to think about what he's going through and how we can help him, not what suits our own mood. I think you know what I mean, so I expect you all to do the right thing."

Wilson went back to his office, settled in his chair and began thinking about what he could do to help his friend get through the next few weeks. If this investigation was handled in a routine manner, given no special attention, and if the perps were young hoods, then months could pass before the case was solved, if in fact it ever was. Detective squads, even those assigned to felony investigations, had been reduced by a half to help the Feds gather bombsite evidence and identify and locate potential terrorists, a statistic that hadn't gone unnoticed by gangs and career criminals. And nothing had been done to relieve court back-logs or the D.A.'s workload, so some offenders managed to slip through the system and its revolving door, further increasing the number of crimes commited. Veterans like Al Wilson knew it was a recipe for disaster, but like everything else dependent upon government action, it would take a major crisis before corrective measures, including the reenforcement of detective squads, were taken. Until then, Dan Costa was going to have to be patient, a trait Wilson knew was not part of his friend's make-up.

# CHAPTER 4

The commuter circled the over-scheduled airport for a half-hour before getting authorization to land. As Dan Costa entered the terminal he could see his friend sifting through the faces of the exiting passengers. When their eyes finally met, they walked towards each other and embraced.

"I don't know what to say, Dan, except he was a great man and I'm sorry as hell for your loss."

Costa just nodded. "Thanks for meeting me, Joe. Do you want to get something to eat before we go?"

"No, that's okay. I had a late lunch. I'm really not hungry. Here, let me carry that."

He reached over and took the handle of a small carry-on, leaving Dan a heavier two-suiter.

Neither spoke again until they were outside.

"The car's right here."

Joe D. had parked in an emergency zone, a portable red light conspicuously perched on the roof of the black Ford Taurus. A small card dangled from the rearview mirror identifying it as an NYPD vehicle on official business.

As the car escaped the protection of the pavilion, Dan got his first glimpse of the snow that had been choking the city. Plows had created waist high roadside barriers, while weeklong freezing temperatures had compressed surface residue into treacherous sheets of ice.

"Someday, Dan, you and me are going to find a way to get out of here when it gets like this. I think the worst part of our job is driving in this city with all this damn traffic, and now we gotta' do it on a friggin' skating rink."

Joe D. drove carefully, his eyes shifting left and right as cars fishtailed attempting to accelerate into lane changes approaching the Brooklyn-Queens Expressway.

"Assholes."

Though he heard his friend's ramblings, Dan was absorbed in his own thoughts, which alternated from the sickening feeling he experienced during Al Wilson's phone call, to the apartment they would shortly visit, to his relationship with his father. His throat tightened as he relived the better moments, the warmth and savory aromas of the little apartment, the exhilaration of a Caruso aria, the quieting peace of the flickering candle before the Madonna. And always the strong, yet gentle, guiding hand of his father. Though he had been a good son, he wished he had spent more time with him, told him more often how much he loved and admired him, perhaps even lived with him after Eileen's death.

"I wish I had been there," he finally whispered.

Joe D reached over and patted his friend on the arm. They rode quietly until he nursed the car to a sliding stop in front of the hundred years old brownstone. He parked halfway into the street, allowing Dan just enough room to open the door. They scrambled over a neatly plowed snowbank, stomping their shoes on a foot-wide path along the sidewalk. As they mounted the steps Dan's heart beat faster. He paused at the top, steadied himself, took a deep breath and looked back into the street.

"No matter how tough you are, no matter how immune you think you're getting to all the violence, you're never prepared for something like this," he said, before entering the foyer.

An ominous quiet magnified the tortured creaks of the worn stairs. As they turned at the top, the door to their left opened and Mattie Turner greeted them.

"Oh, Daniel, I'm so sorry, so very sorry," she said tearfully, before lowering her head and crying openly, unable to say more.

Dan Costa wrapped his arms around her and felt her shaking. After a minute or so, he said softly, "I know Miz Turner. He was a good man and you were a good friend, and I know he loved and cherished the times he spent with you. Now I have work to do. I expect I'll see you at the wake or at church. Meanwhile, you hold up. You know he wouldn't want to see you get sick worrying about him. Besides, he's in a far better place now than either of us."

"Oh, yes, I truly know that, Daniel," she said, as she slowly moved back and closed the door. As they walked away, the two officers heard Mattie Turner break down, her grief rekindling their own.

A large glass vase with a dozen red roses sat in front of the door to his father's apartment. Dan wondered who had brought it, finally deciding it really didn't matter. It was just nice to know that someone cared enough to do it.

Joe D reached in with a small pocketknife and carefully scraped the yellow "CRIME SCENE" ribbon from the side of the jamb. Dan unlocked the door and took a single step into the parlor, stopping before the red stain on the carpet. He knelt and pressed his fingers to it. After a few seconds he stood and surveyed the room before drawing a small white pad and pen from the inside pocket of his jacket. "I'd like you to fill me in on what you've learned so far."

As Dan Costa went from room to room, opening drawers, surveying shelves, inspecting closets, his friend followed, stating events chronologically, describing witnesses, repeating their testimonies. Periodically, Dan would write a word or two. Twenty minutes elapsed before he announced, "I think that does it, Joe. I'm going to call the morgue. If it's okay with them, I want to see my father. You can drop me off at my place and I'll drive up there."

"Unless you want to be alone, Dan, I'd like to go along. You're my friend and the case is mine, so I guess it gives me two pretty good reasons."

"Sure. Maybe we should get a sandwich on the way." He spoke as he dialed.

The Brooklyn Morgue was in the Bay Ridge section, a few blocks from the Verazzano Bridge. Despite the road conditions and a stop to pick up some fast food, they were there in a half-hour. They finished their burgers, fries and sodas in the car.

As they approached the off-hours entrance, Joe asked, "Did you notice anything missing? Al Wilson mentioned a TV and tape player. Anything else?"

"Yeah, a watch, two rings and a gold religious medal and chain. It's odd, but they left a three hundred dollar leather dress coat I bought him last month for his birthday and a two hundred dollar tweed sport jacket I bought him last Christmas. He wore them to church and some social functions around the neighborhood, never to work. They're still like new."

As they entered the depressing two-story graystone, Dan asked, "Does that suggest anything to you?"

His friend didn't hesitate. "Yeah, they couldn't take anything people might recognize, like clothing that could be identified as your father's."

"And that means they probably live in the neighborhood."

Joe D nodded his agreement as they walked towards a guard's desk manned by an overweight, but neatly attired woman in a security uniform.

"May I help you?" she asked in a thick Spanish accent.

"Sergeant DeLorenzo, Brooklyn Homicide," he replied, patiently displaying the gold shield of his office while the guard studied it. "This is Sergeant Costa. We called earlier. Dr. Fiore is expecting us."

"Oh, yes," she smiled. "Just sign in, Detectives, and then take the first left to the end of the hall."

Dante Fiore peered over the top of small, wire-rimmed glasses as the two detectives entered the cluttered room. His clothes were as rumpled as his office. The knot of a comically thin tie, probably from the fifties, was pulled from his neck. The top two buttons of his shirt were loosened, displaying patches of sparse gray hair. He looked not unlike a bassett... baldhead, drooping eyes, long nose...appropriate, most of his acquaintances thought, for his reputation as one of the country's most respected pathologists. Fiore could sniff out findings from evidence most of his peers wouldn't even notice. He remained seated but extended a hand towards Dan, his eyes narrowing as he removed his glasses.

"I can't tell you how sorry I am, Son. Your father was a very special person. I know I'll miss him," he said in a hoarse whisper

"Thanks, Doctor. He spoke about you often. I guess two old widowers like you had a lot in common."

Frank Costa and Dante Fiore had each lost their wives at about the same time, both attended mass at St. Anthony's where they belonged to the Holy Name Society and both were active members of the Brooklyn Italian-American Club and the Knights of Columbus. But whereas Frank Costa had been warm, accommodating and openly friendly, his old friend was a very private, moody person with whom it was difficult to sustain an agreeable relationship. That Frank Costa had done so was just another tribute to his benevolence.

"Yeah, but unlike me your old man was a good person. Rest assured he's in God's hands now," and he made a hurried sign of the cross.

"You probably want an account of the circumstances of his death," Fiore stated as he searched for something amongst scattered papers and folders. "I'm not sure I've got anything of real help to you just yet, but, uh, here it is." He pulled out an acetate-covered report, scanned it briefly and announced in a deliberate tone, "Time of death between 4:00 PM and 6:00 PM yesterday. Probable cause of death, a blow to the head." He peered over the glasses. "I won't be sure of that until tomorrow, but I'd bet money on it." He turned his attention back to the sheet, shifting uneasily in his chair, and continued. "No injuries or marks from the attack except two blows to the head." He hesitated again, moving his eyes from one detective to the other. "It's not written here but I'll include it in my formal report. The first blow came from behind and was probably fatal. The second occurred as he was falling. Can't say if there were two assailants or not, but even so, the same type object inflicted both injuries. My guess would be some kind of pipe; if not that, a curved metal object. In a coupla' days I'll tell you for sure. That's about it for now."

It was cramped and stuffy in the little office so Dan was not unhappy to hear that their meeting was concluded. He asked Fiore's permission to see his father. The pathologist left his chair with no little sign of discomfort and led them into the holding room where a muscular young black in pale green orderlies was unpacking cartons of white linen. Fiore motioned him over.

"These detectives need to view the body of Mr. Costa, the older gentleman from Canarsie they brought in at noon. What's the number?"

"Thirty-two," came the quick reply.

Fiore led them over to a wall that held the bodies in rows of twelve across and three high. He gripped the handle under the small metal plate stamped 32 and turned towards Dan.

"Whatever you see, that's what he'll look like at the viewing. We have to perform an autopsy, 'cause if we don't, some piece of shit lawyer will tear us up in court. I'm not sure I could live with myself if the bastard that did this went free because I screwed up. But I swear to you on St. Anthony, no one will be able to tell."

Fiore slid the drawer out and gently folded back the linen, uncovering the face and upper torso. Dan hesitated before stepping closer. His father's face had a contented look about it, reflecting none of the trauma Wilson had seen. Dante Fiore had been thoughtful. The thick gray hair was combed back and there were no signs of blood or injury except for some red stains on the left shoulder. Fiore had ordered a cleansing, probably immediately upon collection of samples and inspection of the wounds.

Without turning Dan asked, "Were all his personal affects removed?"

"Yes. We have them for you."

Dan reached under the sheet and found his father's hand. It was cold and damp, as he knew it would be. He closed both his hands gently around it, and leaning over to kiss his forehead, he whispered, "I love you, Papa." He stayed a bit longer, racing through the years, envisioning the changes in his father's face as he worked harder and grew older. He pictured his mother together with him, and smiled at the thought that they were now reunited, happy again and looking peacefully down upon him.

As they were leaving, Fiore gave him a large manila envelope, the contents of which included a simple gold wedding band, wallet, eyeglasses in a brown leather case and black wooden rosary beads. There was no money, nor as Dan suspected, anything from his inventory list except the wedding ring.

It was after 10:00 when they reached the front of his apartment on 46th Street off 8th Avenue. He thanked his friend and told him to please call each day with updates, promising in turn to fax him a detailed description of everything missing by noon tomorrow. With some difficulty they got the luggage over the snow-bank.

"You know he's in a good place. If anyone ever deserved what we're promised, it's your father. So let's just nail the bastards that did it and get on with the rest of our lives. That's what he would want. Call me tomorrow." Joe D. turned and carefully rescaled the piled snow.

Dan Costa entered his tidy, well-furnished, three-room apartment, dropped the luggage and laid his coat and jacket on the bed. He walked over to the window, drew back the drapes and raised the blinds. Then he leaned back in a comfortable old recliner and stared at the ceiling. His thoughts were peaceful ones, of family parties, holiday dinners and athletic events at which, with his father's encouragement, he had excelled.

He remembered how his mother would scold them for staying too late at the park or gym. "The supper's ruined. It's dried out, I had to heat it so often. What's the matter with you two?"

With a gentle wave of his hand and a reassuring smile his father would absolve them of wrongdoing, reminding his wife that there was more to life and family than food. "Your heart can't survive on pasta," he would say to her.

He reflected on the times they sat and talked into the early morning hours because his mother's pain was so bad she couldn't lie down, and how on those occasions his father would convince her that God was preparing a feast for when they would arrive at His home.

"We have to endure life's disappointments," he would say. "That's how we cleanse our souls and earn our rewards."

One precious memory followed another until Dan Costa drifted off to sleep. But his dreams were not so gentle, for his deepest thoughts were of the violence and evil that had robbed him of the most cherished person in his life. He awoke suddenly, sweating and breathing heavily. He glanced at his watch;

three a.m. He slipped out of his clothes, pulled back the bedspread and curled up beneath the covers to gaze at a clear, star-laden sky. He envisioned his father up there someplace, smiling down on him, and he could hold his emotions no longer. His throat tightened and tears flowed freely down his cheeks. For just the second time in his life, Dan Costa cried himself to sleep.

When he arrived at the 34th Street police station, most of the dayshift personnel were already in, absorbed with their duties, but they took time to express condolences, offering to help in any way they could. He thanked them but made no effort to extend the conversations. He had carefully printed the list of missing articles and wanted to fax it to Joe DeLorenzo as soon as possible, aware that two days had elapsed, more than enough time for the killers to cash in their spoils. As he waited for an incoming message to terminate, he reviewed the list to ensure the descriptions were accurate and complete, reflecting as he did on the circumstances surrounding each purchase and the sentiments his father had attached to them; the gold and silver watch he had received upon his retirement from the City, the diamond ring he had bought his Rosa for their engagement, the gold and silver crucifix and chain Dan had given him on his sixtieth birthday, a gold tie clasp with three small diamonds his wife had given him for their thirtieth anniversary, just a year before her death.

As the fax signaled the end of the incoming message, he finished reading the list and punched in Joe D's office number, waiting while the sheet was processed. When he returned to his desk he passed the grease board with the detectives' assignments on it, noting that three new cases had been assigned to his shift, one in particular to him. There didn't appear to be any recent additions to the workloads of either the afternoon or graveyard shifts, though he thought little of it.

Comprised of six other detectives, his squad was the largest dedicated to homicide investigation, and because it operated during the day when all the city's resources were available, it stood the best chance of being productive. Most homicides and violent felonies were committed in the late evening and early morning hours, so detectives on those shifts were generally consumed with initial evidence gathering, crime scene reports and file preparation. That left little time for investigative work, so the ultimate responsibility for closing cases fell to the dayshift. Still, he thought it odd that Al Wilson had specifically assigned him a case, when in the past he had always consulted him as the top-ranking detective.

"I'm about ready to head home, but if you want, I have no problem taking your shift if there's things you have to do," Larry Kennedy offered.

Dan shook his head.

"Thanks anyway, Larry, but the best thing I can do right now is work; get my head into other people's problems. I might be a little late tomorrow, so if you could stick around, I have to finalize arrangements for the funeral."

"Sure, whatever you need. By the way, on that Teller case you've got? Carmine Pecora is on his way in from a call. When he gets here he'll fill you in on some information he got that might help."

"Yeah, I noticed that one. Any idea why Al gave it to me?"

"He just thinks you should have something to focus on for a while and that one's not going to be easy. It's drawing a lot of attention because it looks like an old man just got killed for no reason at all. The poor guy lives in the sticks somewhere in Pennsylvania. He comes to the Big Apple to celebrate his birthday and gets blown away during a mugging. Picture how that's playing out with the press and City Hall."

Dan nodded. "Thanks. Al's probably right."

"Take your time coming in tomorrow. I got no reason to hurry home. I talked the wife into getting a puppy, a little boxer, and the damn thing won't house train, so when I get home I get an ear-full and then I gotta' clean up the mess on top of it. Nothin' ever seems to work out," he muttered, as he headed for the stairwell, mired in self-pity.

Shortly before noon, Carmine Pecora returned, offering his regrets, some family sentiments and a comment about the increase in violent crimes since Giuliani left office. Dan chose not to respond so Carmine changed subjects.

"I was told to turn everything on the Teller case over to you and update you on some conversations I had last night. I still haven't had a chance to record them, but I will if you want me to."

"You don't have to. I'll take down what you tell me and add it to the file myself."

"Okay. Well, where do you want me to start? You haven't had a chance to look at the file yet?"

"No, I haven't. I'll tell you what. You go home and sleep. When you wake up, call me. We can probably cover any questions I have over the phone."

"Yeah, sure, there shouldn't be too many, and all I have to add is a conversation with one witness who finally decided to come forward. I'm not sure he's important anyway, the deceased having a friend right there who saw everything up close."

"Okay, go on home and call me later."

Dan picked up the phone and punched Joe DeLorenzo's number. He waited while a clerk tried to find him.

"DeLorenzo here."

"Joe, it's me. Did you get the fax?"

"Yeah, and it's already distributed to all the uniforms, plus Calvin Xeroxed his card on the bottom and is delivering copies to every pawn broker in the Borough as we speak. I also faxed it to all the Manhattan, Queens, Bronx and Staten Island precincts asking them to do the same."

"Thanks, Joe, that's great, and please tell Calvin I appreciate everything he's doing. Anything new?"

"No, but I'm on my way out the door right now to re-interview the neighbors. I started thinking about something Wilson said as he was leaving yesterday and I think he might have something. It involves the Turners. I'll fill you in if there's anything there." He paused briefly before adding, "How are you doing? Is there anything I can help with?"

"Considering everything, I'm doing pretty good, Joe. I don't expect things to be normal, but at least I slept some and I'm not looking to kill anybody, not yet anyway. I'm still remembering and mourning. When that goes away, maybe then I'll start getting pissed. That's when I'll have to worry."

"Yeah, well, whenever you need me you know I'll be there. Just call."

As he replaced the receiver he looked up to see a tired Al Wilson walking towards him. "How about some lunch? It's on me," Wilson offered.

"No, but thanks anyway, Boss. I made myself some eggs and frozen waffles this morning. I got a little *agito* with everything goin' on."

Dan felt Wilson's discomfort. The big man didn't know what to say so he said the predictable. "Well, you know you only have to ask if there's something I can do. Have you made any arrangements?"

"I called Paulie Ippolito. He'll do the pickup when Dante is finished and then I'll meet with him tomorrow to pick out a coffin. He and Father Boland over at St. Anthony's already talked, so there's nothing else I have to do except file for the life insurance."

"Yeah, well," and Al Wilson could find nothing else to say, so he returned to his office, abandoning his decision to have turkey and pastrami on rye at Weinstein's deli on 6$^{th}$ Avenue.

Dan opened the gray folder labeled "Teller, Joseph, 3/9/05." Stapled to the inside cover was a black and white coroner's photograph of a sixty-something, thin-faced man with tight, wavy, gray hair, narrow lips and the unmistakable mark of a bullet hole in the middle of, and slightly above his eyes. A second, larger photo lay atop the report pages. It showed the same man lying on his back in the snow with what appeared to be a bloodstain in the middle of his coat. A wallet lay near his left leg. Dan looked back at the smaller photo. The face seemed peaceful, distant, almost as if it had been staged. It was a gentle face, one that he suspected had seen little violence and few disappointments, but nonetheless the face of a dead man. He read Carmine Pecora's report twice, noting that it left a surprisingly long list of unanswered questions, some of which would have been better served had they been addressed immediately after the shooting. But Dan knew the weather had played havoc with attendance and that everyone was already overworked so he absolved Pecora and his partner of any negligence and began highlighting segments of the report.

*The account of the crime as recorded by Detective Pecora was provided at the scene by the only known witness, Dr. Lewis Berger, friend of the deceased.*
  *Joseph Teller; age, sixty-four, Caucasian.*
  *He and Berger had just left their car in an unattended lot on Third Street and were proceeding towards Liotta's Ristorante on Canal Street when they were approached by two men wearing black watch caps, gloves and ski masks. One had a black ski jacket with silver or gray striping on the sleeves, the other a black or dark blue three quarter length carcoat with hood. The former pointed a gun, possibly a .45, at Teller and told the victim to give him his money. As Teller unbuttoned the top of his coat to reach into his inside jacket pocket, the killer fired twice, hitting the victim in the forehead and heart. Berger sank to his knees expecting the same, but both assailants ran a couple hundred feet down Canal, jumped into a waiting car and sped off. Berger ran to the restaurant and alerted the first person he saw, a waiter named Dominic, who called 911.*
  *According to Berger, he and Teller were research scientists and partners in a small medical laboratory in Nuremberg, Pennsylvania. Weeks before the storm they had made reservations to see Phantom of the Opera and to have dinner at Liotto's to celebrate Teller's sixty-fourth birthday. They planned to spend two days at Columbia University doing some research before returning*

*home. Since all the arrangements had been made and the storm was beginning to subside, they decided to hold to their schedule.*

*Teller's only known relative is a daughter who lives somewhere in Virginia. They were not particulary close. Berger has no idea how to contact her or whether Teller's former wife is alive or dead.*

The follow-up portion of the report was what caught Dan Costa's eye.

*The attendant from a parking lot across the street from the incident was hanging around the shooting site when uniforms arrived. He claims he didn't see anything, but that he did hear the shots and crossed over when he finally saw the victim lying on the ground. Another man, walking on the same side as the shooting, claims that because of the distance and angle of his approach he couldn't see what went down, and that by the time he got to the body, the parking attendant was already kneeling over it.*

*Berger claims the killer fired as Teller was reaching into his jacket, but an empty wallet was found on the ground next to the victim, suggesting the shots were fired after the deceased had removed the wallet. When first advised that Teller's wallet was empty, he said that one of the killers probably emptied it and he was too shaken to notice. Later at the precinct he claimed to remember that Teller had left home with only a few dollars with which they paid the tunnel toll, and that his friend rarely carried money, relying instead on credit cards.*

*Liotto's has its own parking lot, but Berger chose to use one around the corner, one that happened to be unattended. Berger said he was not aware that Liotto's had its own lot. Berger stated that both assailants 'sounded black' and were very nervous, as though they were high on something. He reiterated this at the station house, reinforcing it with the conviction that they were definitely black. This ties the perps into two other muggings in the same general area that were reported last week, though neither of them ended violently.*

Dan wondered why Pecora hadn't closed the report with a list of required follow-ups, standard procedure in a case like this. He should have at least recorded the witnesses' lines of sight and their distances from the murder scene, as well as the distance from the incident to the perpetrators' car and the direction in which it traveled. But what really bothered him was that the victim was a frail old man who offered no resistance or visible threat to his assailants. So why did they have to fire two deadly shots when there was no one around to stop them and while Teller was in the process of extracting his wallet? The possibility that they were high on drugs and not really aware of what they were doing might account for that. Then again, they were organized. They had a getaway car, and according to a witness, had no difficulty running down the block to the car. How is it that neither of the other two witnesses in the area saw or mentioned the car? Had Pecora failed to include their observations in his report? And why hadn't he provided details of the two other muggings so they could build a profile and perhaps tie it into a convicted felon's record. This was all basic police work that a rookie detective would have been smart enough to include, let alone two veterans like Pecora and Zimmerman.

Costa dismissed the drug-crazed theory. He leaned back in his chair, stared at the ceiling and tried to envision the crime scene. Long ago he had convinced himself that coincidence was more often purposeful and that circumstances that made little sense constituted the best clues. Over and over again, despite his efforts to get his mind off it and on to some other evidence in the case, one thought repeated itself. Why had the perpetrators allowed Lewis Berger to escape unharmed? After some reflection, he felt more comfortable believing that there was more to this case than the current evidence allowed and that he would give it all the attention it deserved as soon as the funeral was over.

He was in the process of writing a list of questions to ask the witnesses when the phone rang. A soft, sensuous voice greeted him.

"Sergeant Costa, this is Marilyn Kyme. I'm the Assistant Medical Examiner from Doctor Fiore's office."

"Yes, Ms. Kyme, I recognize your name." He thought too about how others had described her…gorgeous, stacked, sensuous, intelligent… and though they had never met, Dan had thought more than once about arranging to cross her path. But this call was surely about his father and that erased any thoughts he might have otherwise entertained.

"Dr. Fiore asked me to call you and Lieutenant Wilson as soon as we completed the autopsy. The clerk gave you to me first, so perhaps you can relay the report to the Lieutenant?"

The speech was formal, but the tone was sensual, and Dan had to wonder if it was wholly unintentional.

"Certainly, and please tell Dante we appreciate the call. Go ahead."

"There's really not much to say. The victim was struck twice from behind, with the first blow providing the only evidence of reasonable certainty. A left-handed person between five feet-eight inches and six feet in height delivered it. The weapon was something made of iron, badly rusted and dirt covered, suggesting it could have been picked up from a junk pile or garbage dump, certainly nothing new. At the crime scene I noticed a small amount of rust on the rug, some of which had been stepped on by one or more of the assailants, but I'm told we don't have enough imprint to tell us anything about the shape or size of the shoe. Both blows were probably struck by the same assailant, the second landing on the back of the head as your father…" she hesitated, correcting herself, "the victim was falling."

Dan was about to ask something when she interrupted.

"I'm sorry to have personalized this, Sergeant. It was very unprofessional of me."

He believed she meant it. "No need to apologize. Your reference is understandable since he was my father." He wanted to change the subject. "Do you happen to know if Ippolito's has been in yet?"

"Yes, in fact they are at the desk signing the forms right now. They should be leaving in a minute or two."

"Well, thanks again, Marilyn." He purposely used her first name. "I hope someday we can meet on a happier occasion."

The sentiment caught her by surprise. She struggled with a reply. "Yes, yes, certainly…sometime." Embarrassed, she hung up.

Dan replaced the receiver and looked at it for a few seconds, thinking about the probable murder weapon, wondering how he might trace it and if it could lead him to the killer.

He looked down the squad room and saw Al Wilson behind the desk, his head bent over what was probably a report on one of the many open felonies they were investigating. He made his way towards him and stopped in the doorway. Preoccupied, the big man didn't look up. He stared at a sheet, tapping it with a ballpoint pen, alternating each end in a two-step beat. A deep frown lined his face.

"Al, got a second?"

"Sure, come in. Sit down."

Wilson picked up the sheet and stared at it again.

"You know," he started, "there's something that's really been bothering me about your father's murder." He grimaced, as first he arched and then tried to straighten his back. "The man who called 911; he said he came home from work and noticed your dad's apartment door was open. If he's telling the truth, why in hell would assailants who probably knew they had killed your father leave the door open when they left? And if they did close it, in which case the guy is lying and covering up for himself or somebody else, why would he expose himself to suspicion by calling 911? I don't believe the perps left that door open, not by accident and sure as hell not on purpose. If they had left in a hurry…run out of there…somebody would have heard or seen them. We're talking five in the afternoon, for chrissake; there's all kinds of people around…cooking, returning from work, kids playing. It just doesn't fit."

"I agree, Al, the burglars wouldn't have left the door open whether they exited that way or not, not with their victim lying in a pool of blood within three feet of the hallway. Joe and Calvin should have asked the floor's other residents if they noticed the door open, in which case I'm sure their answers would have been negative." He paused briefly before continuing, aware of the implications of his conclusion. "So Mr.Turner is probably lying, not to cover himself because I understand his attendance at work has already been confirmed, but to draw suspicion away from someone he's probably close to. That coincides with a theory Joe D and I have that the assailant or assailants left two fairly new, expensive items of clothing because they would be easily recognized as belonging to my father. And the likely reason people didn't notice or hear them leaving was because one or more of them lived there. They didn't have far to go so they took their time, and so what if anyone saw them."

Dan sat calmly, staring back at his friend who was still absorbing and sifting through the evidence that led to only one conclusion. Finally he said, "It's Joe D's case. I'll let him handle it, because if I do get involved and I get my hands on the bastards, I'm not sure I won't do something we'll all regret."

Costa started for the door. "I have a father to bury. I think I'll take the funeral leave and see you next week.

## CHAPTER 5

The next morning Dan remembered telling Larry Kennedy he would be late, so he called to explain that he had decided to take the three days funeral leave to which he was entitled. Larry said he thought it was a good idea.

"By the way, my guys asked me about the arrangements."

"He'll be laid out tonight and tomorrow at Ippolito's on Bay Boulevard. We'll bury him on Saturday if the snow's not too deep and they can get through the ice to dig the grave. Father Boland's going to say Mass at ten."

"At St. Anthony's?"

"Yeah. Dad was a big part of that place even though it's mostly Hispanic now. Through all those years, all the time he put in...."

"Yeah, he was a really good man, your dad. You're lucky to have had a father like him."

"Thanks, Larry. Cover as best you can. I should be in on Monday."

He had a quick breakfast and drove over to the Ippolito Funeral Home. The sun was warm and bright, an omen of better days to come, of a bitterly cold winter finally on its way out, and Dan privately resented that his father was not around to enjoy it. But as he thought more about it, he reached the happy conclusion that his father was indeed aware of it, though not absorbed by it, for at the moment Frank Costa was surely occupied with a far more gratifying experience. Though neither naïve nor dillusional, Dan was deeply spiritual and convinced there was a Creator and a life hereafter. *How could man possibly be the most intelligent entity in the universe?* That anyone could think so astounded him. He also knew it was childish to think that God got involved in every second of everyone's life. Still, there were times that it simply felt good to believe that on occasion a Higher Power did indeed answer one's supplication and would be there when needed to provide strength, if nothing else. That being the case, God would be more personal in the spiritual realm, and Frank Costa would be rewarded for all he had done in this life.

Paulie Ippolito was seated in his office and rose to shake hands. He was fifteen years older than Dan who still considered him one of his best friends. Dressed in black he looked every bit the somber mortician, though a youthful smile and quick wit revealed his true personality.

"I hope you're holding up well because your father wouldn't want you feeling sorry for him. You remember what he told me when my old man died?"

"No, but I'm sure you're going to tell me."

"He said, 'Your father lived a good life and now he's sitting next to God enjoying everything he's earned. So even if you cry he won't give two shits. He's too happy for himself.' So be happy for him, big guy, 'cause we both know where he is and we both know it's a helluva' lot better place than this."

"I know you're right. It just would be a lot easier if he had gone peacefully."

Dan chose a plain, mid-priced coffin, knowing his father would have objected to anything more expensive. He ordered a limousine and told his friend he wanted the whole St. Anthony's Senior Choir for the funeral Mass, and he didn't care what it cost. He also invited Paulie and his wife, Joanne, to the post-burial luncheon he had arranged at Libretti's near Gate of Heaven Cemetery in Bay Ridge.

"You're going to have an awful lot of people, Danny. Why don't Jo and I skip it? We'll see you around. How about you come over for Sunday dinner? Everybody would love to see you."

"Maybe, but only if you promise to stop trying to fix me up with one of your wife's loony nieces. My God, Paulie, Joanne comes from a nut tree. They could fill an asylum with her relatives. How come she's so normal? Then again, she did marry you."

Ippolito laughed. "Yeah, at least she has good taste. But hey, did you ever notice the bodies on her nieces? *Madonna!* I know a hundred guys who'd give their left ball to nail one of 'em, but they're all scared shitless of Massimo. By the way, you remember Theresa, Massimo's oldest? I said to her once, 'What're you always trying to get Aunt Jo to fix you up with Costa for?' She looks at me like I'm nuts and says, 'He's six-three, built, handsome like a Greek god, toughest sonofabitch in the City and single. And what are you asking me for? I'm gettin' hot here just thinkin' about him.'"

They both laughed.

"Yeah, I remember Theresa, and if she wasn't your wife's niece, I'd think about it. That babe's got a body that doesn't stop."

"And neither could you if Massimo ever found out. You'd be running forever. He loves you, always asks about you, but when it comes to his daughters, he'll kill anybody stupid enough to touch them. I think that's why they're all three still single. I mean, who the hell's going to stand up to Massimo?"

"Speaking of the Capo, how is he?"

"He's fine. He'll live forever. God don't want him and the devil's afraid if he ends up in hell Massimo will kick his ass out and take over."

"You're not far from wrong."

"Remember the time those two *spics* from Bed Sty broke into St. Anthony's and stole everything?" Paulie asked.

"That was about three years ago, right?"

"Yeah, something like that. Well, Massimo gets really pissed. He calls a meeting with Uncle Muzzi and Vito Scarola. Now there's a pair. People think you're tough? When I was a kid I saw Muzzi, a knife in his chest, still beat three guys so bad they were in the hospital a month apiece. To the day they died, none was ever right in the head again. And forget about Scarola. He's thrown so many bodies in the bay the fish think he's Poseidon."

Dan laughed again.

"So anyway, Massimo tells Muzzi and Vito that he wants whoever stole the stuff and he don't give a shit what they gotta' do. So Vito, he knows everybody that's connected, including the *spics,* he gets word to some of them that there's going to be trouble if they don't come up with some names. It takes about a week, but all of a sudden Father Boland gets this big package, and in it he finds everything that was stolen, plus more money than could possibly have been in the poor box, like a coupla' G's. And a week after that, what did those cops find in that warehouse near Yankee Stadium?"

Dan remembered the case. In an abandoned old warehouse in the South Bronx, police found two Hispanic males with criminal records for assaults and drugs nailed to wooden beams. Before bleeding to death, all their fingers had been broken.

They talked all morning about the neighborhood, the tough old Italians, the ones who had been members of the mob and the relatives who had passed away. Irreverence mixed well with nostalgia and their eyes watered with laughter. Finally, Dan said he had other arrangements to make and left, promising to attend a special dinner Paulie would host in Frank Costa's honor with all the old Italian men.

Dan drove to Gate of Heaven Cemetary to meet with another of his father's friends, Jimmy Scanella, the groundskeeper and maintenance supervisor. His real first name was Vincenzo, but in the Italian tradition, the origin of which depended upon whom you asked, he was called "Jimmy". Though he had once been a soldier in the Barracci family, for reasons known only to a select group of insiders, he had asked for and was granted permission to resign, a rare privilege in the days when the code of the *Cosa Nostra* was strictly enforced and release from membership in a family was unheard of. To even ask, risked *bacio de morte*. But rumor had it that Scanella had done his *capo* a service involving one of his daughters that went above and beyond the call of duty and that it would have been dishonorable for Massimo Barracci to have refused so loyal a *soldato*.

Dan recognized him from a distance, for few men in Brooklyn were six and a half feet tall and three hundred ponds. He waved and Scanella started towards him, plowing his way through the snow on legs thick as tree trunks, chewing up yards with the ease of a giant in a field of wild flowers. Unfazed by temperatures in the 20's, he wore dungarees and a turtleneck sweater against which his still massive muscles rippled. With a ragged Yankees' cap pulled hard down over his eyes, Vincenzo "Jimmy" Scanella was indeed a menacing sight and no one to antagonize, despite his fifty plus years.

"My sincerest sympathies, Daniel," he announced in a resonating basso that filled the frigid air, "but now he's with Rose, God bless her. They're happy forever."

Dan thanked him for the sentiment. "We want to bury Dad after Mass on Saturday, Mr. Scanella. What do you think?"

"What are you worried about? I'll have the road plowed and we'll clear paths right to the grave. There'll be enough room for two, three hundred people if you want. You want to say something to your mother now? I'll have Benny cut a path."

"No, no thanks. Saturday will be soon enough. And thanks, Mr. Scanella, I appreciate it."

"Forget about it. You just make sure they catch the *faciems* who did it. Catch 'em and bring 'em here," he said, jabbing a finger towards the ground. "Benny and me'll give 'em fuckin' dirt naps, and if they're lucky they'll be dead when we put 'em under. The *faciems.*" Dan knew Vincenzo Scanella meant every word of it.

He made a final stop to order flowers, two hundred red roses arranged on a stand in the shape of a heart, before going home to shower and dress for the first viewing at four that afternoon. On the way he phoned Joe DeLorenzo but was told neither he nor Calvin Washington were in. He left a message for his friend to call him at home before dialing Al Wilson.

"Lieutenant Wilson here."

"Hi, Boss, it's me. What's up?"

"Nothing, other than your dad's case, terrorists and the usual crap in our jobs. How you doin'?"

"Not bad, probably better than I would have thought. I just hope I'm not going to wake up, realize what's happened and lose it."

"I know what you mean, but you're a strong person, Dan. You come from good stock. Just try not to think about it too much."

"I'm trying, believe me. By the way, I need to speak to Pecora and I didn't tell him I decided to take some time off. He has some information for me on the Teller case and I'd like to have it. It occupies my mind, which is probably good therapy right now."

"I'll take care of it. I'm coming over to Ippolito's tonight, so I'll call Carmine before leaving and get the information for you if he can't call or make it over there."

"Thanks, Al."

"For nothin'. And by the way, Camille just got off the phone. She decided she wants to go to the funeral with me on Saturday, so she won't be there tonight, but she wants you to know her thoughts are with you."

"She's a special lady, Al. You don't deserve her."

"You got that right. See you tonight, kid."

Dan put on the only black suit he owned and was straightening the knot in a simple black and gray tie when the phone rang. It was Carmine Pecora.

"Hi, Dan, how you doin'?" he asked without thinking.

"Okay, Carmine. Just getting ready to leave for Ippolito's. Will it take long?"

"No. I just wanted you to know that the parking lot attendant has come forward with some more information. He called to tell me he wanted to talk but that he doesn't trust the police. Bottom line is that he was in trouble a few years back, spent six months at Riker's for a drug deal and got another six while there for assaulting a guard. Says he's innocent but knows nobody gives a shit. He just doesn't want any grief for what he has to say. Anyway, he claims Teller was shot after he pulled a wallet from his jacket and reached out towards the assailant to hand it to him. He says both perps had to see it was a wallet, that whole side of the street being lit up. He also says they never even looked at the victim's friend, Dr. Berger, like they forgot about everything once Teller got shot, and just wanted to get out of there."

"What do you think, Carmine?"

"I don't know if I believe everything this guy Ruiz is saying. He's got a hard-on for the law, so maybe he's playing mind games, but his story basically backs up what Doctor Berger had to say. It's really starting to look like some junkies who needed a fix, and fast."

"Ruiz. Is that the attendant's name?"

"Yeah. Sorry I forgot to mention it. Jorge Ruiz, age twenty-nine, born in Puerto Rico, lives somewhere up in Spanish Harlem."

"You didn't get his address and phone number?"

"No. Once I got him to tell us everything he saw I didn't see any sense in talking to him again since his story and Berger's are the same."

"Yeah, you're right," Dan lied. "Thanks for the follow-up. I'm on my way out, so if you don't mind, just give everything to Al and I'll put it in with the rest of the file you gave me."

"Okay. I'll see you at Paulie's tomorrow."

Dan's thoughts alternated between the Teller case and his father's until he arrived at the funeral home. He was almost an hour early and wondered if Paulie would be there. As he locked the car and walked towards the entrance, he realized that his hands were sweating and his heart was pounding, the same feelings he had when Eileen died.

Inside, Paul Ippolito was seated at his desk, speaking to one of his sons in the business. Dan made sure he saw him, motioning as he passed, before continuing down the spacious hallway to the main viewing room on the left. Even before he entered, the smell of freshly cut flowers overwhelmed him. There were over a hundred baskets and sprays, some completely covering the wall behind the casket. Together with a dozen or more on the floor, they formed a grotto in which Frank Costa's coffin was comfortably nestled. Flower arrangements continued down both long walls, coming together in the rear, with only the occasional doorway remaining accessible.

His pulse quickened as he approached the head of the room, his father's profile peacefully drawn in the soft glow of candlelight. Instinctively, he dropped to his knees beside the casket, eyes fixed on his father's face, hands trembling, his mind unable to focus on any purposeful thoughts. His breath quickened as he drew in large draughts of air, trying without success to compose himself. Finally, he just gave in, relaxed and let the tears flow, and as they did his breathing slowed and a sense of calm gradually came over him. He uttered no sounds and his body betrayed none of the deep sorrow he felt as he focused on the gentle face of the man he admired above all others. Dan reached out, first to touch the cold, dry hands and then to run his own softly across his father's forehead. He rested it there while recalling memories and praying for his strength and guidance. Only the image of his mother broke his concentration, assuring him that his parents were indeed together and that they would forever be there when he needed them.

Long minutes passed, enough for the tears to dry and for him to sense that others had entered the room, though no one came forward or made the slightest noise. He turned to see Paul Ippolito, Father Boland and a handful of older men Dan recognized from St. Anthony's standing quietly, eyes lowered, their hands folded in prayer. As he acknowledged them with a faint smile, they stepped forward, the aging Irish priest leading the way. He grasped Dan's hands and fought back tears that threatened to fill the normally bright blue eyes. Dan looked into them and remembered that as a child his father had convinced him that Jesus wanted one priest on earth to have His eyes so He could see what everyone was doing. Father Francis Xavier Boland, he had assured his young son, was the priest with Christ's eyes. As he gazed at them and sensed both their sorrow and serenity, he preferred to think as he had those many years ago that his father's story was true.

It wasn't quite four o'clock, but people were already crowding the entrance, so Paul invited them into the viewing room. Uniformed police mixed with elderly and middle aged blacks from the neighborhood. Older Italians and Hispanics from St. Anthony's shuffled in, many drying their eyes as they knelt beside the casket offering silent testimonials on behalf of their deceased friend. Dan stood dutifully to the side accepting the condolences of each mourner, thanking them for attending and promising as he was asked to let each know if there was anything they could do. The room had almost three hundred chairs and all were occupied by 5:00 when Paul took Dan aside.

"They're lined up in the snow outside. I don't think we should shut down, but maybe you should go upstairs and have something to eat. Joanne made you some veal parmigiana. Then you can come back down at seven."

Traditionally, mourners were not allowed in between five and seven at night, and viewing ended at nine, but even Paul was surprised at the turnout and he knew that with the hour or so it took for the queue to cycle, those attending after supper would never get through by closing unless he stayed open.

"These people came to say good-bye to my father, Paulie. The least I can do is be here for them." His smile reassured his friend. "But you can tell Joanne I'll be up for some veal when you close."

It was past 9:30 when the chimes were sounded announcing the closing. All who visited had been afforded the time they needed. Dan had stood beside the casket the entire evening, taking an occasional cup of water, greeting and accepting the condolensces of each mourner. He recognized all the cops and most of the others, though he struggled to remember names and apologized frequently for forgetting. Only once did he begin to choke-up, successfully managing to fight back the tears with what he was certain was his parents' help. The entire St. Anthony's boxing team sporting their "PAL Champions" jackets filed past, each stopping before the casket to raise clenched fists in the fighter's style. These were New York's toughest teenagers, few of whom bothered to conceal their tears, all of whom genuinely loved this man who had offered and shared with them all that he had. It was especially poignant that each youngster was black or Hispanic, and that the fallen hero whom they so respected was white. Dan wondered what the world, or at least this tiny corner of it, would be like if there were more men in it like his father.

Dante Fiore accompanied a stunning young woman who Dan assumed was his Assistant M.E., Marilyn Kyme. When she extended her hand he took it and said, "Thank you for coming, Marilyn."

Fiore looked questioningly at both of them, wondering where and when they had met. Dan noticed but didn't comment, thanking him instead for his years of friendship.

After saying she was sorry for his loss, Marilyn Kyme followed Fiore to the back of the room where they sat with a group of old Italians. During the next hour or so, Dan's eyes sought her out and more than once he caught her staring at him. Her sensuality stirred him, which in turn made him feel guilty.

The grief filled room had an emotionally draining effect on him, but he got through it, and after sharing some parmigiana, salad and a side dish of cavatelli with Paulie, he drove back across the bridge to his apartment to watch the eleven o'clock news that included a segment on his father, highlighted by comments from those standing in line outside in the cold. They spoke of Frank Costa's charity, of his love for his Church, the endless hours he spent teaching and guiding young people and the humility with which he refused rewards and recognition.

Some shed tears as they talked of him being a saint, that they would pray to him whenever they needed help. Despite always knowing what a good man his father was, Dan was only now beginning to realize how deeply so many people admired him and how many lives he had touched. These thoughts brought him great peace and he slept well.

Sunshine forced its way through the drapes, brightening the room and promising some relief from the cold. Still, Dan felt his spirit sink as he recalled the week's tragedy. For a while he lay there, staring at the ceiling, alternating his thoughts between the circumstances of his father's death and the tender moments he had shared with him, his emotions shifting from anger to remorse. If only he could have the last year or two to relive. The more he reflected, the more deeply he regretted, until he realized that there was nothing he could do to amend the past, except to dedicate the rest of his life to the principles his father had taught him.

The phone rang, interrupting his thoughts.

"Good morning. Hope I didn't wake you." It was Al Wilson.

"No. Been awake a half-hour. Just lying here reminiscing."

"You okay?"

"Not bad. Just wish I had spent more time with him. He was a special human being, besides being my father, and a good father at that. I could have learned a lot from him and teaching me would have made him so happy."

"You weren't a bad son."

"No, but I never told him half enough how much I loved him, how proud I was of him, and I never made the effort to be with him. I was thinking how I could have taken him up to a ballgame and dinner, or stayed over and gone to Mass with him on Sunday and then out to breakfast. You know what that would have meant to him?"

Wilson wanted to say something about how the old man was proud of him, but it seemed shallow.

"Anyway, he's gone now and there's not a damn thing I can do about it." Dan hesitated. "Except maybe someday I'll meet a kid who'll listen and I'll make sure he doesn't make the same mistake."

"Don't be too hard on yourself. I don't know of anyone who wouldn't give his right arm to have you for a son. So maybe you aren't perfect…none of us is…but you were a good son and you made your father proud every day of his life."

"Yeah, well, I hope you're right, but deep inside I wish things had been different."

Wilson changed subjects.

"Joe DeLorenzo told me he got your message and he'll see you at the wake, but he doesn't want to discuss your dad's case with you now, not until at least Sunday. He feels you should just get through the funeral and all. Then you can talk."

"He's probably right," Dan admitted.

Everything else they discussed was redundant to the point of being awkward and they both sensed it. They finally hung up with Wilson promising that he and Camille would be at the funeral Saturday.

The Friday afternoon and evening viewings proceeded much the same as Thursday's, with unfamiliar faces and forgotten names amongst the hundreds that waited patiently in line. Women cried, lamenting life's misfortunes, while men shook their heads sadly, recalling special moments. But it was the hundred or so teenagers that moved Dan's heart. As they stood like sentinels before the coffin, two and three across, Dan could sense the genuine remorse that only the highest esteem for a fallen leader could evoke, rekindling the morning's reflections. He could have been part of the great bond between these untamed kids and the father that only now was he beginning to appreciate to the fullest, the father whom others had shared and would miss as much as he. He silently cursed himself for being so blind to the opportunities the fullness of his father's life had offered and he wondered again if this would all have some special significance in his own future.

When the chimes finally rang and the last of the mourners had left, Dan stared at his father's lifeless form and uttered a short prayer.

*Please, Dad, show me the way.*

He felt a hand press lightly on his shoulder.

"Care for some pasta fagioli?" It was Paulie.

They headed upstairs. On the kitchen table Joanne had set a steaming bowl of the Neapolitan entrée that had become a Friday tradition in the Ippolito household. Usually a baked fish and salad followed, but tonight she had indulged her culinary passion, preparing shrimp scampi, baked eggplant and broccoli rabe with garlic and anchovies. A bottle of wicker-wrapped Chianti stood beside an ominous looking homemade Barbarone, a heavy red guaranteed to produce a long, untroubled sleep. Dan wondered which of Joanne's countless uncles had made it.

"Danny, sit down," Joanne ordered. "You must be starved. You gotta' keep up your strength."

Italian women always assume their men are starving, and if they aren't, the added reminder of the uncertainty of one's health usually cements their purpose, calories and cholesterol notwithstanding.

"You gonna' eat with us?" Paulie asked his wife politely.

"No, I ate with Anthony and Junior around seven. You two just sit here and enjoy yourselves. I'm going to go read and maybe go to bed early. I got a lot to do tomorrow before we go to church. Leave the dishes. I'll clean-up in the morning."

She kissed them both on the cheek, left her apron on the counter and headed to the bedrooms in the rear of the house.

Paulie began filling their bowls with the still steaming pasta and beans.

"This is too hot to eat," he concluded. "We'll start with the rest."

One after the other he passed the fish and vegetable dishes, slices of garlic bread and peccorino, a strong grated cheese made from sheep's milk.

"Which wine?" he asked intently.

"How's the Barbarone?"

"Uncle Dominic made it. It'll knock you on your ass, but no hangover. I think that's because he started wearing clean socks last year." His eyes twinkled.

"I think I'll pass. Just a little Chianti."

Dan was surprised at how hungry he was. Joanne Ippolito's cooking was legendary and her dishes tonight were no exception, but he didn't think he'd have any interest in eating. Joanne's skill beat the hell out of his depression.

"Any questions about tomorrow?" Paulie asked.

"No."

"I can't imagine how many people will be here," Paulie continued while dipping a crusty bread into the fagioli, "but Father Boland thinks the whole parish will be at church."

"What time will we have to leave?"

"I don't know. It depends on how many people show up here. It's only five minutes to St. Anthony's, but it could take an hour to get a big crowd into a procession."

"Yeah. Well, I'll leave it all to you." He hesitated before adding, "Before you close the casket, I want five minutes alone with him."

"Sure, kid," Paulie said softly.

For a long while neither spoke, savoring the food, each contemplating quite different subjects.

When Paul finally leaned back in his chair, patted his stomach and announced he was full, Dan wiped his mouth with a napkin and reminded him to thank Joanne again for being so thoughtful.

"Ah, but she loves to cook, and she really loves to cook for you. I think she's still holdin' out some hope that you'll marry into the family."

Dan just smiled lightly. His friend took the hint.

"I know you don't want Espresso, do you?"

Dan shook his head. "It'll keep me awake all night."

"Yeah, me too. But let's have a little Sambucca. It'll finish everything off."

Paul found his favorite, Romana black, a particularly high-octane variety of the licorice cordial favored by Italians. He produced two glasses, each holding the traditional three coffee beans.

"Your father ever tell you the story behind the three beans?" he asked as he poured.

"Father, Son and Holy Ghost," Dan replied.

Paulie cast a questioning glance. "You sure he said that?" He screwed up his face. "I think it's the Holy Family," he said confidently.

Dan shrugged. "Whatever. One thing's sure; the old ones believe in the magic."

They sipped the liquor in silence until Dan drained his glass and stood. "Come on, let's clean up this mess."

"Are you kidding? And spoil her fun? She'd be pissed at me for a week. This is her kitchen, my friend, and nobody besides her does anything in it but eat. You just get going and try to get a good night's sleep."

During the drive back to Manhattan, Dan's thoughts shifted from memories of his parents, the times they shared and the regrets he had, to the circumstances surrounding both his father's and Joe Teller's homicides. During the last he felt his blood pressure rise. Why did two innocent, gentle people have to die at the hands of street scum? Where was the justice? It sure as hell wasn't on this earth, he concluded. Even more depressing was the thought that the future held little promise of change, not with the increase in terrorism, the failure of the Courts to provide the feds and police with broader powers and the reductions in local law enforcement budgets. *Where was it all going to end,* he wondered.

The sun had barely risen by the time Dan Costa studied himself in the mirror...hair combed, tie straight, handkerchief in place. The aroma of freshly brewed coffee lured him to the kitchen where he poured some into a traveling mug, stirred in some sugar and pressed the top on tightly.

Traffic was light in the eastbound direction on both the Brooklyn Bridge and the Belt Parkway. He reached the funeral home just after seven-thirty, making his way to Paulie's office through a side door. His friend was giving instructions to a half-dozen attendants, so he slipped past them to the viewing room where he knelt before the coffin and stared at his father's lifeless features. Memories were revisited, including some with regret, until he sensed that someone was behind him. It was Father Boland.

Dan stood and extended his hand, which the seventy-year-old priest took in a still powerful, reassuring grip.

"You'll do well today, Son, if you just remember that he is where we all hope to be someday."

Dan nodded and found a smile.

"I have a favor to ask, Dan, and please don't feel obligated."

"What is it, Father?"

"The older boys on the boxing team asked if they could be pall-bearers. They really loved your father and in their minds the only fitting tribute would be one they'd share with no one but him. They intend to take turns standing a graveside vigil this evening, which I told them I thought was fitting enough, but they were rather insistent that I ask."

The sentiment touched Dan and he considered it appropriate that the young men whom his father had tried to guide through life should shepherd him into the next.

"That would please him, I'm sure, Father. Why don't you just work out the details with Paulie." With that said, he turned and knelt again as the priest left.

Shortly after, the mourners began filing in, taking seats behind Dan who remained kneeling, his eyes fixed on his father's face, his mind searching for what he was to take from this experience.

Paul touched his arm, breaking his concentration. "We have to start the final prayers." It was eight-twenty.

Father Boland read some lines from the New Testament, something about the rewards for righteous men, but Dan absorbed little of it. He was beginning to sense a purpose to all this and he anxiously focused on it as though this would be his one and only chance. *'Noblesse Oblige,'* he thought. His father's pursuit had been gentle and caring as only a peaceful, loving man's could be. The fact that Dan was less forgiving need not inhibit his quest for purpose. *Someone has to protect the innocent. How else can they fulfill their goals?*

*Wasn't St. Michael a warrior prince? Didn't Jesus, Himself, vent his anger at the money changers in the temple?* The strength he was blessed with must have a purpose of its own, and he began to see it as a virtue to be applied for the protection of others. Only briefly did he consider the violence that could result, dismissing it under the pretext that the end justified the means. Though not entirely comfortable with this position, he turned his attention to the prayers, satisfied that his focus was properly directed, if not entirely clear.

The ceremony concluded, Paul announced the mourners' names, and alone and in pairs they made their way forward for a last good-bye. If their final words had any affect on Dan Costa, he didn't show it. He looked in the eyes of each mourner, returned their embraces and gratefully acknowledged their condolences. Finally, Paul and Father Boland knelt together briefly, and when they left, Dan heard a sliding door close. It had come to this, five minutes alone with a father whom he had loved deeply, but who had perhaps been appreciated more by others. Five minutes to say farewell, to gaze a final time on a once strong yet gentle face that had brought comfort to countless and varied persons Dan had never met and would never get to know. Whether it was the lost opportunities or the realization of finality, something gripped his throat, tightening it, and his eyes watered. He fought to stop the tears, concentrating on the last words he wanted to say, trusting to memory the kindly features, hoping and praying he would be forgiven for his apathy. But they fell nonetheless, for his loss was greater than his resolve, and the only words he could find he repeated over and over. "I love you, Papa. Please help me.

Someone slid the door open and he could hear footsteps slowly approaching.

"It's time we get going, Dan," Paulie said softly.

Dan Costa remained kneeling long enough to wipe his eyes and replace the handkerchief. Then he stood, kissed his father's forehead and walked quietly from the room.

He would remember little of the limousine ride, church procession or eulogies, focusing instead on the times he had shared with his parents. He still remembered his mother's gentle voice and sweet smile, how she would challenge him to study harder or be kinder to people by reminding him that that's what Jesus would have done. He would be a man before he realized that she had never scolded him, that she had raised and taught him by holding him to the highest standards, helping him along the way when he got lost in youthful exuberance. And if by chance he would stray even the slightest, there was his father, equally gentle, but eternally strong, with a work ethic and sense of duty in heroic proportions. Dan learned more from his father's glance than most boys learn from a hundred lectures, for it was what Frank Costa did that taught his son. His words served only as reminders.

Dan took Communion, asking for his parents' help in getting through the next few weeks. For the first time in his life he felt alone and uncertain and he really didn't know how he would handle it. His father had always been there before, when both his mother and Eileen had died, and without realizing it Dan had found solace in his father's strength. No matter what tragedy or burden life held, Frank Costa's indomitable spirit had been the saving grace. Without it his son wondered how he would fare.

A bright sun greeted the mourners as they filed from St. Anthony's, following them to Gate of Heaven in Bay Ridge. True to his word Jimmy Scanella stood proudly with Benny at the head of a six-foot wide, neatly shoveled path leading to Rose Costa's gravesite, where her devoted husband would join her shortly. A fifty by fifty foot square around the grave had been hollowed out of the snow, and though everyone packed in tightly, half the people were relegated to the path and parking area for the final prayers.

Father Boland's last words were short but appropriate.

"Dear Lord, we return to you our father and friend, Frank Costa. We thank you for the days he shared with us, for the love and the peace he brought to our lives, for the courage he showed us and for the righteousness he taught us. He has done all you have asked of him, and more, and in turn we pray that you now reach down and bring him up to live with you in paradise."

One by one the mourners placed a flower on the casket and shuffled down to their waiting cars, until Dan, Paulie Ippolito and Jimmy Scanella stood alone in the bright chill, heads bowed. Dan dropped to his knees beside the flower-covered casket, no idea why, no clear thought filling his mind. Visions of his parents laughing, walking to church, greeting neighbors; the everyday memories of a happy childhood mixed with a foreboding that nothing would ever be the same. He struggled to concentrate on a final thought, something appropriate to take away, to bind him and his parents forever, something to provide strength when all else failed. He stared at the coffin and then at the tombstone that bore his mother's name.

Suddenly, he realized that they had done all they could, that he was on his own, armed with the strength and virtue they had instilled in him by example. They owed him nothing more.

"I love you both. Thank you and God bless you," he whispered softly, before walking away.

# CHAPTER 6

That night he found himself watching an old Sherlock Holmes movie starring Basil Rathbone and Nigel Bruce until 2 AM, before reading a bit from Hemmingway's "A Farewell to Arms" and finally drifting off to an uneasy sleep. When the alarm sounded at seven he instinctively got out of bed, showered and shaved, though he had nothing to do until 10:00, when he would leave for St. Anthony's to attend a special Mass in his father's honor. He passed the time drinking coffee, reading Carmine Pecora's file on the Teller murder and resisting the urge to reflect on the circumstances of his father's homicide.

At church he accepted condolences again, many coming from people who had been at the viewing, funeral and burial. It was becoming tedious…responding to people's advice, comforting others…all the while trying to be attentive. By the time he returned to his apartment he was physically and emotionally spent, so he ate an early dinner and read some of the Sunday Times before drifting off to sleep.

On Monday he arrived at the precinct headquarters before seven, an hour earlier than usual, determined to make quick work of the Teller homicide while consulting with Joe DeLorenzo on his father's case. Once they were cleared up he would decide what to do with the rest of his life.

"How're you doin', Kid?" It was Larry Kennedy, his voice and features unusually grim.

"Good, Larry, though I have to admit, I'm getting a little tired of people asking." A brief smile told the 3rd Shift Supervisor that Dan was serious, but grateful for the interest.

"Yeah, I guess it can get to be a pain. It's just that no one knows what to say, you know? I mean a guy feels like he should say something to show how he feels." He waited for a response, but got only another and shorter smile.

"Well, I gotta' be going," he said uneasily. "If there's anything I can do, don't hesitate. I mean it, Kid, anything at all, and I'll keep you in my prayers." Kennedy felt awkward and wished he hadn't said anything. Sometimes nothing is better.

Dan nodded. "Thanks, Larry, I appreciate it." He watched his friend slowly descend the wooden staircase, fumbling all the while with an absurdly long and uncooperative knitted scarf.

Minutes later Al Wilson reached the top of the stairs, accompanied by a neatly attired, young black man. As he passed Al laid a large hand on Dan's shoulder and gently closed it without speaking or breaking stride. The visitor dutifully followed, though he seemed to hesitate a second at Dan's desk, as if to introduce himself. Dan pretended not to notice, fixing his attention on Pecora's report.

As he heard Wilson unlock his office door, the phone rang.

"Homicide. Detective Sergeant Costa speaking."

"Dan, what are you doin' at work? I thought you were going to take some time off." It was Joe DeLorenzo.

"Changed my mind, buddy. What's up?"

"I called your apartment to tell you Bobby Avent gave me another guy to work the case. He knows Calvin and I are up to our eyeballs with three unsolved murders and at least one more from the weekend that he'll be givin' us. He told me he wants this new guy to just do the legwork on your dad's case. That'll save us some time and keep the pressure on. So at least Avent's heart's in the right place."

"Yeah, but I also think he's gotten some pressure from the top. Everybody wants to see Dad's killers caught. He may even have gotten calls from the Black community. You know, I believe Dad had as many black friends as white."

"If you throw in the *Espanol* he had more minority buddies than white, that's for sure."

"Yeah. Well, keep me posted, Joe." Dan knew he didn't have to remind his friend, but he wasn't in the mood to restrain his instincts.

"Who's the new guy?"

"His name's Ronald Williams. That's all I know except that he's black and served in uniform up in Harlem before getting his shield."

"Listen, Joe, unless it's a coincidence, your new man is probably the same Ronald Williams that drove for Commissioner Jenkins his first year, and if so, be extra cautious about what you say and what you let him in on. Maybe

I'm paranoid, but if black kids are responsible for my father's death, the Commissioner will do anything to keep this from being classified as racially motivated. So far all the victims in cases he's managed to stick that label on have been black and we shouldn't forget how he engineered a cover-up on those two Jewish kids who were murdered last year. Don't put yourself on the spot, but don't let Williams get too close either, at least not until you've got enough to hang somebody. Understand?"

"Got it. I hope you're wrong. We could use this guy's help, but I hear you loud and clear."

Inside Al Wilson's office Rasheed Martin's attention was riveted on what his Lieutenant had to say about his new partner.

"Dan Costa will prove to be as good a cop as this city has ever had, and after that, Commissioner, Mayor, who knows what. So you're getting an opportunity to work with the best. Make the most of it. It's an opportunity that few young men ever get, to work with a real pro. Listen to him, learn and do exactly what he says. Question him only after you've done it. Don't ever doubt what he tells you. You'll find out soon enough that this guy has extraordinary instincts and is smart as hell. That's what makes him special, and you can be just as good. You've got the brains. All you need now is to pick up the skills and maintain your focus. He's the best teacher you'll ever have. Any questions?"

The young man thought for a second before asking, "Does Sergeant Costa have a family? I really don't know anything about his private life except for his dad's murder."

Wilson wondered if he should say anything. It was only after convincing himself that he could oblige Martin without betraying Dan's friendship, and that what he would say was already common knowledge at the precinct, that he decided to answer.

Martin listened attentively as Wilson described the series of events that had propelled Costa's career. Fate pursued Dan Costa and he had the ability to take advantage of it. Nothing ever seemed to deter him. His intelligence and intuition were exceptional, more than sufficient to meet and overcome whatever obstacles were placed before him. He quickly became the surest bet in the City. You couldn't give odds high enough to get anyone to bet against him.

"Before you get the impression he's perfect, let me assure you he's got his human side too, with his own share of weaknesses. I saw him damn near destroyed once because he lost someone he loved so much that he didn't know how to handle it, how to fill the void. Everything about him is so intense, so committed...call it what you want...when it's pulled from him, it leaves a huge vacuum. In the past he had his dad, faith, maybe even my friendship to fill that void. This time I have my fingers crossed. I'm relying on work and a quick resolution of his father's case to keep him focused."

"What was it that brought him to the edge, Lieutenant?"

Wilson leaned back in the chair and swiveled it slightly to his left where he stared at a framed 8 by 12 photo. There were two smiling couples standing side-by-side...beautiful, shapely women standing between tall, understandably proud men. Martin recognized Wilson on the left and assumed the black lady next to him was his wife. A statuesque girl in her late twenties stood next to her. The young detective was taken with her beauty.

"Eileen Murphy Costa," Al Wilson began, and then stopped, as though contemplating everything he could remember about her. A smile creased the corners of his mouth. "Eileen Costa, Dan's wife, probably the most beautiful girl I've ever known."

"She sure is pretty," Martin interjected.

"Yes, she is...was," Wilson corrected himself. "She was twenty-eight when that was taken. We celebrated their third wedding anniversary at an Italian Feast... San Gennaro, I think...no, The Madonna of Mt. Carmel. That was it."

His eyes still fixed on the picture, his smile disappeared and there was no denying the sorrow he felt.

"Eileen Costa was a college graduate, St. John's, smart, beautiful, classy, and most of all, the biggest heart in the world. She could have had a corporate career and made a hundred thousand a year, but she chose a lousy eighteen thousand a year job at a home for wayward girls, battered women and single mothers. All she ever said about it was, 'You have no idea how fulfilling it is to help these poor girls. I'm really fortunate to have this opportunity.' And she meant it," he said with obvious admiration.

"Then one night, three winters ago...I think it was February twenty...yeah, the twentieth...she's leaving work and it's snowing and there's a lotta' ice on the ground. She walks to the corner, 16$^{th}$ Street off Union Square." Wilson's eyes narrowed and his voice softened as his mind prepared to relive the tragedy. "A stupid, twenty year old piece of shit high on marijuana comes speeding across Sixteenth in an old Jeep, tries to beat the light, makes a quick left and runs up the curb and over the corner. Wipes out a street vendor, his cart and two pedestrians, one of whom was Eileen Costa.

They rush her to a hospital. She lies in a coma for two weeks, but Dan won't let them pull the plug. He just sits there beside her bed, holding her hand, twenty-four hours a day, everyday. Friends bring him clothes and he showers and changes, but he never leaves her side. I never saw anything like it and I pray to God I never see anything like it again. It tore everybody up."

Wilson was quiet for a while, drained even by the memory. A minute passed and then he looked at his new detective. "Dan came out of it a quieter, more serious person…if you can believe it, an even more conscientious cop. But some part of him died back then, enough at least to make me worry a little this time around. Keep that in mind. Be respectful, be understanding. Go the extra step. The man deserves it."

"Did they get the guy?"

"Yeah, they got him, not that it matters much. Fact is he'll be out in another two or three years, even though he had a yard long rap sheet for drugs, speeding and disorderlies… another example of the stupidity of the system. The piece of shit will probably screw up more peoples' lives before he's put away for good. "

Martin was about to say something but he was waved off.

"You know enough to understand the man. You don't need to know more. He's become a more private person and you should…no, you damn well better… respect that. If you think for some awfully good reason you should know more or want to discuss it, you see me, and only me. Clear?"

"Yes, Sir."

"Good. Now I'll introduce you to your new partner." He punched an intercom button. "Dan, can you come to my office?"

When he heard the door behind him open Martin jumped to his feet and extended his hand.

"Dan, I'd like you to meet Detective Rasheed Martin. He's been assigned to us for his initial tour."

They shook hands and Costa said, "Welcome aboard," before turning to Wilson. "Lieutenant, there's something urgent I have to discuss with you privately." Without waiting for a response, he turned to Martin, "You wouldn't mind waiting outside for a minute, would you?"

The young officer looked at Wilson who just nodded.

The door had barely closed when Dan said, "I hope you're not going to partner him up with me, Al."

"You're the only one working solo, Dan, and besides, it would do you both a lot of good."

"I've been working solo for two years and I don't need someone to get through this, which we both know is why you're dumping him on me. More than ever I need to be alone."

Wilson knew his friend well and was honestly concerned that depression could consume him as it almost did when Eileen was killed. He just didn't know how to say it without being confrontational.

"Look, Dan, I think you know I'd never do anything unless I was certain it was in your best interest, and right now I'm convinced that having a partner, particularly one that needs time and attention, is good therapy." Before he could say what else was on his mind, Costa jumped in.

"Therapy? What makes you think I need therapy? I've been through this shit before, Al, and I came through okay. It'll take some time but I'll get through it without any special help, however well intended."

"It's not a matter of waiting until you need help," Wilson said softly. "I'm trying to give you one way of distancing yourself from the hurt. Anything that keeps you occupied helps, and if you really work at teaching this guy the ropes it will keep your mind a lot busier than if you were working alone. Besides, you're the best there is and I'd be short-changing the department and this kid if I turned him over to anyone else."

Dan really didn't want Rasheed Martin or anyone else hanging on his tail but he knew there was a lot of logic in Wilson's argument. After a few days he would probably feel differently anyway, but he couldn't resist getting the last word.

"Alright, you're the boss, so I'm going to lose out in the end no matter what. But if you're my friend, you'll leave the door open in case this guy turns out to be someone I don't need right now. Agreed?"

"Like I said, I'll do whatever helps you."

Dan spent the balance of the week teaching Martin the systems and procedures peculiar to Al Wilson and the 34th Street Precinct, as well as the thousand or so points of investigation that John Jay and other formal institutions ignored. Dan was an articulate, well-organized instructor and Martin was an equally intelligent, willing student. The two should have hit it off perfectly, yet neither felt entirely comfortable, each sensing the other's uneasiness. But they stuck to their regimen and managed to wish each other a restful weekend when their Friday shift ended.

Before leaving Dan stuck his head in Wilson's office, "I'll see you, Al. Have a nice weekend and give my best to Camille."

The big man looked up from some papers. "It's supposed to really warm up. Why don't you take a drive up tomorrow night and have dinner with us…or Sunday…whatever's better."

"Thanks, I appreciate it, but I think I'm going to take Father Boland up on an offer. The St. Anthony's team is boxing in a CYO tournament tomorrow. I'm going to work in the corner. Mr. Steele…I don't know if you ever met him…he was Dad's second for years with the kids. He's moving up to my dad's job and I'm going to be his second. I think Dad would have liked that."

"Yeah, he would have. How about Sunday?"

"Maybe, if I'm not too tired. After the fights Father Boland and some of the older men go out for pizza and wine. I feel like I should go, at least this once. But I'll call you early enough Sunday morning if I'm coming. I promise I won't just pop in."

"Pop in any damn time you want. Camille and I would only be upset if you never popped in."

Dan left feeling better about the week than he had thought he would when it started. Outside there were signs that winter was about to give way to spring. The icy slush had disappeared, there was a mild breeze and a bright sun had brought temperatures in the mid-forties. It felt good to see people with their heads up, some even smiling as they passed. Noise and hustle had returned to Thirty-fourth Street. As he rounded the corner he bumped lightly into an exotic looking, well-dressed young woman, her arms overflowing with bulging manila envelopes. It was Marilyn Kyme, Dante Fiore's Assistant M.E.

"Hello, Dan." Her voice was softly seductive. She looked up at him through those tantalizing, almond shaped, green eyes that caught and held his attention.

"Fancy meeting you here. Let me help you with those." He reached out and took most of the envelopes.

They stood closely, staring at each other for a few seconds. Finally, a coy little smile creased her lips. "Are we going to deliver these or just stand here all day?"

He smiled back. "We'll deliver them if you agree to have dinner with me tonight." Her eyes widened. "Why, Sergeant Costa, we hardly know each other," she said demurely.

"That's why we're having dinner, to get to know each other better."

She hesitated, studying his eyes, before smiling again. "Alright, dinner it is. Where and when?"

Dan chose a small continental style restaurant on the west side more famous for its food and intimacy than celebrity patrons. Marilyn arrived a half-hour late, blaming her workload and an uninspired cab driver. "He stayed in lane no matter what," she complained.

They shared a table in the rear where subdued lighting and soft music provided the privacy and comfort both were seeking, though each would later admit to a certain excitement over their first date. They talked about their educations and career choices; she, noticeably impressed with the scope of his experience; he, simply enchanted with her beauty. There was a sultry side to her that blended well with a classic profile, lithe figure and quick smile. He was sure she knew exactly how taken he was with her, but neither her confidence nor his obvious enthusiasm concerned him. Only occasionally did he wonder if the timing betrayed his father's memory, and having decided it would have had Frank Costa's blessing, he enjoyed the evening and indulged his growing infatuation.

Marilyn glanced at her watch. "It's almost ten and I have to be at work at seven, so if you don't mind I'm going to say good-night. I've had a wonderfully relaxing evening and I'd like to do it again." She looked at him earnestly.

"Sure. How about tomorrow?"

She gave a light, girlish laugh that Dan found playfully charming. "Well, I wasn't really thinking that soon. Why don't we wait at least a whole week?"

"Okay, tentatively, next Sunday. I'll call during the week, and if it's nice I'll take you for a ride to New Jersey, to this little Italian restaurant that serves the best saltimbacca in the world."

"New Jersey," she said, as though it were some far-off paradise. "Sounds good."

"Where do you live by the way?" he asked as he helped with her coat.

"That's right, you don't know where I live, do you? Two-ten West Sixty-fifth, Apartment 206. Parking's bad, so I'll wait for you outside."

"Very kind of you, Madame. I'll be sure to be on time."

Dan offered to walk her home or hail a cab. She chose the latter.

"I really do have a lot to do at work and I mustn't be late for services."

Dan reminded himself that she was Jewish and tomorrow was the Sabbath.

A cab pulled to the curb and Dan opened the door. As she stepped towards the taxi he extended his hand to say goodnight. She took it but leaned forward and kissed him lightly on the cheek. She smelled wonderfully.

"I really enjoyed tonight, Dan, and I look forward to next week and Joisey."

"Ditto, Joisey it is. And listen, I want you to know that tonight wasn't just about trying to forget the past few days. I enjoyed being with you. The remedial effect is just icing."

She smiled. "I'm glad."

As he walked to his apartment, Dan Costa felt relaxed and happy for the first time in a week…a little guilty perhaps, but basically satisfied with himself. He thought his dad wouldn't mind either.

He enjoyed the boxing matches at which the St. Anthony's kids distinguished themselves by winning eight of the twelve bouts, clearly establishing them as favorites for the upcoming season's P.A.L. crown. The wine and pizza party that followed was more reserved than usual, owing to the absence of the one man responsible for it all. But they drank toasts to his memory, pledged awards in his name and displayed the kind of interracial harmony that would have made Frank Costa proud. Before leaving, Dan promised Tony Steele that he would serve as his corner's second as long as he wanted him.

He got back to his apartment before midnight and listened to the messages, most of which were from friends offering Sunday dinners. The one he returned was from Joe DeLorenzo who invited him to call anytime before midnight. His watch said eleven fifty-eight.

"Who's this?"

"Goomba, it's me. Whatcha' got?"

"The worst headache in the world, that's what I got. Whataya' doin' callin' me at… Chrissake, it's freakin' midnight, Danny."

"Hey, pineapple, you told me to call if it wasn't after midnight."

"That was before I drank too much and got hooked up with some nymphomaniac. Nobody you know. Besides, I left the message late this afternoon. Don't you check them once in a while?"

"I was down at the Armory for some C.Y.O. matches. Kinda' got caught up in them."

"Yeah, well, look, I feel like shit. Let's not talk now. I'll call you tomorrow."

"But was it important?"

"Yeah. We got word on a watch being pawned over in Bensonhurst. Sounds just like your dad's retirement gift, but the inscription's been scratched off. The dealer had closed up by the time I called, so I'll get on it first thing Monday. Okay?"

"Yeah, thanks Joe, I...."
"Good, now I'm gonna' hang up and die. Goodnight."

On Sunday Dan drove over to Canal Street to question Jorge Ruiz, the parking lot attendant who had reluctantly come forward in the Teller case. There were two Hispanic men on duty when he arrived.

"Jorge Ruiz?"

"Yeah, who are you?"

Ruiz was a fairly big man, six feet and well over two hundred pounds. He had a neatly trimmed beard, thick black hair, angry eyes and what Dan concluded was a permanent scowl.

He showed his gold shield. "Dan Costa, homicide detective out of the 34th Street Station. Detectives Zimmerman and Pecora said you saw the shooting last week. I could use your help."

"I already told them everything," he said with little civility.

"I'm sure you did, but it's policy in these kinds of cases to have a higher ranking officer review what might be a discrepancy in the initial investigative report."

"Whattaya' mean 'discrepancy?'" he asked suspiciously.

"Just a minor error in the report, something the investigating officer missed. I'm sure we can resolve it in a few minutes, but I'd rather not discuss it out here."

The ticket booth was larger than most, with room for two chairs and a small table. You could hang your coat on the cigarette smoke that filled it.

"What do you want to know?" Ruiz asked as he sat, motioning for Dan to take the other chair while lighting up another cancer stick.

"Just tell me what you saw."

"Like I told the other cop, I didn't see everything, but I did see the little guy get hit because the one with the gun was yelling just before he shot. That's why I looked over. I didn't even know they were there until I heard him yelling something."

"Could you make out any of the words?"

"No. Maybe something like, 'Hurry up,' and 'What the fuck ya' doin'?' I don't know. Just yellin."

"Okay, so you look up and this guy's still yelling?"

"Yeah, for another second, you know? And then he just shoots. Bam, bam, twice like that. The little guy goes down right away."

"At the moment of the first shot, what was the victim doing?"

"Looked to me like he was takin' out his wallet, you know, from the inside of his coat, like where you would keep it in a jacket. I mean he wasn't makin' a move at the guy or nothin'. He wasn't doin' shit to make the guy shoot him."

"Maybe he thought the victim had a gun?" Dan asked.

"Man, there was no way you could figure a little old dude like that for a piece. Hell no, I'm tellin' you; I think the guy just felt like stiffin' somebody that night. Just a bad fuckin' dude." He hesitated a second. "But I'll tell you like I told the other cop, those two guys weren't black and they weren't young. Not the way they spoke and not the way they ran."

"I thought you couldn't make out what they were saying?"

"I couldn't, but I could hear their voices, and I'm tellin' you they weren't black." Suddenly, Ruiz changed his tone. "Look, you don't believe me, I don't give a shit. You goddamn cops are all the same, man. You believe what you want and you believe everything another cop says, and it don't mean shit to ya' that the guy could be lyin'. Nothin' changes with you guys. It's always been that way."

Ruiz convinced Dan he at least believed he was telling the truth, so he had no problem maintaining his composure. "I appreciate your help, Mr. Ruiz, but if we find the killers we're going to have to ask you to testify and I have to be sure of what you saw and heard. I or the District Attorney would counsel you not to say anything you can't substantiate." He felt he made his point so he continued. "What about the way they ran?"

Ruiz searched for the right words. "You know how a big fat guy would run, like he wouldn't really run, like he would kinda' slide his feet? You know what I mean?"

"You mean as if he were flat-footed?"

"Yeah, yeah, that's it, man. Flat-foot, that's it."

"Both men?" Dan asked.

"Nah. I don't know. I was only watchin' the shooter. I know there was a second dude, but I really didn't see much of him."

"So he could have been a younger man?"

"I guess so. Maybe. But the shooter, he was older, fat, too. A really big sonofabitch, you know? Moved like you said, flat-footed, not like any young guy like that other dude said."

"How do you know what the victim's friend said?"

"The detective told me. When I told him what I thought about the size of the shooter he told me I didn't know what I was talkin' about, that the dead guy's friend was right there so he should know if the dudes were young and black, or not. I think the guy was probably scared shitless and don't know what the fuck he saw."

"Let's talk about that other man, Jorge, the victim's friend. Do you remember anything about what he was doing during all this?"

"No, like I said, I was watchin' the old man go down and then I watched the shooter. I didn't pay no attention to the other two guys until they all started runnin' and I see the dead guy's friend go runnin' right in front of the car and around the corner."

Dan expressed surprise. "The front of the car? You mean after his friend was shot and the perps headed for their car, the witness didn't freeze, or just fall to the ground? He ran after them?"

"No man, they all started runnin', except the perps jumped in the car on the other side, away from me, you know, and the dead guy's friend just ran straight across the street, right in front of the car. I mean, shit, he was only fifty feet from me. How could I make a mistake about what I saw?"

Dan thought for a moment, staring briefly at Ruiz before continuing. "Can you tell me anything about that car?"

"Yeah. It was a late nineties Lincoln Towncar…black, maybe dark blue."

"But you didn't get the license plate?"

"No, man, everything happened fast. When the car passed me I ran across the street to see if the old man was dead. Then I called 911. I never thought to look at no license plate."

"Did the driver or anyone see you?"

"I don't know. They drove away fast, man."

"Thank you, Mr. Ruiz. You've been a big help. I'll let you know how we make out. By the way, did you tell the other detectives everything you told me?"

"Yeah, I think so, but the little one went across the street, so it was only the big one, the Italian guy, that I spoke to."

"Oh, I didn't know that. Any idea what the other detective was doing across the street?"

"I'm not sure. I just know that they both came over here like they were going to talk to me, and the big one told him to go measure some shit. The little one didn't seem to think it was important but the big guy said somethin' about one of 'em havin' to do it and he wanted to talk to me. Some shit like that. So then we sat down in here and I told him exactly what I told you. Shit, man, he even asked the same questions you did."

"So you told him about the Towncar, why you didn't think the shooter was a young black…that kind of stuff?"

"Like I said, man, I told him everything I told you, but he didn't want to hear what I thought about them not bein' young black guys."

"Thanks again. I'll keep in touch," Dan promised.

"Yeah, well if you really want to catch who did this, I wouldn't go lookin' for no black dudes, 'cause the ones who did this were fuckin' old, man."

## CHAPTER 7

On the way back to his apartment Dan decided to stop at the station and make a call. Convinced that at least some of what Ruiz said was true, the assailants would have had no reason to permit Lewis Berger, the single known witness to his friend's murder, to live. They had more than ample opportunity to eliminate him, yet they chose to let him go, and that could only mean one thing: Lewis Berger was an accomplice. On top of that, Carmine Pecora's work at the scene violated more than one investigative procedure, and the fact that his report omitted important testimony from an eyewitness compounded the problem. He wasn't sure what he would do about it. Pecora's work was occasionally less than perfect, but that could be said of any detective, particularly since the cutbacks had doubled everyone's workload. Carmine was a decent guy, got along with the rest of the squad and pulled his fair share of the load so he didn't want to blow everything out of proportion. Still, his work on this case had been unusually sloppy. He finally decided to postpone any discussion about it, hoping it wouldn't happen again.

When he arrived at the Station it was almost two in the afternoon and he hadn't eaten lunch, so he called the Garden Café on 35th Street and ordered a hot pastrami on rye with spicy mustard, a kosher dill and a Nehi Orange to wash it down. Then he pulled the case file. Lewis Berger's number was a 570 area code in Pennsylvania. The phone rang twice before a man answered.

"Dr. Berger here."

"Hello, Sir, my name is Dan Costa. I'm the homicide detective assigned to Dr. Teller's case. May I take a few minutes of your time?"

Berger hesitated. "I already told the other detectives everything I know. What else can I tell you? I didn't see anything other than what I told them."

"I understand Doctor. Relax, there's no reason to be nervous."

"You'd be nervous too if this happened to you...your best friend shot to death in front of you."

"I can sympathize, Doctor. I'm sure it was and still is a very traumatic experience, and I promise you we will find and prosecute the assailants, but I need your help and it will only take a few minutes."

"Well, alright," he said testily, "but please, make it quick. I have a great deal to do today."

What little there was of the doctor's poise was quickly dissipating.

"I have the investigating detective's report in front of me and I just want to substantiate a couple of statements," Dan said calmly. "You stated that both men wore dark coats and hats... black, I think you said. Could they have been a very dark blue?"

"Possibly. I see no reason why that's important one way or the other."

"Well, we've had a number of armed robberies in that neighborhood where witnesses have reported a man in a very dark blue leather coat and watch cap. And as in your case, the assailant has been a black male, so you see, there might be a connection there."

"Yes, yes, I see," Berger responded less cautiously.

"You did state that you were quite certain the perpetrators were black males, is that correct?"

"Yes, definitely. I could tell by their voices, but I also saw a part of one's neck and the shooter's hand when he extended it to shoot Joe. They were definitely black."

"Any accents?"

"No, I don't think so," Berger responded slowly, as if trying to remember.

"Okay, next we have the shots. You say there were two, and you are certain of that."

"Oh, yes, and the papers substantiated it."

"The papers?"

"Yes, you know, the newspapers. They said Joe had been shot twice."

"Oh, I see. You think they fired twice because your friend was hit twice."

"No, that's not what I said. You misunderstood me. I said I heard two shots and the papers said Joe was hit with both of them. I just was saying there wasn't a third." He waited a few seconds. "Do you understand what I'm saying?"

*Yes, you lying sonofabitch, I understand what you're saying,*

"Sorry, Doctor. Yes, I understand. I was just reviewing these notes of the other detectives and it seems you told them you saw black skin around the eyeholes in the mask, but nothing about the neck area."

In reality, the reports included no statements from Lewis Berger about the perpetrators having black skin, simply that they had sounded black to him.

Again, he hesitated. "Well, your detective got it wrong. I'm sure I said the neck, where the mask wasn't long enough to cover, and I'm certain I said the shooter's hand. I don't know how that Italian detective could have misunderstood. Maybe his notes were translated incorrectly."

"Probably. That does happen a lot, but just for the record it was the Jewish detective's notes; you know, Detective Zimmerman?"

"Oh," was Berger's confused response to another of Dan's fabrications.

"Just one more point, Doctor, and then you can run."

"Good, because I really am late. Please make it quick."

"We are still trying to figure out why you parked in a lot around the corner from the restaurant when it has one of its own right next door."

He replied anxiously, "I know I explained this carefully."

*And,* Dan thought, *you are about to do so again, just as you and someone else have rehearsed a dozen or more times.*

"As we drove towards the restaurant, Joe said he knew of a parking lot that was much cheaper. So I just went where he told me. I wish I hadn't. He'd be alive today if I hadn't listened to him."

"I see. So it was Dr. Teller's choice. Well, that explains that. I guess there's not a lot more to discuss until I talk to the other eyewitnesses.

"What? What other eye witnesses? There wasn't anyone else there. I would have seen them."

"Sometimes in these kinds of situations witnesses like yourself are traumatized. They don't always see and hear what's going on around them. When you ran across the front of that car you were only fifty feet or so from a pedestrian who saw the whole thing, and there were two other men on the opposite sidewalk that saw the shooting, your escape and the getaway car. They said you were really fortunate to have not been killed as well. You see, that's why we had to know the number of shots. We just couldn't understand why they didn't try to kill you as well."

The silence was deafening. Detective Sergeant Costa waited for an explanation.

Finally, Berger offered an excuse that sealed Dan's conviction. If he had harbored the remotest possibility of the doctor's innocence, Berger's attempt to explain away eyewitness testimony negated it.

"One of them did try to shoot me, twice, but I heard the gun misfire. I was that close to them that I could hear the click. The other witnesses couldn't have been close enough."

Dan could picture this frightened little man, but he reserved no sympathy for him. Joe Teller had been murdered and Lewis Berger had played a significant role in it. He was also a likely key to the motive and the identity of the conspirators.

"You're a good witness, Doctor, I just wish you had offered this testimony before. It could be very meaningful. I mean if the gun jammed and we find it, we'll know it's the murder weapon and we can trace it, so you really should have come forward sooner. I think you should drive back here tomorrow so we can resolve this with the other witnesses. It's Sunday, I know, but at least you won't have to take off from work."

"I, uh, I have to see. I don't know if tomorrow's possible." He was near panic. "I have to go. I'll call you."

He hung up before Dan could continue. He redialed but there was no answer, so he phoned Al Wilson. His son, Michael, answered.

"Hi, Mr. Costa. I just want you to know how sorry I am about your dad. I wanted to go to the funeral but they wouldn't let me 'cause they said it would be crowded enough. But I did say prayers for him."

"Thanks, Michael. You're a good kid. Playing any sports right now?"

"Yeah, we still got a shot at the basketball title. We're doing pretty good too, but I'm really looking forward to baseball. I'm a pitcher."

"Yeah, I know. Your father says you're almost as good as your sister."

He laughed. "Oh, Dad always says stuff like that. He doesn't want me to get a big head."

"Is he around?"

"Yeah, I'll get him."

Michael Wilson yelled for his father.

"Hey, Dan, how you doin'?"

"Fine, Al. I just called to let you know I'm driving out to Nuremberg, Pennsylvania tomorrow on the Teller case. His friend, Berger, is involved and I think I can crack him, but he doesn't sound like he's willing to come in. I'm afraid he might run."

"Can you get local law enforcement to help?"

"I'm going to try, but it appears they're under a County Sheriff's jurisdiction. They have a single constable, if you can believe that."

"Give him a call. It can't hurt. He might be a devoted public servant."

"Yeah, one of the dying breed. Anyway, I think I'd better plan to go out there and do some detective work. I'll call in Monday morning if I don't get back. Let Rasheed know."

*LIMULUS*

"You wouldn't want to take him along, huh?"

"Hey, tomorrow's Sunday. It looks like an eight to nine hour round trip. Why ruin his day off? Besides, the department budget can't handle double hotel and food allowance.

"Yeah, yeah, okay."

Dan looked at his watch. Two-thirty. He picked up the phone again and punched in another number.

"Dr. Kyme," a weary voice answered.

"I know you're busy and don't want to talk, but I thought you'd like to know there's one person in the world thinking about you."

"Daniel Costa, ace detective, why aren't you out detecting instead of interrupting me on the single busiest day of my life."

"Because you needed to hear that someone cares."

"You're right, I do, and especially from you," she replied before wondering if she hadn't been too bold.

"Well, well. She let her guard down. What next."

She laughed. "Nothing as intimate as you might think, but you can always hope."

"Proud of yourself for that, I'll bet. You'll be sorry when you hear I'm off to the wars."

"Oh, we're being invaded? By whom?"

"A band of bloodthirsty enzymologists if I don't miss my guess, which brings me to another point. How about a quick lesson in enzymology?"

"Seriously?"

"Yep, since you won't run off with me."

"Well," she started deliberately, "enzymes are complex organisms, usually proteins that are produced by the body's cells. Some enzymologists believe they're the secrets to life and health, but they're not sure if they're cause, effect or both. For example, if you have a heart attack, an enzyme called CPK, Creatine Phosphokinase, jumps like hell. We take some of your blood, mix it with a reagent that contains another measured enzyme called LDH, Lactate Dehydrogenase, and we can measure your CPK to see if it's elevated or not. If it is, you've had a heart attack. If it isn't, you're just in love."

"There you go again, getting sexy and intimate when I'm trying to be serious."

"Oh, okay, I'll be serious."

"Don't you dare. Sexy and intimate fit you nicely."

"I think I'm going to call a detective. This conversation is beginning to sound sultry and lurid."

"Sultry and lurid can be good too."

"Like I said, you can always hope."

Dan searched for a comeback but couldn't find one, so he refocused on his train of thought.

"You still there or are you caught up in your hope?" she asked.

"Still here. Could an enzymologist discover something that could make him very wealthy?"

"Sure. A Dr. Florenz way back in the '30s discovered the relativity of LDH and CPK and how heart attacks affected their levels in blood. By providing such a definitive diagnosis, literally hundreds of thousands of myocardial infarct patients are saved each year. Florenz died a multi-millionaire."

"Any examples more recently? Any research you know about that might have a similar financial impact?"

"It's way outside my field, Dan," she admitted. "Give me a week or so to get out from under and I'll be happy to make some calls. Enzymologists make up a tiny portion of the research community. Theirs is not glamorous work so it doesn't necessarily attract a lot of grants or success oriented people. I've never actually known a research scientist who was totally dedicated to enzyme technology. Most prefer the broader scope of biochemistry…lots of commercial applications."

"Well, thanks for the lesson. I'm not sure I'm smart enough to piece all this together but I appreciate your offer to help. I'm leaving tomorrow morning for Pennsylvania. Would you mind if I call you tomorrow night?"

"Wait until Monday and call me at work. I'm going to be in and out all weekend. By the way, why all this sudden interest in enzymes and money? Looking for a way to become rich?"

"I wish. No, a doctor doing enzyme research of some kind was killed and I always suspect that money is the motive. It's usually that, sex, or rage, and in this case the latter two don't seem to fit, but I could be wrong. I hope to pin some things down this weekend. And speaking of that, have a nice one and I'll call you Monday."

"You too, and Dan, believe me, I'd really rather spend it with you."

Surprised by her comment, he held the phone, conjuring a suitable response when he heard it click.

He ran the Law Enforcement Agency Directory on his desktop and dialed the Nuremberg Police Station.

"Nuremberg, Pennsylvania. Constable Jack Shultz speaking."

"Hi, Constable, this is Dan Costa. I'm a Manhattan homicide detective looking into the shooting of Doctor Joseph Teller. You're familiar with the case?"

Shultz's voice was clear and controlled.

"Familiar enough to wish he had stayed the hell away from New York. Damn shame, Detective. Joe Teller was one special human being, everything you think of when you envision good people. Damn shame," he repeated.

"I'm sure you're right", Dan sympathized. "We could use some help. Dr. Berger was with him and he's being less than cooperative. Can you tell me anything about their relationship?"

"Probably not a lot. I knew Joe well, but I can't say the same about Lewis. I'm not sure anyone here knows him well. Except for his relationship with Dr. Teller, he really seems to be a solitary type, spends all day and early evening at the lab, six or seven days a week. When he's not in the lab or asleep in his room at the local hotel, he's off someplace in New York, twice a month or so. I couldn't tell you exactly where. Like I said, he never really befriended anyone here, though he did seem close to Joe. They were together, working in that lab almost constantly. They'd occasionally go to the local café for breakfast during the week and brunch on Sundays. Sometimes you would see Joe at social functions, mostly church sponsored affairs, and he'd be alone or with a friend from hereabouts, a woman he met a year or so ago. But I don't believe I ever saw Dr. Berger going anywhere or doing anything unless Joe was with him."

The constable hesitated for a second, gathering his thoughts. "I believe they used to drive over the mountain to Sheppton for some dinners, a quiet little place called Anna's. The folks there might know him better than anyone here. Of course he did live at Bottino's Hotel. Joe and Maria own and run it. They're both out-going types, so they'd get him to talk if anyone could. You might ask them. Need their number?"

"I think I'll drive out there tomorrow, Jack. I'm getting the feeling Berger's real nervous about something, so he might run. I need to see him in person before he does. Could you give me directions from the city?"

"Sure. By the way, you do know they're moving the lab?"

"What do you mean?"

"Right after Joe was killed they started moving the lab equipment, cages, boxes of stuff...emptying the place out as far as I can tell. They never have let anyone in the lab itself, just the office area, and that's separated from the lab by a wall and door. I've been in the office a few times and couldn't even tell there was a lab behind it. You couldn't see a darn thing."

"But you're sure they moved the lab?"

"Yeah, they backed in some vans, and two guys, not locals, have been loading and driving off with the stuff all week. I stopped by on Wednesday to see my lady-friend...she worked in their office...and I saw them loading dismantled shelving. She told me last night that they laid her off. Gave her three months' pay though, not bad for less than two years' work."

"Jack, I'm afraid Berger is going to take off. Is there any way you might detain him until I get there? If you can't, see if you can get his new address. At least get me his auto I.D. in case I need to run an all points."

"I can sure as hell try. Give me your number."

Dan phoned Al Wilson and gave him a quick summary of the conversation with Shultz. While he was ending it his other line rang. It was the constable.

"I'll call you back, Al."

"Looks like you were right for thinking he might run," Shultz began. "Maria, the hotel owner I mentioned, said he left with two suitcases less than an hour ago. We checked his room and there are books and papers all over the place...a real mess, and he used to be a neat freak. He's driving a '98 black Nissan Pathfinder. Sorry, I don't have the plates but I did check with the State Motor Vehicle Agency and they have no record of a car registered in Berger's name."

"Okay, Jack, tell me how to find you from New York."

After jotting down the Constable's directions, Dan concluded the call with a promise to stop in at Shultz's office before noon, assuming he made the trip in the three and one-half hours he predicted.

Dan phoned Wilson again. "He's running, Al. I shouldn't have pushed him so hard, damnit. I should have walked in on him tomorrow."

"Maybe, maybe not. If the lab is empty they probably concluded their business, so he was going to leave today no matter what. Get an all points out right now and call me tomorrow when you get there. I'll let you know if we pick him up."

"Thanks, Chief. Give Camille my love."

By 7:00 AM he was on the road, heading down Eighth Avenue to the Lincoln Tunnel and what he hoped would be a pleasant drive through New Jersey to Nuremberg, Pennsylvania. The Internet had told him little about the rural mountain community except that its population was less than six hundred and the nearest city, Hazleton, was twenty miles east. There wasn't much traffic, so within thirty minutes he was on Route 80, a terminally boring, straight line run of almost two hundred miles, broken only by the Delaware Water Gap, a serpentine gorge that separates the Garden and Keystone States. He spent most of the first hour recording the questions he needed to ask, not really certain of what answers to expect. But at the bottom of it all was the issue of motive. Of Berger's involvement he had no doubt. The only question remaining was what prompted it. The image he had drawn was that of a weak, insecure little man whose world was apparently limited to the study of enzymology and the people working in it. According to Constable Shultz, the town consensus was that Lewis Berger had no other life or any interest in developing one. If so, the motive could be academic jealousy. Teller might have stumbled onto something to which Berger felt he had an equal or greater right. Who's to say politicians have a monopoly on greed. But Berger would have needed an accomplice or two, because the profile Dan was drawing was not one of a man who could make the contacts necessary to carry out a murder. Though he couldn't pinpoint all the factors, he was comfortable concluding that there was at least one other conspirator and that the motives lay beyond professional jealousy. For these reasons he formed his questions to determine which other scientists or businessmen were associated with Teller and Berger, what the nature of their work was, what successes they had achieved and what their circumstances were immediately prior to the murder.

Confident that he had thought everything out well and not missed any important issues, he relaxed and tried to enjoy the scenery. Though spring had just begun, the sun was bright, the sky was clear and green patches were beginning to dot the fields. A sign announced that he was passing the Allamuchy exit, that Hackettstown was next and that the Delaware Water Gap was just fifteen miles further. *Almost halfway there.*

His thoughts shifted to his brief conversation with Joe DeLorenzo. Tomorrow his friend would interview the pawnbroker who had reported receiving a watch that matched the description of his father's. If luck was with them, it would be his and they would get a positive I.D. on the seller. That's when Dan would want to talk to Joe, to make sure he did everything by the book. This was one case that wasn't going to be lost or dismissed due to police oversight or legal technicalities. Dan had seen enough of those, and enough of judges and trial attorneys who seemed preoccupied with nuances of the law rather than guilt or innocence. Throw in juror prejudice and it was easy to understand why barely twenty percent of felony assault cases resulted in prison terms, which was in turn the reason for the proliferation of violent crimes. Fewer than ten percent were committed by first time offenders. Until the system was changed there wouldn't be any reduction in crime because the people most likely to commit them were being recycled to the streets.

This was the source of his greatest frustration and the main reason behind his growing dissatisfaction with the job. He would always do his best as long as he carried a badge, but he was beginning to think about a life outside the force, away from the violence, free of the politics and indifference that nursed it. Still young, he was more intelligent than most and there was nothing in his background to discourage a prospective employer. Friends in real estate and the stock market had encouraged him to think about a career in their fields, but until recently he hadn't seriously considered it.

"I'd be bored to death behind a desk," he had told them.

But politically correct officials, an antiquated justice system and a prejudiced Police Commissioner had made him think more seriously about alternatives. What good was he really doing, putting ten, maybe fifteen murderers away a year? Twice that many got off on technicalities or soft sentences. The whole damn mess was so twisted, so insanely ineffective, it depressed him to think about it, though he was beginning to do so more frequently.

He knew enough good people like Al Wilson and cared deeply enough about them that he wanted to hang in there, hoping that the pendulum would swing back towards the middle. Terrorism had reduced the public's appetite for violence and there were signs from the black community of a growing disenchantment with certain activists and their never-ending excuses. Even the New York press had begun to question the Commissioner's motives and tactics, a privilege they had rarely if ever exercised. True to form, Jenkins had accused them of "confederate journalism," a charge he repeated so frequently that despite their liberal nature, they were obliged to refute. He had lost his last ally amongst the establishment, so there was a light at the end of the tunnel and that encouraged Dan. Besides, the actual work of a detective invigorated him, something sales in the private sector could never do.

The road ahead curved sharply to the right. He was entering the Water Gap. With the sun still behind him, the broad expanse of the Delaware shimmered in sharp contrast to the dark, tree covered Poconos straight ahead. The scenery distracted him and more than one nervous driver blasted a warning as Dan drifted from his lane. The road mirrored the contours of the river, which as the map had predicted, cut frequent and sharp angles through the granite bedrock. Not until an eighteen-wheeler appeared ominously close did he decide to pay closer attention to his driving.

Finally, the maze concluded, he paid the dollar toll and collected the obligatory receipt. Immediately, his attention was drawn to a large highway billboard: "Welcome to Pennsylvania. America starts here."

Given his mood, his father's death and the terrorists' activities, the assertion seemed appropriate. Yet for the next five minutes what he saw was not unlike North Jersey or parts of Staten Island. Stroudsburg was a city with its fair share of malls, traffic and enough litter to draw attention, though miniscule in comparison to New York's.

Once clear of it, he began an ascent to the top of the Poconos through quaint little towns named Scotrun, Jim Thorpe and White Haven. All around him were forests of oak, maple and white birch, their budded branches intruding into the rich green of robust spruce and eastern hemlock. Thick clutches of wild rhododendron and mountain laurel, seemingly resistant to the noxious fumes of passing traffic, formed a delicate barricade. The ribbon that was Interstate 80 nestled comfortably in the lush landscape that stretched to the horizon. Dan forgot everything else, absorbed the natural beauty and wished Marilyn Kyme was there to share it.

Another hour passed before he saw a sign that told him it was time to turn onto Route 81 towards Hazleton. The Jeep began a steep descent into the Conyngham Valley, a wide, earth-tone patchwork of evergreen and dairy farms. Once in its depth he faced the reverse climb to Hazleton, Pennsylvania's highest city, snuggled amongst the peaks of the Green Mountains. There, a right turn would put him on a one-lane road atop the Pismire Ridge that ran above the richest vein of the Llewelyn Foundation, America's anthracite treasure.

Throughout the nineteenth and the first half of the twentieth centuries anthracite, the world's hardest, hottest burning coal, had fueled the nation's industrial complex. Together with Pennsylvania's iron ore deposits, it provided the ingredients for manufacturing steel, solidifying the State's claim as the nation's industrial leader. It had spawned the country's largest canal system, running ore and minerals from the Great Lakes region to the foundries, as well as thousands of miles of railroad track carrying coal and steel to and from the furnaces.

Dan recalled schoolbooks with pictures that told another story, one of abject poverty and hardship to which immigrant miners from Eastern Europe were subjected, of the Lattimer Massacre, in which unarmed miners marching for basic rights were shot down by mine owners' guards and of the ultimate collapse of the coal processing empire. He remembered reading how these people suffered starvation and black lung, marveling as he did at their perseverance, work ethic and spiritual commitment. He reflected on how peoples' attitudes had changed, from selfless dedication to duty to the "me" generation.

There had always been and would always be the coal barons, men so blatantly obsessed with wealth that the killing of starving miners meant nothing. Today they masqueraded as drug dealers, stock manipulators and politicians, some occupying the nation's highest offices. What bothered him most was that an increasing percentage of society was adopting the same callous, self-serving attitude. The more he thought about it, the more convinced he became that it would never get better, that whatever had been in the hearts of those whose dedication made this country great was slowly and forever disappearing. It was only a matter of time before everything hit rock bottom, a helluva' price for what some labeled progress.

Annoyed with himself for what he considered a growing obsession, he sought refuge in a silent prayer, remembering something he had read in a book on meditation:

*God, give me patience to accept the things I can do nothing about, the strength to overcome the others, and the wisdom to know the difference.*

A sign ahead alerted him to his next turn: "Oneida." He passed quickly through the old mining town named after one of the Iroquois tribes, with its one room wide duplexes bunched in straight lines along a narrow road. Well-used pick-ups hinted at the standard of living, though carefully manicured front yards spoke of pride and self-respect.

Oneida's lone thoroughfare turned sharply right, following a sign informing him that Nuremberg was five miles ahead. The road plunged abruptly, narrowing and twisting as it did down the face of a Green Mountains ridgeline. He couldn't help but think of the consequences for indecision or lapsed concentration, especially in the winter.

White birch hovered above, supported by thickets of healthy rhododendron, laurel and wild azaleas. Juniper and hemlock fought their way through the tangle for a share of the filtered sunlight.

Each time he shifted his attention from the road to the beauty surrounding him, the Jeep would kick up shale fragments on the shoulder, reminding him to stay the course. Large moss-covered out-croppings of limestone and granite provided more ominous warnings, flowing to the very edge of the roadway.

The two-mile downward spiral was followed by a series of rises and descents, each with its own challenge of sharply banked turns, first to the left and then abruptly to the right. His admiration for the driving skills of the natives was growing. He slowed to take in a waterfall cascading from high above to a rock-lined trough that funneled beneath the road and into the woods beyond.

The road began a gradual climb through the tilled fields of a dairy farm. In the distance he could see the cow barn, just opposite a white, two-story farmhouse complete with red brick chimney, wrap-around porch and a cluster of well-preserved outbuildings. With a broad tiller in tow, a tractor plodded in straight lines across the landscape. As he passed the barn the unmistakably earthy aroma of fresh cow dung invaded the car. Dan didn't mind. He was caught up in a nostalgic slice of Americana.

The road began another ascent towards a cemetery on a hillock at the foot of a spruce covered mountain. Wind and rain had erased the names and dates of more than a few headstones, suggesting that the plot had been there for centuries. He was still searching the markers when the road suddenly played out and he found himself staring off into space, across a green valley to a tiny town nestled in the hillside of a cone-shaped mountain.

*Nuremberg,* he thought, recalling Jack Shultz's description. The road turned sharply right and he again negotiated a steep, twisting descent, across a wooden bridge that spanned, according to a well-weathered sign, Black Creek, and back up the reverse side towards the town. A single road, flanked on each side by white clapboard houses and the steeples of two churches seemed to disappear in the pine and hardwood forest that covered Sugarloaf Mountain. He slowed, looking for some edifice that might suggest a police station. Halfway up he noted a green trimmed house with a modest "U.S. Post Office" sign hanging from the eave, followed by another of identical design notifying those interested that this was "Leon's Café." Almost to the top, the multi-colored façade of "Moretti's General Store, Founded 1898" reminded him that he had reached his destination. Jack had said his office was right next door.

Dan pulled to the curb and parked in front of a one room wide, two story, fieldstone house of undeterminable age. A small black-on-white sign identified it as the property of "Luzerne County Law Enforcement."

Before exiting the car he pulled hard on the handbrake, ensuring it was well set. Nuremberg's one and only street could easily double as a ski slope.

A knock on the door brought a welcoming "Come in."

In what had once been a miner's parlor, Jack Shultz arose from behind an old but sturdy wooden desk that occupied most of the space, leaving barely enough for a three drawer file and two well-worn chairs. The smell of recently laid institutional green linoleum was only slightly more offensive than the glare from fluorescent lights set in a tiled drop ceiling.

"Glad you made it," the constable welcomed him with a warm smile. He was a trim, broad shouldered man in his early forties, with bright blue eyes and a firm, reassuring handshake.

"For a while I didn't think I would. That road from Oneida is a trip."

"Hell, you should try it when there's ice and snow. Just three weeks ago we had a late storm. Had to close it for two days. Couldn't even get the plows up or down. Happens every couple of years."

"How do the people get in and out?"

"Well, if you continue up Main Street, it turns right and runs along the face of Sugarloaf until it gradually drops into Fern Glen. Then you can follow the Tomhicken Road about eighteen miles into Hazleton. It's a little longer that way, but people have to eat."

"You have no food store?"

"Not since old Henry Bottino closed up. He used to have a store and butcher shop on the bottom floor of his house. Was there about fifty years before he packed it in. His younger brother, Joe, owns the hotel."

"I didn't see a hotel."

Jack laughed. "Sure you did. It's right next door," and he pointed his thumb up the hill. "They have a little sign next to the door. They rent three rooms on the second floor. Not bad now since they added a bathroom. At one time Joe and Maria shared one downstairs bath with the guests. They've gone modern," he said with a grin.

"Have you had breakfast yet?"

"No, Jack, just a glass of juice. I wanted to get out here early."

"Well, it's Sunday," Shultz said, checking his watch, "and the churches will be emptying just about now."

Right on cue, bells started ringing.

Proud of himself, the constable continued.

"Don't look surprised, everything around here is done according to schedule. Mountain people have their ways and they won't change them, not in the least, not by a minute. That goes for the preachers, too. Anyway, Leon prepares a super brunch on Sundays. Let's head down there, because some of the people you'll want to talk to will be there. I can point them out, maybe set up the interviews."

As the constable led the way, Dan noticed the neatly starched, perfectly cut blue uniform, polished shoes and gleaming waist holster. For whatever evil lurked in their idyllic setting, Nuremberg's citizens had chosen a formidable guardian.

"Larry Moretti runs the General Store," Shultz advised as they passed it. "Fourth generation. Guy's got everything, no lie, and if he doesn't have it in stock, which is rare as hell, he knows where to get it in a day or two. It's like having a Home Depot without the crowds. Larry's one of the folks you're going to want to talk to."

They crossed the street and descended on Leon's as twenty or so worshippers in their Sunday best trudged up the hill toward them.

Shultz checked his watch again. "Good, we're here first and the door will be open."

The constable was two for two. They entered a twenty-by-twenty room with neatly covered tables and chairs lining the walls, a serving table overflowing with food occupying the center. A broad expanse of a man in a white tee shirt and chef's hat peered from behind a serving counter cut in the back wall.

"Mornin', Jack," he said without looking.

"Good morning to you, big guy. What's on the menu?"

"Got a surprise today," the busy owner promised. "Got my hands on some lamb's kidneys. Peppered and sautéed them with venison in some of old man Nahas's wine. Came out better than I thought," he said proudly, finally looking up for approval.

"Sounds great, I'll try 'em," Jack said, handing Dan a plate. "Charlie Nahas's wine ain't made for no human man's stomach," Jack whispered, " but you can't beat it for removing rust from metal or frying up sausage and venison." Shultz nodded an assurance that that was fact.

As they surveyed the piles of food, people began filing in, eyeing Dan while greeting Jack and their host. Everyone smiled. Dan was sure they were permanently etched.

"Real nice people here," Jack confided, as he piled thick slices of bacon, over-sized link sausages and squares of dark brown something-or-other onto his dish.

"You gotta' try his scrapple," Shultz ordered as he forked a slab onto Dan's plate. "Makes it himself. Best damn scrapple on the mountain. Everything but the oink."

Scrambled eggs, steaming buckwheat pancakes, the kidney and venison special and a greasy potato and onion concoction called "bubble and squeak" followed. After choosing a table, Jack returned to fill another plate with toasted black bread, scoops of butter and generous slices of country cured ham. "Just in case we get hungry later."

Dan observed the people as he ate, washing everything down with a thick brew of hot coffee and fresh, rich cream. They all looked happy and healthy, if not just a bit overweight.

"Anyone around here ever die of a heart attack?" he asked.

"Sure, but only when they're ninety and only if they're ready, unless of course," Shultz added seriously, "they were miners. Not too many of them lived to see sixty, and the lucky ones died by accident."

Dan was about to ask what he meant, but Jack continued with his thought. "These people work hard all their lives, but they do it with a lot of love. It's the caring for their families and each other that keeps them young, I think. They've got a lot of pride, comes from knowing they do their best and it's usually good enough. Their kids never starve or go without the necessities." He paused. "Too bad so many of these kids don't take after their parents."

Dan looked surprised.

"The young people here aren't like their parents, at least not all of them. We have our share of problem teenagers and young adults."

"What are they into?"

"No drugs, at least not the heavy stuff…marijuana, maybe. The big problem is alcohol…alcohol and sex. The parents in these parts…my generation, my parents' generation…they tried to raise their kids right, taught them right from wrong, what self-respect is all about. He looked around the room. "What have you got here, twenty-five, thirty people? And how many are less than fifty years old?"

"There's only two young couples."

"Right, and only one of them is married. The other," and he motioned to his right, "is the Heller kid, one of the few with his head screwed on right. His old man, Hank, wouldn't have it any other way, but most can't overcome the peer pressure these kids are under. It's not like it used to be, that's for sure. Maybe having to go to a big regional high school in Hazleton is the problem."

Dan glanced again in the direction of the Heller boy, easily his height, but a lot closer to three hundred pounds with shoulders as wide as a bull's. "I can't imagine that kid being intimidated by anyone."

Jack smiled. "Neither can I. Besides, just about everyone in these parts knows that the only person stronger than the Heller boy is his dad. Push comes to shove, they'd make a helluva' pair. I'm glad they're not the type to raise cane, 'cause they'd sure make my job a hell of a lot harder." Jack gathered his thoughts and said almost to himself, "When I was a kid I could have a fever and I'd still go to church. That may be the biggest part of what's missing," he concluded, as he looked around the room again.

For the next five minutes neither spoke as they finished stuffing themselves with Leon's cooking, reminiscent of the sumptuous breakfasts Dan had enjoyed in the Corps. It seemed that Jack Shultz was really concerned by whatever run-ins he had been having with the local youth, but it had to pale in comparison to New York's problems. Teenagers in the city weren't just the fruits of the problem; they were their own damn trees. They weren't headed in the wrong direction. Many of them had been there and back, some more than once.

"Hey, Dan, here's Jim Franco," the constable exclaimed. "You'll want to talk to him."

Jack stood and extended his hand. A smiling red face with clear, bright eyes and a tuft of silver hair headed towards them.

"Looks like you've added a little around the middle," Jack kidded the older gentleman.

"Yeah, well, I can't play golf in the snow, you know," a wide grin accompanying the handshake.

"I want you to meet Dan Costa, a New York City detective assigned to Joe Teller's case."

The smile disappeared as Franco took Dan's hand, grasping it firmly.

"You knew Doctor Teller well?" Dan asked.

Franco nodded. "Joe Teller was as nice a guy as you'd ever want to meet. I met him when he moved up here with Berger about four years ago. Taught him how to fly-fish and play golf. He never got very good at either, but he was good company, a good friend."

Jack patted Franco on the shoulder, prompting a little smile. Jim looked back at Dan. "If you want, I can talk to you today or tomorrow. I've got time before the course opens Tuesday."

"Play a lot of golf, do you?"

"Oh, yeah," he beamed proudly, "every day, unless it's raining too hard," he reminded himself. "Do you play?"

"Not enough to be any good, Jim, but I'm going to get serious about it someday."

"You should. It's too damn expensive not to. If you're just going to chase a ball in the woods you might as well trade it in for a walking stick and do some serious hiking." Both younger men nodded their agreement.

"Well, I see you two have eaten so I'm going to do the same. I'll join you afterwards. Where are you staying?"

Dan looked at Jack.

"Why don't you walk up to my office, Jim? I'll leave the door open in case we're not there. I want to run Dan over to the lab. It should only take an hour."

"That'll give me enough time to eat and do some socializing," Jim said, searching for a table with an empty chair and faces he knew.

At the top of the hill Dan followed Main Street as it twisted across the lower face of the mountain to a half hidden road on the right that Jack told him to take.

"What did you mean when you said the lucky ones died by accident?"

"You ever see a man die of black lung?"

Dan shook his head.

"You don't want to."

After a quarter mile or so of towering pines with mountain laurel undergrowth, they came to a tall, one story, slate-roofed, red brick structure not unlike the design of the turn-of-the-century townhouses on New York's Upper Eastside. Wide sandstone steps ascended to a set of fortress-thick, eight feet high wooden doors flanked by two sets of only slightly shorter double hung windows.

"This was Nuremberg's Grammar School from 1902 until the '70s. Originally it had four rooms, but they were converted to eight in the late 40's," Jack informed him.

Dan pulled into a small parking area that wrapped around the back of the building. "Unusual architecture for up here," he said admiringly, "but you can see it's really well built."

"Yeah, a lot of Italians settled in these parts in the latter part of the nineteenth century. Some came from Tyrolia, mostly to work the mines, but they were the best damn stonecutters and masons these mountains ever saw. My grandfather told me they built the foundation with the sandstone they excavated right here and got the bricks from a furnace on the Susquehanna about seven miles that way," he said, pointing to the west. "It was pretty damn mildewed and overgrown with wild grapevines when Berger and Joe bought it, but they had it sandblasted before they moved in. Had all the trim repainted, fixed the roof, put on new gutters and cleared out all the weeds and overgrowth, too. Funny though; after all that work, clearing everything out, fixin' everything up, they go and put these heavy black drapes up, floor to ceiling. Couldn't see a damn thing in or out."

Dan noticed that there was no sign, only a stone lintel over the center entrance: "Nuremberg School, 1902."

"Did they ever put a sign up, Jack?"

"Not that I can recall. Come to think of it, I'm not sure I ever heard anyone refer to it as anything but 'the lab.' But you should ask Jim Franco. He would know."

Dan followed the constable as he walked to the rear of the building, past a ground level garage door that had been a recent addition. They entered a personnel door into a storage area and then through a second door into a single large room that took up half the building. Paper and cardboard debris littered the floor. Along one wall stood lab benches that held a number of sinks and metal framework to support a distillation process, or something very similar. Bits of broken glass, some lined with blue markings, lay where they fell.

Jack Shultz looked around disbelievingly. "They took down most of the walls," he said, his voice touched with nostalgia. "There used to be four rooms here."

Measured markings on the wood-plank floor, one inch or so squares, darkened the surface, drawing Dan's attention. He bent down for a closer look.

"What do you see, Sherlock?" the constable asked.

"Looks like mold around the edges."

"Is that significant?"

"Probably not."

Against the opposite wall there were more measured markings, three sets of four each, and then another group in the left front of the room that covered smaller areas. He studied each.

"Notice anything?" Shultz asked again.

Dan just shook his head "It's been pretty well cleaned. They sure didn't want us to know what they were working with."

Dan carefully paced the distances, drew a rough diagram and recorded the measurements in a small pad. He went outside, withdrew a camera from his car and returned to take pictures, while Jack Shultz stood by and watched quietly.

"Any idea who might have done the interior work, Jack; you know, the renovations?"

"No idea. I didn't even know the inside had been changed. Better ask Franco."

"Is that the office area?" Dan asked, pointing to a door at the front of the building.

"Should be," the constable responded as he approached it. He pulled some keys from his jacket pocket, selecting what looked like a common skeleton key. Within seconds he opened the door. "Yep, it's the office."

What had been the school's vestibule was empty except for an inexpensive, metal secretarial desk and chair. Dan breathed deeply, exhaled and walked back into the lab where he repeated the exercise two or three times.

Shultz observed curiously, dying to ask what the hell he was doing.

"Take a couple of deep breaths, Jack, and tell me what you smell."

The constable did as he was asked, screwed up his face and inhaled again.

"It's different. I don't know that I've ever smelled it before."

"How about salt water?"

"Yeah, maybe," Shultz replied without conviction. "Almost like stale water. Do you think stale water can smell like brine?"

"Possibly," Dan said as he carefully placed some glass shards in an evidence pouch, before picking up something tiny, studying it and finally wrapping it in a separate piece of paper.

"Is there a basement?"

"Yeah, it has an exterior storm door. Wanna' see it?"

"Sure, might as well. We're not learning much up here."

A padlock barred their entry, but it offered little resistance to Shultz's talented fingers and cache of picks.

"You're pretty good at that," said the impressed New Yorker.

"Should be. After my dad was injured in a mine accident he became a locksmith. He wanted me to be one too, and I was basically his apprentice until I graduated high school. Together we made enough to keep food on the table. But I joined the Army, and after that, installing locks seemed too damned boring, so I joined the Washington D.C. force. Put in twenty years and moved back up here to my roots. Haven't regretted it."

The constable flipped a light switch and they found themselves standing on a hard-packed earthen floor in a musty, rock-walled room half filled with brand new lab benches, stocks of cartons and assorted equipment. Stenciling on unopened boxes indicated a supply of beakers, petri dishes and glassware.

"I thought they cleaned this place out," Jack exclaimed, surveying the stores.

"They did," Dan responded thoughtfully.

Shultz cast a questioning glance.

"They cleaned out everything they had to."

Dan broke out his notebook and went around carefully recording each bit of information on the boxes, including the manufacturers' names, product descriptions and part numbers. He opened every box, studied its contents and compared them to their container's description. Two aquariums, each about twenty gallons in size, attracted his attention.

"Did either Teller or Berger have an interest in tropical fish?"

"Not that I know of. Maybe they used those tanks in the lab?"

"Yeah, but for what?"

Upon their return to Shultz's office they found Jim Franco comfortably seated, studying an Appalachian Mountain Club pamphlet. He greeted them without looking up. "Find anything interesting?"

"Lots," said Dan, "but I'm not sure I know what it all means."

"Well you sure scraped enough stuff off the floor to impress me," Jack said, while carefully measuring coffee and pouring it into a water-filled pot.

"Jim, did you ever get inside their lab?" he asked after turning on the burner.

"No. I asked Joe a coupla' times for a tour but he said he couldn't oblige me. Said he had agreed to some strict protocols, whatever the hell they are." He looked at the two officers for an explanation, but neither offered one.

"Did Joe Teller ever talk about the work he was doing, what he was trying to accomplish?" Dan asked.

"Only that they were enzymologists, that they were extracting enzymes from vegetables and animal tissue."

"But not the reason they were doing it?"

"Well, he did say that pharmaceutical companies made what he called diagnostic reagents out of them. Joe made it sound like there was a lot of money to be made, but that he and Berger hadn't gotten rich over it yet."

"Did he give you the impression he thought he would be rich someday?"

Jim Franco thought for a minute. "Yes and no. He never said anything specific to me, but he was getting pretty excited lately. I mean he was really in a great mood for a while. I think it was about six months ago, we were sitting around the store over at Moretti's and he looked at me, happy-like, and said, 'Jim, we're getting real close to something special. You'll have a famous friend someday soon, and then we're going to just play golf until I finally beat you.'"

"And that was six months or so ago?" Jack interjected.

"Yep," Jim responded, nodding slowly.

The questioning continued for another hour, Dan covering all the subjects he had intended, from the name of the lab company and those on the boxes to other scientists and whatever subjects Joe Teller had voluntarily brought up. Though his witness tried hard, he could offer little information of any value. No one had ever mentioned a corporate name…Teller had insinuated he had a proprietary interest…no other business associates' names had been discussed except for Berger's.

"How about customers, companies that they sold the enzymes to?"

Franco shook his head. "Nope. I don't believe Joe ever mentioned a customer to me. Fact is, the more I think about it, the more I'm sure he never said anything about them selling enzymes, only that pharmaceutical companies used them, like I said before."

Dan's questions about the identity of tradespeople and craftsmen familiar with the lab or its business resulted in similar responses.

"We're almost finished, Jim," Dan promised, as he watched him shift uncomfortably in the chair. "Just two more questions. You mentioned that six months or so ago Joe seemed pretty happy. Did his mood change anytime after that?"

"Sure as hell did. He got pretty quiet about a month before he was killed. In fact, I called him twice and he seemed preoccupied, didn't want to talk. During that period I only saw him a coupla' times and then once the week before he died. I think it was Tuesday morning." He deliberated. "Yeah, Tuesday morning at the Post Office. He had just opened his box and there was nothing in it, but he looked like he expected something and it wasn't there. He wasn't happy." He thought again. "Maybe he was disappointed or depressed, not angry though. Joe never got angry."

"And that was the last time you saw him?"

"Yeah, come to think of it, it was. I asked if anything was wrong and he kinda' looked at me and said, 'Sometimes life just stinks, Jim. You think you know people, but….' He never finished the sentence. He just walked past me and out the door. I called him that night to see if he was okay, but there was no answer. I never saw or talked to him again."

Dan nodded sympathetically. It was clear the two men had formed a close friendship.

"Last question. Is there anyone else in whom Joe might have confided? Anyone else as close to him as you?"

"Well, he did like to sit down at Larry Moretti's on Saturday afternoons. That was about the only time he took off...late on Saturday afternoons and most Sundays. I don't know if he talked much to Joe and Maria Bottino, but I do know he thought the world of Maria, so you might want to check with her, too. He lived at their hotel, you know."

Dan was about to thank him for his time when Franco thought of something else.

"You know, there is one more person. Jack, you know Marcy Holland from over in Eagle Rock. I recall that she and Joe met at the Episcopal Church picnic a year or so ago and that she had him over for dinner quite a bit. You might want to check Marcy out," Jim suggested.

Dan smiled. "Sure will, Jim, and thanks for your time."

"Care for another cup?" Jack asked as Franco left.

"No, I've got more than enough caffeine in me. Besides, I'd like to interview the Bottinos and Marcy, if that's possible. I can catch Moretti tomorrow."

They walked next door to Nuremberg's hotel. Inside it looked like any house in which two retired people might live, with a comfortably sized sitting room in front, a kitchen and dining room behind and what appeared to be a bedroom and bath in the rear. Maria Bottino looked younger than her years, her short-cropped black hair, dark eyes and trim figure suggesting a healthy woman with considerable energy.

"Hey, Jack," she squealed, "watcha' doin?"

"Stayin' out of trouble until you ditch your old man, gorgeous."

"Aah, you say that to all the girls. You better watch it or one of these days one of us is gonna' take you up on it."

Her laugh was infectious, her smile warm and friendly.

"Want you to meet Dan Costa, a New York City detective."

"Pleased to meet you, Maria."

"Same here, Dan." Her face quickly lost its exuberance. "Are you here because of Joe Teller?"

Dan nodded. "I'd like to ask you a few questions if you don't mind."

"Not at all. If I could help catch whoever killed him...."

"I know. Apparently, Joe was a helluva' nice person."

"Oh, yes," Maria started, as she motioned for them to sit and headed for the cupboard. "One of the nicest gentlemen you'd ever want to know, and bighearted. He was forever contributing to different church functions, and we got three, counting Sacred Heart in Weston. They're Catholic you know. You must be one, right?"

"Yes, I'm a Catholic," Dan answered as he watched her carefully select cups, saucers and cake dishes.

Jack spoke before Dan could get the words out.

"Please don't fuss, Maria, we had a big brunch at Leon's."

"Oh, just some coffee with a couple of scones. Nothing fancy."

Jack looked at Dan and shrugged.

"I understand both Dr. Berger and Joe lived here," Dan continued

"Yes, they had the two front rooms upstairs. Would you like to see them?"

Dan nodded. "When you get a chance," he said as she set the table.

"We can talk over our coffee and then go up," she suggested.

Maria's responses were not unlike Jim Franco's.

Yes, she had spent a lot of time talking to Joe, sitting on the back porch on warm nights, looking out over the valley, or drinking cocoa and sharing a warm fire in the parlor during winter.

No, he never talked about his work after their first conversation.

"I know he was an enzymologist," she said, pronouncing the word carefully, "but I really couldn't tell you what he did."

"Apparently, they both worked pretty hard?" Dan asked.

"Oh, yes, my God, they were hardly ever here. I offered to cook for them, but they left so early and usually came home so late that it just wasn't practical. And even when Joe would come down to talk, nine or so at night, Dr. Berger would just stay in his room. God only knows what he did up there," she said.

"Did they ever argue?"

"Not that I know of, but no thanks to Dr. Berger. He wasn't the most pleasant person in the world. More than once he said something sarcastic, but Dr. Teller would just look at me, wink and smile, so I knew not to get upset. But I would have kicked Berger out of here a long time ago if it hadn't been for Dr. Teller."

"Did anyone ever come visit them here?"

Maria looked off, trying to recall. "You know, I never realized that they never had company." She thought again. "Nope, never once... unless," she said deliberately, "you count the time Joe ducked in with Marcy Holland to get a photo album. But they headed right back out."

"Were Marcy and Joe close?"

"He seemed to enjoy her company. He told me so once, but I don't know if there was any romance there, if that's what you mean."

"How about phone calls, letters?"

"They had phones installed in their rooms when they first got here. I couldn't say how much they used them, certainly not often. They weren't here that much, and it's so quiet at night, I'm sure I would have heard if the phones rang."

"And mail?"

"They always got their own."

As Franco had testified, Maria stated that she never heard either scientist mention the names of associates, a sponsor, or anything else that might suggest that the two were not alone in the venture, nor could she ever recall either of them mentioning a customer. "Maybe they were just doing research?" she offered, cocking her head to the side, as if that could be an option worth considering. "But in that case, where would they get the money to keep going? Joe told me enough that I'm sure he wasn't a wealthy man. In fact, I seem to recall that he once told me his wife left him because they had so little, and she never believed he would ever amount to much, financially speaking."

Berger's room was as Jack had described, littered with papers, periodicals, books and a few articles of clothing.

"Can you believe this," Maria asked, "and this man was a neat freak. I mean everything was always in its place. Whenever I came up here to clean the windows and vacuum, nothing was ever out of place."

"I'll need a few hours up here tomorrow, Maria, if you don't mind. Please don't touch anything until then, okay?"

"Sure. Wanna' see Joe's room now?"

It didn't take long to figure out that Teller's room had been gone over with a fine-tooth comb. Other than his clothing, a few non-fiction books and some generic texts, nothing remained to suggest anything about him or his work.

"Some of his personal stuff is gone," Dan heard Maria exclaim as she pointed to the dresser, bare except for a small lamp and a man's jewelry case.

"What stuff?" Jack asked.

"He had a heavy cardboard file box." She sheepishly admitted, "I looked in it once. Besides that jewelry case, it held a briefcase and an old leather-bound notebook, a really big one, and I don't see either of them," she said, "an old, beat-up, brown notebook and a burgundy colored briefcase," she repeated slowly, while searching the room with her eyes.

"From the time you got word of Joe's death, who could have gotten into this room?" Dan asked.

"Just my husband or me, I think. I never gave Dr. Berger a key. Of course, that doesn't mean he couldn't have had one made. Oh, I feel terrible. I should have kept a closer eye on everything."

Shultz consoled her. "There's no way you could have suspected anything, Maria. I probably should have sealed everything off when Donna called."

"Who's Donna?" Dan asked.

"She's the lab receptionist I date. Berger called her from New York the morning after the shooting and she called me. Damn," he said regretfully, "why didn't I think to seal this room."

Dan could have said something reassuring, but didn't. The room should have been sealed. A rookie would have known better.

"Maria, I need a place to stay tonight. Why don't I just use this room," Dan suggested.

"Sure. I changed the sheets the day they left for New York."

"I'll be back with my bags after supper, maybe sooner if we can't find Marcy Holland. Will your husband be around tonight?"

"He better be. He went over to his cousin's in Shenandoah, but he promised to be home for supper. He usually keeps his word," she said cautiously. "Wanna' eat with us?"

"Not tonight. I owe Jack, so I'll take a raincheck."

As they drove down the valley in the direction of the Eagle Rock Resort, Dan asked if Jack had a fingerprint kit. "I'd like to know if anyone besides Berger was in that room, even though I'd bet he's the one that went through everything."

"I'll have one tomorrow," Shultz promised.

## CHAPTER 8

The Eagle Rock gate guard inspected their credentials, called Marcy Holland and gave them directions to her house. They drove through a very private, wooded community with lakes, riding paths, golf and tennis facilities, an impressive year-round resort. As they negotiated a steep turn running parallel to the ski slopes they spotted her chalet style home perched on a hillside. An attractive white haired woman in her sixties greeted them. She had the compulsory blue eyes, rosy complexion and broad smile of the Pennsylvania mountain people. A beagle pup named Toby barked a protest as they entered an antique-filled sunroom complete with a modestly stocked bar, library and assorted snacks.

"Just some diet soda," Jack answered, as Marcy played hostess.

"Sounds good," Dan seconded.

For the better part of an hour Dan asked the same questions and for the most part heard the same answers as he had during the previous interviews.

In response to her question, Dan admitted that the absence of any evidence related to other business partners, the project's goals, or eye witnesses to the lab activities was making it difficult for him to establish a motive.

"Then you don't think it was a random mugging?" Marcy asked.

Dan had been too obvious, but now that it was out, he didn't mind exposing the possibilities in the interest of soliciting more information.

"I really can't tell you anything else," she asserted, trying to recall anything that might help. "Joe was so secretive about his work. More than a dozen times I asked about the lab, Lew Berger, the project. He would just smile and remind me he couldn't discuss any of that; that if he did, he would forfeit his continued involvement and any rewards he had coming."

The words had barely left her mouth when her eyes suddenly narrowed.

"There was one funny episode about nine months ago," she started, deliberately looking off, searching her memory. "I had invited him for dinner.

It was a hot, humid evening and he arrived a bit late, in a good mood, but looking very tired. He gave me a quick little peck on the cheek, which he did whenever he saw me," she said nostalgically, "and I couldn't help but notice a strange odor. He must have seen me twitch my nose or something because he asked me what was wrong. In my own subtle way, I said, 'Pardon me for asking, but have you been playing in garbage?' Of course, I laughed along with him, but he apologized. And then he said, 'Horseshoe crabs do tend to stink in the summertime.'

"I repeated, 'Horseshoe crabs?' and then he just kind of shook his head as though reprimanding himself and said, 'Forget it, Marcy, it's a private joke.' But he did go in the bathroom and scrub his hands and arms. When he came out I asked him what he was doing with horseshoe crabs and he looked at me seriously and said, 'I told you it's a private little joke and it's really something I wish you wouldn't mention again. Promise?'

"I put it out of my mind because he asked me to, and he had never really asked me to do anything else. It's funny," she said, "because from that point on I think I detected some fishy kind of smell half the times we were together, but never anywhere near as strong as that night."

"Did Dr. Berger ever have the same odor about him?"

"I never got close enough to him, but I also wasn't in his company much, only when I invited him over for dinner. Joe never asked me to so I didn't invite him all that often. I'm not sure Joe enjoyed his company socially. Dr. Berger had no sense of humor and rarely contributed anything to a conversation, so I think it was a relief for Joe to be away from him."

With scores of ideas and possibilities racing through his head, Dan turned from his hostess. "What are the chances of getting the phone records tomorrow, Jack?"

Shultz looked surprised, trying to figure out what Marcy had said to prompt Costa's request. "No problem. I'll get on it first thing in the morning," he promised.

Dan's mind poured over a list of possible leads, thinking aloud. "Bank records? Where did they bank and under what names? They had to have money and a checking account. They had to pay for supplies, insurance, the building." He looked at the constable. "We have a lot to do tomorrow, Jack."

Still feeling guilty for not sealing Teller's room, Shultz promised, "I'm here to help however I can, Dan. Just rattle off the orders."

"Anything I can do?" Marcy asked hopefully.

"Sure, tell me what was in the photo album."

"Goodness, I forgot all about that. Sorry. Let's see. Most of the pictures were old, thirty, maybe forty years old...his wife, a baby daughter, then when she was a little older, not quite a teenager. It seemed all the pictures of his family stopped when he got a divorce. That fits because his wife took his daughter and moved south."

"Where was Joe living after his divorce? Did he ever say?"

"Somewhere in Virginia, I think." She thought for a few seconds. "Funny, I'm not even sure why I said that. He never really told me Virginia and I never asked, but he must have said something that convinced me it was Virginia."

"And you don't know what he was involved in down there?"

"I only know that he's never done anything except work in a lab. That's all he ever told me when I asked him about his life, but he was very secretive, kind of gave me the impression he might have worked on some secret government project at one time or other, though I can't recall exactly what he said to make me think that."

"Did he ever talk about enzymes? I mean, I know he didn't talk about the specific project and lab, but what about enzymes in general?" Dan was searching for clues that Marcy might not recognize as important.

"Well, I did ask him what enzymes were the very first time we talked and he said they were like proteins and that their levels in the body indicated generally how the body was doing."

"Uh-huh. Anything else, like what they could be used for or how they were identified?"

Again it was obvious that Marcy Holland was struggling to recall anything that might help. "The only other thing he did say was that they were found in every animal and vegetable, and that science had only scratched the surface, that someday we would recognize that enzymes were as important as blood and tissue, maybe more so."

"Did he ever tell you who they were selling to?"

Marcy thought hard. "You know, I don't believe he ever did mention a customer or a company. I wonder if they had any customers?"

"Well, you've been a big help, Marcy. I can be reached through Jack if you think of anything else."

They stood to leave.

"Don't you want to know about the rest of the album?" she said quizzically.

"Of course, how stupid of me."

"Don't feel badly, I forgot about it altogether, remember? Anyway, there was a final leaf with four pictures on it, all taken within the last four years.

One was of Joe and Lewis standing in front of the old Nuremberg School before it was all cleaned up. That was right before they moved in. There was another of them with four other men standing in front of the school after it had been cleaned and repainted. There was a picture of Joe looking up from some kind of table in the lab, and then...." Her eyes widened. "I've got it," she shrieked. "Virginia, the fourth picture. Joe was shaking hands with one of the four men and there was a sign behind them: 'Chincoteague Island, Virginia.'"

Proudly, she paused before adding, "The guy looked just like Sean Connery. He towered over Joe."

Dan exited the Eagle Rock gate and drove south along the Pismire Ridge past birch-covered mounds of anthracite culm to Anna's Restaurant in Sheppton. They entered the side door of what had been a simple four or five room dormored cottage, the front of which had been converted to a bar and the back to a one-room restaurant. The kitchen was located to the side behind a trophy-covered wall of impressively racked bucks.

The Caramel Porter from a local microbrewery was superb, the roasted quail with rice and raisin stuffing exquisite. Homemade rice pudding, espresso and sambucca completed the feast. Dan couldn't believe the check: $34. He gave the grateful waitress $45, told her to keep the change and asked for a receipt.

"Do you think Anna could give us a couple of minutes?" Jack asked when she returned.

Shortly, an attractive blonde who looked to be in her early fifties emerged from the kitchen wearing a chef's suit and welcoming smile. Nothing suggested she had been cooking for thirty or more guests, her clothing still spotless, her hair and make-up perfectly in place.

"Someday I'm going to come in here and catch you with your hair up and your guard down," Shultz joked. "Don't you ever feel guilty looking so good?"

"He serves this crap all the time," Anna confided, seating herself between the two officers. "Thinks it'll get him a free meal. Pleased to meet you, Detective. My name's Anna."

"Like I said, Dan, gorgeous, witty and a great cook," Jack continued. "Marry me."

"What happened to 'and I'll take you away from all this?'" she asked.

"Hell, all this is why I'd marry you. Whoops, I don't think that's what I was supposed to say", he joked.

"You got that right, flat-foot," she said smartly, turning her attention to Dan. "Maria Bottino called and told me about a hunk of a New York City cop that's going to stay at her place tonight. I guess you're the man."

"Well, I don't know about the hunk, but I did meet her today and I am staying there tonight. Do you mind if I ask you a few questions?"

"I'd be insulted if you didn't."

*Anna must have been a hell of a woman in her day.*

She contributed little beyond what the others had already told him, reinforcing the image he had of the two scientists. Frequent diners at her place, particularly during the week, they had always arrived together and been quietly sociable, until a few months ago. Then they began coming less frequently, or in Teller's case, with someone else, namely Marcy Holland. On at least two occasions Anna could remember Teller and Berger momentarily raising their voices, and when alerted to the attention they were drawing, suddenly going silent.

"They seemed to change a few months back. I mean, God, I'd see them damn near every night in the beginning, laughing, talking to my other guests, usually about hunting or fishing. Well, maybe Joe, not Lewis too much. He wasn't really a sociable person. But in the first three years he and Joe looked like they were really good friends. Then it sure seemed to change," she said sadly.

"You didn't know what they argued about?"

"No. I did ask Joe once when he came in alone why he and Lewis weren't dining together like they used to. I thought maybe they had tired of my cooking, so I was going to come up with some new dishes for them. He started apologizing, saying it had nothing to do with me or the food or anything like that. I must have really made him feel bad because that night, after dinner, he asked me to sit and have a drink with him, and he told me that Lewis and he weren't spending as much time together because they had had some disagreements and he needed to be away from him to 'clear his head,' I think he said. We never talked about it again."

"When was that?"

"Maybe a month, six weeks ago at most."

"Just one more question, Anna. Did you ever see either of them in here with anybody you didn't recognize?"

"Recently?" she asked.

"From the first time you saw them to the last."

"Sure, in the beginning. They were both here with a couple other gentlemen, but that had to be four years or so ago."

"Would you recognize their pictures if I showed them to you?"

She deliberated. "I gotta' be honest. I'm not even sure I know how many different ones there were... two, three.... I'm not sure."

Dan was about to ask another question.

"But I sure as hell remember one of them," she said with a wink, "a real matinee idol. Looked just like Sean Connery."

On the way back to the hotel Jack asked about the bombings and how they were affecting life in the Big Apple.

"It's getting tough on people," Dan started. "Guys get up, go to work, wonder if they'll ever make it home at night. It has to be especially tough on the ones with a family. There were sixteen school kids killed in that subway bombing and people know that could happen again, and probably will."

"They still don't have any leads?"

"Yeah, about ten thousand of them. That's how many illegal Arabs there are living in the five boroughs, guys whose visas have run out, not to mention the ones who never had them to begin with."

"How's it going to end?"

"I wish I knew. I'm not sure life hasn't permanently changed for the worse. But I'd also bet that if some big-shit politician or somebody in his family were to become a victim, you'd see a lot of changes, and fast. For one thing, the press would give us a little support, not like now when they hear about some mistake we've made and pounce on us. You'd think that under the circumstances they'd put the lives of innocent people ahead of selling papers, but they sure don't seem to. Even when one of the terrorist groups called in to take credit for that subway bombing a writer refused to cooperate with the feds, claiming he didn't have to disclose his sources. And half the print and electronic media types supported him. By the time the feds got a court order the suspects went underground, free to do it all over again, and don't bet they won't."

Jack Shultz shook his head. "It still amazes me that some people are more worried about how we treat the terrorists than about what they're trying to do to us. Don't people understand this is a war, different maybe from any other one we fought, but still a war?"

"The man in the street knows exactly what it is, but he's not the one making the decisions or shaping policy. It all goes back to politics, Jack. There isn't a liberal in Congress who wouldn't do exactly what a lot of the hawks have been campaigning for if they weren't worried about votes, but to make the opposition look bad they accuse them of trying to rewrite the Constitution, or that we're violating constitutional rights, like the men who wrote it really intended freedom of speech to protect child pornography and terrorist meetings, shit like that. Then the same activists who lie awake at night trying to think of how to make our jobs even harder are the first ones to accuse us of incompetence when there's a bombing. I don't really think they're that stupid. I just think they pander to the least intelligent in the hope of getting support for their agendas and they don't give a rat's ass how many people have to suffer. It's a real mess and it's not going to be resolved anytime soon because the courts still have a lot of the ultra liberal judges from the '90's who refuse to recognize that the environment in this country has changed and they have to look at life as it is today. Until they do, the feds have to rely as much on luck as the law to do their jobs."

Neither spoke for a while until Dan said, "I'm not naïve enough to suggest that anybody has all the answers right now or that every civil rights activist is a self-serving jerk who just wants to pull down the fat cats or hear himself talk. I believe most of them genuinely feel for the little people and have got their hearts in the right place. But they've got to root out the ones that don't and begin to realize that an awful lot of innocent people are going to die if we don't face reality and permit the feds some leeway. Hell, Jack, this is war of the worst kind, fought in our streets, with our kids as targets. They've gotta' let us do our jobs," he repeated.

"Folks out here are really confused by all the debate over this deportation issue. So what if one or two innocent Arabs get sent back to Iraq or wherever. If it helps keep two American kids alive, it's worth it." Jack sat mulling a thought before adding, "Man, I can just picture what would happen out here if some Muslims paraded around protesting deportation of illegals." He didn't bother to elaborate.

Dan said wistfully, "I wish everyone would try to live in peace, just live and let live, without the prejudice and intolerance that seems to be at the root of all our problems. The world could be a decent place to live. Too bad it'll never happen."

When they arrived at the hotel, Dan reminded Jack to call Donna Schulman, the lab receptionist, and arrange for an interview in the morning.

"I can have her here by eight, eight-thirty, if that's okay. It'll give me time to get the finger-print kit and call the telephone company."

"Sounds good. What do you want to do for breakfast?"

"It's on me. Meet me at Leon's at 8:30. I'll see if Donna can join us"
"See you then."

Joe and Maria Bottino were sitting in the parlor watching television, a chocolate cake, dishes and silverware neatly arranged on the coffee table before them.

"You timed it perfectly, just in time for dessert. I made a Bavarian chocolate cake, Joe's favorite. Sit down while I get the tea." Maria was her lively self.

Dan guessed that her husband was at least ten years older, but every bit as friendly, just like everyone else in Nuremberg.

"Have a seat, Dan. Joe Bottino," and he extended his hand. "I come from a Tyrolean family that settled here right after the Civil War. I'm fourth generation and the only one who didn't work in the mines." He rambled on with an amusing, loosely jointed family narrative until his wife, carefully transporting an expensive looking porcelain teapot, rejoined them. Her entrance gave Joe time to take a quick breath.

"Ever have Bavarian chocolate cake?" he continued. "I mean the real stuff, not like the sugary crap you get in New York."

"I think I had some once."

"Well you're about to taste the best there is. Nobody can bake that cake like my wife," he said proudly. "There's only one thing she does better, and that's something you'll just have to take my word for."

His laughter was cut short by a stern look from Maria.

She ignored Dan's protest, handing him an oversized slice of her masterpiece. Never a big fan of chocolate, he required two mugs of tea to get it down, succeeding without offending his hostess, while concealing a conviction that his digestive tract would never recover.

"I guess Maria told you that we're not certain Joe Teller's murder was the result of a routine mugging," Dan stated, "so anything you can tell me that might provide a clue to the motive would be a big help."

Joe Bottino wiped the final traces of chocolate from his mouth and reached for the tea. "I was surprised to hear some of the questions you asked Maria. Do you really think Berger could have been involved?"

"What do you think?"

"I don't know. I didn't like the little creep," he confessed, "but murder! Christ, who can you trust if not your best friend?"

His wife scolded him. "Don't use the Lord's name like that, Joe. There's no call for it."

"Now, them other guys," Joe continued, a look of deliberation crossing his face, "them I didn't like right from the start, did I, Babe?"

Puzzled, Maria asked, "Who are you talking about?"

"Them guys that came up in the beginning, don't you remember? They stayed here a coupla' nights. You even said they were…what…arrogant?"

Maria recovered. "Oh, yes, yes, I know who you mean. Dr. Teller had introduced them as scientists, but you and I thought they were bankers or something."

"Why bankers?" Dan asked.

"Well," she hesitated, searching for a reason, "they were dressed up real snappy and they talked different; sure didn't have time for us. Walked right past you like you weren't there."

"And remember the cars?" Joe interjected. "Hoo, boy, were they nice, or what? Mercedes, two of 'em, brand new and big. Biggest I've ever seen."

"And they were only here a few days?"

"Yes," Maria responded, "they stayed here two nights. There were four of them, two to a room. I remember now, they complained about the single beds."

"Yeah," Joe interrupted, "you'd think they'd be happy to each have their own bed. What'd they want to do, sleep together in a double?" his intention poorly veiled by laughter.

"No, Joe," his wife corrected him, "in a regular hotel there's either a king-size bed or two doubles in a room. You think hotels in the city have single beds?" She grinned, looking to Dan for confirmation. He offered a supportive smile.

Joe continued, "Well, anyways, they didn't look like they belonged with either Joe or Berger. That's the only point I was trying to make."

"Did any of them say anything to give you an idea of what the purpose of their coming up here was? I mean, it is kind of odd that they would choose such a secluded place…no other scientists, no universities."

"Joe told us one night over supper that what they were working on required peace and quiet," Maria stated with certainty, "and that because it was going to take a while, they needed to conserve their money. The building was inexpensive and so were the living accomodations. That's what he said."

"But never why the project would take so long?" Dan asked.

The two looked at each other, then at Dan, before shaking their heads in unison. "It's funny, but all that time they lived here," Maria concluded, "we never learned anything more than what they felt comfortable telling us. We never felt we had a right to push them. I mean it's their business. People have a right to their privacy."

*This sure as hell ain't New York,* Dan thought.

He thanked Maria for the dessert, both of them for their help and wished them goodnight. He climbed the thinly carpeted stairs to sleep in a bed previously occupied by a man whom everyone had described as gentle, kind and generous.

*Just the type predators take advantage of.*

The next morning he was up early, showered and dressed by six, and carefully screening the debris in Lewis Berger's room before the Bottino's began stirring. Maria asked if he would like some coffee and toast. It was 7:15.

"I'd love a cup, Maria, thanks, but no toast. I'm meeting Jack at 8:30 over at Leon's. He's buying," Dan added with a wink, as though that were the reason.

In the kitchen they shared cups of robust dark coffee sweetened with generous dollops of thick, freshly whipped cream.

*I could get used to this,* Dan thought.

"Find anything up in that mess?" Joe Bottino asked, scratching his backside through a fluffy old bathrobe as he shuffled into the kitchen.

"No, not really. What amazes me is that I haven't found a scrap of evidence related to anything that was in that lab or what they were working with."

"You haven't spoken to Larry Moretti yet," Joe said. "I know he ordered stuff for them and he and Teller got to be good friends, probably closer than Joe and Berger were after a while. Teller spent a lot of his time down at Larry's. I bet he'll know something."

The thought was encouraging.

"I'll be back later, Maria. If you don't mind, leave Berger's room as it is. I may need another hour or so in there."

"Sure thing. I just remembered. I have some boxes with lids on them. Would you like to have them to maybe take some of those papers back to New York?" She stretched her arms to form a two-foot square.

"That's a good idea. Thanks, Maria."

She beamed happily as Dan left for his appointment with Jack and Donna Schulman.

His body drifted downhill as he crossed the steeply inclined Main Street. Just ahead a car pulled alongside Leon's Café, the wheel turning sharply into the curb. A stunning, well-endowed blonde in her early to mid-thirties slid from behind the wheel, straightening herself before closing the door. She peered over her shoulder at Dan and allowed just the slightest hint of an encouraging smile before wiggling her way to the café entrance.

*Please, God, make my day. Let that be Donna Schulman.*

Inside he caught Jack planting a light kiss on the lady's cheek. From behind, Donna Schulman looked every bit the consummate object of men's fantasies. Perched on three-inch heels and poured into skin-tight black ski pants and a white turtleneck, her figure was enough to stop traffic anywhere. What she was doing in rural Pennsylvania was anybody's guess.

Jack saw Dan and waved.

"Good morning, Dan," he said, trying to suppress a sheepish grin. "Want you to meet Donna Schulman."

*You devil,* Dan thought.

"Hi, Detective." The voice was softly enticing. Her figure blended well with a fresh-scrubbed look, full red lips and broad smile. Luxuriant waves of blond hair encircled her face and fell softly past her shoulders. Up close she looked even better than she had outside.

"Good morning, Donna, pleased to meet you," he managed to mumble while still surveying her curves.

The subject of Teller's murder didn't surface until they had finished eating and were settled in Jack's office. Dan took the chair next to Donna, enjoying the scent of "Nina Ricci". *Eileen used to wear it; L'Aire du Temps,* he remembered.

He found nothing about Donna to dislike. In fact, during breakfast she proved to be intelligent and refined, yet very down to earth in a most likeable way. He was dying to ask why she had settled in Nuremberg, but knew that it was hardly appropriate, at least not until he got to know her better.

In the interest of time, he summarized for Donna what he had learned from Jim Franco, Anna, Marcy and the Bottinos, expressing concern that both Teller and Berger had told them little else that he could use in his investigation.

She waited for him to finish. "I might be able to help fill in some of the missing pieces. Let's see, where do I start?"

Before Dan could suggest a direction she began an articulate review of the names and places she had read, seen or heard during her employment as receptionist at the lab, none of which seemed important. She identified two doctors who had phoned on rare occasion as Steinberg and Norville. "If either one of them called, I was to immediately notify Dr. Berger."

"Did you ever meet them?"

"No, in fact, while I worked there the only people I ever met were a dozen or so tradesmen and salespeople who came to the office. None of them ever went into the lab, at least not while I was there, and I can't think of more than a handful that either Dr. Berger or Dr. Teller came out to speak to."

"So you never saw the faces of these other two Doctors?"

"No, I never even saw their pictures."

"Anything that could tell you where they lived, what they did, or what their relationship with Teller and Berger was?"

"If I use my imagination, I could picture them both in New York. They had accents like you sometimes hear on TV, you know, like deep in the heart of Brooklyn." She wrinkled her nose and smiled.

*Enchanting,* Dan thought.

"How about the mail? Do you remember seeing any return addresses?"

"Believe it or not, I never saw any mail except for the junk mail they gave me to throw out. We had no post office box. Each of them had one, but they never gave me anything to open, just junk to get rid of."

"Who was the junk mail addressed to?"

"Either to 'Occupant' or one of them."

She could see Dan found it difficult to believe.

"You don't believe me, do you? You think I'm trying to cover something up, but I'm not," she said flirtatiously, without the slightest hint of concern.

She paused, expecting Dan to dismiss the idea.

"It does seem strange that you were paid to just sit there, look pretty for an occasional salesman, answer the phone that never rang and get rid of garbage."

He smiled, waiting for a response, but Donna Schulman just smiled back and shook her head slowly.

*The woman is positively disarming.*

"Okay, so what did you do all day? Write checks? Balance books? Type reports? Clean glassware?"

"Nope, nope, nope and nope," she replied musically. "I did what I already told you, plus, I read a lot of books and magazines, I kept my office clean, and oh yes, did I forget to tell you I plotted numbers…hundreds and hundreds of numbers?" And she giggled, not like a little girl, but like a sexy, clever woman who liked to tease overly masculine Manhattan detectives.

"Plot numbers? What kind of numbers?"

She could see Dan's interest peak, so she stopped flirting and answered seriously.

"Daily, every couple of hours or so, they would bring me out a long, computer generated list of numbers with a three digit number written in red at the top with the date. I would enter them in certain sequences into a computer. That work took up at least half of my time. I think the purpose of my input was to generate graphs."

"What did the graphs look like?"

"I don't know. The printer was in the lab, so I never got to see one. Dr. Teller just told me once that the reason I was inputting all those numbers in different sequences was so they could print out different types of graphs."

From his expression Donna was satisfied that the detective believed her.

"Do you know why they worked with horseshoe crabs?"

"Is that what that fishy smell was all about?" she asked, surprised by the question. "Both doctors warned me never to mention any odors or things I might see or hear, and believe me they warned me more than once. Berger told me a hundred times he'd fire me on the spot if he ever heard that I had discussed anything about the lab with anybody. It never bothered me because I honestly didn't know anything." She paused briefly. "Horseshoe crabs. I never would have guessed."

"You mean you never saw them?"

"The windows were blackened, the doors were kept locked from the inside and there was a black curtain partition on the lab side of the door to my office. Even if I was staring at it when they brought me the tapes, I couldn't see anything but black." Convincingly, she emphasized it. "Absolute black. I couldn't tell you anything about that lab."

Dan mulled everything over while Donna accepted Jack's offer of coffee. She neither received nor sent mail or checks, so she had neither names nor addresses of people they dealt with.

"How did you get paid?" she heard Dan ask as she stirred sugar into the richly strong coffee.

"By cash, off the books. That was their condition when they hired me. I just filed taxes as a kind of free-lance typist."

Dan changed subjects abruptly, thinking he had finally hit on something. "Horseshoe crabs can't live out of water. Somebody must have brought them on some kind of schedule, maybe dragged out dead ones."

Donna turned to Jack. "Do you think that's what that van was for?"

"Maybe," Jack nodded in agreement. He hesitated, as though trying to recall some misplaced details. "On a couple of Saturdays Donna and I hiked along the crest of Sugarloaf and we spotted an old van, a Dodge, I think, at the back of the building. It was backed up to that rear overhead so we couldn't see if they were loading or unloading, but Teller's or Berger's car was always in the parking lot."

"Did either of you notice a name on the van, a license plate, anything we might be able to trace?"

The two looked at each other before shaking their heads. "We were pretty far away. I'm not sure we could have read a license plate even if we had had reason to," Jack responded.

"They both worked nearly every Saturday, at least in the morning, so I never took much notice if there were other vehicles there with them," Donna admitted. "But I really can't remember any other truck or car, other than that one we mentioned, at least not on Saturdays."

"Okay, but give it some thought. You might come up with something we can use. How about shipments to customers? Did you package and mail anything for them?"

A quizzical look crossed Donna Schulman's face, as though she had never given the idea of customers a thought.

"You know, it's hard to believe, but I'm not sure we ever shipped or mailed anything to anybody, at least not something other than a simple envelope." She looked at the ceiling as if in deep thought before turning to Dan. "Honest, Dan, I really can't remember ever having been asked to package or mail anything to anybody that might have been a vial or any kind of drug container. Maybe they hand delivered the stuff themselves?"

In closing, Dan asked about the relationship Joe had had with his partner, and Donna's opinion, supported by first hand evidence, matched that of the other witnesses.

"They had some awful rows at the end, and it was odd because it was Dr. Teller who did most of the yelling. He had been such a reserved, gentle person, but the last month or so he would really let loose some hateful things at Dr. Berger, calling him greedy, inhuman, despicable…what else…uh, oh yes, and shameful. He said those things on two occasions that I know of, and he had to really be screaming for me to hear him because those walls are extra thick and he had such a naturally soft voice."

Dan looked at his watch, almost ten-thirty. "Where did the morning go?" he said to no one in particular.

"Time flies when you're having fun," Donna replied, with a look that said more.

Dan instinctively winked, then wished he hadn't. "I'd better check in with the office, Jack. Mind if I use your phone? I've got a toll free."

"Sure. Need privacy?"

"No, but it might take a few minutes. Would you mind seeing if Larry Moretti can afford us some time. Maybe we'll do it over lunch?"

"Larry won't turn that down even if he has to close up," Donna said.

Ignoring procedure for the umpteenth time, Dan told Donna she was more than welcome to join them. "I'm sure he won't mind you sitting in. It might even make him feel more comfortable."

Jack gave her a reassuring shrug. "Why not?"

"Thanks, and I promise not to eat too much." The look she gave Jack suggested that her one or two extra pounds had been a subject of debate.

Dan couldn't imagine why the constable would have complained.

"Lieutenant Wilson here, may I help you?"

"Good morning, boss."

"Hey, Dan, how you doin'?"

"Fine. It's beautiful out here and the people have been great. I haven't found anything that'll break the case yet, but I am convinced Berger's involved in a conspiracy, something to do with what they were working on up here."

He took a few minutes to give Wilson a summary of all he had learned since Sunday morning, tying aspects of it into Carmine Pecora's report with which he knew his supervisor was familiar. The fact that there were no company names, checking accounts or accounting records concerned both men and led Wilson to the same conclusions Dan had reached. The subject of the lab experiments had been significant enough to warrant extraordinary security measures, and something had been said or done to necessitate the murder of one friend by another.

"What's on the agenda?" Wilson asked.

"The local constable is getting phone records and a fingerprint kit. I need to establish Berger's presence in Teller's room because a number of personal items are missing. I also want to make sure no one else besides the hotel owners left prints. I'll wrap up the interviews today and return home tonight."

"Good. Do you want to fax the phone bills here? I can put Rasheed on it."

"Maybe, but I do have something more important I'd like him to do." Dan gave Wilson the two doctors' names, Steinberg and Norville. "Have Rasheed go through the five boroughs' phone books first. I've got a hunch the former receptionist at the lab may be right about something. If he can't find them there, he'll have to go to the A.M.A. Directory on the Internet. If that doesn't work, have him use the Net to identify universities and foundations doing research in enzymes, biochemistry and microbiology. All those sciences are kind of tied together and it's not so big a field that prominent players will go unmentioned."

"I'm sure he'll be glad to have something to do."

"He'll have plenty to do when I get back. I don't think this is going to come together easily." He paused for a second. "It's important that he get the ball rolling on those doctors, but there is one other thing if he has the time. It's been bothering me that the pedestrian who told Carmine he saw Jorge Ruiz cross the street after the shooting didn't bother to mention the getaway car, or at least not according to Carmine's report. The suspects had to be heading in his direction and there were snow warnings posted, which meant there were no cars parked along his side of the street. The guy had to have a very good look at the car."

"Yeah, you're right. I'll call Carmine myself, because it wasn't in his report and it should have been. He missed it."

"Yes he did. By the way, did Joe DeLorenzo call?"

"No, was he supposed to? I'll check with the Desk Sergeant."

"A pawnbroker reported receiving a watch that fit the description of Dad's retirement gift. Joe and Calvin were going to interview him this morning."

"I'll call Joe and let you know if anything big broke. You just wrap things up there so you don't get home too late. Anything else?"

"No, I think that does it. We'll have plenty to do if we don't catch Berger. Right now he's our only promising lead."

"Yeah. I've been checking the wires every half hour. He seems to have slipped through. You did put out an APB, right?"

"Yep, to all Pennsylvania's border states, but he probably couldn't have made it out of Pennsylvania, except for Jersey. I got it on the wire within an hour of his leaving the hotel. I'm beginning to think he's still in PA. Maybe we can get the State Police to canvas motels along Route 80. It's just a hunch, but I keep tying Berger to conspirators in New Jersey and New York, so that's the route he would take if he was running scared, and I definitely feel he was panicking."

"Makes sense. I'll see what I can do. I may call you back after I talk to Joe D. What's the number there?"

"Call my pager. I'm leaving for an interview."

Jack and Donna were standing outside the General Store with a man in his mid to late forties. A neatly trimmed beard his only distinguishing feature, he was otherwise of average height and build.

"This is Larry Moretti, Dan. We've told him all about you," Jack said.

Dan anticipated the blue eyes, unaffected smile and firm handshake. He couldn't help asking as they crossed the street towards the café, "Do all you people up here have blue eyes? I'm beginning to suspect inbreeding," he joked.

"Most of our grandparents came from Tyrolia," Larry answered, "so we're half Italian, half Austrian. I guess that's where the blue eyes come from."

"Do you remember your grandparents?" Dan asked, trying to relax Moretti.

"Oh yeah. My grandmother lived with us until she died a coupla' years ago. She was ninety-two. My grandfather, he was the smartest man I ever knew," he said proudly, "never went past the fifth grade but read the papers every day. Worked in the mines all his life, first as a breaker boy when he was ten, then as a mule tender until he made miner and and at the end as a gangway boss. Retired with black lung at forty-eight and died from it at fifty-six. He read damn near a book a day once he stopped working."

Larry Moretti looked off to Sugarloaf Mountain. "He's buried up there. Smartest man I ever knew."

The special of the day, pot roast with onions, carrots and potatoes, was served on stoneware dishes, accompanied by thick slabs of black bread, a tub of fresh butter and mugs of hot tea. Dipped in the rich, brown gravy the bread alone was worth the price of the meal, $4.50.

Dan was astounded. "How can he afford to stay open at these prices?"

"He earns enough to make a living," Jack assured him, "and he loves to see people enjoy his cooking. It's not as fancy as Anna's, but it's always fresh, hot and filling."

"Besides," Larry added, "most folks around here couldn't afford to pay more. He'd be out of business if he raised prices."

Moretti could think of nothing that wasn't already on Dan's meager list of leads despite having spent a couple of hours nearly every Saturday afternoon for the past two or three years with Joe Teller. In the winter they would sit around the stove and talk sports, politics and books they had read. Larry had inherited his grandfather's library, so he and his friend shared a bounty of printed treasures, from James Fenimore Cooper and Mark Twain to Rudyard

Kipling and Arthur Conan Doyle. Aside from the occasional historic account of World War II, they gorged themselves on nineteenth and twentieth century classics.

"I'll really miss Joe," Larry said with obvious feeling. "He never accomplished much that I know of but his heart was sure in the right place. He would say to me, 'I'd give up ten years of my life to do something really good for people.' I'd ask him what he meant, and he'd just say, 'Oh, I don't know, maybe discover a cure for a disease, find a way to feed the world, something like that.' And he would always look off as if he could picture himself doing it, or maybe regretting that he would never have the chance."

Dan asked, "If you had to come up with a reason why Berger would have murdered his friend, and remember I'm not saying he did, just suppose he did…what would it be? And think about the two men, what they said, what their personalities were like."

The proprietor of Nuremberg's General Store thought about it for a while and seemed ready to answer a few times, but he rethought each conclusion. Finally he said, "I'd be guessing, 'cause I'm still shocked he could have done anything to hurt Joe, but I do know that a month or so ago Joe was in my store one really cold afternoon. I wasn't feeling all that well and was thinking of closing up early, like four or so. He was sitting in the back in his favorite chair by the stove and I walked back and mentioned closing up. He looked up at me and said, 'Larry, do me a favor and let me just sit here for a while. I'll lock up for you.' Well he looked so damn lonely I told him I really didn't feel all that bad and I'd sit with him for a bit and we did. I got out a bottle of Wild Turkey and we had a coupla' shots each, and that's the most I ever saw him drink. His mind seemed a million miles away, 'cause we sat there for damn near two hours and he hardly spoke at all, until he finally said he had kept me long enough. When he got up he held his hand out and said, 'You've got a good heart, Larry, and you've been a good friend, a good friend to me and everybody in this town. Don't ever change, because there's not enough people like you to go around.' I didn't know what to say then, but I realize now that something was depressing the hell out of Joe and I wasn't smart enough to see it and ask him about it. If I had, maybe things would have worked out different and he'd be alive."

Dan shook hands with Larry Moretti and hiked back up to Jack's office. He was about to open the door when he heard Moretti call out to him. "By the way, Joe gave me a journal, a kind of history of his work to hold on to. Would you be interested in seeing it?"

# CHAPTER 9

Jack and Donna drove into Hazleton to pick up the fingerprint kit and telephone records while Dan settled in the constable's office to study the beaten leather notebook Maria Bottino had alluded to and Joe Teller had given to Moretti for safe keeping. The pages were dated, some going back to the '50's when Teller was an organic chemistry major in college.

It didn't take Dan long to realize he would learn nothing on his own by studying the scientist's notes, for the pages were filled with complex equations comprised of enzymatic symbols and abbreviations. Only once did Teller refer to a proper name, "Snively," and in a manner that suggested he hadn't known him directly. So Dan resigned himself to reviewing Carmine Pecora's report, his own notes, and deciding what his next step would be. Beyond the observations in Pecora's report and the fact that Berger had fled the interview, he had little hard evidence to implicate him as an accomplice. But the extravagant steps taken at the lab to conceal their research were an indication of the magnitude of whatever the two had been working on, which Dan was now convinced had something to do with the motive for the murder. He was equally certain from the comments of the Nuremberg witnesses that Joe Teller's optimism dating back about six months ago and continuing up to a point at which he appeared depressed and at times uncharacteristically angry a month or so before his murder was related to the successful closure, or near closure, of some research of significance. The key to everything lay in whatever caused his sudden change, so he began considering a long list of possibilities.

*The project began to fail because of something Berger did or perhaps failed to do, something that either way was not just a mistake, because Joe Teller wasn't the kind of person that would turn on a friend for making an honest mistake.*

*Maybe Berger had sold them out, given up whatever they were supposed to get out of all their effort, or even worse, made arrangements to somehow siphon off more of the reward for himself. But Teller agreed to go with him to New York, so maybe Berger agreed to make things right? Then why was Teller murdered? Because Berger woudn't or couldn't keep his word, so he lured Teller to New York and set him up.*

*Or maybe the project was near closure and Berger wanted more credit, more reward. So what? Not enough reason to murder your best friend who by all accounts would have shared whatever fame and fortune came his way.*

*Maybe the project was near completion but the financial support that was promised was being pulled and maybe Berger was the reason. But what about other money sources? If Teller was that close, why couldn't he find other backers?*

He tried to concentrate, running the only consistent facts over and over again in his mind...Teller's personality and goals, his optmism and sudden depression. There were dozens of possibilities, but he ultimately settled on one that seemed to accommodate all the evidence or at least everything he had been told. Teller, or he and Berger jointly, had completed or nearly completed a project of some scientific and perhaps, financial significance, putting him in a very positive mood. But then the plug was pulled, some promise was broken, some support withdrawn. They were almost there and suddenly, their work was terminated or delayed for reasons unacceptable to Teller, reasons that infuriated him enough to threaten to do something drastic. That's when Berger managed to patch things up and convince Teller to go to New York, not for a play as Berger testified, but for a meeting to correct whatever differences they had. New York fits because it's convenient to the accomplices and because it's the one place that supports whatever excuse they gave Teller. To murder him in Nuremberg or the surrounding area where tragedies of that nature just don't happen would have appeared far too suspicious. But a mugging turned fatal in New York? Hell, it happens every day.

Convinced that his imagination needed a break and that further study of the Teller notebook would prove as unproductive as the first, Dan decided to search out some other townsfolk Maria Bottino, Anna and Jim French had mentioned.

He stopped by the Nuremberg Post Office, a converted turn-of-the-century, two-story, one room wide house perched on the sloping main street next to

Leon's Café. The postmistress, a middle-age woman with distinctively Italian features appeared from behind the counter. With a broad smile and youthful exhuberance she welcomed Dan to Nuremberg and asked what she might do for him. He explained what he was doing there, the people he had met and the basics of what the town's other citizens had told him.

"I was just wondering if you might be able to add anything that might help me in the investigation."

"I can tell you that Dr. Berger once threatened me…told me if I ever again gave Dr. Teller any of his mail, he'd see to it that I lost my job."

She went on to explain that on one occasion, shortly after they had moved into the hotel, Joe Teller had come in for his mail and offered to take Berger's back to him. She thought nothing of it, since she knew they were partners, had bought the old schoolhouse together and had come in to purchase their postal boxes together. "They sure seemed to be really close friends, so I was more than shocked when Berger acted the way he did. I guess he expected some mail he just didn't want his best friend to see."

"And you say that was when they first got here, like three or four years ago?"

"Yep, and his attitude about it never changed either, because Dr. Teller asked me another time and I told him what Berger had said. Dr. Teller seemed a bit confused at the time, but the very next day he apologized to me for putting me on the spot, so I guess he got told the same thing by Berger."

Dan learned nothing more from the postmistress, so he walked further down the hill to the little Lutheran Church where Joe Teller frequented services with Marcy Holland. The minister, a tall, studious looking fellow with thinning gray hair and a neatly trimmed salt and pepper beard was quietly reading a book in a tiny anteroom of the church. He welcomed Dan, pointed to a chair and asked if he'd like something to drink.

"I've converted this into something of a private study, a place where I can meet one on one with parishioners or simply find some peace and quiet. It used to be a good place to hide from my wife until she found me here once too often," he laughed, "but I'm sure you don't want to hear about the trials of a country minister, so what can I do for you?"

The minister listened to Dan summarize his previous interviews, before filling his pipe and settling back in his reading chair. "I never got as close to Joe as I would have liked," he started, "though not because I didn't try. He was a man of simple tastes, but extraordinary wisdom and humility, the kind of person we all can learn a great deal from. But he was absorbed with his work…obsessed by it is more accurate…to the point where he didn't really let anyone or anything interfere with it. It was like everything else in his life was competing for a little slice of his time, if any was left. Only once did I even have the opportunity to discuss it with him. It was about eighteen months ago. He and Marcy had just begun seeing each other and they came to a dance one Saturday night. Well, as you might expect, Joe was no hoofer and Marcy could dance all night, so she proceeded to wear out the rest of the men while Joe and I sat and talked away the evening. He relaxed, told me about his kid, a marriage gone bad and how all he had left was his work. But he also said that someday he hoped his life would have served a good purpose. I asked him what he meant and all he said was, 'Scientists like me labor in obscurity, but if we do just one thing to open other people's eyes, people who can do something with what a guy like me starts, well then, it's worth all the heartache and all the disappointments of a lifetime.' I tried to draw him out, to learn something about what he was working on, but he cut me off. The last thing he said about it was, 'For every Jonas Salk there's a thousand Joe Tellers, who just stumble around in the dark getting more confused every day.' I saw him twenty, maybe thirty times after that, and he never seemed to have changed his attitude, but he also never spoke about his work to me again."

The last stop Dan made was to a farmer in the valley at the bottom of Nuremberg's main street, a big, burly German with calloused hands, a leathered face and the requisite smile of Pennsylvania's mountain folk. He was the sixth generation to till the soil of Cemetary Farm, first settled by his ancestors in 1794.

"Sure, I knew Joe Teller," Clyde Kohler responded, while leading Dan into a newly restored, century old cow barn, "and a first class fellow he was. Never should have gone to the city. Knew nothing good would come of it," he reminisced. "But Joe told me he had no choice, that he had to go to finish what he had started."

Carefully avoiding the dung trough, Dan asked, "Did he tell you what he meant by that? Did he say anything else at all?"

"Nope, and I didn't think it was my place to ask."

"But he seemed reluctant to go, as though he knew something might happen to him?"

"Oh, I don't know if I'd go so far as to say he had any premonition; more like he didn't want to face what was going to be an uncomfortable situation. Joe didn't like confrontations, used to come down here and walk the fields with me, watch me milk the cows or just sit in a rocker up on the porch and look at the sunset; said it got his mind off his problems and away from people he didn't like. I told him I'd be more than willing to talk to anyone giving him any trouble, but he just thanked me for the offer and said there probably wasn't anything anybody could do to change certain people."

The long walk back up the hill to the constable's office at the foot of Sugarloaf Mountain took long enough for Dan to review everything he had learned during his visit. There were more questions than answers, but of one thing he was certain: Lewis Berger was no friend of Joe Teller's, and had lured him to the city to be murdered. The motive remained a mystery, but certainly related to the work in the lab.

The phone rang as he entered Jack Shultz's office. Concerned that it might be Wilson or Joe D, he picked it up.

"Nuremberg Police, may I help you."

"Good, I was afraid you wouldn't answer." It was Jack Shultz. "I've got good news and bad. The Jersey State Police found Berger in a motel near Hackettstown. The bad news is he has a bullet hole in the back of his head. He's been dead about twenty-four hours. No witnesses. He had checked into the motel yesterday afternoon and the cleaning lady found the body at eleven this morning."

"Well, I can't say I'm surprised. Do me a favor, Jack, and use whatever influence you've got to have them hold the crime scene as is. I need to get to it before they destroy what little evidence there might be. Can you do that?"

"I can try. It's New Jersey jurisdiction, but I can fill them in on your case and that should help. How quickly can you get there?"

"Within two hours if you don't mind doing the fingerprinting at Bottino's."

"Sure. What about the telephone records? They've got the last twelve months here and they're running the previous twenty-four as we speak."

"Will they fax them to my Manhattan office?"

"I'll see to it."

Dan gave him the precinct's fax number and the file number in case the information came in before he did. Then he got directions to the motel.

"Thanks an awful lot, Jack. I owe you a few."

"Don't mention it, and keep me posted, okay? I'd sure like to know how everything plays out, and if there's anything you need, just yell."

"Thanks again and say good-bye to Donna for me, you lucky stiff."
"Hey, I'll even kiss her for you."
"I'll bet you will."

Dan retraced his route along Pismire Ridge, across the peaks of the Green Mountains, down into the Conyngham Valley and across Route 80. It was almost four when he arrived at the Castle Tower Motel outside Hackettstown. A New Jersey State Police cruiser was parked alongside door number seven. Yellow crime scene tape cordoned off the area.

Dan showed two State Troopers his credentials. They explained that their people had removed the body, dusted for prints and left everything else exactly as they had found it. "We're also to advise you that you can't remove anything, but that we're to make a list of whatever you want and try to accommodate you later on," one said formally.

The room was nondescript; a double bed flanked by two nightstands, a long, four-drawer chest supporting a TV on one wall and a small round table and armchair on the other. A chalk profile of a man's legs protruded from the bathroom, the torso portion outlined directly in front of the sink. A large bloodstain appeared where the head would have been.

An attempt had been made to simulate a robbery and struggle by tossing clothes and toilet articles about, pulling out the drawers and uncovering the bed. Dan searched for papers but could find none. *A research scientist with no briefcase and no papers. What are the chances?*

"Any personal items such as wristwatch, rings, wallet?" Dan asked.
"Not a one, Sergeant. Looks like robbery."
Dan didn't bother to correct him. "The body was lying face down?"
"Yes, sir."
"Fully clothed?"
"Yes, sir. Sportshirt, cardigan sweater, trousers and shoes."
Dan got on his hands and knees, closely inspecting the carpet in front of the bathroom door. "Has this been vacuumed?"
The trooper responded hesitantly. "I'm not sure. Do you want me to find out?"
"Yes, please. Make a note that if it has, I'd appreciate knowing what was found. If not, I'd really appreciate having them do it."

It was obvious that Berger had trusted the assailant enough to let him into the room and to turn his back on him as he entered the bathroom. Ballistics would prove whether the gun was the one that had killed Teller.

"I think all I'll need is the vacuumed debris, a ballistics report and any other signs of violence on the body," he stated, though he expected none of the latter. "Any objection to my speaking to the cleaning lady?"

"No, sir. In fact, we have her and the motel owner waiting for you."

"Good. Let's just check his car first, if you don't mind."

Dan was not surprised to find that it was unlocked and void of any documents. Except for two suitcases stuffed with clothes the car was clean. The killer or killers had been thorough.

The manager's office reeked of cigarette smoke. Dime store prints of Elvis and cheap reproductions of his concert posters covered the walls. An overweight redhead on the wrong side of forty rumbled forward as Dan entered, the alcohol on her breath reaching him before she did. Her eyes undressed him as he introduced himself. He took in the garishly smeared lipstick, blue eye shadow and fake lashes, and felt kind of sorry for her. She motioned him to a table in the corner where a thin young woman with long, mousy brown hair, wearing a tee shirt and jeans, was seated on one of four rickety folding chairs.

"This here is Dottie, my cleaning lady. She found the body," the redhead announced in a harsh smoker's voice.

Nervously, Dottie stood as Dan approached. His smile relaxed her as he asked if she had disturbed anything before noticing the body.

"Oh no, sir. As soon as I opened the door I could see the man's legs and I knew they weren't moving, so I rushed right out and yelled for Madeleine."

"That's me," the redhead volunteered, seeking some attention, frowning when she received none.

"Did you notice any strange odors in the room?"

"No, sir, I don't think so," Dottie replied after considerable deliberation, "but like I said, I ran out right away. Nothing like this ever happened to me. I was really scared."

"Sure, I can understand that," Dan said sympathetically. "Can either of you recall seeing a car other than the victim's Pathfinder in front of the room after Berger checked in?"

Neither volunteered an answer, looking to each other for help.

"How about strangers?" Dan asked. "Men milling about, asking for the deceased... anything like that?"

Madeleine commented, "We were both working, so you can understand that we wouldn't see people or cars that just came in and went out."

"Don't you have a trip line that rings when a car pulls in?"

"Well, yes," the owner replied a bit defensively, "but I don't look out every time the bell goes off. Christ, I'd be gettin' up every two minutes, 'specially when the regulars start comin' in."

"Regulars?" Dan asked.

"Yeah, you know; wham, bam, thank you ma'am, half-hour sessions." She laughed, promoting a series of smoker's coughs.

"Oh, I see," Dan said, backing up to avoid her breath. "How about the victim's mood when he checked in?"

"Nervous as hell," Madeleine stated after a long puff. "Didn't I mention that to you, Dottie, that he was sweatin' and jumpy? I even asked him if he was all right and he just looked at me as if to say, 'mind your own damn business.' Little creep."

Dottie listened, nodding as her boss spoke.

"Did he ask if anyone had been in to inquire about him?"

Madeleine forced her fleshy lids open. "Shit, you're right, goddamn it, he did ask something like that. Let's see, what did he say…was it…no, shit…oh, yeah, he said, 'I'm expecting a couple of friends…males.' He said it like I was thinkin' some broads were gonna' do him. Then he said, 'They'll be driving a Lincoln. It's okay to give them my room number, but only if they're driving a Lincoln. Anybody else asks for me, I'm not here.' That was it, I'm sure of it."

She stared at Dan expectantly.

"And did they ever arrive?"

"If they did, I never saw 'em. You, Dot?"

The maid replied that she had not seen anything resembling a Lincoln.

Before leaving, Dan reiterated for the troopers what he would need, adding to the list a set of morgue photos. He didn't know why he asked for them, chalking it up to habit. A faithful student of A. C. Doyle, he never forgot Holmes' famous reply to Watson when the good doctor asked his friend what he was searching for. "I have no idea, Watson, but when I find it, I shall know."

As he started the Jeep, he noticed a split rail fence separating a narrow back street from the motel. Had a Lincoln parked there, neither Dottie nor her boss would have seen it or whoever got out, climbed over or through the split rail and entered room number seven.

He arrived at his apartment a little after nine, the trip having been extended by the security checks at the tunnel and the increased volume at the Lincoln Tunnel now that the Holland was closed. Dan wondered how many years a man lost just from the stress of driving in traffic. He hated it with a vengeance, promising himself that whenever he retired his home would be somewhere in the quiet country as far from the city as possible.

He was anxious to speak to Joe DeLorenzo, for even though the Teller case was developing into a real challenge, the anxiety he suffered over his father's murder made everything else in his life secondary. Temporary respites such as the Nuremberg trip and Marilyn Kyme helped, but Dan knew that recovering from what he was feeling would be a long process and that it couldn't begin until his father's killers were either in prison or dead and buried.

He dialed his friend's number.

"Hi, Joe, it's me."

"Hey, Dan, you're back from the woods?"

"Yeah. How'd you make out today?"

"Not bad. It was your dad's watch and we got a good description of the guy from the pawnbroker. He described him as black with an average build, in his late teens, early twenties, mustache and a scar on the left cheek just below the eye. He was wearing a black woolen watchcap, blue carcoat, dark trousers…the baggy kind…and white sneakers with gray side trim. The name he signed on the register, Joe Rollins, is a phony, but I'm having the computer check it for corresponding initials. Some of these shits aren't the sharpest knives in the drawer."

"It's a start. Did you have Kuhn there?" Dan asked, referring to the department's best artist.

"Sure. Calvin and Ronald Williams are meeting me in the neighborhood first thing in the morning. We're going to canvas the area with Kuhn's sketch."

"How has Williams fit in?"

"So far, no complaints. He's quiet as hell, just asks what he can do and goes about doing it. If Jenkins has something up his sleeve, Williams sure hasn't shown his hand. He's been a model assistant."

"Good, just don't let your guard down."

"I won't and I'll check in with you sometime tomorrow."

Dan popped two frozen chicken potpies into the microwave, showered, put on a comfortable old sweatsuit and dialed Al Wilson's home number.

Camille answered. "Hello, Dan, how are you? When are we going to see you?"

"I'll make a dinner appointment with Al soon, I promise. I've just been really busy with a special case your husband dumped on me, sending out thank-you notes to people who sent flowers and donations and just trying to accept what happened. How are you and the kids?"

"Oh fine. They ask for you all the time. Michael keeps wanting to know if you're going to make it to one of his games. Did Al tell you he's the only sophomore on the varsity? And he's starting at point guard."

"You sound just like a proud mama."

"Yeah, disgusting, isn't it? Well, listen, here's Al, and don't forget, I expect you for dinner within the week."

"Evening, Dan." Wilson sounded tired.

"Hi, Boss. You sound like you were sleeping."

"No, just relaxing. Listen, you got a fax from that Nuremberg constable. He's having those phone records you want delivered tomorrow. There were too many sheets to fax. He also says a guy named Larry Moretti remembered seeing New Jersey plates on the Dodge van. That mean anything to you?"

"Yeah, an old heap that might have been delivering some things connected to why Teller was murdered. Anything else?"

"Rasheed found your doctors in the A.M.A. register. He was searching for professional and hospital affiliations when I left the office."

"So they're MD's?"

"Must be. Last time I checked they're the only ones that could get into the A.M.A."

"On that sarcastic note I'll say good evening to you, Lieutenant, and see you in the morning."

He wanted to hear Marilyn Kyme's voice but her number wasn't listed in either the phone book or with "Information." He toyed with the idea of driving to her apartment but he knew she wouldn't' appreciate that. If she had wanted more attention she would have given him her phone number, but since she hadn't, he concluded that she wanted to regulate both the frequency and timing of their contact. Though he knew their mutual attraction was strong, her control of the relationship to date frustrated him. At this point he wanted to move it forward, but he couldn't help feeling that she was less enthusiastic about taking the next step, at least for now. All he could do was allow things to move at a pace with which she was comfortable, share in whatever she thought appropriate and wait until she decided it was time to get serious.

Marilyn's intelligence and maturity were as obvious as her beauty. If she were as attracted to him as he thought, sooner or later she would express her feelings and that would justify his patience. The more he thought about it, the more convinced he became that it was a small price to pay, for no one in his life had ever made him feel this way except Eileen and he knew how happy he had been with her. He went to bed thinking about his wife, but Marilyn Kyme filled his dreams.

The squad room clock read seven sharp as he finished climbing the stairs. Larry Kennedy's third shift detectives were all at their desks pounding out reports.

"Hey, guy, this was delivered for you about an hour ago," Kennedy informed him, holding out a brown paper-wrapped package.

"Thanks. How ya doin'?"

"Not bad, yourself?"

"Okay. I was in Pennsylvania yesterday," he stated as he opened the UPS parcel from Shultz. "I wouldn't mind settling down out there. Love the people...simple, honest, gregarious, too. Always smiling."

He rambled on in half sentences about the mountains, food and the voluptuous Donna Schulman while thumbing through four sets of telephone company records. One was in Joe Teller's name and three were in Berger's. Teller's had to be the one in his hotel room, as was one of Berger's. Dan concluded that one of the other two was on Donna's desk and that the last was in the lab. He drew a cup of coffee and sat down to begin his instructions to Rasheed Martin. As he leaned back to review what he had written he saw his new partner reach the landing at the top of the stairs, an armful of books and papers precariously balancing an oversized breakfast sack from McDonalds.

"Ptomaine time," the fledgling detective announced to no one in particular. "Come and get 'em. We got McMuffins, biscuits and sausage and lots of greasy potato whatever."

He dropped the load on his desk. "See you made it back from Whitelandia," he teased, a broad smile replacing his usual early morning frown.

"What are you so happy about?"

"Hit four of the five lottery numbers last night," he beamed, "worth $570."

"Don't be offended, but I hope you never win some real money. We wouldn't be able to stand you."

"Sergeant, trust me, if I ever win some real money you will not have to worry about seeing me. I'll phone in my resignation, assuming I have the time before I jump a plane outta' here."

"I thought you were the soon-to-be super cop that's gonna' clean up New York."

"True, true," he said in mock seriousness, "but only for as long as I need a job. If I have to work, this is as good as it gets. But it's still work."

Dan watched Rasheed bounce around the room, offering the food, tossing it behind his back and over his head to any takers. He was beginning to think Al Wilson's opinion might be right. Rasheed Martin had something to offer, at least that is, until he hit the jackpot.

"You finished?" he asked as Rasheed returned.

"Yes sir, all set," he replied enthusiastically.

Dan told him to take notes as he began explaining the details of his trip, omitting only the personalities of Nuremberg's citizens and his growing fondness for them. He emphasized the absence of clues, the steps taken by Teller, Berger and their associates to ensure secrecy and the probable importance of whatever discovery they had been pursuing in the lab. A summary of Berger's flight and demise concluded the summation. Dan glanced at his watch; nine-fifteen. He had been talking and answering questions for half an hour, enough time for his eager partner to fill a small notebook. It also reminded him that he hadn't yet seen Al Wilson, the man renowned for his punctuality.

Kennedy was preparing to leave, his reports for the day concluded.

"Larry, any idea where the boss is?"

"Yeah, I forgot to mention it. He called just before you got in. He had to stop off at City Hall. He'll be in around noon."

Rasheed spent the next half-hour detailing what he had learned about the Doctors Steinberg and Norville. Both were apparently very successful, holding executive positions in two of New York's most prestigious hospitals, in addition to being the principals in one of the city's largest private medical groups. Both were in their fifties, married and with large families. Each owned palatial homes on Long Island and in Florida, plus condos in an Upper East Side co-op that included some very impressive luminaries.

Martin confessed that he hadn't expected to uncover much, since everyone to whom he had spoken were senior staff personnel at the hospitals and the medical group. But he did learn that the suspects had spent very little time at the hospitals in the past year, working instead at the medical group offices in mid-town, something they hadn't done in years. According to their office manager, they hadn't come in more than once a week for a three or four year period, and then only to sign checks and conduct cursory reviews of patients' records. Then, without notice, she began seeing them daily, though they would seclude themselves in a boardroom immediately upon arriving and remain sequestered for hours at a time. The doctors kept the room locked, but she knew there was a good deal of equipment in it since she had overseen its installation to Dr. Norville's specifications. Her summary description of it had to suffice since she had no key or any other means of gaining entrance.

"What were the medical group's specialties?" Dan asked as he continued scribbling notes.

"Family practice," Rasheed answered, proud that he had thought to check, "and Internal Medicine. There are six doctors in addition to our two principals."

Dan continued writing for a minute, then tore off two pages and laid them face-up so his partner could read them. They were the questions he wanted Rasheed to ask the office manager, but without implicating the Doctors as suspects in Teller's death.

"How did you gain her confidence?"

"I'm not sure I did. I just told her we were conducting a confidential investigation, that nothing she said would be publicized to anyone, most notably her employers, and that she shouldn't assume that they were suspects in anything. At one point when she asked why their schedules were so important, I told her they related to establishing whether or not they were at the hospitals on specific dates at specific times. I'm not sure I convinced her of anything other than my promise to keep things strictly confidential."

"Good thinking. Now let's go over these," he said, sliding the papers closer to his partner.

Dan had to establish that there were direct communications between the Nuremberg lab and the doctors, which he felt certain would be accomplished through the phone records now stacked on Rasheed's desk, but corroboration by the office manager wouldn't hurt. Any knowledge on her part of the Doctors' interests in studies concerning enzymology, horseshoe crabs or Chincoteague Island would help link the suspects to the victims.

Rasheed looked questionningly at Dan when he mentioned the crabs.

"I'll explain it as soon as I know what I'm talking about."

A third set of questions related to the associations and universities with whom they were or had been affiliated, any outside interests and the sites to which they traveled or vacationed. Dan relayed the Sherlock Holmes anecdote to explain his purpose.

Finally, he wanted him to ask questions that might connect the Doctors to some unsavory or at least unlikely characters. "The dark blue Lincoln belongs to someone and that someone is connected to our trigger man. Maybe you'll get lucky."

"Now I've got to get to Forensics," Dan reminded himself, checking his watch. "Before you hit anything on those lists, go through the phone records until you find a number on the Jersey shore that belongs to a commercial fisherman, a co-op, or anybody that could supply horseshoe crabs to the lab. The only clue I can give you is that it would be in area code 609. And it probably wasn't called too often, because it's an obvious link to the purpose of the lab. They would have only called it in an emergency of some sort. Leave whatever numbers fit the bill on my desk. After that make your visit to the office manager; then come back and do the rest of the work on the phone records. Check off every call to any of your doctors' numbers. Use some code to indicate home, office, hospital…whatever. Remember, these may end up being the only evidence we can rely on to connect Steinberg and Norville to Teller and Berger."

He thought for a few seconds before concluding his instructions. "We need to find some people who have knowledge of the experiments. I'm really hoping those phone numbers include suppliers of the crabs and lab equipment, maybe a software development guy for the computers. We're going to have to prove a motive and I'm pretty damn convinced it's connected to whatever research they were conducting in that lab."

As they gathered their things, preparing to leave, Dan suggested that they meet back there by four.

A short ride to the Forensics Lab in midtown was made easier by the lull between rush hour and lunch, before the streets would be jammed with people anxious to get outside and enjoy the warm sun, particularly after such a long, hard winter. Even the fear of looming terrorists couldn't restrain enthusiasm for the promise of a spring day.

Bill Mason was Forensics' answer to Dante Fiore. Overweight, overworked and overbearing, he grunted his understanding of Dan's request and shuffled back to his office, not bothering to say anything pleasant, or for that matter, decipherable.

Costa punched in Al Wilson's number. No one answered, so he waited for the tape. "You have reached Lieutenant Wilson's desk. Please leave a brief message after the tone."

"Al, it's Dan. I'm at Forensics and heading downtown to talk to a Mr. Kaplan, the pedestrian in the Teller case that identified Ruiz as an eyewitness. Rasheed is on some follow-ups. We'll both be back by four. Hope everything's okay," he concluded, still wondering about the purpose of Wilson's appointment at City Hall.

His destination was Kaplan's Electrical Supplies, a contractor's store around the corner from where Joe Teller had been shot. Its proprietor, Sidney Kaplan, was a white haired, paunchy, grandfatherly type with a friendly but nervous smile. Obviously uncomfortable with the impending interview, he warned of a tight schedule and limited time.

They sat at a small table in the corner of a dusty antique of an office, surrounded by stacks of paper, yellowing catalogues and obsolete fixtures. Dan was already convinced Kaplan knew more than Carmine Pecora had reported and decided he wasn't going to leave without getting it all. By a series of questions and assumptions he carefully positioned Kaplan on the sidewalk heading in the direction of the shooting. He voiced his understanding of the angles and the lighting, confirming Kaplan's assertion that Jorge Ruiz, not he, had sight of the murder. Following that, Dan asked a series of innocuous questions that did nothing more than establish the positions of some parked cars, all of which were on the opposite side of the street, and of the angle of approach that finally gave Kaplan a view of Teller's body. With each confirmation Dan would add to a sketch that he held from the witness's view, finally laying it face-up on the table when he had seemingly completed his questions.

"I'm no Rembrandt, but I guess this is pretty much a picture of what you described, isn't it?" he asked in a friendly tone.

Sidney Kaplan looked it over, confident that he had said nothing to arouse suspicion or to further implicate himself in the affair. Looking relaxed, he said, "You did a pretty good job, Sergeant. You're right, you're no Rembrandt," he laughed, "but the drawing is accurate."

Dan just smiled as he reached over and drew a small rectangle between two stick figures, one representing the deceased, the other, Kaplan. The witness frowned as he shifted in his chair, a nervous little smile curling the edge of his mouth.

"What's that supposed to be?"

"That, Mr. Kaplan, is a mid-nineties, dark blue Lincoln Town Car in which the murderers of Joe Teller made their getaway, the same car you failed to report to the investigating detectives. Someone who conceals information during an official investigation is referred to legally as an accomplice after the fact. Is that what you want to be, Sir, an accomplice to murder?"

A long minute passed during which Sidney Kaplan's complexion turned an alarming crimson, and though he said nothing, it was more from fear than an unwillingness to cooperate.

"I'm sure you had nothing to do with the murder, Mr. Kaplan, but even as an innocent bystander you're required by law to tell us what you know. I promise you that absolutely nothing will happen to you despite your previous failure to tell the truth, as long as you do so now." He paused, hoping that one final nudge would convince Kaplan to come clean. "But lie to me now, tell me you don't know anything, and you'll leave here in cuffs because we both know exactly what you saw. The difference is it's your legal responsibility to put it on the record."

Kaplan raised himself unsteadily and made his way to the desk, leaning heavily on it for some time. Then he opened the top drawer, withdrew an envelope and a pharmacist's bottle and took some pills. He breathed deeply and slumped into a leather swivel chair. Without a sound, he held out the envelope. Dan opened it and withdrew the crudely written note in black ink on unlined white paper.

*"We know who you are. Talk to the police and you will live long enough to bury your family."*

"I have a wife, four children, seven grandchildren," he said barely above a whisper. "That was delivered to my home…not here…to my home. What am I supposed to do?" and he looked pleadingly at the detective who felt just a little guilty.

"No one's going to know you said anything. I have more than one way of ensuring that. Just tell me everything," Dan said earnestly, "and I'll make sure these people are put where they can't hurt anyone else again."

Sidney Kaplan shook his head. "I know what people like that are capable of," he said softly, "and if killing me…." He shook his head again, took a deep breath and slowly, reluctantly, began recounting what he had seen.

"I was walking down the street to my car when I heard the shots. It scared me. I don't even know why I kept going, but I did, until I got next to the appliance store. That's when I could finally see everything, the car, two guys getting into it, another man running across the street away from the shooting and Ruiz standing there on the sidewalk looking at everything."

He breathed heavily a few times, looking down at his hands and then to a framed picture on his desk. Turning his eyes towards Costa, he continued, "About then the car, the Lincoln, it started down the street towards me. I moved over to the appliance store windows. I was trying to hide but there was no place to hide, and I looked at the car as it passed under the streetlight just in front of me, no more than thirty feet, and I saw the man in the front seat. He took off his mask and that's when he saw me. The car was alongside me then and we were looking at each other. It was still moving but we saw each other, and he raised his gun and I just knelt on the ground, covered my head and waited for the shots. But they never came. By the time I looked up the car had gone around the corner, so far that I couldn't even hear the engine," and he turned from Dan to the desk photo. "My Rachel, she'll be sixty-two next month and we'll be married forty years this summer. Do you think I could live with myself if anything happened to her?"

"There's no way they will ever know what you told me, Mr. Kaplan."

Dan's cool, professional manner was gaining the witness's confidence. "I hope you're right, Sergeant, because all I care about is keeping my family safe. I don't care if they kill me, I really don't, just as long as they leave my family alone. I often wonder why they didn't just get out of the car and shoot me when they had the chance."

"Because that would have made the victim's murder seem like something other than a mugging gone bad and that's the way it had to look. If the killer hadn't removed his mask there wouldn't even be this note."

Sidney Kaplan understood. "So the poor man wasn't mugged? Everything was staged?"

"It's possible. Do you think you could identify the guy in the passenger seat if you saw a photo of him?"

"Maybe," he said thoughtfully. "He looked like he had a square face, dark features and a good head of black hair. It was very disheveled when he pulled off the mask."

"Dark features?" Dan asked. "Like an Arab or Puerto Rican?"

"No. He looked more Italian or Greek."

Dan nodded. "And how about the driver or the passenger in the back?"

"Sorry, I only saw the large man in the front."

"License plate number or anything else about the Lincoln?"

"Isn't it funny, but the first thing I saw was the license plate. It was definitely New York, but I couldn't tell you the numbers."

"Anything else about the car? Dents, extra chrome, flashy hubcaps?"

"No, nothing else. Sorry."

Dan gave Kaplan his card, offered more encouragement and a final promise to keep everything confidential.

"Nothing will break in the newspapers to alert the killers to your involvement, so don't worry. When I catch them you'll be the first to know."

It was after three when he arrived at the 34th Street Precinct. Rasheed hadn't yet returned, but Al Wilson was seated in his office so he knocked and walked in.

His friend looked over the top of his glasses. "Have a good day?"

"Not bad. The guy that owned the electrical supplies business had reason to be afraid, but he came forward and cleared up some issues. I think I'm on the right track."

"Care to give me an update?"

Dan summarized everything, including what Rasheed had learned about the two doctors who Dan was beginning to think were the brains behind both murders. "I haven't ruled out the possibility of other conspirators, but I'm betting that one of them, if not both, financed the project and masterminded the murders to cover up something that went wrong or was about to go wrong…more likely the latter.

"Sounds like you've made some progress. Keep me posted."

"Sure. By the way, if it's not too personal, what went on downtown this morning?"

"Nothing much, just some policy discussions."

Wilson tried to downplay its importance, but Dan could not recall his friend ever having been invited to Gracey Mansion before.

"Anything I should know about?"

Wilson looked up. "Nothing you have to know about, Dan, or be concerned with. You and I agreed a long time ago that Donald Jenkins couldn't always be trusted, but we also agreed some of his goals were decent. To him the ends always justify the means and that's just the way it is. If we knew and worried about every little thing he said and did we would drive ourselves nuts. Besides, his days are numbered, so put him out of your mind."

Back at his desk Dan had to resist the urge to speak to his boss again about the morning's meeting, having convinced himself it had something to do with his father's murder. Only the pile of work on his desk dissuaded him. He picked up the phone and dialed Jack Shultz's number.

"Constable's office, may I help you?"

"Hi, Jack, it's Dan Costa."

"Hello, Big Guy, how ya doin'?"

It took five minutes to summarize his visit to the Castle Tower Motel as well as what Rasheed Martin had uncovered about the doctors. He had no obligation to do so, but felt that Jack had been a big help and was genuinely interested in the case, so it was a courtesy if nothing else.

"I need for you to speak to Donna. There's got to be some way of tracing the people that met with Teller and Berger at the lab. Remember her telling us that a handful of men got to go into the lab? Well, we need to find them and she's my only lead. Tell her to try hard to remember anything that might give us a clue…business cards, brochures, invoices, maybe their cars and license plates…anything. I've got to pin down that project, Jack, because it's the key to everything. Without it I have no motive."

"I understand. I'm picking her up in an hour for dinner at Anna's. I'll talk to her and call you in the morning."

*Tough life you've got there, Jack,* Dan thought, before thanking him and hanging up.

While debating who he should call next, Joe DeLorenzo or Marilyn Kyme, Rasheed appeared at the top of the stairs. It was exactly four o'clock. The morning's broad smile was gone, replaced by the look of someone who had accomplished little despite considerable effort.

"You look like a man with troubles."

"Yeah, well, I can't say I was a blazing success. That Office Manager must have told one of the doctors that I had been in asking questions because she told me absolutely nothing this time."

"Was she belligerent?"

"No, she just kept saying she didn't know nuthin' about nuthin', and believe me, I covered everything we discussed, plus a few thoughts of my own. But I did hit a couple of raw nerves. When I mentioned Chincoteague her eyes opened real wide and she turned a little red, like she was shocked I even knew the place existed."

"Is this woman attractive?"

"Maybe a middle-aged white guy would think so, why?"

"Could she and one of the doctors be doin' each other?"

"Maybe, I don't know. I've never seen the doctors."

Dan looked away from his partner, rapidly sorting the input.

"We can't rely on her, Rasheed," he concluded shortly. "We need another source."

"I might have one," Martin replied, barely suppressing a grin. "There's a good lookin' sister workin' in that office. I came this close to asking for her number," he said, holding his thumb and forefinger an inch apart. Then, checking his watch, he said, "I can get back there in time to catch her when she leaves."

"You sound pretty damn certain she'll talk to you."

The morning's smile returned. "Sergeant, a man should know when a woman wants him, and this man knows that woman wants him."

"You sure are a cocky bastard for someone so ugly."

"Ugly? Who's ugly? How much money you got says the lady doesn't open up this evening?"

"What, her legs? I don't give a damn about that. You know what we need to get from her."

"And I'm sayin' I get both, but the money's on what we need to know."

"How do I know you'll tell me the truth?"

"You don't," Martin said. "You'll just have to take my word that where a case is involved I'll never lie to you."

"You got a deal. Come up with something by tomorrow morning and dinner's on me."

"Surf and turf at the Palm," he shouted over his shoulder as he flew down the stairs.

Dan's list of things to do and evidence to consider was longer than it had been when the day started. One particular subject, heavily underlined for emphasis, drew his attention. Who were the triggermen and how were they to be found? The New York plates didn't necessarily mean Manhattan or even one of the boroughs, so tracking down and interrogating the hundreds of owners of mid-nineties blue Town Cars in New York was out of the question. Unless the doctors slipped up, the killers would remain anonymous, and without the killers, it would be virtually impossible to convict the doctors. Catch twenty-two.

For some reason, and it could have been the type car, the m.o., or Sidney Kaplan's comment about the shooter looking Greek or Italian, he began to suspect the possible involvement of the Mob, or at the very least, professional hit-men. Dan believed that made sense if the lab project was one of unusual significance, something the Mob wouldn't mind underwriting, financially or otherwise. It was within the realm of possibility that one of the two doctors could have knowledge of such a contact, and even more probable, that one of their attorneys would. Now that he was giving the idea some thought, it was beginning to appear increasingly plausible. To explore it further he would need someone connected, and for that the starting point was obvious – Massimo Barracci. He would phone the Don that evening and arrange a meeting.

His spirits lifted, he dialed one of the Coroner's numbers.

"Dr. Kyme's office."

"Hello, this is Sergeant Costa, thirty-fourth precinct. May I speak to Dr. Kyme?"

"She's extremely busy, Sergeant, and asked not to be disturbed."

"Please tell her who it is and see if she can call me sometime later today."

Though she held her hand over the receiver, he could tell that whoever had answered was relaying the message.

"You are absolutely the only person for whom I would take a break right now. How are you?" Marilyn's voice could melt an iceberg.

"Hey, you keep talking like that and I'm going to start believing you mean it."

"Sometimes I do."

"That's better than never." He paused. "I'm doing pretty good, but I guess I'm supposed to assume you're up to your beautiful green eyes in cadavers, paperwork or both?"

"Oh, it's a lot higher than that, Sergeant. If you ever want to see me again you're going to have to find a way to prevent all this killing." Seriously, she said, "For the first time since I joined this office, we have more bodies than places to store them. There are four on the tables in the surgery and three on gurneys waiting to go in. I've never seen anything like it."

"I know we had a drug hit over the weekend, but that's all we contributed. If I knew it was going to keep you from seeing me I would have had the body dumped in Joisey."

She laughed lightly, the way Dan loved to hear her.

"I guess there's no way of getting to see you this week," he said, praying he was wrong.

"You're not getting off that easily, Sergeant. Remember? You're taking me across the river to Joisey this weekend."

"So you think you can still make it?"

"If you promise not to call until five p.m. Friday, I promise to get all my work done and spend time with you Saturday...maybe even Sunday, if you like."

"You strike a hard bargain, Doctor, but I'll do my best." In a more serious tone he added, "It would make it a lot easier to get through these periods if we could just talk for a few minutes each night."

He anticipated her response.

"Let's talk about it this weekend, Dan."

"Sure. I'll call Friday."

"Oh, I almost forgot," he added, "you're so busy, don't worry about helping me with that enzyme problem. I'll find another way to tackle it."

"Thanks, but I already made a phone call for you. There's a Doctor Clarence Worthington at Columbia University who will be happy to give you some time." She gave him the number, and sounding very tired said, "Now I must get back to work. Thanks for calling. Hearing your voice does help. I'm really looking forward to Saturday."

The next call was to Joe DeLorenzo. The desk sergeant answered, telling Dan that his friend and Calvin Washington had left around two to investigate a shooting. Neither had returned, so Dan left a message with the sergeant and on Joe's home recorder. Then he began preparing what he would say to Barracci. Without deliberation, he decided that the best approach would be complete honesty, since there was no downside to it. If he tried to be circuitous and the Don saw through it, he would be offended, and there is nothing worse you can do to the head of a family. By being truthful he would show his faith in Barracci and reflect his belief that the Don would neither condone the murder of an innocent man nor expose Dan to any danger.

Barracci's family was heavily involved in illegal gambling, high priced prostitution and some influence pedaling, in addition to a number of otherwise legitimate enterprises through which they laundered money, the most notable of which were a pier container service and a nationally prominent trucking company. But law enforcement agencies on both the federal and local levels believed that no one in the Barracci family had anything to do with drugs and that the executions in 1996 of two former members were the result of their having violated the old man's edict against the trafficking of narcotics. Though he could be ruthless, Barracci generously supported charities, particularly those involving disadvantaged children, the elderly and the Catholic Church. Consequently, he enjoyed a special position in the community and with the police, each appreciative of his benevolence while wary of his connections. The fine line he walked made him the target of less accommodating people on both sides.

Dan searched his book of private numbers and phoned Barracci's office near the Brooklyn Navy Yard.

"M.B. Enterprises. May I help you?" a pleasantly feminine voice inquired.

"Mr. Barracci, please. My name is Dan Costa."

"Sergeant, how are you? I was so sorry to here about your dad."

His memory failed him. "I apologize. Your voice sounds familiar," he lied, "but I can't quite place it."

"It's Pam Donaldson. We've met a couple of times here."

"Oh, yes, I'm embarrassed, Pam. Please excuse me. Of course I remember, and thank you for the Mass card. It was very thoughtful of you."

Pam Donaldson was Barracci's *goomadda*, or mistress. In her mid-forties and still single, she retained both her beauty and stunning figure. She also provided a steadying influence on her lover's business decisions, altogether a showpiece the Don was proud to display, and he did so unabashedly. With blazing, past-the-shoulders red hair and a Renaissance model's body she turned heads easily, yet the two frequented popular mid-town bistros, the Metropolitan Opera and other public places with impunity. If Mrs. Barracci was aware of the relationship, and most suspected she was, she accepted it for what was probably a long list of accommodating reasons.

"I would have attended the wake but we didn't think it was appropriate at the time," Pam confessed, alluding to some influence from the Don that would remain private.

"The Mass Card was more than I expected, Pam, and thank you again."

"You're very welcome. I'll find Mr. Barracci for you."

Shortly, the familiar voice boomed over the phone: "Daniel, *come sta?*"

"*Mezza, mezza, Si Massimo.*"

"And when am I going to see you? You never come around anymore now that you're a big shot detective. You forget your roots?"

"No, never, I've just been really busy. You know you can't believe the papers. They keep telling people that crime is down, but it's all bullshit. We're up to our eyeballs, and with Dad's death I haven't had any time to myself. Plus, they keep cutting the budget so we have fewer men on the streets and that means more work for all of us. But enough of me. How are you doing?"

"I'm really good, had a great check-up last week…turning sixty next month. You gonna' come to the party? My daughters are arranging it, so I'm sure you'll get an invitation and you'd better come. No excuses. *Capisce?*"

"I'll be there, I promise."

"*Bene, bene.* Now, what can I do for you?"

*The old man's not stupid,* Dan reminded himself.

"I've got a case involving the murder of someone a lot like Dad, a good person who didn't deserve to get killed. For reasons I don't want to discuss over the phone, I think you might be able to help me. Could you afford me some time this week?"

"Of course. Don't even ask. What are you doing tonight?"

"Actually, nothing," he replied, pleased that the Don would be so accommodating.

"Alright. I'll have Pam make reservations at Belmonte's on 16$^{th}$. You know where it is, right? How about seven?"

"Seven it is, Uncle, and thanks."

## CHAPTER 10

Belmonte's was small and exclusive, very protective of its clients' privacy, an ideal meeting place for business negotiations and wise guys with women who were not their wives. Though expensive, the food was superb and worthy of its clientele. The lighting, positioning of tables and placement of large plantings combined to afford the patrons quiet seclusion. Covert schemes and multi-million dollar transactions could be concluded without fear of compromise.

Dan could see only two small tables to his left, though laughter and the voices of those trying to talk over it could be heard from somewhere beyond a jungle of fern and ficas trees. From one particularly dense arrangement a maitre 'de in black tie emerged, a patronizing smile permanently affixed to an otherwise unremarkable face.

"May I help you, Sir?"

"Mr. Barracci's table, please."

The man tilted his head slightly, raising his eyebrows. "We have a table reserved by Ms. Donaldson for her friends. The gentleman you refer to may well be there. I will check," he said, disappearing into the foliage.

It was possible but unlikely that the man had never heard Massimo's last name, in which case, Belmonte's was the only ristorante in the five boroughs in which the Don wasn't on a first name basis with the waiters. Before he could consider other possibilities the tuxedo returned, parted some yellowish grass, apologized for the delay and asked Dan to follow him. After negotiating a half-dozen turns through a diminutive forest they arrived at their destination, a circular table in a rear corner bordered by a variety of leafy hedges and the ubiquitous grass.

The flaming red hair and alabaster skin of Pam Donaldson caught his eye, indeed a rose amongst the thorns. She wore an emerald green dress that further enhanced her Irish beauty. *You too have a tough life, Uncle Massimo.*

"Hey, here he is," Barracci bellowed, rising to embrace the detective he would have as a son-in-law, not altogether a poor reason to be so accommodating.

"Uncle Massimo, it's good to see you," and in truth Dan did enjoy the Don's company. As far as he knew, the Capo had never ordered or permitted an innocent to be injured, had done a lot of good with his money, protected his family and friends, and didn't flaunt his position. He could be boisterous at times and was a notorious womanizer, but the majority of politicians Dan knew were all those things, and worse.

Mussolino, or Uncle Muzzi, as Dan had been taught to call him, Vito Scarola, Anthony Lacozza, the balding family consigliere and the Don's personal friend for more than thirty years, and a fourth gentleman Dan didn't recognize all stepped forward to shake his hand before Massimo ordered everyone to be seated. He motioned for Dan to sit next to Pam, which he did after kissing her on the cheek and commenting for all to hear, "She grows more beautiful every time I see her."

"Why thank you, kind sir," she responded playfully.

"Dan, I want to introduce Nicholas Santucci, my, shall we say, business developer. Now you know everybody, so let's eat."

Muzzi and Scarola, each in his late sixties, had retained their impressive bulk and legendary appetites. While the others laughed their way through the five-course dinner, the two Barracci soldiers, infamous for their brutality and cherished for their loyalty, devoured their food without comment. Dan ceased wondering how each had sustained his strength despite their years, as they consumed everything in sight. The others took reasonable portions from the family style servings Massimo preferred, leaving more than half the food for the grateful old warriors. *Manasta fagioli*, a greens and bean soup, was followed in order by a light pasta in olive oil, garlic and basil, a medley of fried and broiled seafood, and finally, saltimbacca ala Romano, accompanied by spinach Florentine. Generous cubes of pungent garlic were difficult to avoid, though everyone except Vito and Muzzi did their best. Dan admitted it was as fine a meal as he had ever eaten, regretting the two glasses of Chianti that had repressed an excellent veal.

The host announced a bit formally, "We will have some business to discuss as soon as the Sambucca and Espresso are delivered. Obviously, we repeat nothing that we hear unless I give permission." He looked for and received silent assurances. "Dan, you know Anthony is my attorney. I wanted him here in case we need a legal opinion, and of course, you can trust him as you do me," he assured his young guest. "Is this all satisfactory?"

"Absolutely, Uncle. As always I trust your judgment."

"*Bene.* Now let us enjoy our drinks as you explain your problem."

Having expected the presence of Lacozza and the two soldiers, Dan had prepared an explanation that would neither offend the Don nor jeopardize his investigation should his trust be misplaced. Reluctantly, he had to expose the names of the doctors, since he believed it was through them or their attorneys that the mob contact would have been initiated, a logical conclusion given Berger's personality. Doing this without knowing anything of Santucci's background was risky, but he did trust Barracci. Besides, he had little alternative.

His story began with Teller's murder as it had been reported in the papers, further explaining that there were two unnamed witnesses in addition to Berger that saw the killers escape in the blue Town Car. To avoid a discussion he fabricated a story that the perpetrators had been identified by Berger as middle aged white men with New York accents, an account supported by the evidence, most notably the testimony of the two witnesses. The placement of the fatal shots, absence of site evidence and the threatening letter to one of the witnesses added to his conviction that professionals had been hired, thus his call to the Don for assistance. Any insight his people might provide would be kept confidential as to its source, adding a final assurance that since he was the responsible investigator there would be no pressure to disclose informants.

If he was getting through to any of them, their expressions didn't confirm it. Only Santucci seemed riveted to every word, his eyes fixed on Dan's, an occasional movement about the mouth betraying a point of particular interest.

When Dan finished, he drank his espresso and Sambucca in order and waited for questions. Barracci looked at Muzzi and the giant Scarola, who only stared back without comment, as if to say, *"What do we do next, boss?"*

Aware that the responsibility to fulfill the Don's obligation in the matter would fall to another, Lacozza said nothing, deferring to Santucci who seemed lost in thought, his eyes having shifted to his Sambucca and the three coffee beans floating in it. Finally, he addressed Dan.

"Sergeant, suppose we find a connection with the Lincoln and it turns out to be family. How do you accuse them without disclosing our involvement?" he asked, sweeping his arm around the table.

"The strong probability is that the shooters have some kind of police record. I'll just testify that I tied the names of the Lincoln owners from D.O.T.

records to those with convictions and brought the only matches in for questioning."

"Why don't you just do that now?" Santucci challenged.

"Because I can't narrow the year of the Lincoln down to a manageable number. Once you give me the contact, I can adjust the testimony of the witnesses to the correct year, making the search more believable. I'll also know the borough in which it's registered, and I'll cover that by saying we had put out an all-points and that a uniformed patrolman in that borough identified it."

Santucci remained unconvinced.

"If, as things develop, that scenario won't play out to everyone's satisfaction," Dan countered, "I'll just rely on an old stand-by, the word on the street. We can testify that we put some money up to entice street informants and a tip came in that we simply followed up on."

From the look on Santucci's face, Dan knew he was not completely comfortable with either story, fearing that there could be ramifications to the Barracci family, a concern that he relayed to the Don.

Massimo nodded, appreciative of his vigilance. He turned to Pam Donaldson. "Time for you to be going," he said softly, bringing her hand to his lips. A simple look to Scarola brought him to his feet. As he slid Pam's chair out the other men stood, wished her goodnight and watched her disappear before the hulking soldier.

Lacozza began to speak but Barracci held up a finger quieting him. "We wait for Vito," he said.

"You got her a cab?" the Don asked, as the legendary enforcer returned. Scarola nodded and reseated himself.

Then the Don spoke. "We are obliged to help Dan Costa," he stated, looking in turn to each of his people. "I personally trust him with my family. Therefore, we will put out the calls and leave it to him to ensure no one ever learns of our involvement. That's the way it will be."

He turned to his attorney. "You speak to no other consigliere. You are the one person I do not want involved. If you ask questions, that will be enough to implicate us."

To Muzzi and Scarola he simply commanded, "*Star zitto*. When it is time I will tell you what you must do."

Then to Santucci he confided, "I know you suspect Savarese and Codella because of the money that may be involved, but you forget that each is being closely watched by the Feds. For them to order a hit of an innocent at this time would be *stupido*, even for them. Still, their families may be good starting points, because some underboss could be involved without one of the *capos* even knowing it, so look at everybody out on the Island where those doctors live." He pondered a thought, raising a finger to prevent an interruption. "Daniel is correct. The Doctors hold the key, so you look into their lawyers, anybody that might be able to connect them to a hit man. Any mouthpiece on the island could have connections to Savarese, Codella, or one of the underbosses...they all mix with *'Mericans'*. Where money is involved, there are no longer two sides." Almost to himself he concluded, "But Savarese and Codella will be clean on this, I know. They have too much to lose."

Addressing Santucci, he completed his edict. "If either of their families is involved, it's probably without the *Capo's* permission, and so, without his knowledge. Would one of their people order the hit?" he asked aloud. "Absolutely, particularly if the money is what Daniel says it could be. There are more every day that break the old rules, that don't follow the code. Now it's what 'I' can get, not what's good for the family, not what the *Capo* decides. So you look at them all from top to bottom, but remember, we must also find the connection to those doctors. *Bona fortuna*," he said, raising his glass, fully recognizing the magnitude of his charge.

Despite his father's murder, the intricacies of the Teller case and his growing infatuation with Marilyn Kyme, Dan was able to clear his mind and sleep well that night, awaking only when the alarm sounded at six. Shortly after seven he was in the office, completing notes from the previous evening and closeting them in a separate file in a locked drawer of his desk. A few minutes before eight he heard Al Wilson and Rasheed Martin climbing the stairs.

The Lieutenant said good morning as he passed on the way to his office, Rasheed doing the same as he settled into his chair. Dan sat patiently waiting for his partner's report.

"Can we renegotiate a cheeseburger?" Martin asked with a grin, suggesting to Costa's dismay that whatever he had learned didn't warrant dinner at the Palm.

"So you struck out?"

"Not entirely. The lady was willing, she just didn't know much."

Costa waited for more. His partner held out for a reduced reward.

"Cheeseburgers on me if you learned anything helpful."

Gratified, Rasheed disclosed that his last night's date was the assistant office manager responsible for patient appointments, billings and insurance paperwork. Only in the office manager's absence did she have any communication with Doctors Steinberg and Norville.

"She said they were both pretty much cut from the same tree; serious, arrogant and secretive. Whenever they showed up they spent some time with the office manager and then holed up in a converted conference room where they would remain for hours. She didn't say anything interesting until I asked her whether or not she had ever heard or read anything connecting them to Nuremberg, Pennsylvania, Joe Teller or Lewis Berger."

According to Martin, the assistant manager had taken a call a month or so ago from a friend of Steinberg's who gave his first name as Lewis. She had never heard anyone refer to a "Lewis" before and she was certain it was the first time she had spoken to him. She advised him that the doctors weren't in and asked if she could take a message. He started to give her his phone number, mentioning an area code 570, but stopped and told her to have Steinberg call him. She relayed the message to her boss who seemed to know who Lewis was, mentioning that he worked in a laboratory in Pennsylvania and that she would take care of it. Later that day she came back and told her to forget what she had heard because it involved work that was very confidential and that Lewis shouldn't have called there to begin with.

"Did she say anything else?" Dan asked.

"No, not really. She was naturally suspicious and I tried to make it sound innocent enough, but she knows I'm a homicide detective so she probably didn't believe me."

"Nothing else about Teller, Berger or a research project?"

"Nope. I even said I couldn't believe she worked for two men she knew so little about and her response was, 'I hardly ever see them. Besides, I have a lot to do. That's a big practice, you know.' I couldn't argue that point."

"Okay, at least we're on the right track. You have to get through those telephone lists today. Agreed?"

"Got it. I isolate all the calls to the doctors' homes, hospital offices, the group practice and their condos."

"Don't forget their Florida homes," Dan reminded him. "This deal's been going on for at least five years."

"Right. What about the Lincoln and Berger's murder?"

Dan hit an automatic dial-up and then chose his words carefully. "I'll be talking to the Teller witnesses again to try to pin down the year of the Town Car. Then I'll check New York State Driver Registration. I'm also putting it out on the street through informants that have turned up some stuff in the past, some ex-junkies that can use the money. I'm waiting for word from the State Police in Jersey on some scene evidence before I do anything else on Berger." He was about to elaborate when Jack Shultz answered his call.

"Hey, Jack, how's it going?"

"Fine, Dan, fine. I was just getting ready to call you. I spoke to Donna last night and she's here with me now, so I'm just going to put her on and let her speak for herself."

"Hi, Dan, how's the Big Apple?"

"Big as ever, Donna, not as safe as it used to be, but I promise to protect you if you two want to come over for a weekend. The treat's on me. You can even stay at my place."

"It would be more fun if I came alone," she teased, before embarking on the only addition she could make to her previous testimony.

"One day a young, good-looking guy came in, said his name was Greg, that he was a computer specialist and had an appointment with Dr. Berger. Since the doctors were at lunch I told him to have a seat, that they would be back shortly. He was a real flirt, telling me how beautiful and all he thought I was and would I consider having dinner with him…that kind of stuff. I tried to change the subject…really I did…stop looking at me like that you jerk," she laughed. "Sorry, Dan, Jack's being a real jerk. Where was I? Oh, yeah. So I asked him what he did and what was he there for. Now, I don't know if he was lying, but he said he had designed the computer systems the doctors were using…analogs he called them…and that Berger had phoned and asked him to come up as soon as possible because he wanted to make sure everything was working right."

"When was this, Donna?"

"Eighteen months ago. I'm sure I had never heard his name before, so any connection he had with the lab would have been before they hired me, or maybe he called on the inside phone, the one in the lab. Anyway, I never saw or heard from him again."

"His name was Greg? Any last name, address, phone numbers, anything?"

"Nope. Never heard from him or saw him again. When the doctors returned, I went to lunch and when I got back his car was gone."

"How do you know what kind of car he was driving?"

"It was the only one in the parking lot when I left for lunch, a bright red Corvette with the prettiest Jersey plates I ever saw."

"Jersey, you say. What made them so pretty?"

"They had a red, white and blue lighthouse on them. Really pretty."

Dan recalled having seen a plate of the type Donna described, but he didn't know whether it represented a location or an historic symbol. So he phoned the Hackettstown State Police barracks where he could follow-up on Berger's murder and get an explanation of the plate at the same time. A Lieutenant Brady took the call.

"Sergeant Costa?"

"Yes, Lieutenant. I'm the Manhattan homicide detective that your troopers were kind enough to assist at the Castle Rock Motel murder."

"Oh, yeah, I remember your name. You're the one that wanted the carpet dust," he said jokingly. "I'm supposed to call you if we turn up anything. Well, we haven't found anything we wouldn't have expected to find on a floor in a Hackettstown motel. There was residue from red shale that we found on the victim's shoes, so we assume he brought it in. There's a ton of smudged fingerprints, but you'd expect those in a well-traveled motel. I'm sorry, but I don't think we're going to be much help to you."

"It was a long-shot anyway, Lieutenant, but while I have you on the phone, could you tell me what a lighthouse on one of your license plates means?"

"Sure. That's Old Barney, the nickname the historical society people gave to the lighthouse at the southern end of the Barnegat Bay. It was built around the Civil War...still standing. It guards the entrance from the ocean to the Barnegat Bay, probably the roughest piece of water on the whole coast, a real boater's nightmare. The Corps of Engineers has to dredge it out every five years or so. The wrecks really pile up at the mouth."

"Is it common for folks living on the bay to get those plates?"

"No, I don't think so. I've got an uncle who lives right on the bay in a town called Lanoka Harbor and he doesn't have them."

"Can anybody in the State get them?"

"Yeah, now that I'm thinking about it, there are a few people I know who have them and they live in North Jersey, but they have summer homes on the shore. I wouldn't think I'd pay an extra hundred bucks for those plates if I didn't at least vacation down there."

"Thanks for your time, Lieutenant, and if you ever do turn up anything in your investigation, please let me know."

"Will do, and good luck."

## CHAPTER 11

The phone was ringing as Dan entered his apartment. It was Joe DeLorenzo.

"You're a tough guy to get a hold of, Joe. What have you been up to?"

"Man, you cannot believe my caseload. The shit's really hit the fan and Avent's been busting everybody's balls. I don't mean to make excuses, but I'm sure you don't want me calling at 2:00 A.M. and that's when I got in last night. No shit, Dan, heaviest damn workload I've ever had."

DeLorenzo explained that he, Calvin Washington and Ron Williams had canvassed his father's neighborhood, speaking to over fifty people and leaving the pawnbroker's police sketch in all the local stores, restaurants and apartment foyers. "We spent all day yesterday out there," he said. "No one claimed to have definitely seen such a person, but a few held it out as a possibility.

"There's this one woman, Tonee Feathers, an exotic dancer that we interviewed before, lives in your father's building. Anyway, she looks at it for about a minute, then says, 'If he was skinnier I might be able to say I've seen him around here. He looks like some young punk who made a wise-ass remark to me once, but that kid wasn't as heavy as the one in this picture.'"

Joe continued with similar comments from other people in the neighborhood, a few of whom also referred to a thinner person. "In fact, a good friend of your dad's, a Mr. Gadsden, he says there's a guy who hangs out around the apartment house that has a hat and coat like the pawnbroker described, but he didn't think the sketch looked much like him. He told me he wasn't even certain the man he saw had a mustache and beard. And like everyone else, he couldn't put a name to the face."

"People look a lot thinner clean shaven. Have Kuhn do a drawing without any facial hair and see what your witnesses think."

"I thought of that, but you gotta' remember I'm only looking to see if somebody can give me a name, not pick a guy out of a line-up. The only evidence that will convict is a confession. We haven't won a felony case in years based on possession, you know that."

"Yeah, you're right," Dan admitted without trying to hide his frustration. "Well, keep me posted, okay?"

"Sure, and keep your chin up. We'll get this piece of shit. It's only been a coupla' weeks. Now that the word's out on the street we'll start getting some names."

The next day Al Wilson asked Dan for another update on the Teller case. Normally he wouldn't, because in the past Dan had always volunteered new information as it developed, holding back only when its relevance was at issue. For no particular reason Dan suspected that Wilson's visit to Gracey Mansion had something to do with either his father's or Teller's case and that the request for an update was a follow-up to that visit.

Dan disclosed everything, including his appeal to a mob connection, though he never mentioned anything to suggest Massimo Barracci, and respecting Costa's position, Wilson chose not to ask about the contact's identity. Dan summarized what he had learned from Ruiz and Kaplan that had not been included in Carmine Pecora's report. He spent some time detailing Kaplan's testimony because it lent credence to his belief that some professionals had carried out the orders and that he was sure they could lead him to the conspirators. A condensed version of his written report on the trip to Nuremberg and the Berger murder followed with the promise that the typed report to which he alluded would be on the Lieutenant's desk by noon. He discussed Rasheed's interviews with the medical group's office personnel, complimenting his partner's ability to obtain information of a confidential nature. The talk concluded with references to Rasheed's telephone lists, the computer programmer's red Corvette with Old Barney plates, Dr. Worthington's pending interview, the dead-end at the Castle Rock Motel and his anticipation of a report from forensics.

"What do you hope to get from Bill Mason?"

"A lead on what they were using in the lab, which might get me to somebody who knew what that damn project was all about. I'm convinced that Teller was murdered because of his research and Berger was killed because his accomplices were afraid he might crack and disclose the details, not just of what they were working on, but of the identity of everyone involved."

"It's sure a complicated one, but you seem to be making some progress, so just stick with it. Handle it your way."

"Thanks. By the way, you made a good choice. Rasheed is beginning to work out well, now that he's loosening up. I never have to tell him anything twice. He's a quick learner."

"That's good to hear. I kind of noticed a change in his attitude myself. I think you intimidated him a little in the beginning but he seems to have found his confidence. You really think he'll be a keeper?"

Dan nodded. "Unless he hits the lottery."

Rasheed called to say that by morning he would finish identifying the people whose numbers were on the telephone lists.

"Good work. How many are down around the Jersey Shore?"

"Four. Two each to two individuals."

"Any ID yet on them?"

"Yeah. One's Greg Chadwick, a computer programmer. The other is a fisherman, a guy named Ron Symanski."

"That's the best news I've heard since we got this case."

"Then you're not going to like hearing this. Chadwick drowned in a boating accident last week. His body floated up on the beach in Seaside Park, not a hundred yards from the wreckage. The boat blew up, burning his body pretty badly, but they got positive IDs from his dental records and old x-rays of a double fracture of his right leg. There's other corroboration too…not much doubt."

"Sonofabitch, I should have guessed it." He thought for a few seconds before adding, "Rasheed, forget tomorrow morning. Do you have Symanski's address?"

"Yeah, eight-fifteen Twin Oaks Drive, Toms River."

"Good. Get your ass down there now. If Symanski is the fisherman that supplied Teller with the crabs, his life could be in danger and he probably doesn't know it. Chadwick's death was no accident. He was murdered and it won't be long before the perps realize we're onto Symanski. So get down there on the double. When you're on the road, call me here and we'll go over the questions. Got it?"

"Roger. I'm on my way."

Martin called within a half hour to report that he was clear of the Lincoln Tunnel and heading towards the Garden State Parkway that would put him in Toms River within two hours. "When you hang up I'll call their police headquarters to get directions."

Dan began detailing what they needed to ask the witness and what each answer he gave might suggest. "You'll have to determine from his answers and body language if he's an accomplice, and if he is, you back right off. Got it?" Dan's voice left no doubt as to the urgency of his instructions. "If this guy's part of the problem and we disclose what we know, we'll blow any chance of them slipping up."

"I understand, and I'm not going to screw up," his partner promised.

"I know you won't. Call me when the interview's over and don't try to drive back up here tonight. It'll be late. There's enough left in the budget for a good meal and a decent motel."

Dan dialed the number Marilyn had given him for Dr. Worthington's lab at Columbia. After introductions and a summary lesson in enzymology Worthington agreed to meet with him the next morning.

As they descended the stairs together, Dan advised Al Wilson of his and Rasheed's schedules.

"Camille's going to kick my ass for not dragging you home for dinner tonight, you know that, don't you?"

"Then don't tell her I left with you," Dan suggested.

"Hell, man, the woman knows what I'm thinking even when I'm not thinking it."

"Good thing the kids took after her – brains and beauty."

"Yeah? You wouldn't think so if you had to pay their college tuitions. Sometimes I wish my boys were just smart enough to graduate high school and motivated enough to go to a tech school. They'd probably make more money bein' plumbers or electricians than whatever they'll end up being after I spend a couple hundred thousand on college."

"Ah, you love it. Stop feeling sorry for yourself." Dan knew there was no sacrifice Al Wilson wouldn't make for his family.

At precisely 9:00 A.M. Dan arrived at Columbia for his meeting with Clarence Worthington, a short, bald, overweight Doctor of Enzymology, with a distinct lisp that seemed particularly comical for a man of his age and position. His accent was strongly Victorian, the result of his formative years in London and an extended education at Cambridge and Oxford. Approaching seventy, he had been one of the world's more renowned microbiologists for forty years with over a hundred process patents to his name. Costa felt honored to meet him and fortunate that he was so accommodating.

Worthington expressed his remorse at having heard of Teller's and Berger's deaths.

"I knew neither of them extremely well, having only been in their company a handful of times," he said, "but of Teller in particular, I had heard some promising things. No more than five years ago he was credited with a breakthrough in the separation of GPT and GOT from proteinacious mass in bovine pancreas, a considerably more effective process than that which science had been pursuing with porcine liver." Unaware of Dan's confusion, he stayed his course. "It is one thing to hypothesize on the probable value of an identifiable enzyme, quite another to extract, isolate and purify it, and then sustain its homogeneity during application. The latter was apparently Teller's given talent though he rarely received the acclaim he deserved. Amongst his peers, however, he was extremely well-respected."

"You speak as though you knew of him and were quite familiar with his work. Why is it you didn't know him personally?"

Hesitantly, Worthington said, "Joe Teller associated with some very undesirable sorts, at least from my perspective. Now please don't misunderstand. I don't mean to say they were dishonorable. They were simply absorbed with the commercialization of our science, and that regrettably, is something to which I cannot accede. The financial rewards for scientific research are not great, but they are certainly adequate. Our purpose must be to open doors to as many applications as possible and Teller's mind was capable of creating numerous opportunities for mankind. To have wasted any of his time on the commercial application of just one or two developments was most disappointing, particularly when there were countless others who could have carried on the menial work."

"So you're saying that he abandoned his research to participate in product development?"

"Well said, young man," Worthington beamed, "you have a firm grasp of the situation."

*Wanna bet?*

The doctor proceeded with a further explanation of what enzymes were, addressing some thoughts he had missed over the phone but employing essentially the same terms and descriptions Marilyn Kyme had used. He moved onto the scope of their presence in nature, how that was manifested in human beings, and closed with a prediction that the next quantum leap in both genetics engineering and health science would be propelled by enzymatic discovery. He displayed what would have otherwise been described as youthful enthusiasm, impressing his listener and leaving little doubt as to why the man was considered foremost in his field.

When Worthington stopped to remove some petri dishes from an oven, Dan asked, "Are the kinds of enzymes in man also found in other animals or vegetables?"

"Absolutely," he stated as he aligned the samples beneath some strangely colored lights. "In fact the greatest aid we have to digestion is an enzyme called pepsinogen that we extract from horseradish root. It's used in every digestive tablet on the market and it obviously assimilates easily into the human body's biochemical process. Then there are others that so perfectly match the molecular structure of a coenzyme in our own bodies that we can use them as magnets to attract and measure the latter. As an example, we use the LDH in bovine pancreas to measure Creatine Phosphokinase in your blood to determine if you've had a heart attack." He paused. "Oh, we discussed that on the phone yesterday, didn't we?"

With unguarded enthusiasm the aging scientist went about presenting further evidence of enzyme compatibility between vegetables and the whole of mammalian creation, leaving the young detective a bit jealous.

"Are you still with me, Sergeant?"

"What? Oh, yes, of course, Doctor."

"You seemed a bit lost there for a moment, perhaps in your own thoughts?"

Dan apologized. "My mind only wandered to the extent that I'm so impressed by the fervor you display for your work."

"Then it is I who should apologize, Sergeant. It is as arrogant to carry on about one's conventions as it is one's grandchildren," he exclaimed. "That's why I won't have any of the little brats about, afraid I might become one of those prattling old fools with an arm's length of photographs and countless vignettes."

"But you do love your work, Doctor, and that's marvelous."

"Yes, well..." he paused briefly, reflecting on a half century of devotion, "I fear there has been so little time for anything else, my affection can find no other object for attachment."

Dan's mind was beginning to focus more clearly than it had since his father's death. He was slowly emerging from his depression, regaining energy and feeling more alive. Neither his friends, nor his work, not even Marilyn Kyme, had fully awakened him to the excitement that life's opportunities offered, but this devoted scientist had showed him that without any other apparent reason for contentment, he was able to embrace every minute enthusiastically, absorbing in return a lifetime of fulfillment. To some it would seem tedious, certainly monotonous, but to Clarence Worthington it was challenging, exciting and sufficiently rewarding.

Refocused on the object of his visit, Dan advised his host of Marcy Holland's comment about horseshoe crabs and the on-going work Teller had been doing with them. As he spoke, Worthington's interest grew, his expression reflecting a change from curiosity to deliberation.

"Any idea why they would be using horseshoe crabs, Doctor?"

Worthington stopped puttering, sat in an overstuffed leather chair behind his desk, partially obscured by a mountainous pile of books and papers, and began recalling facts from years of study. He seemed about to speak when Dan's cell phone interrupted his concentration.

"Sergeant Costa," Dan answered.

"Hey, partner, it's me. How ya' doin?"

"Fine, Rasheed. You had me worried. I thought you were going to call last night."

"Sorry, long story, but it's not all bad. Can you talk?"

"Not right now. Where are you?"

"Leaving the Garden State toll booth at the Raritan River Bridge. I'm thinking of taking the Staten Island Outer Bridge Crossing to the Verazzano and the Midtown Tunnel."

"Don't. It's out of your way. Stay on the Parkway to Exit 164…I think that's it… and it'll dump you off on Route 3 to the Lincoln Tunnel. You'll be in the office in an hour. I'll meet you there."

"Roger. See you soon."

"Sorry, Doctor. My partner."

Worthington waved away the apology. "I'm accustomed to interruptions – learned a long time ago that they are inevitable. After all, we do have to eat and sleep on occasion," he stated before embarking on his disclosure.

"Many years ago, sixty perhaps, a biochemist living and working in Virginia by the name of Richard Snively pursued the study of Limulus polyphemus, horseshoe crab to you. He was, like many biologists and enzymologists, intrigued by the singularity of its blue blood and the fact that it is not a true crab, but a descendant of the extinct trilobites, the first arthropods, or animals with jointed legs. He built a small research laboratory along the ocean where the crab was generously available. I should mention that trilobites first appeared during the Cambrian Period over five hundred million years ago," he reminded himself, "and that although we cannot be certain as to precisely when Limulus polyphemus first appeared, it is quite definitely the oldest still living creature, mucking its way through inland rivers at least two hundred million years ago." He paused, allowing the magnitude of the statement to sink in, continuing when Dan acknowledged his amazement.

"Snively believed there was something in the animal's blue blood that permitted it to withstand the ravages of time. Through eons of disease, predators, privation and climatic change, only Limulus and a fish, coelacanth, have survived sufficiently long to be referred to as living fossils." He paused briefly again to consider how to proceed, ultimately concluding that the detective's interests would be best served by moving onto the practical aspects of Snively's study.

"Snively's thesis…not a written one in the educational sense, but rather the conclusion he reached after years of study…was founded on his belief that Limulus had developed some biochemical quality that made it immune to disease and adaptable to virtually any external influence, so changes in climate or habitat would have had no terminal effect upon it. Regrettably, he didn't live long enough to further his studies and no one to the best of my knowledge has ever picked up the gauntlet. Interestingly enough, Doctor Teller would have been the man to do it," he hinted, "because he had that special gift of finding the proverbial needle. I assure you, Sergeant, I am not a betting man, but were I, my money would have been on Joe Teller if we were choosing someone to isolate a Limulus agent."

"Is it reasonable to suspect that either Teller or Berger would have had access to something more than Snively's theories, such as his notes or an unpublished report?"

"Possibly. Though Snively was a uniquely private person, he shared his research with whoever would listen, for if nothing else, he was a man deeply devoted to academia. He would prefer to go the route alone, but given a choice between failure and cooperative success, I feel confident he would choose the latter."

"If no one decided to pursue Snively's thesis because no one believed he was correct or cared to follow another scientist's lead, then the work on it could have laid dormant until something occurred to motivate Teller and Berger. Is that possible?"

"Yes, your approach may very well have merit, but I don't think I would include Berger in the same breath as Teller and Snively. The man simply wasn't up to the task."

"You knew him?"

"We had some brief encounters and I quite frankly found him to be a leech of the worst sort, worming his way into circles in which he simply didn't belong and largely wasn't welcome. The man never had an innovative, much less original thought in his life."

Perhaps feeling a bit guilty, Worthington added, "Mind you, I never collaborated on a project with him, so given the benefit of the doubt, he could have been an excellent assistant, performing menial research, the less ingenious lab work."

"If you were to pursue Snively's work, Doctor, what would you need, and in layman's terms, how would you do it?"

"Quite simply, you would need Limuli, a device to immobilize them while extracting the blood, tanks of saltwater in which they could replace their own blood..."

"What?" Dan exclaimed, cutting the Doctor off.

"Limuli are fully capable of reproducing their own blood, provided you leave just a tad in. You can't bleed them totally, you know, since their blood is so singular."

"I see. So the lab would have to have large aquariums?"

"Perhaps not as large as you might think. The crabs are rather sedentary when removed from their habitat. They might need a bit of mud and sand, saltwater, and fish or mollusk cadaver. That would suffice nicely."

"Thank you, Doc, sorry I interrupted."

"Yes, let's see. Where were we? Oh yes, we would need a chromatographic column or two, a bench size Delaval...that's a small centrifuge...and of course, the normal compliment of laboratory supplies and equipment...tubing, beakers, a refrigerator, perhaps a freezer, and so on."

"What's that chromatographic column?"

"It would look to a layman to be a large styrated beaker. In reality it is a glass tube with separating filters and compartments that permit physical and chemical separation of ingredients as the subject passes from top to bottom through successive media, the desired end product collecting at the bottom."

"I think I'm beginning to understand," Dan stated. "The type of filtration medium used is the result of scientific trials. Knowing the contaminants and how to pull them out of the mass is at the crux of the whole science."

"You almost have it," the Doctor promised. "Finally, you must know what you're looking for so that the filtration media you use neither contaminate nor bind your object, but allow it to pass through. Secondly, you must be aware of all the so-called contaminants, for some of them are quite invisible, and while they remain in the mass they can even change the identity of the object of your experiment, much the same as oxygen in the presence of hydrogen appears as water."

After making a few notes, Dan said, "We're almost finished, Doctor, if you don't mind."

"Not at all. I'm quite enjoying the respite, and I don't mind telling you, it would give me no small degree of satisfaction to play the tiniest part in helping to apprehend Teller's assassin. The scoundrel did us all very great harm. I'm certain Doctor Teller still had a few good years left in which to display his mettle."

"It seems everyone speaks well of him."

Worthington nodded appreciatively.

"If you were either Teller or Berger, and you decided you wanted to make a lot of money off Snively's theory, what precisely would you be looking for?"

"I won't deceive you, Sergeant. On past occasion I have thought of possibly pursuing Snively's theories, though not for monetary reasons, and I have to tell you I have yet to feel comfortable with the prospect. It is simplistic to say a life sustaining ingredient, or a disease prevention, though I truly believe Snively had that in mind somewhere down the road. He believed that old Limulus did indeed have some factor in its makeup that warded off infection, but how that could be identified, much less isolated, is quite another matter. Still," and he hesitated, pensively looking off, "if one did recognize the protein or the gene, I would imagine that by trial and error it could eventually be isolated. After all, that would simply become an issue of time and effort, neither of which is alien to the scientific makeup. However, in the short term and at the time of his demise, the object of his trials was a blood-clotting agent which he had at one time assured all was well within his grasp."

"And he died before completing his work?"

"Yes, though I cannot tell you how far along in that regard he was, nor do I know what became of his notes. I heard, though I can't remember from whom, that his wife received quite a nice sum from a pharmaceutical firm, presumably for rights to his research. If so, we have the deceased Mrs. Snively to thank for one of the many clotting compounds on the market. Then again, each of them displays some rather undesireable side effects, so it is quite possible that further purification of the known substrates could produce a more efficacious product, one that would bring considerable reward to its founder."

"Would that kind of research require great secrecy?"

"Heavens, no, nor would an enterprising scientist even resort to bleeding limuli. He would simply purchase existing clotting agents, identify non-essential elements and experiment with some revolutionary filtration media. Quite frankly, it's not the type of research that Teller would either enjoy or find academically challenging, not for five years or more, anyway."

"So it's not likely that Teller was working on that particular project at the time of his death."

"I think I would have to agree with that conclusion, Sergeant, unless...."

Worthington sat quietly deliberating for so long that Dan wondered if he had drifted off to sleep. He was about to speak when the good Doctor suddenly restarted.

"Unless that same agent contained properties that held promise for other applications."

"Such as?"

"The aforementioned anti-infection factor."

"You really believe that's a possibility?"

"Snively seemed to think so."

"What do I do to determine if Teller was on to that idea, and more importantly, had made significant progress towards isolating it, or at least, identifying it?"

Worthington considered the prospect a minute. "Give me a day or two to think that one out, Sergeant, and though I can't promise I'll come up with an answer to please you, I will at least provide you with a number of options."

"Can't ask for more than that, Doctor, and to perhaps help you in your effort I'll turn over this journal Dr. Teller had been keeping. Just before his death, he gave it to a friend for safekeeping. I've thumbed through it a few times but it only seems to contain some symbols and abbreviations for chemicals in equations, certainly nothing I could possibly understand. It might be useful in court so please don't let it lay about. I have a feeling that for some reason the people behind Dr. Teller's murder would love to get their hands on this."

"I shall guard it carefully."

"And now, if you'll afford me one more minute, I'll leave you to your work. Have you ever heard of either a Doctor Norville or a Doctor Steinberg? They're MD's in Mid-town who might have financially backed Teller."

Worthington shook his head. "My memory fails me on occasion, but I am quite certain I am unfamiliar with those names."

After thanking Worthington for his time and promising that he would keep him posted on his progress, Dan hurried back to the office where he found Rasheed on the phone hastily scribbling some notes.

"Okay, Doctor, I'll tell him as soon as I see him."

"Was that for me?"

"Oh, Dan! Yeah, it was. Sorry, but I didn't see you coming in."

"That's okay. Who was it?"

"Dr. Mason from the forensics lab."

"What did he say?"

"Not much. The thinner glass shards had traces of alcohol on them and nothing else, as though they had been sterilized. The styrations were blue etchings of the type used on laboratory beakers for gradiant measurements," he reported, with eyes fixed on his notes. "The thicker glass had traces of seawater, but the samples were too small for him to determine what the trace contaminants in the salt were." Rasheed looked up for a moment, lowering his eyes again when Dan motioned for him to continue. "The packet marked 'floor residue' had more seawater in it, but was diluted with traces of a heavily chlorinated cleaning agent like a Mr. Clean."

"And that was it?" Dan asked, hoping for more.

"Yep, I got it all, but Mason said if you need to speak to him, he'll be at work until seven tonight and all day tomorrow."

*Say what you will about Bill Mason, but the man doesn't cheat the taxpayer,* Costa thought.

"Do me a favor and get your notes typed up by Monday morning under 'Teller, Joseph; Nuremberg Lab Samples, Forensics Report.' That'll do it."

"Got it. Now you want to hear about my trip?"

"I'm all ears."

If Dan were meticulous to a fault, he could have found little in his partner's report to criticize. It was chronological, easy to follow, and included scores of names, dates and places, leaving nothing to the imagination. Had he gone in Rasheed's place he would have fared no better.

Ron Symanski was married with three very young daughters. His home, a small bi-level in a pleasant middle-income neighborhood, was clean and orderly, but modestly furnished. The one car garage housed a five-year-old station wagon, while a tired old Dodge van occupied the driveway. If Ron Symanski had been making serious money from any criminal activities, he certainly hadn't been spending it.

Originally a Chesapeake Bay commercial crabber, Symanski had inherited a 1980 thirty-six-foot Silverton from an uncle, which he had modified for deep sea and sport fishing. About five years ago a Doctor Norville and two friends engaged his services to do some shark fishing in Hudson Canyon. During the trip, Symanski mentioned his crabbing background, which interested Norville and eventually led to a contract that had only recently been terminated. Every Saturday at five a.m. he would haul up king crab pots he buoyed along the southern end of the Barnegat Bay just beyond the rush of the Barnegat Inlet. Each such effort would net him from twelve to twenty horseshoe crabs which he would nestle in wooden crates stuffed with moist seaweed, load them into his van and drive four hours to a little town in Pennsylvania's Green Mountains. There, with the help of two scientists he came to know as Joe and Lewis, he would place the crabs in large aquarium tanks in an old red-brick laboratory and remove those he had delivered the previous week to the crates. Upon his return, he would release the crabs into the Barnegat and be home in time for the Saturday evening meal with his family. For his efforts he would be paid fifty dollars per crab, netting him an average of about six hundred dollars a trip, almost as much as he made from the rest of his week's effort. So he had been less than elated to receive last month's news that his services would no longer be required, and was in fact wondering how that source of income was to be replaced.

He could recount little else of importance to the case, in that he had never met anyone at the laboratory other than Joe and Lewis, knew nothing of the project and could only describe the room in the simplest of layman's terms. Rasheed had, however, asked him to draw a floor plan that Dan studied.

"It looks something like I imagined," he said after scanning it. "See here, these tables with tanks, the lab benches, and here, the trellis type arrangement they bled the crabs from."

"I felt sorry for the guy, Dan, 'cause at first he thought I was there to talk about taxes on the cash he had received, but I told him that was our secret. And it is, right? I mean we're not thinking about turning this guy in?"

"Of course not. No need to mention how he got paid in the report." He visualized the fisherman with his wife and daughters in their little home, wondering how they would replace half their income, a job made doubly difficult by dwindling stocks of sport fish and heavier competition from massive commercial trawlers. *'It's always the little guy that gets screwed,'* he thought.

"How about Greg Chadwick?" he asked, his attention shifting again to the case. "Did you ask Symanski if they had ever met?"

"Yeah, but he didn't know him. Toms River's a pretty big town. Anyway, as to Chadwick's death, it could've been an accident, believe it or not.

Apparently Chadwick liked to run his boat in rough seas. It was…let's see," he stumbled through the pages of a small notebook, "a thirty foot Sea Ray, a fast ocean-going speedboat according to the Marine Police at Point Pleasant. They're the ones handling the investigation. But I gotta' tell you, Dan, I don't think they're taking it anywhere. They're convinced that kind of accident can happen with that kind of boat. It was still pretty cold out in the surf and they figured he had all the hatches closed tight so fumes could have built up, and blooey!"

"You really believe that?"

"Hey, what do I know about boats. I'm just relaying what the so-called experts have to say."

"Did you interview anyone at the marina?"

"Yep, the dock supervisor on duty, a nephew of the owner. Claims he never even saw Chadwick get on the boat. When he took a walk to get a sandwich he saw the red Vette in the parking lot. That's when he noticed the boat was gone. Next thing he knew was from the radio the following day – heard about everything washing up on shore ten miles south in Seaside Park.

"So Chadwick was in the habit of running the boat in cold weather?"

"Yeah, according to the owner's nephew and a friend of the deceased that the Marine Police spoke to."

"Did he always take it out alone?"

"Not always," Rasheed answered, "but enough so that no one down there was surprised to hear that no other bodies washed up."

"Did you speak to his employer?"

"Didn't have any. He was a free-lance electronics engineer. But I did get the names of some people he did project work for and the president of a former employer of his. I'll make sure I talk to them first thing Monday."

"Good. You did well, partner. It's not your fault that we're hitting a lot of dead-ends."

"Well, we've still got those phone numbers," Martin said hopefully, looking at his watch as he spoke. "I'll wrap those up on Monday, too. If you don't mind now, it's after five and I've got a date, so I'd like to shove off."

"Wouldn't be an assistant medical office manager, would it?"

"Can't put anything over on you, detective," Martin joked, while throwing on a lightweight leather topcoat and hustling down the stairs, flashing a broad smile at his partner as he disappeared beneath the landing.

# CHAPTER 12

"Hi, you're late," Marilyn Kyme greeted him with a big smile.

"Sorry," Dan replied as he watched her slide into the car. She wore mid-season black pants and a matching jacket, fashionably offset by a white cotton turtleneck. "I got a call just as I was leaving." He continued looking at her until she felt uncomfortable.

"Come on, drive," she said, still smiling, avoiding his eyes. As they pulled away she glanced up and to her right.

Dan noticed. "Anything wrong?"

She just shook her head lightly.

It was a perfect spring day, bright, warm and with just the slightest hint of a breeze, so it wasn't surprising to find a lot of weekend drivers exiting Manhattan for the Jersey shore and mountains. Dan took the Lincoln Tunnel, explaining how that would lead them to routes 3, 80 and 280, eventually depositing them in Orange and the Villa Italia.

The time passed quickly as they light-heartedly exchanged comments about the weather, their work and the more newsworthy events of the week. She was describing a particularly gruesome knifing in the South Bronx when Dan blurted, "Almost missed it," and swerved to the right, just managing to get off 280 and onto the Central Avenue exit ramp. "We're almost there."

He drove about a mile through a well preserved, low to middle income neighborhood.

"This used to be all Italian. Now it's mostly black, a few Hispanics, but it's still a good neighborhood."

"You said that as though you're surprised."

"A little bit," Dan admitted. "Being a cop in New York tends to make you cynical; not that I'm proud of it, but your experiences do tend to contribute to your thinking." He wondered if she understood, but didn't bother to ask.

They passed a small park where teenage boys played in-your-face basketball, encouraged by the admiring glances of passing teenage girls. Spring was in the air.

The car slowed as Dan turned into a parking lot alongside a Mediterranean style building with a sign proudly announcing "VILLA ITALIA." His Grand Cherokee looked out of place amongst a fleet of Cadillacs, Lincolns and Mercedes. Conspicuously occupying two spaces up front was a burgundy colored Rolls Royce Corniche.

"Yeah, you're right, this neighborhood has certainly gone to the dogs," she teased.

"No, just to the mob."

"You're kidding. You've brought me to a den of criminals."

"No. Criminals are people found guilty of having committed a crime. Believe me, no one you'll see in here has ever been found guilty of anything, though a few probably should have."

The Villa Italia was appropriately named. From niches high in the walls marble statues of ancient Romans softly illuminated by crystal chandeliers surveyed the guests. Gold velvet chairs surrounded linen covered tables adorned with Venetian goblets, Florentine dishes and gold plated utensils. A plush red carpet and tuxedo clad waiters added to the ambiance, but it was the melancholy strains of a mandolin that transported the soul to a world an ocean away.

"I love it," Marilyn whispered as the maitre 'de approached. "Thank you for bringing me."

The dining area held about twenty tables of assorted sizes, almost all of which were occupied, mostly by families with freshly scrubbed, well-behaved children, some by couples immersed in romantic conversation.

Marilyn stole a quick look at a table in the far corner occupied by six men nattily dressed in dark suits.

"Keep looking over there like that and I'm going to have to defend your honor."

She turned her eyes towards him, playfully biting her lower lip. "Wouldn't want you to do that. They don't look like they'd fight fair," she whispered.

"Well, let's see. Nicky Nose...he's the one with the schnozzola...he'd pull a gun right off. Nicky's never been known to waste time. Joe Pinocchio...he's the other one with the banana beak...he'd probably wait until I was shot and then shove some unmentionable down my throat. Then there's...."

"Cut it out. You don't know those men. Do you?"

Dan smiled back. "Of course I do. Every mob has a Nicky Nose and a Joe Pinocchio. You can bet on it. I mean, what are the chances of one or two Italians out of six having a nose like Durante."

She laughed. "Tell me about when you were young."

"I can't. I don't remember."

"Yes you do. I mean like when you were sixteen. Did you belong to a gang?"

"Sure, every New York kid belonged to a gang. I was with the East Side Barons. We were throw-backs to the fifties...black leather jackets, DA's, shades...the works."

"I'll bet you were cute. What was your nickname?"

"Can't tell you. It's embarrassing as hell."

"I'm a doctor. Nothing embarrasses me," she said, sipping the Valpolicella he had ordered.

"Alright, but you can't laugh."

"I won't laugh, I promise," she said earnestly.

"Mule."

"Mule?"

"Yep, Mule."

"Why mule?"

Dan just widened his eyes and grinned broadly. Marilyn Kyme got a napkin to her mouth just in time.

He ordered for both of them, beginning with a roasted peppers and mozzarella salad, followed by a delicate cheese and spinach manicotti topped off by veal francese with vegetables.

"We'll never eat all that," she complained.

"Sure we will. We'll take our time, you'll relax, tell me how much you want me, and the food will just go down without us knowing it."

She reached for his hand. "I do want you, you know." Her eyes would have told him even if her lips hadn't. "Especially now that I know."

"Know what?"

"Your nickname," and she giggled until heads turned.

"You're wicked, you are," he said in his best cockney. "You'd have your way with me, you would."

"Hey, that's really good." She leaned over, careful not to speak too loudly. "Any other talents?"

"Of course."

"Like what?"

"They don't call me mule for nothing."

"If there's better food than this anywhere in the world, it should be illegal," Marilyn sighed, leaning back and staring at her empty plate. "I should be ashamed of myself. You knew if you brought me here I'd make a pig of myself, didn't you?" She smiled, waiting for him to say something, but he just stared at her.

"Stop looking at me like that, Daniel," she scolded him, squinting. "I know what's on your mind."

"Oh, yeah? What's that?"

"Well, as the mule once said to the lady, 'I can't say. It's embarrassing as hell.' "

Both wondered as they tried not to laugh too loudly: Would it always be like this?

As he opened the car door for her, she put her arms around his waist, reached up and kissed him gently on the lips. "Thank you for the best meal I've ever had and thank you for making every second perfect. She kissed him again, this time letting her lips linger. "But most of all," she whispered seductively, "thank you for making me feel like a woman every minute we're together," and she pressed her body to his, parted her lips and allowed him to hold her closely.

The sound of a car entering the parking lot pried them apart. "I'll shoot that guy," Dan promised.

"You'd be shooting a dead man because I'm going to strangle him."

They continued to stare at each other, sensing what the other felt, knowing that a threshold had been crossed and something new and exciting awaited them.

"It's so very easy to think wonderful things about you," he finally said, "that scarcely an hour goes by that you're not on my mind."

"Me, too. Sometimes I hate both of us for it. I can't get my work done."

"How about a ride down the shore? We could walk on the boardwalk, have a light dinner and be back in the city by eleven."

"I'd love that, but you have to promise to pick me up at noon tomorrow and think of some wonderful things for us to do, so I'll be as happy then as I am now."

"Oh, I can think of a whole bunch of wonderful things for us to do."

"Oh, that's right. I almost forgot, they don't call you Mule for nothing."

# CHAPTER 13

It wasn't easy for Dan Costa to get through the next few weeks. He had never been handed so many drug related shootings, the solving of which almost always depended on some embittered rival stepping forward to give up the killer. That seemed to be happening less and less as gangs consolidated, eliminating the smaller players and enforcing codes of silence.

On the Teller front the phone numbers Rasheed researched pointed to a five-year relationship between Steinberg, Norville, Teller and Berger, but the elusive motive for the murders still hadn't been found, and until then, the D.A. wouldn't support any requests for wiretaps or search warrants. Nicholas Santucci had not yet identified the hit men, so Massimo Barracci had begun to think mob members might not be involved, though he obligingly kept his lieutenant on the job when Dan managed to convince him that there were no reasonable alternatives.

His partner's failure to locate the company that had removed the contents of the lab added to his frustration. None of the phone numbers were traceable to a van company, another indication that Berger had had well-organized accomplices orchestrating everything.

As for his dad's murder, neither street informants nor the Brooklyn Police had turned up any leads beyond the vague recollections of neighbors who had been shown John Kuhn's sketch. The lack of progress on his father's case troubled him more than anything, as he started to believe the assailants would never be found. In similar cases, most of the convictions resulted from arrests made within the first two weeks of the felony and more than a month had already passed. Unless the killers made a mistake, bragged about it, pissed somebody off or got caught committing a similar crime, they could easily go undetected, a prospect that haunted him.

And there was Marilyn Kyme. Though they were greatly infatuated with each other, perhaps in love, they still hadn't made love. Whenever he touched on the subject she would switch topics or tell him how deeply she cared for him and that he would have to be patient a little longer. Any effort on his part to convince her of his intentions had been met with gentle kisses and more assurances, so he resigned himself to accepting things as they were, trying to focus his energy on his work, while looking forward to their next date with youthful anticipation.

He was drinking his morning coffee and considering his options for the coming weekend when he saw his partner doggedly making his way towards him.

"Good morning, boss," Rasheed intoned as he dropped into his chair, searching drawers for medicinal relief.

"You look like shit. Another night with the office manager?"

Martin didn't bother looking up. "A gentleman never tells," he mumbled, despairing as he lifted an empty aspirin bottle.

"Catch," Dan warned, as he tossed a box of Tylenol.

"You're a good man, but next time buy aspirin. It helps your heart, too."

"Yeah? Well, you definitely need help with your heart. How many nights have you seen that girl? You only met her a coupla' weeks ago. What's her name?"

"Tonya, and I can't help it man," he confessed, "the lady is absolutely perfect. I mean, she looks good, she smells good…you know what I mean."

"Yeah, I know what you mean. You're pussy whipped and banging the hell out of her."

"You're talking about the woman I may really love, you know that?" Martin warned.

"Sure, at least for another week."

"Man, you are so cynical. What makes you so cynical?"

"Bad guys make me cynical, Rasheed, bad guys on the street, in Washington, at City Hall, and all of them getting away with it."

"I know what you mean," Martin concurred. "I try not to think about them…the hypocrites, I mean…because I don't think I could concentrate on my work if I let them get to me."

Dan told himself it was advice worth taking. "Listen, there's one thing we haven't looked into on the Teller case."

"Just the way you said that is enough to tell me I am definitely not going to like what I'm about to hear."

"It's not that bad," Costa promised. "I just want you to go down to Chincoteague Island and see what you can dig up about the time Teller and

Berger spent there. I'm convinced the Nuremberg lab project started on Chincoteague, so somebody there may know something about their research and other players that were involved."

"Man, do I hate it when you make sense. Alright, when do I go?"

"I'll make a call to the job down there to see what they know. You call ol' Tonya and see if she wants to take the ride this weekend. The budget will cover the motels and most of the food."

Rasheed Martin lit up. "Daniel, that is one hell of an idea. Why didn't I think of that?"

"Because you're in love, and while men are in love they're not too smart, unless of course they're Italian, to whom all things come easily."

"Yeah, right."

Dan had dialed the Chincoteague Police and was waiting for them to pick up when Rasheed gave the thumbs up, the delectable Tonya having excitedly agreed to the trip.

"Chincoteague Police, Sergeant Kichel speaking." The voice had a distinctive southern drawl.

Dan introduced himself, summarized the Teller and Berger killings, explained what he needed and concluded the conversation by thanking the sergeant for his help.

Kichel hadn't known anyone Dan mentioned since they had already left the island by the time he joined the force, but he was aware of a small research lab on the southwest corner of the island that closed about five years ago. Some of the fishermen who frequented his favorite watering hole spoke of the money scientists there had paid for horseshoe crabs and a couple of senior officers had on occasion mentioned the scientists' names. He would be happy to escort Rasheed to the old lab site and see to it that at least one of his superiors was available for an interview. He also provided directions to a good motel, an excellent restaurant and police headquarters.

"So you're all set," Dan concluded. "When are you leaving?"

"Tomorrow night. She's taking Friday off so we'll make a three-day weekend out of it. I'll pay out of my own pocket."

"You don't have to. The motel and half the food bills are on the department. Now, if you don't mind, let's go over all the possibilities."

With Martin recording, the two exchanged ideas about possible leads, ranging from fishermen who might have provided horseshoe crabs, to laboratory equipment distributors, to physicians and dentists who might have treated Teller and Berger. The list was finalized with Rasheed's inclusion of the local barbers and clergy.

"With that many people to see you're going to have to get a good night's sleep," Dan warned.

Rasheed countered, "Hey, no disrespect intended, but you do your job your way and I'll do mine my way." He delighted in the prospects.

The clock above Al Wilson's door read four, the hour Dan had promised to call Marilyn. He was about to when the phone rang. It was Pam Donaldson.

"Good afternoon, Dan. I hope all's well."

"Not too bad, Pam, yourself?"

"I'm fine. I'm calling to see if you're available for dinner tonight."

He couldn't resist. "You've made my week. I never knew you cared."

She was surprised by the response, taking a few seconds to think of an appropriate comeback.

"I've always wanted you," she whispered seductively. "I've just been too shy to admit it. All I've ever needed is some encouragement from you."

It was Dan's turn to come up with something but he failed miserably. "You got me there," he sputtered. "I think I'm out of my league."

"Some ladies might consider that an insult."

"Oh, yeah, it didn't come out quite right. Sorry."

She laughed. "Don't be. I've had a lot of experience with flirts. Not too many can handle a woman who plays their game."

Dan hated pregnant pauses but he couldn't think of anything to say, grateful when Pam continued.

"Mr. Barracci has asked me to make reservations for seven-thirty this evening and thought you might want to pick the place."

Without thinking he said, "It's Friday night, Pam, I've got a date." Then, realizing it would be insulting to refuse the invitation he added, "It's someone very special and we don't get a chance to dine together often." He still felt uncomfortable.

Pam sensed it. "Please feel free to bring her along; that is, unless you feel your friend would be uncomfortable in our company?"

"Of course not, not in yours, nor in Massimo's," Dan replied, while assuming that the dinner was being arranged to provide him with information Nicholas Santucci had uncovered, something in which he did not want Marilyn involved.

Both knew Massimo Barracci considered a refusal to break bread a personal insult. Dan would have to cancel his date with Marilyn, and having advised Pam of his decision, selected Belmonte's for the meeting.

He called Marilyn to reschedule their date, but once he heard her voice, he regretted the decision.

"I'm surprised you answered," he said. "Tired?"

"Not as much as I thought I would be. Maybe the thought of seeing you energizes me."

Now he felt worse. "I'm afraid I've got some bad news. I have to cancel tonight. Believe me, if there was an alternative, I'd be with you."

"I'm jealous," she pouted, in a way that begged for an explanation.

"It has to do with the Teller case." He debated telling her more, finally deciding she deserved it. "You know some of my closest friends and relatives have mob connections. Well, a while back I solicited the help of one of them, someone I trust who is not really a bad person. No drugs or anything like that. He wants to meet…something important."

"What time are you meeting him?"

"Seven-thirty."

"That's early," she said hopefully. "Why don't we meet for dinner after the meeting?"

"The meeting is a dinner," he admitted.

"Oh." Now she really seemed disappointed.

"I'm sorry. Believe me, I can't just refuse the invitation. It would be a big offense."

"Did he know you had a date?"

"His secretary made the arrangements, so no, he didn't know."

"I'm surprised she didn't tell you to bring me," she said suspiciously.

"Actually, she did in a way, but I knew you would feel uncomfortable so I chose the only option."

Marilyn didn't hesitate. "You're wrong, Dan, there's another option. You could have invited me to accompany you."

"You don't think you'd have a problem in the company of men like that? That's certainly not the impression I got when you saw those men at Villa Italia."

"This is different. These are your people; people I have to get to know if we're ever going to mean anything to each other."

She hadn't spoken like that before, as if she had decided that Dan Costa was going to be a part of the rest of her life and that they had to begin taking steps in that direction. It made him happy.

"Or are you ashamed of me?" he heard her say. "Maybe not ashamed, I don't think you're that, maybe just not willing to let your family meet me because you're not sure."

"I love you, I'm proud of you, even when you jump to crazy conclusions like that, and I'll pick you up at seven."

"Good boy. Now what should I wear?"

"Well, you'll be in the company of loose women. You'll have to look the part," he teased.

"You're definitely asking for it, Sergeant, and tonight you are just liable to get it."

"Promises, promises," and before he could say more, he heard the receiver click.

As he pulled to the curb he could see her exit the lobby. She wore a long lightweight black coat and unusually high-heeled pumps. Her scent preceded her into the car.

"Lord, you look good," he said, admiring her lightly waved hair parted slightly off-center, "and you smell even better." For the first time she had applied a daringly red, high gloss lipstick and green eye shadow that added a sultry tone to her natural beauty. "I hate having to share you tonight," he continued, while she just looked at him, enjoying the same romantic thoughts.

"Dinner won't last forever," she said softly, before looking ahead and exclaiming, "Now drive you gorgeous hunk of a man before I attack you right here."

"Promises, promises."

She looked from the corner of her eye and purred, "You just wait and see, sergeant wise-ass."

The cadaverous head waiter Dan had met on his first visit to Belmonte's appeared and greeted them with the same fixed stare, this time acknowledging Dan with a slight tilt of the head. "Follow me, please. Your party is already seated."

As Dan helped remove her coat, Marilyn stepped forward and turned to reveal a tight fitting black dress supported by two barely visible straps. An uplift bra, or some other gravity defying foundation, supported two milky-white globes of matching perfection. The dress stopped well above the knee, further enhancing her long, shapely legs enticingly concealed within shimmering black nylons. By the time his eyes reached the black patent leather, open toed pumps, his heart was racing.

If there were words to describe his feelings, the sight of her robbed him of them. He just stood there, taking her in, wishing he could press her to him and never let go. She finally stepped toward him and took his hands.

Softly, she whispered, "I love you, Dan Costa, and I love the way you look at me, and think of me and want me, but most of all I love you because you love me and are trying so hard to be perfect for me."

They stood there, indifferent to the maitre 'de waiting for them to follow, to the people watching them; people wondering just who this extraordinarily attractive couple was.

The men stood in unison as they emerged from the greenery, Dan noting that all eyes were fixed on Marilyn. Only Pam Donaldson bothered to acknowledge him, casting a look of approval.

The Don was accompanied by his attorney, Anthony Lacozza, the enforcers, Muzzi and Scarola, and the reliable Nicholas Santucci. Barracci pulled out the chair to his right, the one Dan was certain had originally been intended for him, but which Barracci was now holding for Marilyn. Not until she was comfortably seated did he even bother to recognize Dan.

"It's good to see you, Daniel, have a seat," he said, indifferently waving his hand towards the opposite end of the table. Turning his attention again to Marilyn he remarked, "We are rarely privileged to be in the presence of two such beautiful women. I hope you enjoy the food and the company."

Massimo was being disgustingly charming.

Dinner consisted of the usual five-course Friday fare…soup, salad, a light pasta, fish and pastry. To everyone's amusement Muzzi and Scarola ate as though they were starved, consuming more than the limits of mortal men. Occasionally, Dan caught Santucci studying him but neither spoke to the other except when passing the family style dishes. Lacozza, looking nervous and worried, was particularly reticent.

"How have you been, Anthony?" Dan asked the consigliere as a waiter served linguine in an oregano flavored white clam sauce.

"Pretty good, Dan, yourself?" he responded, trying to summon some enthusiasm.

"Not bad…not as good as the Don," he said in a low voice, nodding towards the laughing Barracci, who was alternating his attention between the red and raven-haired beauties on either side of him.

Dan tried to draw Lacozza out, thinking that might encourage Santucci, but neither would commit, not until their boss signaled his approval, which Dan knew would not be given until they were finished dining.

As a waiter offered and poured a variety of after-dinner drinks from a small cart, Barracci leaned over and whispered something in Pam's ear.

She turned to Marilyn. "I need to powder my nose. Would you mind joining me?"

"Of course not," Marilyn replied, and the men stood until the ladies disappeared into the Belmonte forest.

Reseated, Barracci gave a sign to Lacozza who reached beneath the table for a briefcase that he opened, extracting a large manila envelope. Cautiously, he looked around while Dan wondered for whom. The table was completely concealed from the view of the other diners. Satisfied, he handed the packet to Dan. Another signal from his Don and Santucci began speaking.

"Don't open the envelope here," he warned, "but when you do, you'll find my name and number on a card in case you have any questions. There are photographs of the two men you want. On the backside are their names, last known addresses and some other pieces of information you may need to find them. On the typed sheet is an explanation of how they were recruited, plus everything else we could find out about the deal they made and what kind of people I think they are." His speech concluded, he looked to Barracci.

"Daniel, the service Nicholas has provided must never be disclosed. To do so would place everyone at this table and others at very great risk. If you are asked if I or any of my people were ever solicited by you or your department, you must tell them that you approached me and that I refused to even comment, that I only said I knew nothing of the incident. Do you understand?"

"Perfectly."

Later that evening as they were driving up Park Avenue towards Marilyn's apartment and she was happily telling Dan how much she enjoyed the food and company, she sensed his preoccupation and asked why Pam had been told to visit the ladies' room.

Though he was tempted to say more as a sign of growing trust, he chose to be cautious. "The old man had a private dealing with people that concern him...that he doesn't know all that well. He just wanted to know if I had heard anything about them."

She moved closer to him, encircling his arm in hers. "Pick me up tomorrow morning?" she asked, leaning her head on his shoulder.

"Sure, where do you want to go?"

"Away for the weekend," she said softly, "anywhere you want."

He leaned over and kissed the top of her head. "I love the hell out of you, even though you dress like a whore."

Expecting a poke, her response shocked him as she nuzzled closer. "Yes, your little whore."

The message light on his apartment phone was blinking.

"Hi, Dan, it's Jack again. Guess you're out partying. Donna thought of something else, so give me a call when you can. I'm taking her to the Bloomsburg Fair on Sunday. Why not join us?"

He got into bed and opened Santucci's package. The first photo was of a thin-faced man, unremarkable except for a distinctively aquiline nose and a scar that ran above his left jaw-line. He could pass for almost any age from thirty-five to fifty. On the reverse side a carefully printed biography identified the face as that of Carlo Rinaldi. His address and phone number in Brooklyn followed.

The man in the second photo resembled Sidney Kaplan's description of the gunman in the passing car. With a thick, curly hairline that descended almost to his brow, wide face and menacing scowl, Albert Tataro could be Hollywood's perfect hit man. Only Muzzi and Scarola fit the role better.

Santucci's letter told of their relationship to the doctors for which Dan had been searching.

Rinaldi had been arrested for extortion two years earlier. As part of the Anthony DePalma family, a small-time Long Island syndicate suspected of drug trafficking and racketeering, he had been represented by Richard Musto, a well-connected mouthpiece who just happened to be the attorney for a limited investment partnership that included Doctors Steinberg and Norville. Rinaldi had gotten off, but didn't escape the wrath of DePalma who hadn't authorized the extortion. He was stripped of his status, along with most of what had been a healthy share of the family's income. Relegated to the rank of a lowly soldier, the same shared by Tataro, they had resorted to moonlighting, taking on enforcement jobs for the limited partnership. Word had it that DePalma was furious and was exacting payments through Musto in lieu of cutting both men off permanently. Whether this indicated that DePalma knew of their involvement in the Teller/Berger murders remained uncertain, though it had been made abundantly clear to everyone that he would tolerate no further infractions of his authority.

What sealed Dan's conviction that Santucci had found Teller's murderers was his closing paragraph.

*Apparently, these two morons don't listen too well. Rinaldi told one of my informers that they had taken some other more recent jobs.*

*On one, Tataro was in the process of getting off one boat and onto another somewhere down in Jersey when he slipped and fell into the ocean. Damn near drowned to death. Rinaldi and another guy had to haul him back in with boat hooks. They don't say who, if anyone, was killed but my informer seems to think it involved murder. He says Tataro is crazy, never leaves a guy with just a beating. Always ends up killing him. If that's all true and DePalma finds out, these two are shark meat.*

Dan leaned back and ran the growing list of evidence through his mind, hoping somehow to close in on the motive for Teller's murder. Except for that, everything was fitting nicely. If he could uncover the motive and Joe D could solve his father's murder, he could free his mind to do nothing but think of Marilyn Kyme, ultimately convincing her that they belonged together. He had no doubt she would agree.

She bounded down the brownstone steps, a bulging knapsack cradled in one arm and an enormous tote bag dangling from the other. In one motion she hurled them onto the backseat, jumped in and closed the door.

"Let's get out of this city," Marilyn said, playfully poking Costa in the ribs. "Ooh, I do love those muscles. Can't wait to see them," she squealed lustily.

He drove off laughing. "You're turning into one beautiful, lovable nut, you know that?"

"You say the nicest things," and she leaned over to plant a wet kiss on his cheek, lingering to run her tongue up and around his ear, down his neck.

"Knock it off, at least until we're through the tunnel," he pleaded, as a cab cut him off from the right, making an almost impossible left turn off Eighth Avenue.

"Okay, but your body's mine once we hit Joisey," and she gave him a final poke.

Clear of the tunnel and its helix, she slid as far towards him as her seatbelt would allow, and without warning put her hand inside his shirt, slowly running it across his chest.

He didn't want her to stop, pleasuring in her newfound boldness, particularly when she again pressed her lips to his cheek, nibbling her way down his neck.

"Oh, woman, am I going to love you tonight," he moaned.

"Where at?" she blew the words seductively into his ear.

"All over."

She laughed. "Not where, like on my body, you adorable nut. Where, like in what city?"

"Nuremberg, Pennsylvania."

Marilyn Kyme had never been to Pennsylvania, in fact nowhere west of Paterson, New Jersey, so the rural hills of Sussex County and raging waters of the Delaware excited her. "It's so beautiful, Dan. I love it."

Her excitement turned to wonder as they cleared the Poconos and began their ascent of the Green Mountains. Dan entertained her with stories of the immigrant miners, their deeds of courage and selfless devotion.

"I think it's terrible what they did to those people," she reflected sadly.

Marilyn delighted in the descent on the narrow road from Oneida to Nuremberg. Some of the rhododendron and mountain laurel had blossomed since Dan's visit and the ash and birch were in full foliage.

"It's absolutely enchanting. I had no idea it could be so beautiful," she marveled, as they neared the bottom of the valley. When it came fully into view she yelled, "Stop. Stop the car! I want to take a picture."

He pulled over to the right as far as he dared while she rummaged through her tote bag, finally extracting a throwaway camera. She snapped a few pictures of the mountain stream and dairy farm in the distance. Back in the car and ignoring the seatbelt, she threw her arms around Dan's neck and kissed him playfully. "Thank you again and again. I love this place."

"And I love you like this. I never thought I'd see you acting like a little kid. It's out of character but I love it."

"I am a little kid, so you'd better be gentle with me."

"Will you please stop talking like that," he begged, "at least until we can do something about it."

She licked her lips suggestively. He just shook his head, feigning hopelessness.

She made him stop the car twice more, once so she could take photos of some of the late eighteenth century grave markers and again at the top of the hill when Nuremberg first came into view. Each time she would cover him with kisses, thanking him for bringing her and reciting a litany of lascivious promises.

"If this is what mountain air does to you, we're moving up here," he vowed, as the Jeep climbed Main Street and strangers waved their welcomes.

He parked in front of the hotel.

"Is this where we're staying?"

"Yep. The Nuremberg Hotel, Joe and Maria Bottino, Proprietors," he announced, pointing to the small sign.

Maria greeted them as if they were life-long friends, throwing her arms around Dan and kissing him on the cheek. Joe did the same to Marilyn, surprising her and drawing a disapproving look from his wife.

"Joe's just a big flirt, but he's harmless," she assured them.

"Whataya' talkin' about? She's like family," he said, excusing his indulgence.

"We're leaving in about an hour. Joe's nephew is getting married in Philly, so you'll be on your own until tomorrow. We should be home around noon and there's no other guests," Maria said, suggestively winking at Dan. "Just help yourself to tea, coffee and whatever drinks are in the fridge. There's some wine and liquor in the cabinet above the counter. I made you a cake and some scones. Eat whatever you want."

She led them upstairs to room number four, the only one Dan hadn't seen during his first visit. "I put on fresh sheets, vacuumed and dusted," she assured them.

It was in the right rear and had the best command of the valley that stretched five miles through the patchwork towns of Weston and Tomhicken. A sturdy, canopied four-poster dominated the room.

"Oh, Maria, it's absolutely perfect," Marilyn exclaimed.

"Yeah, it sure is," Dan agreed, his imagination already kicking in.

"It was my grandmother's," Maria said proudly, "the only thing I have of hers. We save it for young couples." She looked around the room. "We call it the honeymoon suite, but it's really a collection of family heirlooms."

Beneath the windows that overlooked the valley was an ornate cedar chest, badly scarred but still lustrous.

"Joe's grandmother bought it for her daughter as a hope-chest." Two matching alabaster porcelain lamps flanked the bed, perched on spindle-legged, hickory nightstands. "The lamps were in my great aunt's parlor. They're over a hundred years old. The tables were in Joe's parents' bedroom. He thinks they inherited them from grandparents, so they're even older."

She pointed out the mirrored chest-of-drawers from a great-uncle, her mother's dressing table and a handsome, cherrywood butler that had been her great-grandfather's. "There's a lot of memories in this room," she said dreamily.

"Dan and I appreciate your letting us share them," Marilyn said warmly.

When Maria had left, Marilyn put her arms around Dan. "Hold me. Hold me and never let me go." They stood like that, embraced for a minute, making no sound, feeling each other's warmth and heartbeat.

Finally, softly, she said, "When they leave, I want you to make love to me. I want to shower and come to you in this bed and give myself to you. I love you so very much."

The nightstand clock said three p.m. Dan listened to Marilyn's steady, restful breathing, her head nestled between his neck and shoulder, her body curled over his right side. He looked at the transparent black negligee draped over the bedstand and thought of how she had trembled at his touch, finally relaxing and sharing an ecstasy that transcended their expectations. He moved his hands across the smooth skin of her buttocks.

"I thought you were going to let me rest until after dinner," she whispered sleepily.

"I'm sorry. Did I wake you?"

"Unh-unh. I've been awake for awhile thinking of you."

"All good, I hope."

"All wonderfully, magnificently good. I think I'll make you kiss me and love me and do all those other delicious things to me every day. You'll be my love stud forever."

"Then I'll have to charge a fee."

"Shut up," she teased. "Don't ruin anything. It's all too perfect and I don't want you to spoil it."

"Yes, ma'am."

She rolled on top of him, rubbing her body against his. "I want to feel you inside of me again, and don't stop until I tell you."

When they finally walked into Anna's restaurant at seven that evening all heads turned, some recognizing Dan, but most taking in the sultry, long-haired beauty with him. Anna joined them for coffee after they had finished their dinners.

"So what brings you back?" she asked.

"I wanted Marilyn to see your town and I'm meeting with Donna Schulman tomorrow morning. She thought of something that might be important."

"We're having the Firensi's play tonight," Anna said, referring to four aging brothers who played a decent medley of ethnic music in the local clubs. "Why don't you stick around? You'll enjoy them."

"Thanks, maybe we'll do that," Dan stated, before a gentle kick from Marilyn prompted him to add, "but we did have an awfully long drive and we're both kind of tired, so we might take a rain check."

Anna smiled knowingly.

"Are you having any success with the investigation?"

"It's like most of them, Anna, either you know how it happened and why, but don't know the perp, or you know who and how, but not why. This one's really complicated by the nature of their work. We know it had something to do with the motive, but not understanding the details of their science makes it hard to figure out what there is to gain. You know a bank teller gets shot to steal his money, but why do you shoot an innocent old scientist?"

"Well," Anna said, "my father always told us there were only two things on a man's mind. I guess money can motivate men to do some pretty ugly things, so that has to be your answer…money…because with Joe, God bless his soul, it sure wasn't sex."

"Yeah, I think you're probably right," Dan agreed, "but we haven't been able to figure out how money fits into it. Teller only alluded once to the possibility of money being a factor in his research. Otherwise he kept referring to personal satisfaction, that he'd never get rich doing this work."

"Are you sure about that?" Anna asked.

"Why? Do you know differently?"

"You can talk to Marcy Holland to be certain, but I'm pretty sure he had indicated to her and Larry Moretti that he expected to come into a lot of money someday. Hell, I can even remember one night in here, me and him and Marcy, we were sitting right over there next to the fireplace," she said pointing, "and Marcy was all upset that they had only raised two thousand dollars for a cancer research group. He said to her, 'Don't worry about it. In another month or two I'll personally cover the shortfall, I promise.' That was eight thousand dollars he was talking about."

"How long before his murder was that?"

"Oh," Anna thought, looking off, "no more than two months."

"And that was before the argument in here with Berger?"

"Yeah, just before that."

*So,* Dan thought, *Teller thinks he's coming into some money, gets ticked at Berger when he doesn't, but goes to New York with him to share dinner. Somebody bullshitted somebody.*

"If you and Anna are going to solve this crime, at least you can buy a lady a drink," Marilyn complained.

"Sure," Dan said, "I could use one for the road myself."

"They're on me," Anna exclaimed, "and so's the dinner."

"You can't do that," Dan protested.

"Sure I can. I own the joint. Besides, I know someday you'll lock up the creeps that killed Joe and I'll be grateful. This is payment in advance."

"Thank you," Dan said, leaning over to give her a kiss. "That's very nice of you."

Anna smiled and turned to Marilyn. "If I were twenty years younger, Honey, you'd have more competition than you'd want."

Back in the car, nestled amongst clusters of mountain laurel and blue spruce in Anna's parking lot, Dan and Marilyn kissed and groped each other until the windows fogged, shielding them from prying eyes.

"Now look what you've done," he scolded, "I can't see out." He couldn't repress a grin.

"Good," she panted, placing his hand beneath her skirt, "no one can see in either."

His hand slowly traced her legs past the top of her stockings, gently feeling his way along the inside of her thighs, tenderly touching and stroking until she began to moan softly. He licked her ear. "You must be cold down there," he breathed. She groaned, kissing him hard, closing her thighs tightly around his hand.

They remained locked together long after it was over, her face pressed between his neck and shoulder.

"Can you drive like this?" she asked. "I don't want to move."

"No, but I'll make a deal with you," he said, leaning back slightly so he could see her face. "If you let me drive, I'll make love to you until the sun comes up."

She looked at him adoringly. "And I'll just bet you could do it."

He drove carefully back down the Oneida road, through the unlit forests of hemlock and birch, past the dairy farm and along the creeks, finally up Main Street, stopping at the foot of Sugarloaf Mountain. As he followed her up the stairs, watching her sway immodestly, anticipating the soft warmth of her body, he knew that this was all he would ever want or need, and he hoped it would be enough for the woman he loved.

They awoke to church bells calling worshippers to Sunday service, but chose to lounge in bed a while, rollicking to each other's touch, ultimately concluding with more love-making.

Before crossing the street and walking down to Leon's Café, Dan knocked on the door of the constable's office, but no one answered. He had arranged to meet Jack and Donna for breakfast, a good idea since he and Marilyn were famished. Making love can build an appetite. It was already past ten, so most of the tables were filled with parishioners looking forward to Leon's brunch. It would hold them until the traditional evening roast.

Dan and Leon acknowledged each other, though the chef quickly shifted his attention to Marilyn, as did just about every man in the room.

She wore her hair lightly pulled back, making it look even thicker as it cascaded between her shoulders. Form-fitting blue slacks and a simple white pullover made her appear taller, enhancing her curves. Even without the almond shaped green eyes, olive complexion and rich, flowing hair, Marilyn Kyme would be a showstopper.

They had just finished filling their plates with eggs, hotcakes, a variety of breakfast meats and the special of the day, poached kippers, when Donna entered with Jack close behind.

Dan stood and reached to take Donna's hand, but she moved through it and kissed him a bit longer and harder than Marilyn would have liked. Dan sensed that Donna knew exactly what she was doing.

"Hey, Jack, I'd like you to meet my girlfriend," he said purposefully. "Donna, Jack, this is Marilyn. I've told her all about you guys and she said she'll be nice anyway."

They laughed, though the looks the girls gave each other lingered, something like two prizefighters feeling each other out.

Donna shed a light three-quarter coat to reveal a pink pantsuit that would probably have fit better and been more appropriate ten years earlier. Dan couldn't help but notice how it strained to contain her ample figure. From the corner of his eye he could see Marilyn watching him, so he riveted on Donna's backside as she moved towards the buffet. These were hot times in Leon's Café.

"What an ass," he whispered in mock admiration. Turning to face Marilyn he added, "Oh, sorry, that was kind of insensitive. I promise to never again let you see me ogle another woman's ass."

She couldn't help laughing, but kicked him anyway. "Get a real good look at it, sweetheart, because it's the only ass you're going to see for a while."

"I love you when you're clever like that."

They ate and made small talk. When Donna tried to insinuate that they had spent more time together during Dan's last trip than they really had, he made sure to correct her, giving Marilyn little reason to even think about being jealous. She relaxed and listened to the give and take, confident that Dan Costa would always be faithful and that the chance at a lifetime of happiness with him was solely in her hands.

"I understand you may have thought of something that could be important to the case," Dan finally said to Nuremberg's one and only sex symbol.

"I've thought of a lot of things I'd like to tell you," Donna replied seductively. When no one found it particularly humorous, she shrugged and turned her attention to the purpose of their meeting.

She related that, depending upon the weather, Berger had driven to New York City every other Wednesday or Thursday, returning each time with a white box, a variety of colored labels affixed to one panel. It was roughly three to four cubic feet, and judging by the way Berger carried it, Donna didn't think it weighed more than a couple pounds.

"One week last winter…I think it was in January…he got the flu," she recalled, "and he must have asked Dr. Teller to go in his place because they had an awful row over it. Dr. Teller rarely drove, and never to New York, so he refused to go. Well, Berger had his usual tantrum, darn near passed out, and finally stormed back to the hotel. Maria even called to find out what had happened…he was that pissed. Anyway, the next day a man from a messenger service walked in carrying the box, or at least one that looked exactly like the kind Berger usually brought back. He asked for Dr. Teller, who happened to be in the bathroom. I said I'd give it to him, but he wouldn't leave it, said he had to give it personnaly to Doctor Teller. When Joe came out the guy just handed it over. They never said a word to each other. As far as I can remember, that's the only time anybody ever brought that box to the lab besides Dr. Berger, and I'm sure I never saw that guy again."

"Did Berger come to work that day?"

"No," she said with assurance, "he was really sick. He was out from the Thursday they had the argument until the next week. I remember Dr. Teller telling me how he took him to the emergency room Saturday afternoon. He was that sick, and he still looked a little washed out when he came back to work."

"Whatever was in that box was valuable enough for Berger not to trust it to anyone else," Dan observed. "Any ideas as to the contents?" he asked, directing the question to Donna.

"No, but whatever it was, it was cold."

"Cold? What do you mean cold?"

"Cold, like ice."

"How do you know?"

"Because when I asked the delivery guy for it, I reached to take it and my hands were on it for a second. It was cold, as though it contained ice."

Dan looked at Marilyn. "Plasma? Blood?"

"Perhaps," she said thoughtfully, her mind searching a long list of possibilities, "but it also could be a biological culture, or tissue, maybe bone."

She turned to Donna, "Can you tell me any details about the labels?"

"There was always one light blue and one bright yellow, and then a bunch of smaller red ones with handwriting on them. I'm sure of that."

"Sounds like blood samples," she concluded, "infected ones at that. I'm just not sure what the blue is for." She hesitated a second. "Donna, did the light blue label have any print on it?"

"I don't believe it did."

"Dan, that blue label may be a project symbol. Sometimes blood labs will use different colored stickers to designate samples for specific projects. When I take blood from an overdose victim it goes into two vials and then into a small sleeve with a circular dark green sticker on it. Samples from poisoned victims get a lighter green and if we suspect lead poisoning it gets a small gray square. I just don't know if light blue means anything special," she confessed, "but tomorrow I'll make a call to the blood lab and let you know."

They finished breakfast and piled into Dan's Grand Cherokee. It was time for the Bloomsburg Fair, the second largest one of its kind in the nation. In the middle of the quaint central Pennsylvania college town stood a three hundred acre fairgrounds built in the latter part of the nineteenth century to accommodate livestock auctions. Over the years buildings had been added to house equipment exhibits, auctions, craft competitions and animal shows, with separate buildings for swine, goats, sheep, fowl, bovine stock and horses. With exhibitors from every corner of the state, 4H Club and Inter-County competition was fierce. It spoke of a lifestyle that would both fascinate and bewilder the New York couple.

"Park right here," Jack said. "I brought a pass. Stick it on the windshield," he ordered, handing Dan a red and white Official Police Business placard.

They had parked within a hundred feet of the main gate, beneath boldly lettered NO PARKING signs, drawing suspicious stares from people queuing before the ticket booths.

"Follow me," Jack said confidently, as he strode past the crowds before turning towards a portal manned by an armed State Trooper. Terrorism casts a long shadow. The two spoke briefly before the officer opened the door and motioned them in.

"How did you swing that?" Dan asked.

"I just showed him my badge and told him you were President of New York City's PBA, an honored guest. He was impressed."

Before them stretched an endless series of intersecting promenades, each lined with stalls and tents hawking clothes, ethnic foods and crafts of every sort. In the distance towering ferris wheels, a roller coaster and other rides attracted a dozen teenagers who raced past the amused couples. To the right the clickety-click of carnival wheels drew Marilyn's attention.

"You have to win me something, Dan. Our first carnival date. It's good luck."

He watched her move down the walk with girlish delight, the heads of more than a few men turning as she bounced past them. A voice boomed over the loudspeakers advising that tickets for the Garth Brooks' show at eight that evening were available at the fairgrounds grandstand. She stopped in her tracks.

"Dan, did you hear that? Jack, do they really have Garth Brooks here? "

Surprised, Jack asked, "You really like that guy?"

"Like? I adore him. Of course, not the same way I do you, Darling," she said quickly, planting a kiss on Dan's cheek.

"Well, in that case," Jack replied, " I guess we'll have to use these. I was gonna' give them away." He handed her four bright red tickets.

"Front row," she shrieked. "Jack, I love you," and she threw her arms around the grateful constable.

"Just like a groupie," Dan kidded. "What about me?"

"Just wait till you see what you get if you win me something," she promised, racing towards the wheels with their stuffed and glittering prizes.

Lured by the smell of sausage and peppers, skewered lamb and fried fennel cakes, the two men ate their way around the fairgrounds, sampling an array of spicy, grease-dripping, ethnic foods, their digestion aided by generous doses of Bavarian Bock and homemade wines. Marilyn pledged undying love when Dan shot enough clay pipes to win her a stuffed Pinocchio. "Now I have two Italian dolls," she cooed.

"Oh, that's a relief. I thought you were going to say two blockheads."

"That too," she added laughing."

She hugged him proudly when he pounded a spring-mounted lever, driving a metal ball to the top and ringing a bell to the delight of on-lookers who avowed it couldn't be done. For his effort he won their adulation and an enormous Wiley Coyote.

"I am not carrying something bigger than me around this fair," he protested.

"You can leave it here and pick it up on the way out," the beaten operator offered. Marilyn thanked him and sped off in search of Dan's next conquest.

They joked their way through the animal exhibits where Marilyn made some erotic comparisons between her lover and a Hereford bull named Donald. When the opportunity arose, Donna whispered to Dan, "She certainly has let her hair down, hasn't she?" and strode off, having made her point, whatever it was.

The Garth Brooks show ended at ten. They had eaten and drank to excess, braved the wildest rides, endured the smelliest livestock and captured a bounty of prizes. All that remained was a four-hour drive back to Manhattan by way of Nuremberg.

"Do we really have to go back?" Marilyn wondered after they had said good-bye and thanked Jack for planning the day.

"You really like it out here?"

She sat up and faced him. "Dan, I never knew I could feel this way, not even close. I never knew I could be so completely happy and it's all because of you. Right now I think I could be happy anywhere, as long as I'm with you, but everything here seems so perfect. It's quiet and peaceful and the people are so warm and generous. Hell," she snickered, "I was the most obscene person at the fair."

"Take a nap," he said, reaching over to massage her neck and shoulder. "Put the seat back and get some sleep. It's a long ride and you have to go to work in the morning."

"I'm staying with you tonight. I wish I could stay with you every night," she added, before tilting the seat back and surrendering to her fatigue.

Dan was annoyed that he hadn't yet unraveled the purpose of the lab project, certain that it had hastened Joe Teller's death. He realized his attention had been diverted by his father's murder and his budding romance, and though neither made him feel guilty, he was uncomfortable with his failure to make sense out of the evidence he had. As the car climbed the north side of the Conyngham Valley towards Route 80 and the long stretch to Manhattan, he concentrated on the facts in hand, determined to construct some viable scenarios before arriving home. Somewhere between the Water Gap and the

Lincoln Tunnel bits and pieces of testimony from Nuremberg's citizens, Clarence Worthington, and in particular, Donna Schulman began to form some incomplete but feasible possibilities. A lot more supporting evidence would be needed, and he wasn't sure where he would get it, but at least he had a general direction to follow.

At precisely two-thirty A.M., he pulled to the curb in front of his apartment.

He nudged Marilyn gently. "Wake up, Darling, we're home." Within minutes they were in bed, she, sleeping soundly; he, lying contentedly, softly tracing the naked curves of her back, confident of the prospects his imagination had stirred. Only time would tell if any of his choices were correct, but the fact he had finally cleared his mind and pieced some of the evidence together in a reasonably logical fashion was enough to satisfy him. That and Marilyn Kyme's warm, smooth body brought him a brief, but restful sleep.

At seven the alarm sounded, much too early for the exhausted couple. Dan made a heroic effort, bounding from the bed, throwing the covers off his groaning lover.

"Up and at 'em," he encouraged, until the sight of her lying unclothed, arms outstretched, aroused a more natural reaction. He slid between her legs, running his tongue down her neck, around her breasts and across her stomach.

"This is the way I want to wake up every morning," she moaned, digging her nails into his back as he entered her. The thought made their lovemaking all the more enjoyable.

# CHAPTER 14

Rasheed Martin was laughing at something a caller was saying, but as Dan seated himself the young detective's demeanor changed and he mumbled a promise or two before hanging up.

"Did I interrupt something?"

"No," Rasheed replied unconvincingly, "just finding out how Tonya's feeling."

"And how does Tonya feel?"

"Real fine," Rasheed grinned, dragging the words out slowly. "And you look pretty damn pleased with yourself if I do say so. Nice weekend?"

"Best weekend in years, but it's time you, me and the boss got together. Is he in?"

"Does a bear shit in the woods? He was over here ten minutes ago wondering where you were. I told him I thought you were downstairs. I don't know where he went after that."

"Okay, it'll give you a chance to tell me about your trip to Chincoteague, and please spare me any details that don't involve the case. I already know more about your budding romance than I can stand. "

Rasheed smiled broadly and began.

On Saturday morning he had found Ron Kichel, the sergeant at the Police Headquarters to whom Dan had spoken on the phone. He brought Martin out to the island's southwest corner, a narrow sand spit renowned as the debarkation point for the wild horses that routinely swim the strait between Assateague and Chincoteague Islands. A decaying laboratory with living quarters still stood, slowly surrendering to the relentless ocean winds and salt air. For more than five years it had gone unoccupied, condemned for habitation and too costly to purchase and renovate. Kichel predicted that next year's budget would include an allocation to level the building.

Nothing inside the structure hinted at its purpose, much less its research objective, other than some rusting lab benches and tiled walls and floor.

'Your best bet is to talk to some guys at Fish's, a local bar that fishermen and odd-job guys hang out at,' Kichel had suggested. He led them there and wished them good luck after introducing them to some men, two of whom would prove helpful.

"The first was a guy they called Jersey Joe, a semi-retired fisherman. He used to net horseshoe crabs, bring them back and forth to the lab, even helped Joe Teller bleed them on occasion. He liked Teller," Rasheed said aside. "Thought Berger was a real asshole."

"The second was an itinerant handyman named Sam, one big sonofabitch that had been a decent heavyweight club fighter until someone cracked his head with a two by four in a brawl."

"Sounds like you met some real characters," Dan observed.

"Yeah, and none of them had last names in that place. Kind of made me feel like I was in Little Italy. You know…Sam the Plumber, Tony the Nose, Joey the Bat."

"That's Nicky Nose to you."

Rasheed laughed. "I'll get it right one of these days. Anyway, this Sam was hired to keep the place clean, not just sweep up, I mean really clean," he emphasized. "Every night at six he would go in and scrub the floors, walls, benches, everything, with a strong disinfectant. He said it smelled worse than a hospital. Berger screamed like hell at him one time because he saw some dust on the ceiling." For emphasis Martin added, "The whole room wasn't more than five hundred square feet and it took this guy like six hours every day to scrub it, so you can imagine what they expected. Jersey Joe said you could eat off the floor."

"Sounds like they required sterile room conditions."

"I don't know, but here's the interesting part. We talked about a lot of things and then I hit on the other lab people. Apparently, there was only one other guy who spent more than a day or two there during the whole period that Teller and Berger worked there, another scientist named John Kempler who just happens to have died in a mysterious one-car accident about four years ago. Kempler had told both Sam and Joe he was a former NIH scientist who was being paid a lot of money by some New York people to help set up an experiment. You know what Kempler's specialty was?" Martin asked, heightening the drama. "Blood disease. Human blood disease."

Rasheed let it sink in and was about to continue when Dan's phone rang.

"Hi, love you," Marilyn greeted him, "and can't wait to see you."

"Hi yourself. Same here. I'm in a meeting. Can I call you back?"

"Better not, I'm inundated. Just two quick things. Okay if I stay over tonight? I'll cook," she promised.

"Silly question. Be there at seven and I'll cook. What's next?"

"The light blue label on your blonde girlfriend's package?"

"She's not my girlfriend. What about it?"

"It's not a universal symbol, so it must represent something private. Does that help?"

"Almost as much as your love," Dan said. "See you tonight."

Martin watched as his partner furrowed his brow and stared at his desktop, seemingly oblivious to his presence. Finally, turning again to Rasheed, he suggested he finish his story, though it now attracted less of his attention.

Martin concluded, "That's about it. Kempler told them what he did at the lab and I thought you'd like to hear it."

"I did, and it's important. What about Kempler's accident?"

"Apparently he got drunk and drove off a causeway down in the Tidewater area late one night. They dragged out the car and body."

"Hmm, a convenient coincidence."

Eventually they found Al Wilson and Dan orchestrated a ten minute update, disclosing everything but his most recent dinner with the Barracci family, referring instead to an anonymous informant as a lead to Albert Tataro. "He's our next target," Dan said, finishing the briefing. "We'll tackle that together," he promised his partner.

"What will you do with Dr. Kyme's lead?" Wilson wondered.

"Rasheed's got some pavement work to do, notifying every Manhattan hospital that we need a records check on HIV samples sent to the doctors' group practice."

"Why not to Nuremberg?" the Lieutenant wondered.

"Because Berger picked up the samples and I think he got them at the group practice. That would deflect anyone's interest away from Nuremberg. Besides, I'm not sure all those samples were filed and handled properly. Everything was treated so secretively, I wouldn't put anything past those doctors, including the stealing of blood samples."

"The problem I see," Wilson predicted, "is that you'll alert the doctors to how close you are. Someone at some hospital will let them know you're snooping."

"Good point," the Sergeant conceded. "We need a cover."

"NIH always works," Wilson reminded him. "Those bureaucratic bastards are forever auditing records."

"Sounds like a winner."

Costa called a regulatory officer at NIH in Atlanta, advising him of their plan. He received no objection, but was asked to forward an advisement of any impropriety they uncovered, which he promised to do.

Rasheed was given a phony NIH ID and briefed by Dan as to how to act and what to ask for. "Remember, you're an obnoxious, pea-brained bureaucrat who wouldn't recognize a violation if it bit you in the ass."

"Who should I call to make an appointment?"

"Nobody. NIH has the same audit authority as OSHA and FDA. Just show up, announce yourself, ask for the Blood Lab Manager and tell him or her that you're conducting a random audit. They won't like it but they'll have to comply. The nice thing about it is that they'll leave you alone, won't even know what you're recording. Start with the hospitals that Steinberg and Norville are affiliated with. Those bastards may have built a hell of a network so you'll have to move fast."

Martin loaded a briefcase with a small camera, some pads, an audio recorder and the computerized hospitals file.

"I'm on my way," he announced. "See you in the morning."

"I don't want to see you until you've hit every hospital," Dan told him. As an afterthought he added, "And I wouldn't tell Tonya what you're up to. I'm sure we can trust her, but to let her in on anything would only place her in jeopardy."

"Gotcha'," Rasheed concurred as he rushed off.

While Dan was debating exactly how he would approach Rinaldi and Tataro, Al Wilson dropped himself in Martin's chair, stretching to ease his ever-aching back.

"Why don't you try an acupuncturist?" Dan suggested. "They help a lot of people with stiff backs. What have you got, arthritis?"

"Yeah. They call it degenerative spinal arthritis. I call it a pain in the ass."

"I'm sure it's not fun," Dan commiserated.

"So, when you comin' for dinner?" Wilson asked, shifting uncomfortably. "Damn, how does the boy sit in this thing? Damn thing's not designed for no human backside," he continued complaining, as Dan picked up the phone and dialed a number.

"New York City Morgue, Dr. Kyme speaking."

"Thought you were inundated."

"I am. Just stopped because I knew you were calling."

"Beautiful and clever. How lucky can I be? We've been invited to my boss's house Wednesday night. Is that okay?"

"Only if you'll love me to death afterwards," she said, lowering her voice.

"Sounds good. I'll tell Lieutenant Wilson, he's right here."

"Don't you dare. Love you," and she hung up.

"Would Camille mind if I bring a date?"

"Of course not. May I assume it's a shapely cadaver carver?"

"Yep. Disgusting occupation, but she has a way of making me forget it."

"Be careful boy, that kind can get you hooked and married real easy."

"The hookin's already done," Costa admitted, "and I'm not sure I'd object to marriage."

"Well, if you feel that way, it might not be so bad," Wilson said approvingly, wincing as he started to stand. "Wednesday it is. I'll tell Camille seven?"

"Seven it is."

Dan called Massimo Barracci. Pam Donaldson answered and made some small talk until the Don picked up. They exchanged traditional respects before he got to his point.

"I'm getting ready, today, maybe tomorrow, to talk to Rinaldi and Tataro. Normally I would just go to their homes or businesses, talk to them there, but I'd appreciate your opinion." Barracci reveled in such displays of respect.

"They hang out at the Medici Social Club on Riverside Drive," the Don said. "They'll probably be there all afternoon, but they're not going to say anything in front of the family, you know that."

"Yeah, but sooner or later I have to talk to them. I've got to start the ball rolling. After two, maybe three interrogations one of them will slip up, contradict something the other said. Then maybe we'll have something to turn one of them. I don't see it happening any other way."

"Yeah, I guess you gotta' start someplace," Barracci conceded, unhappy that he hadn't come up with a better idea, "but better crack them fast, because if DePalma thinks they pissed in his face, like makin' a hit he didn't order, those two guys are already dead. I mean they won't last the night."

"I understand and I know that could happen. They could also let those doctors know we're onto everything and that could make them run where we'd never find them. They've got enough money to do it."

"Except," the Don reminded, "you said there's a lot of money involved in whatever that project is. If those doctors are the greedy bastards you think, then maybe they won't want to bail out. Maybe they'll think they can get around an investigation and still end up with the money. You know what I mean?"

"Yeah, that's a point," Dan agreed.

His pride and position restored, the Don excused himself, wishing Dan good luck. "And watch your back. Tataro's too stupid to be afraid of anything."

Barracci's last advice haunted Dan as he drove down the BQE towards the Verazzano and Riverside Drive. He would soon be very visible to both the mob and the suspects, including the psychotic Albert "Two Ton" Tataro. He began to consider the feasibility of fermenting a confrontation and blowing Tataro away just to keep him from killing anyone else. The thought warranted more consideration as he realized that Marilyn's inclusion in his life couldn't be concealed forever, particularly if they wanted to find a way to get to him. Exposing her to such a danger wasn't acceptable under any circumstance.

The Medici S.C. resembled most Italian-American clubs in New York. Disguised as a tavern to justify its liquor license, admittance was restricted to the few dozen members of the DePalma family, some fringe associates and "wannabes". From the latter were chosen the bartenders, cooks and cleaning men, ensuring secrecy without privation.

On the first floor there was a bar and restaurant in which the card games, dining and drinking took place. A private room or two might be reserved for high-level meetings, craps and money counting. Upstairs there were bedrooms for sexual activity as the needs arose. Wise guys were notorious for womenizing, something of a right of passage that escalated to a way of life, and it wasn't restricted to maintaining a mistress. Most clubs regularly invited young prostitutes who could earn a couple of thousand dollars an evening without working very hard, a nice arrangement if you were indifferent enough to ignore the cigar smoke, garlic breath and same old ugly faces.

The door was locked, so he knocked, took out his gold shield and held it before the eyehole, waiting while curious pedestrians slowed to see what was going on. He was about to pound the door when it opened and he was confronted with the sullen face of Albert Tataro.

"What do ya' want?" he grunted.

"Sergeant Costa, NYPD. I'd like to speak to Albert Tataro and Carlo Rinaldi."

"They ain't here," and the door began to close.

Dan stopped it with his foot.

"Albert, I don't think Mr. DePalma wants to hear that the police forced their way into his club just to drag you and Carlo downtown, particularly not when you had been given the opportunity to talk to me right here."

Tataro turned away to listen to some muffled instructions. Shortly, he opened the door and motioned Dan in.

Thick cigar smoke clouded the Medici, though the expected bouquet of simmering tomato sauce and garlic held its own. He was ushered to a table in the rear, past glowering unnamed faces not unlike those of the bocci alleys and card-rooms of his youth.

Italian men took their cards and dining seriously, and in that respect, they all looked and acted alike, basically ignoring their uninvited guest. Dan Costa would have been treated no differently had he been a made man.

Tataro stopped beside a table at which three men with napkins efficiently tucked inside their shirts were busily attacking piles of linguini, meatballs and sausage. A plate holding a half-eaten portion belonged to Tataro. They stopped slurping long enough to measure Costa.

"What can we do for you?" a short, rotund under-boss asked while prying particles from his teeth with a fork.

"I need to talk to Albert Tataro and Carlo Rinaldi about a problem we're having over in Manhattan. Maybe we could use one of those rooms?" Dan suggested, pointing to the two doors along the back wall.

"You gotta' talk to Carlo and Albert, huh?" he asked as if to ensure he had heard correctly. "Suppose they don't want to talk because they haven't done nothin'?"

Dan listened while he studied the man's features, finally deciding that his baldpate and wide-set bulging eyes made him look like a frog.

"Then I'll come back with a warrant, search this place, arrest them and embarrass the hell out of Mr. DePalma. I'm sure he'd love to know that you brought all that down because you're a little asshole trying to play big-shot." Dan fixed his eyes on the pudgy little toad whose expression changed suddenly, reflecting newfound concern and diminishing confidence.

"They're my employees," he protested. "They don't talk to no one unless they're told why."

"Fine. I'll be very happy to tell them, in private, back there," and he pointed again to the doors.

The frog deliberated, looking first at Tataro and then Rinaldi.

Alright," he conceded, "but neither one of you guys has to say anything you don't want to. Understand? He starts strong armin' and you come out here. We don't need to take any of his shit," he assured them, his confidence partly restored.

"After you," Dan said to Tataro.

The toad interjected. "No, you gotta' start with Carlo. Mr. Tataro just got a call from his sick mother. He gotta' return it."

Dan couldn't help laughing, but agreed. His concession was unimportant. DePalma's lieutenant would counsel Tataro, obviously believing he was the bigger risk, though Dan believed he was unaware of what had brought him there. Now he would have the opportunity to play Tataro against whatever Rinaldi said. It might work out better that way. He just had to be careful not to push either man to a point where they would alert the doctors.

*'What a menagerie,'* Dan thought as the rodent-faced Rinaldi seated himself.

"Mr. Rinaldi," he started, "I suggest that you come up with an excuse for this little talk, because I don't think you'll want your bosses to know why I'm really here."

Rinaldi's expression didn't change.

"You may have had absolutely nothing to do with it, but we have two different informants…you know, mob informants…who swear that you arranged the shooting of Joseph Teller and Lewis Berger, that you did it for some unknown conspirators and that you did it for money."

Rinaldi continued staring at his interrogater without flinching.

"Our informants also suggest that we offer you protection because even though Mr. DePalma knows nothing of your involvement right now, when he does learn of it, your lives will be forfeited, or so our informants believe."

Costa waited for a reaction. Rinaldi gave none.

"We can sit here all day, Carlo, or you can offer a comment. It's up to you, but I wouldn't stay in here too much longer if I were you. Froggy out there might take it the wrong way, if you know what I mean."

Without taking his eyes off Dan, Rinaldi pulled a pack of cigarettes from a shirt pocket, lit one and blew the smoke towards him. "I don't know what you're talking about," he finally said.

Dan was impressed with his cool confidence.

"Does that mean you don't know Teller and Berger, or that you didn't kill them, or that you don't think Mr. DePalma will have you anchored to a garbage scow when he finds out?"

"It means I don't know what you're talking about," he repeated in the same monotone.

"You know, Carlo, if you weren't such a piece of shit, I'd probably let you listen to the informants' tapes. I think they know Tony the Hand better than you, and if they say he'd wax you, I think I'd give it some thought." Using DePalma's sobriquet, which Barracci had disclosed, got Rinaldi's attention.

"I told you, I don't know what the fuck you're talking about," he repeated, this time with less composure.

"Come on, Carlo, am I supposed to believe those two guys don't know what went down. The Attorney General's office pays them ten times what you earn to keep us posted on everything from drugs to money laundering. Some unauthorized hit on the side by two nobodies…they're going to lie about that and get thrown off the gravy train? They'd be crazy to bull-shit us."

Rinaldi snuffed the cigarette and lit another, his eyes no longer settled on the detective. Costa felt the vibration from the suspect's foot tapping nervously, watching as he rolled the lighter between his fingers. Playing a hunch, he changed strategy.

"Look, Carlo, we all know those guys aren't lying, and if you heard the tapes you'd understand why. I won't eliminate the possibility that they're wrong for putting you at the scene, but they swear Albert made the hit and that you helped him set everything up, which makes you as guilty as that gorilla. If they're wrong about you, I'll listen to whatever you have to say. I'll keep an open mind and maybe work out a deal for you."

Dan had given Rinaldi an out and he was seriously thinking about it until the door flew open.

The frog entered first, followed by a stuffed suit and the simian Tataro.

"This is Richard Musto, Mr. Rinaldi's attorney. He says you have no right to force anyone here to talk to you," the underboss announced.

The attorney stepped forward, a gratuitous smile etched on his chubby face.

Dan couldn't escape the irony. "I must say, you do fit, Counselor."

Musto cocked his head. "I don't understand, Sergeant. It is Sergeant, isn't it?"

"Yes it is. Sergeant Costa, to be exact. What is it you don't understand?"

"Your reference to my fitting something."

"Oh it's nothing. I was just thinking of how people sometimes look like their dogs, maybe other animals…that's all."

"So? What the hell's your point?"

"Nothing much. It's just odd how...now please don't take this the wrong way...but all you guys, you kind of look like, well, it's like a zoo in here."

"You're real funny for a two-bit flatfoot I can buy and sell with the change in my pocket. So what does that make you?"

Tataro stood behind Musto, nudging him forward, eager to make his move, but the lawyer restrained him.

"Relax, Albert, there's no need to lower yourself to the Sergeant's level. Besides, he'll be leaving now."

"Right again, Counselor. Just as soon as your client gets his hat and coat we'll be leaving together."

All eyes turned towards the suddenly nervous Rinaldi.

Surprised but still confident, Musto said, "Oh, really? Just where and why are you taking him, may I ask?"

"To jail for murder."

"What the fuck's he talkin' about, Carlo?" the frog croaked. "What'd you tell him?"

The lawyer kept his composure. "Just what murder are you accusing Mr. Rinaldi of having committed?" he asked calmly.

"Mr. Rinaldi? Who said anything about Mr. Rinaldi? Did I say anything about you?" he asked the relieved Carlo before turning a serious eye towards Tataro. "It's Mr. Tataro who's going to jail for the murder of Joseph Teller. Mr. Rinaldi is only a witness."

It took a few seconds for everything to register. Then simultaneously, the toad hurled threats at Rinaldi who shrieked his innocence while the slowly calculating Tataro began moving forward, not sure whether the cop or his friend would be his first target. Musto, unfortunately in his path to both, was catapulted over a table and chair in the process. The ape's progress now unimpeded, he charged Costa who deftly pivoted on his left leg, drawing his right back and delivering it with the greatest force possible to his assailant's groin, turning the Tataro family jewels to a darker shade of blue. The floor shook as it absorbed the falling giant, who lay there, frozen in pain and gasping for air. Dan poised for another attack but no one moved. The missing portion of the fourth plate of linguini spilled from the stricken Tataro as Dan stepped over him. Musto lay motionless, a trickle of blood oozing from what looked like a badly broken nose.

"I'd take care of him if I were you," Dan suggested to the speechless underboss, as he extracted his phone and called for assistance. "You sure you don't want to accompany Albert and me downtown, Carlo?"

"Fuck you, cop. I didn't say nothin' and you know it. And I ain't your damn witness because I didn't see nothin' and Albert didn't do nothin'."

"Didn't do nothin'? You better get your eyes checked, Carlo. I clearly saw your friend toss Mr. Musto about ten feet, not to mention the fact that he attacked a police officer in the routine performance of his duties."

To the still recovering frog he simply wondered, "Who do you think is going to cause you more grief over all of this...us poor cops, or Mr. DePalma?"

The frog swallowed hard.

Tataro's trip to Manhattan's Thirty-fourth Street Stationhouse was rerouted for a visit to Mt. Sinai Medical Center where he was delivered in the same fetal position in which the EMTs had found him. The doctors administered drugs to reduce the swelling and ease the pain, before retaining the victim overnight for observation. Dan got the call as he completed the paperwork on Tataro's assault charges. It was a small victory, but he knew bond would be posted before daylight. Still that would give him a chance to interrogate that evening. He filled Al Wilson in as they left headquarters, the Lieutenant for his trip home in the tedious, never-ending West Side traffic, Dan for his drive to Mount Sinai.

"Remember; dinner tomorrow evening. Don't even think about canceling," Wilson warned as he carefully positioned his back on the seat of the unmarked Buick LeSabre, property of the NYPD.

"We'll be there," his friend waved. "Just don't bust chops."

Wilson smiled. "You're in no position to give orders, lover boy," he called out as he drove off, determined to find a suitable test for the younger couple's sense of humor.

The uniformed officer posted outside Tataro's room recognized Dan.

"He hasn't moved much, Sergeant. Moaned a few times, cursed a lot. That's about it."

"Anybody try to see him?"

"Just doctors and nurses."

"You going to be on all night?"

The young officer looked at his watch. "No, Sir, I've already pulled a double. In ten minutes I'll be relieved."

Dan checked his own watch; five-fifty. "Okay, let me know when you leave."

## LIMULUS

Albert Tataro looked gargantuan lying on the diminutive hospital bed, his oversized head covering the pillow. Stretched out straight on his back, a sheet covered a large, humped object resting on his lower abdomen. Dan guessed it was a bag of ice.

Tataro's eyes were closed, his face periodically wincing in pain.

Dan heard the door behind him open. A blonde pixie in a starched nurse's outfit quietly glided in. As she passed, he caught an unusually heady scent, one he didn't recognize but thought he liked. He waited for her to check the cold pack, take a pulse and record it on the patient's chart.

"You smell very nice," he whispered. "May I ask what it is?"

"Capricci," she responded with an inviting smile, drifting over next to him. "Would you like a closer smell?" she asked, arching her feet and tilting her neck.

Caught off-guard he stammered, "That's a very tempting offer." He bent his head, breathed in and smiled. "Capricci," he repeated. "I gotta' remember that."

"Maybe you should remember this, too," she said, pulling her ID badge closer to him. "Barbara Trent. I get off at six, but I'm in the phone book if you're busy tonight. Call me sometime," she suggested as she left the room with Dan's eyes following her out the door.

*Marilyn, the things I sacrifice for you.*

Tataro forced his eyes open and struggled to focus, finally signaling with clenched fists that he recognized his visitor. A painful reaction cut short his attempt to speak.

"I'm sorry I had to do that, Albert, really I am," Dan lied, "but I didn't feel like getting killed, and you looked like you were in the mood."

He sat down in a chair beside the bed "You got a bigger problem than some busted balls, because Carlo won't provide you with an alibi for the night Joe Teller was killed. You remember Teller, the little old guy you killed down by Canal Street? You tried to make it look like a mugging, and you know what? If your friend...yeah, Carlo...if he hadn't shot his mouth off to some wise-guys about how you plugged Teller, then we would never have been able to trace it to you. You would have gotten away with it, but then he bragged to a guy who's an informant and we got everything. I knew the only stumbling block would be Rinaldi swearing you two were off someplace else together, but he's not offering that, probably figuring he can cut himself a deal if he turns on you."

Tataro gave no hint of what he was thinking, but Dan sensed he was holding out the possibility that his friend could have told some other wise guys about the killing, and if that were true, then there might be something to his refusal to offer an alibi. The other possibility was that he was just trying to figure out how to get out of bed and strangle the guy who had ruptured his balls.

Tataro's hate-filled eyes remained fixed on Dan until the officer-on-watch opened the door.

"I'm off, Sergeant."

Dan left the room to meet the replacement, Patrolman Luis Sandoval, one of the many minorities that were changing the face of the uniformed ranks.

Dan summarized the circumstances that had landed Tataro in the hospital and of his involvement in Teller's murder. Sandoval acknowledged remembering the case.

"So, no one, and I do mean no one, enters this room unless you eyeball their ID and ensure it's a legitimate doctor or nurse. Unless you're positive, you tell them to come back with the nurse-in-charge."

Before he left that evening, Costa introduced the head nurse to Sandoval, repeating his precautionary instructions.

Another attempt to get Tataro to talk failed, so Dan gave up, but not before promising him that he was a walking dead-man, if not by DePalma's order, then by his own hand.

"One way or the other, Albert, you're going to pay. Your easiest way out is to talk. That way you only have a judge to worry about. At least you'll have your life. Any other way, you die. If the capo doesn't do it, I will," he threatened as he left.

Tataro had plenty to think about. Tony DePalma may not have been the most influential family head in New York; in fact, he was probably the least respected, but he was one of the most feared. A long-time soldier, he had paid his dues with more than a dozen rumored killings and a reputation for carrying out his threats. Word had it that you could trust him implicitly, as a friend or enemy, to do what he promised, and both Rinaldi and Tataro had been warned to lay low, advice they had ignored. Coupled with the risk to which they had exposed Steinberg and Norville, and the futures of the two wise guys were understandably in doubt. On the doctors' behalf, and for a healthy fee, Musto could easily persuade DePalma to give the orders, while making Tony the Hand believe it was in his best interest. Dan wondered how much time he would have to break one of them. Keeping Tataro in protective custody was important enough to speak to the D.A. first thing in the morning.

On the way home he stopped to purchase an ounce of Capricci and two bottles of Asti Spumante. The sweet, sparkling wine seemed expensive at twenty dollars a bottle. The perfume cost more than twice that. Both, he thought, would be well worth it.

He pounded the boneless chicken breasts with the flat of a cleaver before dipping them in a butter, garlic and lemon mixture and coating them with flavored flour and breadcrumbs. Sautéed in butter, olive oil and a squirt of Marsala they would emerge as his version of Chicken Francese, a treat for which more than a few Manhattan ladies had shown extraordinary gratitude.

The fresh asparagus spears were tenderized in a steamer while he washed escarole and rudiccio for a salad that would include sliced cucumbers, tomatoes and red onion. Balsamic vinegar and olive oil spiced with basil and oregano would serve as dressing. He had considered the addition of stuffed mushrooms, opting instead in the interest of time for fresh garlic bread, the specialty of a nearby bakery.

He covered the chicken with tin foil to keep it warm, set the table and lit two candles. As he was checking the temperature of the chilling Asti, the doorbell rang.

Marilyn Kyme had to be tired, but all he saw were the soft green eyes and tantalizing smile. He took the overnight bag from her before wrapping his arm around her, kissing her and kicking the door shut.

"Missed you."

"Me, too," she said in that way of hers that made him want to undress and love her on the spot. He pushed himself away, toting the bag and her coat to the bedroom.

"Everything's ready," he announced on his return. "Wanna' freshen up first?"

"I'd rather have you make love to me," she said lustily, "but I'm absolutely starved, so I need nourishment first, then a shower. After that, Daniel Costa, I am going to let you ravage me, but only if you do it slowly and gently."

"That's not being ravaged," he corrected her as he discarded the tin foil and placed decorative lemon wedges around the chicken.

She came up behind him and pressed her body to his. "If you want to ravage me you have to do it my way," she demanded. "Otherwise, I might eat, drink and go to sleep. Then what will you have to ravage."

"Ravaging a beautifully erotic woman in her sleep can be fun," he replied, turning as he did and running his hands over her backside, cupping her tightening cheeks.

"Oh, God, stop," she pleaded with a smile, pushing him away. "What are we going to do, Dan? We can't even look at each other without wanting to jump into bed."

"We're going to sit down and eat this artistically prepared cuisine. Then you're going to shower while I wash the dishes. Then I'm going to take my shower."

He began serving the food.

"Then what?" she asked petulantly.

"Then, Susan," he started in his best Cary Grant, "I'm going to start kissing you at the top of your head and not stop until I reach the bottom of your feet. Now you might not like that, Susan, but that's the way it's going to be, even if it takes all night."

"Don't say another word. Just hurry up and eat," she begged.

"That was exquisite. My compliments to the chef," she said dreamily, draining the last of the Asti. "Time for my shower."

"Got something for you to wear. Here," and he handed her the Capricci.

"Hmmm, I love it," she said, sniffing the tiny cap, "but I hardly think it will cover me. What else should I wear?"

"That and your birthday suit will do just fine," he replied, as he gathered the dishes and carried them to the sink.

When he had finished he peeked in the bedroom to see her lying on her back beneath the covers, eyes closed. He started to wonder, but was shortly relieved when he heard her whisper, "Don't take too long or I'll start without you."

Within minutes he had showered, run a razor over the day's growth and patted on some French-sounding aftershave that promised to drive women to unspeakable lengths. As he flicked off the switch and rounded the corner the bedroom lights suddenly went on, exposing Marilyn, lying buck-naked on the bed. She bit her lip, watching him react to the sight of her writhing, before closing her eyes and throwing her head back in anticipation.

## CHAPTER 15

Convinced by Dan's report that Rinaldi was not likely to turn against his friend and face the wrath of every wise guy in the city, the D.A.'s office hesitated to charge Tataro. The absence of corroborating eyewitness testimony, a murder weapon and other tangible evidence at the scene made the securing of an indictment improbable at best. A sympathetic Assistant Prosecutor acknowledged Dan's reputation and trusted his judgement, but predicted that under the circumstances nothing short of a confession was going to justify issuance of a warrant.

"I know you wouldn't be here unless you were convinced of the suspect's guilt," he had said, "but you've got to give us something we can use in court."

Al Wilson and Rasheed Martin were listening to his account of the meeting when the phone rang.

"It's for you," Wilson said, handing the phone to Costa.

An excited Joe D exclaimed that he had an i.d. on his dad's killer, a young black male who had tried to pawn a gold and silver crucifix and a diamond studded tie clasp at a shop on Avenue J, just six blocks from the apartment. The shop owner had picked the guy out from a mug shot.

"He's not exactly a dead ringer for John Kuhn's sketch, but he's close enough for me to believe we got the right guy," Joe said.

"What's his rap sheet?"

"Name's Jesse Booker, age 20, Afro-American. Last known address is up on 169th Street. He's been arrested fourteen times with eight convictions; only served time twice because he was still a minor when six of the charges were made. This piece of shit has served a total of eight months in jail. Can you believe that? Eight months for five burglaries, two possessions with intent to sell and an aggravated assault. One of the six arrests that was never prosecuted involved a fatal beating. When the victim died they had no witness, and in another two he beat women senseless, but they wouldn't testify because he lived in their neighborhood, was underage and they figured he'd come back for them."

"What are his personals?"

"Let's see, uh, five-foot ten, one-sixty."

"Left-handed?"

"Yep, left-handed, just like Dante said."

"What's your next move?"

"Calvin and I are waiting on Ron Williams. He'll be here any minute. I've already got the warrant."

"That's good news, Joe. Let me know how the arrest goes, and thanks for calling."

Costa relayed the report to his boss and partner, both of whom expressed relief that his ordeal might soon be over.

"It might be good that you've got a heavy caseload right now, something to keep your mind occupied," Wilson noted. "Why don't you two go over what Rasheed got on those HIV samples and then let me know what you intend to do next."

Costa and Martin retired to their desks where the younger officer provided copies of his findings. Over a three-year period twelve area hospitals, including two in New Jersey, had forwarded almost a thousand blood samples to the doctors' group practice in Manhattan, the majority suspected of being HIV infected. Those that weren't seemed to be random samplings with no particular contaminants, or at least none that had been recorded. All were supposedly for their analysis prior to recommending treatment programs, advice for which they were handsomely paid. Whether in fact they had conducted any tests, analyzed the results or done any of the work for which they had been compensated, Martin hadn't yet determined. What he did establish in a hundred of the instances was that taped recommendations, each accompanied by a signed statement by one of the two doctors, had been sent back to the patients' attending physicians, all in conformance with government and insurance carriers' regulations. Rasheed had scanned the doctors' letters and found that only one drug in two different dosages constituted the full scope of their recommendations.

"They could have thrown darts at a board or picked numbers from a hat and a clerk could have printed the letters. The victim's name, blood sample number and testing dates were the only things different," he concluded, "and I think you know the address of the doctors' analytical lab."

Dan just nodded. "I'm sure I do. What did they call it?"

"Oh, they were very creative: The Nuremberg Life Science Laboratory."

"I was so damn worried these bastards had covered their ties to that lab. Here it is in official records. It just proves that sooner or later, every shit screws up somehow. All we gotta' do is keep snoopin'."

His partner agreed. "What do I do next?"

"What do you think?" Before he could respond, Dan said, "Keep in mind that everything you do should be with an eye towards having to build a case in court."

Martin understood the point. "We got a tie to the lab, we got the samples going there and we got these analyses going back to the victims' physicians." He kept thinking. "But we don't have actual lab test data. The computers? Is that what you mean?"

"That's one thing." Dan gave him another minute to think before making his point. "There has to be an inspector from some agency like the FDA's Bureau of Biologics that's familiar with the lab because the ones dealing with human blood are under strict government control. Start with them. Find the inspector that licensed or audited that lab. He should be able to provide us with everything that went on there, including the purpose of those crabs. The more we understand about their work, the easier it will be to figure out a motive."

When Rasheed left, Dan began wondering if in fact the lab's sole purpose had been HIV detection in blood samples, in which case, Teller could have been murdered because the test results were being dummied in order to sell certain drugs. He dismissed the idea quickly. Two of the world's foremost enzymologists wouldn't have been needed for such a mission, nor would the extraordinary security measures have been required. Blood labs were widely publicized, their work hardly sensitive, at least not that of the analytical labs. Dan assured himself that the blood samples were diverted to Nuremberg for a far more important and lucrative purpose than HIV detection.

He phoned his favorite MD.

She sounded tired. "You're making me feel guilty," he said.

"You should be," Marilyn said, before admitting, "I'm fine, just absorbed in my work and thinking about seeing you tonight."

"Yeah, well, we got the Wilsons tonight, don't forget. I'll pick you up at work around five."

"Okay, but let's not stay too late. I'm sleeping at your place. So did you call to make sure I hadn't forgotten about the Wilsons?"

"Nope, got a question for you. How does a lab determine if blood is HIV infected?"

"Simple. If it's taken from a person with HIV, it's infected."

"Ha-ha. Now be serious."

"You put a smear on a slide, stick it under a microscope and if it looks like HIV and swims like HIV, then it's HIV."

"So it's visual."

"Bingo. Give that man one hot and hungry lover," she said, lowering her voice.

"Don't start, the day's too damn long." He asked, "So we don't need those horseshoe crabs, or a lot of secrecy, or anything like that?"

"No, just a way to get rid of the blood because it's contagious as hell."

Dan realized he should have thought of that. "How does the government require you to dispose of HIV infected blood?"

"There are companies licensed to treat it. All the labs have to do is package and label it a certain way and contract with a licensed disposal firm. Both have a lot of paperwork to do and the files have to be kept for, I think, seven years, but it's all spelled out for them. Why don't you call the FDA? They have a Manhattan office and I'm sure they can put you on the right track."

When he hung up, he called his partner and filled him in on what Marilyn had recommended, reminding him to locate the disposal firm and secure their records of any Nuremberg pickups. Then he called Clarence Worthington and summarized the evidence indicating Teller's involvement in some sort of blood research, possibly HIV. The good Doctor agreed to meet him after two, enough time to drive to Mt. Sinai Medical Center where he found Albert Tataro sitting in bed watching cartoons.

The ill-tempered giant clicked off the TV before bellowing, "Waddaya' doin here? My lawyer says I don't hafta' talk to you about nothin', so get the fuck out."

"Hey Albert, relax. I've already told you I'm sorry, but I wasn't about to stand there and let you take me apart." Dan wondered if the big dunce might be stupid enough to be conned by someone who had almost turned him into a eunuch.

Tataro wasn't a total moron. "Fuck you," he repeated, "and fuck all you asshole cops. I ain't forgettin' what you did."

"You don't want to do anything stupid, Albert, because the whole force knows you want a piece of me, and that just gives me license to blow your head off. Anyway, I don't want to see you dead," he lied, "because I know you were put up to the Teller murder by Carlo. I'll bet he didn't even split the two hundred thousand with you."

That got Albert's attention. He eyed Dan suspiciously.

"Aha, so you didn't even get a hundred g's, and here you are takin' all the heat. How much did he give you?"

Tataro thought for a while. "You ain't trickin' me," he finally announced. "I don't know nothin' about no two hundred big ones, no guy named Teller and no killin'. And I'm still gonna' get ya' someday."

Dan reminded Tataro that connected people were willing to swear to his having been the triggerman and that calls last night and again this morning had linked him to Lewis Berger's murder at the Castle Rock Motel in Hackettstown, the last a complete fabrication, but it sounded good.

"I'm your only hope of not frying, Albert. You think Carlo or Tony DePalma is going to sit in your lap when they pull the switch? Why protect them if they don't give a damn about you? You ever think of that? I feel sorry for you, I really do. You'll go to the chair, Carlo will get off and DePalma will keep your share of the two hundred big ones. You're a fuckin' dummy." He let it sink in before heading for the door.

"And think about this. Everybody in the family knows you and Carlo took the contract because Tony was pushing you out. So now the sonofabitch that put you on the spot to begin with, he's the one who winds up with your money. Nice move, Albert, you dumb piece of shit," and he walked out, not altogether convinced he had accomplished anything.

Tataro hadn't given up anything Costa hadn't already known…that he was the trigger, Carlo had been the point, that they had gotten paid and therefore DePalma, the family head, had probably not been involved. That Albert Tataro would ever testify against the doctors was a longshot, and without that, the case against them would require significantly more evidence and a great deal more effort. How much of either remained was a growing concern.

Unhappily, he drove to Columbia University where he found Clarence Worthington immersed in an experiment, surrounded by bubbling beakers, acidic fumes and billowing vapor. Unwashed glassware and lab apparatus covered the bench tops.

"How are you, Sergeant? Come in, please," he offered. "After studying Teller's journal, as coded and proprietary a document as I have ever reviewed, I decided to embark on some work on your behalf. I'm well into it, though to the present not wholly successfully, I'm ashamed to report."

"Nonetheless, I appreciate the effort."

"Yes, well, I also decided to restore my memory of what little I once knew of Snively's work. I convinced myself after considering our first go-round that if Dr. Teller had been eliminated due to a disagreement over a discovery of some magnitude that it might indeed be related to our limulus friend. Some entries in his journal seem to support that line of reasoning, though as I first alluded, he coded everything so well that I am having difficulty synergizing his entries with Snively's text. Upon revisiting Snively's publication I now recall just how taken he was with the prospects of his thesis. Teller might well have been equally enthused and therefore, took up the proverbial gauntlet."

The transition Dan's mind had to make from the one syllable obscenities of Albert Tataro to the scientific jargon of Clarence Worthington, Ph.D., was not an easy one, though he enjoyed the challenge as well as the professor's company.

"Snively was an interesting fellow," Worthington reminisced, gazing out a window, "quite intelligent, very creative and industrious as the proverbial beaver, just not overly considerate of the feelings of others. To the contrary, he could be quite offensive and almost always arbitrary. Small wonder that anyone ever remained in his employ long enough to really determine precisely what he was about. Mind you, the bleeding of limulus for analytical purposes was not peculiar to Snively's research. Others had done it before, and in fact, during the period of his experiments. It was the blue blood, I think, that so fascinated them."

"Well, to continue," he said, turning his attention back to his visitor, "I secured some limulus serum from a colleague out on Long Island and have been busy separating dissimilar proteins. I was about to chromatographically purify them when you arrived, so if you'll permit me a few minutes, I shall complete the set-up and we shall see what the gods have in the offing." Without hesitation he moved off.

The Detective Sergeant watched as the aging scientist hoisted glass columns from beneath the benches, setting them on the lab tops, pouring and layering an assortment of powders, liquids and what looked like fibrous paper filters. Briefly holding one up for his benefit, Worthington told Dan that it was comprised of silica and salt, first suspended in a solution and later lyophilized and pressed into a disk.

"We can't expect to achieve in a matter of days what Snively and Teller might have accomplished after years of work, but with the journal and a very large dose of luck we might be able to prove that there is an anti-bacterial agent capable of being isolated. If so, we could assume that Teller had been successful in all of the steps that followed…stabilizing the agent during the chromatographic process, neutralizing its side effects and suspending it in a solution that did not substantially change its structure. Those are the challenges that would have tested their resolve and that kept me from pursuing Snively's lead when I was still young enough to do so."

A half hour passed during which the kindly professor jumped back and forth amongst stations, tweaking here, stretching tubing there, absorbed in, but not quite satisfied with, his effort. Dan looked on, convinced that in his next life he would accept almost any vocation except that of a research scientist. Everything they did, he surmised, took forever.

"If I'm not mistaken, we should be set to proceed," the professor proclaimed, and not a second too soon to suit his visitor.

Worthington turned some T-valves, releasing a brilliantly blue, translucent fluid through a maze of glass rods and plastic tubing into six carefully aligned columns, each filled with a variety of dissimilar materials. From the expression on his face, Dan concluded that the professor was pleased with his progress.

"Now, we must be patient for an hour or so," Worthington announced. "Upon our return we might see a clue to our next step. We serve no catalytic purpose standing here, so let us adjourn to the cafeteria for some refreshment."

Dan convinced him to allow the NYPD to pay for lunch, in which case they needn't suffer Columbia's cafeteria fare. They walked to a small café on the north side of the Museum of Natural Science.

"I applaud your choice," Worthington stated, savoring the baked eggplant with garlic bread. "You appear quite comfortable here," he observed. "A frequent visitor?"

"When my wife died three years ago…."

"Oh, my dear boy," he interrupted, "I am deeply sorry. Please forgive me for exposing old wounds."

"Quite alright, Doctor," Dan assured him. "I'm as over it as I'll ever be. As I was saying, after she died I used to go to the museum every weekend, spend the day from opening to closing. It occupied my mind. It was peaceful, I guess, and gave me a chance to recover." For a brief moment he envisioned Eileen smiling, as she always seemed to. His mood didn't escape the professor's notice.

"We all have our crosses to bear, Sergeant. How we do so dictates how many of life's few pleasures we will get to enjoy."

Upon their return, Worthington went about his work with renewed energy, barking instructions to Costa who had volunteered his assistance. Shortly, they had collected teaspoons of syrupy liquids, which with great care were spread in petri dishes until their surfaces were covered. One by one the scientist examined them in a space age microscope hooked up to PCs and a series of busy printers. On a CRT screen Dan followed the erratic movements of some sperm-like creatures, his attention diverted by the sudden rush of his host to the far wall where row after row of books in apparent disarray were stacked. He selected and discarded a number of them, searching their spines for a specific title or author.

"Here it is," he exclaimed with the enthusiasm of a successful prospector. The manuscript he carried with noticeable care to his desk resembled an old volume of the Britannica Encyclopedia, oversized, maroon leather binding, quite cracked and well used.

Worthington explained as he carefully turned the pages. "Not to bore you, Daniel, but I'm sure you're curious…you are curious about all this, I assume?" He looked to Costa for assurance.

"Of course," Dan replied.

"Very well," he responded intently, though he said nothing more, mystifying his guest as he poured through the manuscript, turning pages with a care worthy of a Gutenburg first edition. He soon laid Teller's brown leather notebook alongside it, comparing entries, jotting numbers. At times perplexed, at others animated, but continually engulfed in deep thought, he remained silent for a quarter of an hour, oblivious to his visitor's presence. Ultimately, he leaned back and studied Dan for a while as if to focus on some indifferent object while his mind took him on a distant journey, before relaxing his frame and rising. He paced thoughtfully, finally turning his attention to his guest.

"Do you think you might be able to secure a small quantity of HIV infected blood for our analysis?"

"I think so. How much would you need?"

"Twenty milliliters would do nicely for now."

Dan dialed his partner's cell phone. He relayed the request together with instructions as to the paperwork he would have to complete, how to find Worthington's office and a reminder to deliver the samples before six. "Take care of it yourself, Rasheed, and give the samples only to Dr. Worthington."

"Got it. Will you be there?" he asked.

"I don't think so," he responded, checking his watch and reminding himself of the traffic he faced in getting to the morgue. "I'll see you in the office in the morning."

"My partner will deliver the samples before six, Doctor. Did you see anything in those dishes that's interesting?"

"Possibly. There are signs of anti-bodies that appear to have properties similar to some described in Snively's initial reports which suggest that we might well be on the right track. That may not be as decisive as you would like, but at the risk of raising your hopes prematurely, I would have to admit that I am surprised by our good fortune. It seems that by a strange combination of design and providence we have deciphered the bulk of Teller's coded formula which in turn appears to duplicate what Snively used to separate a limulus enzyme that once free of accompanying proteins has self-generating properties that are indeed quite singular. It appears to have traits that would allow it to dominate any interfering organisms. That in turn opens up the possibility of anti-viral or anti-bacterial properties. We still have to harvest them properly and find a way to test their resistant strains without destroying them, and that is just the beginning of our effort, but at least we have reached first base, as you colonials are fond of saying."

Dan tried to follow but his expression betrayed his confusion, which didn't escape Worthington's notice.

"Don't be alarmed. If my suspicions are founded, I will be in a position to explain in layman's terms precisely how Snively and Teller uncovered an enzyme in Limulus's blood that absorbs and transforms invasive bodies into harmless waste matter. For now, you need only know that the enzyme in question appears to have characteristics that would not permit it to passively exist with any other aggressive intruder. If so, it would identify itself to a scientist seeking a cure for one of the forms of hepatitis as a potential treatment, and one I might add that would be totally compatible with human blood cells, with little or no chance of serious side-effects."

"Why did you say hepatitis?"

"Because HIV was unknown when Snively first began his limulus based research, and because if I have interpreted his notes correctly, hepatitis was a virus with which he was experimenting long after the introduction of HIV, along with a host of other viruses and bacteria. So you see, we still face a great deal of work, but your access to the infected blood will hasten things along."

"Then why ask for the HIV sample?"

"Because I assume time is somewhat of the essence and there are too many hepatitis strains to test. Secondly, we're not looking to produce a cure overnight, but to put ourselves in a position where we can state with some certainty that there exists a limulus enzyme that can destroy viruses in humans. Finally, none of Teller's working formulas suggest the identity of his objective, but knowing his passion for exploratory research I believe he would prefer to sow his seeds in virgin territory, not in soil planted by another. For now I think we should simply pursue his notes to completion and see what we harvest."

Dan thanked Worthington, reminding him that not only had Teller and Berger been victimized by this intrigue, but that a young programmer had been murdered and countless HIV infected patients had probably received indifferent, if not ineffective, care. He closed by promising that if the scientist provided a clue to the determination of this case, however arcane, he would pursue it to the end and not rest until those guilty had been punished.

"Then it's worth my every effort," Worthington avowed, "and it shall receive it."

Dan was relieved that he had the attention of someone who seemed capable of clarifying the scientific aspects of the case. Confident in the belief that input from an FDA inspector would corroborate whatever Worthington's experiments uncovered, he looked forward to an evening with Marilyn and dinner with the Wilsons.

The traffic was as congested as they expected, but the time passed quickly as it always did when they were together. Marilyn alluded to having purchased an unusually enticing negligee that was secured in her overnight case, but no amount of exhortation on his part could encourage her to reveal more of its design, so he contended himself with fanciful visions of her in a multitude of colors and various degrees of exposure. To entertain those thoughts while conversing on other topics and navigating in heavy traffic took all the concentration he could muster. By the time they arrived in White Plains, he regretted having agreed to a mid-week visit, speculating instead on what they could have been doing in the privacy of his apartment.

The dinner proceeded as Dan had expected, the teenagers behaving perfectly, exhibiting a maturity beyond their years, yet reflecting the energy and outgoing personalities that one would expect of children who had been raised with the right mixture of compassion and discipline. Dan made no secret of his admiration for Al Wilson, secretly hoping that some day he would find the same degree of satisfaction. As for Camille, the years had been more than kind. Though in her early forties, she looked ten years younger, having maintained her figure and avoided telltale wrinkles. Only a few strands of gray were detectable in the rich ebony luster of her hair, a small price to pay for a mother of three and wife of a New York City police officer, enduring sleepless nights, awaiting his safe return from late shift patrols. When they had finished dessert and the children had been sent off to their studies, Camille took Marilyn on a quick tour of the house, narrating the history of her teapot collection, while the men adjourned to Al's basement study. There he poured two snifters of his favorite after-dinner brandy, Chartreuse, a distillation of some twenty herbs concocted by monks in a cloistered French monastery.

"Ever hear the history of this stuff?" Wilson asked.

"No, but I'll bet I'm about to."

"You need some culture, man. Life isn't all about crime and the streets. It's good to learn about things outside your urban existence."

"No argument there. Tell me about Chartreuse."

Only slightly mollified, Wilson handed Costa a half-filled glass glowing with the distinctive green shade that gave the brandy its name.

"A couple of centuries ago," he started, settling himself comfortably in an oversized rocker, "three monks in a cloister outside Lyons began experimenting with wild herbs, at first for medicinal purposes, or so they claimed. Pretty soon they had perfected it to the point where the good friars were belting it down in sickness and in health. Afraid that some of his charges might run off and sell the stuff commercially, that being in violation of their vows of poverty, the Abbott devised a simple scheme. He divided the brandy-making chores into three and then met with each of the monks separately, giving the first brother the job of collecting, storing and measuring the ingredients. He charged the second with the sequence and timing of the addition of the herbs and the third with the temperature and duration of the distillation process. But he also changed some aspect of what each of the three did and then made them swear under oath not to disclose the changes."

Satisfied that he had his friend's attention, Wilson continued. "As he grew older, in fact not much more than a year before he died, he devised a scheme to ensure the continuity of his original plan. To protect against the inevitable deaths of the aging friars, the Abbott had the first learn the job of the second, the second studied the third's and the third apprenticed to the first. As one died, the living backup would train a replacement, ensuring the secrecy of the process."

"Good story, isn't it?" Wilson asked, confident that Dan would have to agree.

"Not as good as it tastes," Dan responded, enjoying the herbal flavor, appreciating the mellow essence.

Wilson shook his head disapprovingly. "No, man, you don't get it. It's the story that distinguishes it…gives it its soul."

"A rose by any other name," Dan reminded him.

"You're hopeless, you know that? Italians are supposed to relish culture. The story is culture."

"Yeah, and probably mythical as hell. I'll bet the Abbott made off with the proceeds and half the monks were drunks. Some enterprising citizen probably paid them all off and the stuff is distilled in a Parisian factory," he said, though he preferred to believe that everything was exactly as Al Wilson had related.

"You are really hopeless," the Lieutenant repeated. "Turnin' into a damn cynic."

The ladies rejoined them. Seeking a more appreciative audience for his tale, Wilson retold the story for Marilyn's benefit. His wife stoically endured her fiftieth or so recital.

"That's really fascinating," Marilyn said with apparent interest. "How did you ever learn about it?"

"Please, Al, not tonight," his wife implored him. "Let's save that for a leisurely barbecue when these two don't have to drive back to the city and be up early for work."

Dan could have kissed her. "Yeah, we really do have to be going. Marilyn has to be in at seven," he lied.

"Been busy?" Al asked as they headed for the stairs.

"Yes, a lot more than the papers or City Hall would have anyone believe," she answered. "Contrary to what the Commissioner says, crime is not really down, at least not from what the M.A.'s office can tell. And on top of our normal workloads we've had to help out with the terrorists' victims. The feds require so much more paperwork. That's the real time killer."

In the car Dan said, "I know you're exhausted. Thanks for agreeing to come tonight."

"It doesn't matter how tired I am or where we go or what we do, as long as I'm with you. Besides they're really terrific people."

"That's what I like, a well-trained woman who knows her place."

She reached down and gently squeezed his genitals. "Wanna' rethink that?"

"Uncle, uncle," he cried, before they just leaned against each other and enjoyed the trip across the Tappan Zee and down the Palisades to Manhattan. They were back in his apartment before ten.

"Take your shower and wait for me in bed," she suggested. "Then I'll take mine and surprise you."

He did as she asked. He was sitting up, reading, naked under the covers when she sang out, "Get ready, I'm coming in."

She stopped in the doorway, posing seductively, her left arm stretched above her head, her right hand resting against her waist. She wore a sheer black triangular bra that covered little more than her nipples, a see-through G-string and fishnet stockings secured by a black garter belt.

"You look fantastic, good enough to eat," he whispered.

"You really think so?" she taunted, subtly altering her pose.

"Oh, yeah," he assured her. "You're definitely making an impression."

"Show me."

He pulled down the covers.

"Oh, my," she giggled, "it's my turn to be impressed."

# CHAPTER 16

Rasheed Martin called in a few times, first to confirm that he had secured some HIV infected blood from the FDA and delivered it to Dr. Worthington, and later to report his progress in documenting the dates on which blood samples had been sent from hospitals to the suspects' Manhattan offices. His last call at about four in the afternoon was to report that he had identified an FDA official named George Richards as the person who had inspected and later qualified the Nuremberg lab for its original license application. Richards had also been the ongoing field auditor of record, something the field supervisor to whom Rasheed had spoken found curious. But since this gentleman was not Richard's manager, he wasn't able to provide an explanation.

"Normally we don't permit officials charged with the initial qualifying audit to conduct re-certifications," the official had stated. "A qualifying audit requires a great deal more engineering experience, a working knowledge of the involved scientific processes and familiarity with the local and federal environmental impact regulations. The people who do this type work are extremely valuable and not worth wasting on follow-up checks, which we call re-certifications. We can get recent college graduates to conduct those."

"So why did Richards do both?" Rasheed wanted to know.

He was promised it would be looked into. When told of the conversation, Dan reminded Rasheed that Richards could easily have surmised the real purpose of the lab and was later included in the conspiracy to keep him quiet. The younger detective agreed, suggesting that he bring Richards in for questioning.

"Let's wait and see what else that supervisor has to say," Dan said. "The more we know, the more confidently we can handle Richards. Is there any reason to believe he may be aware of our interest in him?"

"Not that I know of, and I warned the supervisor twice that everything is confidential."

Satisfied that there was nothing left for him to do except wait for Clarence Worthington's call, Dan phoned Joe DeLorenzo and hoped his friend would answer. He was disappointed when the tape came on, but he left a message that he would be home that evening and would appreciate hearing from him. He was about to call Marilyn Kyme when the phone rang.

"Detective Sergeant Costa, Homicide."

"Worthington here," the excited voice replied. "I have news of some significance, certainly worth your driving over here. I think we might be approaching the next step."

"Really? Can you tell me about it?"

"I'm in the process of tending to some further experiments. Can't spare the time. But suffice to say that Limulus has not let the side down. The old boy certainly appears to have some unique self-defense mechanisms. Get over here at the earliest possible." He hung up before Dan had the opportunity to say anything else.

He was about to call him back when Carmine Pecora walked by, heading for Al Wilson's office. Dan had put off a conversation he wanted to have with Pecora and for some reason felt compelled to have it now

"Carmine, you got a minute?"

"Sure. Waddaya' got?"

"On the Teller case, I've just been wondering why your report didn't include Ruiz's comments about the car and the perps. That all should have been in your report unless you knew for sure that he was lying, and in that case, you should have brought him in for questioning. You didn't follow the book and I'm curious as to why."

"I made a judgement on the spot that Ruiz was lookin' for a way to get us off Berger's testimony about the perps sounding black, in which case anything else he said about them was probably bullshit. I didn't bring him in because even if he was telling the truth, he was too far away to have seen any details that would be of help to us."

"That's still no reason to not record eyewitness testimony or ignore procedures. I think Ruiz's testimony is right on and if we had had it from the start Berger might be alive today, in our custody and spilling his guts."

"Hey, I'm up to my neck with work, Dan. Excuse me if I'm not perfect," Pecora muttered as he walked off.

Costa tried Worthington's number but there was no answer, so he waited until Pecora had left Wilson's office and then went to tell him about the call and that he was going to Columbia to learn what had developed.

Wilson said, "Sounds interesting. Mind if I join you? We can both take our cars and drive home from there."

Dan cursed the unyielding traffic that stretched the four-mile drive to thirty minutes. Though corporations were fleeing the city in droves, Manhattan's streets remained as congested as ever. Some blamed it on the reluctance of people terrified by the bombings to use the subways. Others pointed to the increase in police checkpoints. Whatever the reason, Manhattan's gridlock was a constant annoyance, no longer dependant upon the rush hour to fray a commuter's nerves.

As they walked down the long corridor that serviced a dozen laboratory-office suites reserved for federally funded programs, Dan saw people in white smocks milling about in the vicinity of Worthington's lab. "I hope he hasn't said anything about his findings," Costa remarked, picking up his pace. "I don't trust anyone in this case."

For a different reason, his concern grew as he approached, for some in the group were wiping tears, others struggling to hold them back. He excused himself as he pushed his way through the door and into the crowded office area, his way further blocked by a mix of lab and office personnel.

"Police," he yelled. "Let us through."

A path opened and he recognized the cluttered desk and the scientist seated behind it. He set his jaw and bit hard as he focused on Clarence Worthington who was sitting upright, head back, eyes fixed squarely on the young detective he had been expecting. Dan Costa walked around to him and gently lowered his eyelids, taking care not to touch the blood that had oozed from a hole between his eyes. He looked at Al Wilson who just shook his head sadly.

Now there was something personal in it. As Dan had listened to people speak of Joe Teller he had come to appreciate the humility and kindness of the frail little scientist whom he had never met. But in Clarence Worthington he had found an ally with whose help he was going to get to the bottom of a conspiracy involving a very significant scientific break-through, a task he would now face without the aid of the one person who could have deciphered the Limulus puzzle.

The two detectives reacted instinctively, ordering people away from the crime scene, asking if anyone could offer any information that might help.

A young couple stepped forward and identified themselves as graduate assistants to another research scientist whose lab and office were in the same complex. A half hour earlier the girl had wandered down the hallway during a break, and noticing Worthington's door ajar, stepped in to say hello. "We all liked him so much," she explained. "He was a real inspiration. I used to enjoy talking to him whenever he had the time."

Her scream had brought her boyfriend running, closely followed by a score of others. No one reported having heard a shot, and except for a lone witness, no one had seen anyone leaving the area. A young assistant said he had passed a couple of men wearing suits in the hallway just before five, but hadn't bothered to look at their faces, so he couldn't even guess at their ages, much less what they looked like.

"Average height and build," constituted the sum of his description. Pressed on the issue he would only confess that he hadn't really look at them, but that he was fairly certain neither was a large man as Dan had expected.

It wasn't long before the room began to fill again, this time with homicide detectives from Manhattan North accompanied by a team from Forensics. Dan explained his involvement to the senior detective, Joe Ryan, an officer familiar to both himself and Wilson.

"Stick around if you want, Dan, I can use all the help I can get. Another homicide to add to my workload is about as welcome as a case of AIDS."

The irony escaped neither Costa nor Wilson.

"Thanks. I'm interested in any notes he may have written within the past couple of days."

Ryan advised his crew not to remove anything until Costa had seen it.

The desk looked much the same as it had the previous afternoon. The beaten encyclopedic manuscript lay closed before the dead scientist, suggesting that at some point he had seated himself to study it. A small white pad lay near it, curiously turned away from the victim, not the position it would have been in had he been writing. The top page was blank. Dan took a pencil and lightly ran it across, hoping Worthington had pressed hard enough to make an impression. A faint, indiscernible scribble was raised, one that would require enhancing by the forensics lab to be of value. Nothing else seemed remotely tied to the experiments being run for his benefit.

Before joining Wilson in the lab area, Dan gave permission for the Coroner's personnel to begin work on the body, reminding them that he needed to review whatever contents they extracted from the victim's pockets. He told everyone that he was looking for names of people, companies, perhaps even hospitals and doctors, anything that might provide clues as to whom Worthington had been speaking or meeting with recently. Ryan didn't object.

"All I can find here is a lot of lab apparatus," Al admitted, "not to say that I know what I'm supposed to be looking for."

"Notes, scribbles, marks in the dust, blood, anything," Dan said.

"You know," Wilson observed after some deliberation, "that's what's missing. There are no lab notes. Every scientist makes notes, leaves them all over the damn place. Where the hell are his?"

"He knew precisely what he was looking for, I'm sure of that," Dan said, "so we won't find tons of notes on the subject. But he did run six simultaneous tests while I was here. He had to have left some notes concerning those, unless of course, his killers knew enough to take them."

Wilson continued searching, opening cabinet doors, turning over anything that might conceal the tiniest scrap, unaware that Costa had returned to the office area now being scrutinized by a horde of investigators.

"If you had to guess," Dan asked the senior forensics person, "would you say the killer was within ten feet of the victim?"

"I'd think so," he said with some assurance before remembering departmental protocol, "but I'll reserve judgment until we run some tests."

He asked Joe Ryan if he could have one more go at the desk's contents.

"Sure. What are you looking for?"

"Names that your men wouldn't recognize."

Dan opened each drawer, ignoring long-forgotten papers that should have been discarded years ago, articles on subjects alien to his case and a collection of some archaic lab utensils. As he touched each he seemed to bond closer to the man he had known briefly, but had come to accept as a kindred spirit despite their radically different interests.

*The absent-minded professor,* Dan reminisced. *Each in our own way, we shared a passion for the truth.*

In the large center drawer he found what he was looking for. He called Wilson and Ryan over. "You'll both note that I've taken this card from the victim's desk drawer," he stated, handing it to Ryan. "Book it as evidence. I'll explain later, and if you could send me a copy of whatever the lab raises from that notepad, I'd appreciate it."

He headed for the door with some apparent purpose, but stopped short of it to return to the desk where he picked up the old leather bound, maroon colored manuscript.

"Let me have this overnight, Ryan, and I'll help you solve this case."

"You're welcome to it," the detective said. "I don't read anything thicker than the sports pages."

As they walked towards their cars Costa told his boss that he was beginning to understand how the circumstantial evidence fit together. "What I'm not sure of, Al," he lamented, "is how I'm going to get what the D.A. will require for an indictment."

"Any resources you need, just ask."

"Thanks. Rasheed and I can handle it."

Back at his apartment Dan heated some leftover meatballs and sausage in tomato sauce and settled down with the maroon manual that he was certain held the clue to what Worthington had found so exciting. He turned the parched and faded leather cover: "SCIENTIFIC COMPENDIUM OF LYSIN CHEMISTRY IN BACTERIAL REDUCTION." He regretted his decision, but aware of Worthington's suspicions, he began review of the seven-hundred-page manuscript. At some point he decided that knowing what Lysin was would probably help. He consulted a dictionary. L*ysin: an antibody causing the disintegration of bacterial cells.* He recalled that the suffix, "lysis," meant a breaking down or decomposition.

The phone rang, interrupting his thoughts.

He glanced at his watch…eight-fifteen…and hoped it was Joe DeLorenzo.

"Hi. Miss you like crazy," Marilyn said. "How come you didn't call today?"

He told her about Clarence Worthington and the book he was studying.

"Oh, Dan, when will it all end? I'm beginning to worry about you. Would they come after you if they knew you were getting close?"

"No, never," he lied. "They'd prefer to think we're not tying everything together. Homicide detectives don't get killed without the world being turned upside down. They wouldn't risk that."

"I hope you're right, but I'm going to worry just the same. Now that I've found you, I never ever want to lose you. I love you so much."

As happy as she made him and as good as she sounded, he had committed to getting through the book that evening so he could move the investigation forward.

"Think about someplace you'd like to go this weekend and we'll leave Friday night. Won't even wait until Saturday," he promised.

"Anywhere?" she asked, hinting at some far off, exotic retreat.

"Anywhere that I can afford that will allow me to get back in time for work Monday," he said seriously. "And once I solve this case, even that won't be a condition."

The prospect thrilled her. "And we have vacation time coming up, too. Oh, Dan, I do love you," she repeated, before he assured her that he felt the same. "Now I really do have to get back to this. Call me tomorrow."

He had turned and scanned half the pages without noticing anything familiar when the phone rang again. It was Joe D.

"Sorry again, Dan, but I just got in," he said, excusing his failure to stay in touch. "Avent keeps giving me more cases. I don't understand it. I've got double what anyone else has and I'm primary on everything he's given to Calvin and me. I'm starting to wonder."

"Wonder what?"

"Ah, forget it, I'm just paranoid."

"Wonder what?" Dan insisted.

"Your dad's case," he finally admitted. "We're not moving as fast as we should. We haven't even staked out the suspect's last known address."

"Did you discuss it with Avent?"

"Yeah, and all he said was he couldn't drop everything else and that he would ask for some off-duty patrol officers if we were still jammed by the end of the week."

"So this suspect, Booker, he has no job, nowhere to hide, and we can't find a way to just go pick him up?"

"No lie, Dan, since the pawn shop operator ID'd the mug shot, we've done nothing, and I've been putting in twelve-hour days, working my ass off on seven other homicides, most of which are drug related. You know how many people you gotta' talk to before one of those gets to the D.A. Christ, I must have ten suspects for every murder."

Too tired and too intent on getting through the book to get annoyed by the game Avent could be playing, Dan told his friend to just keep him posted. "You can always leave a message if you can't reach me."

But he also decided to speak to Al Wilson in the morning, hoping he would talk to Avent to see if there was some purpose to Joe's work assignments and his apparent indifference towards his father's case.

He brewed some coffee, determined to finish the book.

It was one a.m. when he turned to page four fifty-seven and saw the tiny, torn strip of white paper, a remnant of a larger sheet apparently employed as a bookmark. The page contained two photo reproductions of tiny sperm-like creatures swimming amongst some dark, irregularly shaped cells of approximately equal size. In the photo on the left there appeared to be a few more of the cells than in the one on the right. Upon closer examination, he noticed that the ones missing on the right were, in the left, a bit larger and darker than the others. He began reading the chapter's text, more than fifty pages, stopping frequently to re-read sentences and consult his dictionary. Two hours passed before he reached for a pen and some paper to copy selected quotes while adding editorials of his own. Lastly, he retrieved his police issue Polaroid, moved the book under a light and photographed a few pages. It was well past two in the morning when he slid under the covers, and after three by the time he fell asleep, his thoughts alternating between what he would say to Al Wilson about both cases.

At eight he and Rasheed were seated, facing the Lieutenant in his office, the giant size coffees and still warm Danish products of Dan's visit to the local Jewish deli. Before beginning, Costa directed Martin to record everything and have it typed for eventual review by the D.A.'s office, heightening Wilson's interest, since he knew Costa did this only when he believed the case had been solved.
  "By the way, Al, when we're done I'm going to need a minute of your time in private. It's strictly a personal thing," he said, turning to Rasheed. "Nothing to do with our work."
  Martin understood, confident that his relationship with his partner, both professionally and personally, had been proceeding well.
  Dan's monologue took fifteen minutes as he restated the evidence at the scenes of Teller's and Berger's deaths, the lab in Nuremberg and at Worthington's office. He alluded to the untimely and highly suspicious accident that claimed the life of Greg Chadwick, the programmer who had designed software for the computers in Nuremberg, and to the very irregular assignment of George Richards as both qualifying and re-certifying auditor of the Nuremberg lab. Then he began to tie it all together.
  "There is one explanation for everything, the murders included," he began. "I've thought long and hard about the evidence, the security precautions, the players and their scientific backgrounds, and only one scenario fits everything. I'm convinced Joe Teller was murdered because he had found what he, Berger and their investors believed is a cure for viral or bacterial infection, probably the former, possibly hepatitis or even HIV. Based on his studies of a Dr. Richard Snively's research and his later work

with horseshoe crabs at the Chincoteague Island laboratory, Teller was able to isolate an enzyme in their blood that acts as a lysin, a parasitic cell that destroys bacteria."

"But AIDS is a virus, not a bacteria," Rasheed interrupted, for which he was going to apologize before his partner nodded his agreement.

"You're right, and I'm not sure how it all fits scientifically, but the crabs either have a second property attached to the lysin, that if isolated, attacks viruses, or if the lysin mutates into some form that can attack viruses. Either way, the chromatographic separation of the components of the blood was critical to Teller's discovery, just as it was to Snively's determinations. Unless separated from all other protein in the blood, whatever form it takes won't react to a virus. It'll stay at home, so to speak, protecting against the millions of bacteria to which horseshoe crabs are exposed in seawater. But freed of that responsibility, it will attack any aggressive cells, viruses included, certainly ones as aggressive as hepatitis or HIV, if in fact Teller got that far. We know Snively got pretty damn far with his work on hepatitis, so considering the time Teller put in after that, it's reasonable to expect that he was after even bigger fish, something like HIV."

"Nobody ever said we didn't pollute the hell out of our water," Wilson commented, still intrigued by the crab, its blue blood and its properties.

"By constant exposure through the milleniums, these crabs eventually engineered a remarkably powerful immune system that has allowed them to survive millions of years, because unlike just about every other creature, their lysins are potent enough to withstand any bacteria, or at least any we've managed to dump in our oceans so far, so it's possible Teller had some other targets, but you have to keep Steinberg and Norville in mind. They were involved in HIV treatment programs and would have been targets for Berger's fundraising effort. The continuation of the research depended upon two things in addition to Teller's participation…money and HIV infected blood. Berger knew that Steinberg and Norville were able to supply both."

He let everything sink in before moving on to another thought. "I'm still not sure why they chose Nuremberg, except that it's within hours of Manhattan, yet remote and rustic enough to afford them the secrecy they wanted. I can't think of any other reasons."

"Finally, Worthington had told me that trial experiments on any in-vivo would have required three to five years of scientifically collected data and that the record keeping would have demanded very explicit trials, which explains both the time Teller and Berger spent on Chincoteague Island and in

Nuremberg, as well as the custom-designed software system. Our suspects probably believed that the deaths of Teller and Berger would arouse Greg Chadwick's suspicions, and since he knew the purpose of the computers, he too had to be eliminated."

"What's that word in-vivo mean?" Rasheed wondered.

"It refers to a drug taken internally, either swallowed, inhaled or injected, as opposed to an in-vitro that stays outside the body."

His partner was impressed.

"Dictionaries help," Costa confessed. "Anyway, I suspect that Berger wanted to cash in on their discovery, but Teller wouldn't agree, maybe because he didn't think they were ready, perhaps because he wanted to involve others so that the greatest good could be done in the shortest time possible. Whatever the disagreement, the two men argued openly, which surprised everybody who knew them. At one point, Teller even confided to an acquaintance that Berger was proving to be a big disappointment, as though he never really knew him. I suspect that Teller was about to break off the studies or bring them somewhere else when Berger reconciled their differences somehow and convinced Teller to take the trip to New York. There he was murdered by Albert Tataro and Carlo Rinaldi, a pair of disenfranchised wise-guys, solicited by the doctors' attorney, James Musto."

"This is getting tough," Wilson observed. "We're going to have a helluva' time bringing some of these fat cats down."

"Not if we get Rinaldi and Tataro to talk," Dan reminded him before continuing.

"Berger panicked when I called, and now I wish like hell I hadn't," he said with obvious regret. "Anyway, he called one of the doctors and they called Musto, maybe Rinaldi directly, though I doubt it. Telephone records from their offices the day Berger was murdered will tell us who called whom," he reminded Rasheed.

"Berger is given some reason to stop at that motel in Hackettstown where Tataro puts him out of his misery. Next we get the tip on Tataro and Rinaldi," Dan added, still protective of Barracci's involvement, "and through our questioning of them, the doctors are alerted to our investigation. When George Richards learns of Rasheed's visit to his FDA offices and then of his request for HIV samples for Worthington, he puts two and two together and notifies the suspects."

Wilson interrupted. "First, how does this Richards guy figure in this?"

"He initially certified Nuremberg to handle the blood as a diagnostic lab, but he probably figured out its real purpose. Either that, or Steinberg and

Norville realized having him on their side would guarantee secrecy. That's when he asked for or was offered a share."

"And just a year later, he took a cut in pay and a demotion to a field auditor's job so he could continue to cover up the trials," Rasheed jumped in.

Dan smiled. "Elementary deduction?"

"Got a call from my FDA contact," Martin confessed with a grin. "But I am pissed at that guy," he said, the smile removed, "I specifically told him not to say anything to Richards or, in fact, anyone else in his office about our discussion. He opened up his big mouth and got Worthington killed."

"Probably," Dan added, "I can't think of who else would have put them on to him."

"But what made Richards finger Worthington?" Wilson asked, still a bit confused.

"I found his card in Worthington's drawer. It had Richards' old title on it. I suspect he visited the good doctor a while back, possibly to audit him for one project or other, but most likely to ask him more about Teller and Berger's work. Richards may not have known the specifics of what they were doing in Nuremberg, only what they were using, and possibly their final objective. To visit Worthington and learn more may not have been a poor decision at the time. For whatever reason, the fact that he did so and later asked questions about the blood samples Rasheed requisitioned, point to him being the person who fingered Worthington. I'm just not sure who did the shooting because neither description of the only two strangers seen in the area fits Tataro. I suspect it could have been Rinaldi and Richards, himself. Who else could have identified the professor? Remember, they had to move quickly. No time for photos and stakeouts."

"I still can't believe that supervisor talked to Richards after I asked him not to," Rasheed mumbled, mostly to himself.

"Like I said, it's the only way the doctors would have known to eliminate Worthington," Dan reminded him.

Everyone was quiet for a while until Dan summed up what had to be Wilson's concern.

"Al, I know it's all circumstantial. Without the lab records we can't even prove what they were working on, but give me one other scenario that covers all the evidence. There is none. There's no other reason for the players, the years of work, the secrecy, the crabs and the murders. Anything else doesn't justify the investment or the risk. You don't kill four people for a Nobel Prize in meaningless research, enzymes or otherwise. Big money had to be the prize and nothing would have been bigger than a universal hepatitis or AIDS cure."

## LIMULUS

"Or a preventative," Rasheed submitted.

"Possibly," Dan conceded. "Either way, very big money, enough to kill for."

"Okay," Wilson said, yielding to the growing possibility that Costa had reached the right conclusion, "suppose you've figured it all out. Where's the proof, and don't tell me about phone calls that can be dismissed under client-attorney privilege. Where's the test results, the computers themselves, the blood…where's anything that can back up your assumptions?"

Wilson's point was well taken, for without hard evidence, it would be difficult to implicate the doctors or Richards in the Nuremberg lab activities. At worst Richards could confess to having done a less than thorough job of monitoring the records. As for the doctors, they had been there so infrequently they could admit to a total absence of knowledge concerning the actual work. Just another arms-length investment gone awry might do very well in court. Short of a confession, it wasn't even worth discussing with the D.A.

Costa was formulating his next move when Wilson's phone rang. It was Joe Ryan with a message for Dan.

"Hi, Joe, how's it going?" Costa listened for a minute before thanking Ryan and hanging up.

"Forensics raised most of Worthington's last notes," he started. "He scribbled the names of some chemicals in six different columns…I'm guessing a set for each of the chromatographic experiments he ran. At the top of the sheet he wrote 'L. lysate,' which probably represents 'Limulus lysate,' virus or bacteria eaters from a horseshoe crab's blue blood. Joe Teller isolated a cure, maybe for HIV. I'll bet on it. He was killed because he didn't agree with whatever his backers wanted to do next. I'm going to nail their asses, Al. You just give me some time to think and I'll give you a case even our D.A. can win."

"I'm sure you will," a tired Al Wilson said. "Now you had something personal to discuss? I got a million things I still gotta' get to today."

"Rasheed, get a hold of the blood disposal company that handled Nuremberg. We're going to need their retention samples, one from each month. If I'm right, they'll prove our contention that Teller isolated an antibody that digested whatever viruses were in that blood. I may be gone by the time you get back, so leave me messages. I'll check in."

"Will do, but first I'm going to call that FDA guy and find out why the hell he let Richards know we were on to him."

When Martin left, Dan filled Wilson in on DeLorenzo's call. "Please don't misunderstand Joe; he's only concerned that he's not moving Dad's case fast enough to satisfy me."

"You don't have to make excuses for him, Dan, I know the kind of police officer he is. He's as good as it gets. I'll feel Avent out, and don't worry about anybody being put on the spot. I'll chalk it up to your anxiety."

"Thanks, Al. I'm going to make some calls and then visit Carlo Rinaldi."

"Want some backup?"

"If I meet him at his club I might, otherwise I can handle it. I'll let you know if I need help."

There was one final note from his previous night's work that he hadn't addressed. Back at his desk he punched in a phone number and waited while it rang.

"Constable Shultz, Nuremberg Police."

"Hey, Jack, Dan Costa. How's it goin'?"

"Great, Dan, how about you?"

Dan gave Shultz a quick summary, including his interview of Rinaldi, the Tataro skirmish, Worthington's death and the final conclusions he had just disclosed to Wilson and Martin.

"Whew, that's heavy," the constable admitted. "How are you going to go about putting the case together? Doesn't sound like you've got enough evidence to indict."

"And you sound like my boss," Dan replied good-naturedly, "but you're right. So far everything's circumstantial."

"Is there something I can do to help?"

Normally, Dan Costa didn't struggle with anything involving police work, but he was more than a little uncomfortable with what he had to say.

"Jack, I'm not sure Donna has told us everything she knows. I checked the phone records and found calls to her desk from private rooms at the doctors' group practice. There's also a number of late evening calls to her apartment from a Manhattan condo owned by Alex Norville, one of the doctors we suspect. I apologize for bringing this up but I have to at least ask her about it. I didn't want to do that until I spoke to you."

Jack's response was slow in coming, his tone betraying his concern.

"Well," he hesitated again, "I guess you gotta' do what you gotta' do, Dan. I'd be shocked if she was involved in anything as sordid as all this, but...." A second or two passed before he added, "Anything else I should know about?"

"We have reason to believe she visited Norville at that condo. We showed a picture of her that Marilyn had taken at the fair to the doorman who ID'd her as a friend of Norville's. Said he saw her a couple of times," Costa lied. Donna Schulman had been a regular visitor, at least one weekend a month for almost a year."

"I see," was Shultz's only response.

"When did you begin dating her, Jack?"

"Oh, let's see, probably two years ago, just after she showed up."

"Do you recall her being gone on weekends?"

"Yep, lot's of 'em, particularly in the past year. We weren't engaged or anything, so I never had the right to say or do anything about it, but I sure was disappointed and she knew it. When I'd ask where she was going she'd tell me that she had family in Philly and New York State that she wanted to visit. I never doubted her. You obviously didn't trust her, did you?" he reminded himself. "What made you check her out?"

"The phone calls," Dan replied, concealing the fact that he felt from the beginning that she didn't belong in a town like Nuremberg. That and her testimony that she had never seen the inside of the lab, heard any conversations or taken any calls from the doctors all seemed too improbable.

"Where do you go from here?" Shultz asked.

"I'm going to have to come out there and talk to her again. I don't want to make the same mistake I made with Berger and scare her off. Either that or I'll ask her to come into the city, maybe to ID some photos, something like that."

"Funny you should be telling me all this now. She left here about an hour ago. I asked her out this weekend and she told me she was meeting some girlfriends in Philly."

"I'm sorry, Jack. I really wish I didn't have to tell you all this."

"Hey, don't feel that way. Like I said, you got a job to do." He tried to put up a front but Dan could feel his disappointment. "It's not like she had ever given me reason to believe I was the only man in her life."

Dan didn't know what to say to make it any easier. Jack Shultz didn't deserve any of this. *Just another good guy getting screwed.*

"I can hold her here if you want," he offered.

"No. No point in alerting her. You don't have any time off coming up in the next week, do you?"

"I got a year's worth. As long as I give the sheriff a week's notice I can take off. Anything less than that has to be a real emergency. What do you have in mind?"

"I keep offering to have you guys over here for a weekend. I thought maybe we could hook up that way."

He had barely spoken the words when he realized he had asked his friend to set up the woman he loved, insensitive even for a New York City cop.

"That's stupid of me, Jack, forget it. I think my brain's beginning to run on fumes. I'll see what I can do to free up a day early next week and I'll come out there on some pretext. I'll call you as soon as I work out a schedule. In the meantime, just keep our little talk to yourself. I'm asking that more because I'm worried about her safety than for what she can tell me. I'll nail these bastards with or without Donna's help."

"You can trust me, Dan. I may not be too smart, but I am honest. This won't be the first time I've been hurt in my life and it probably won't be the last. If anything, I feel stupid for not having suspected something myself. It's been two years and I never did meet one of those relatives or friends she supposedly visits. Makes me feel like a jerk, now that I think of it."

"Being in love with a beautiful woman is the best excuse for doing stupid things, Jack, and we're all guilty of it."

He stared at the phone long after he had hung up. He could kick Donna Schulman's magnificent ass for what she had done to Jack Shultz. The problem was, any price she might pay would only increase his anxiety, and it was very possible that she was in over her gorgeous blonde head. This case had no upside, and for the first time in his career he was working on one to which he had become personally attached, feeling emotion for and against people, finding it increasingly difficult to divorce himself from it long enough to attend to other investigations. It frustrated, even angered him that he had become so obsessed with seeing it to its final conclusion, interfering with everything else in his life except Marilyn Kyme. But Teller was so much like his father, while Steinberg and Norville epitomized the hypocrisy and greed he despised. Together they provided the impetus to see it through, and quickly. His life would return to normal once he could put it all behind him.

He was preparing to call Massimo Barracci when the phone rang.

"Eagle's Mere," Marilyn shouted before giggling.

"What about it?"

"You don't even know what it is."

"Sure I do. It's where you want me to take you this weekend."

"How the heck did you figure that out?"

"Elementary, my dear lover. Firstly, you never call me unless you want something, and you did say you wanted to go away this weekend, to which I responded that you should pick a place. Secondly, it sounds like a place. Ergo, that's where you want to go this weekend."

"Okay, wise-ass, where is it?"

"Pennsylvania mountains," he replied without hesitation.

"You're unreal. I don't even want to hear how you figured that out."

"And lastly, you'll want to know if we can still leave Friday night, and the answer is still yes."

"Suppose it's a ten hour drive."

"But it isn't, because I gave you conditions last night and you wouldn't be so enthusiastic right now if it didn't meet all of them. So I figure it's probably no more than a five hour drive, five and a half, tops."

"You're scary," she said. "I think you read my mind. Do you know how I found it?"

"My first guess is those brochures you picked up at the Bloomsburg State Fair. You sure as hell didn't call to ask Donna Schulman, or anybody else in Nuremberg for that matter, because they might tell her."

"Right again, you damn genius. You've just given me another reason to love the hell out of you and I think I'm going to do just that tonight," she promised, lowering her voice to a whisper.

When he didn't respond she asked if anything was wrong.

"Everything's fine." No point in worrying her, he thought. "But I think we'd be better off tomorrow and on the weekend if we skip tonight. I'll be getting home pretty late and we should both get a good night's sleep before all that driving."

She wondered about what he had to do that would keep him out late, but she trusted and cared about him enough to let it go at that.

"You're right, darling. We'll enjoy the weekend that much more if we're rested."

It was almost noon. He dialed and Pam Donaldson answered.

"It's Dan Costa, Pam. Is the man available?"

"For you I'm sure he is. I'll get him."

"Dan, how's my favorite cop?" Massimo Barracci roared. "When am I going to see you?"

"I thought I'd come over and take you out for lunch if you're available."

"I'm always available to you," he said, "but lunch is on me. Is Dabatto's okay? I gotta' stay close. Got a meeting at two."

"Sure. I'll leave now," Dan said, checking his watch. "Should be there by twelve-thirty."

He got up to leave when the phone rang again. He debated answering it, finally giving in, thinking it might be Jack Schultz. It was Rasheed.

"Nothing important. Just thought I'd let you know I spoke to that FDA contact and he swore up and down he hasn't seen or talked to Richards since I met with him, so he couldn't have told him anything about Worthington. I believe him, Dan, but where the hell does that leave us? What would have made the suspects take out Worthington? I mean, how the hell did they even know you had spoken to him?"

"Good question," a confused Dan Costa replied, but he had something more important on his mind and he didn't want to keep Barracci waiting. "We'll both have to give that some thought, but right now I've gotta' get going. I'll talk to you later."

The drive across the Harlem River and down the Brooklyn-Queens Expressway to Hall Street, just south of the abandoned Brooklyn piers, went well, as it often did at midday if there were no accidents. Without stop-and-go traffic Dan was able to give his conversation with Rasheed some thought. If the FDA officer was telling the truth, then someone else had uncovered Worthington's involvement and gotten word to Musto, the doctors or Richards.

Could Richards have coincidentally visited or spoken to Worthington, and could he have mentioned the tests he was running on Dan's behalf? Did someone hear of Rasheed's pick-up and delivery of the HIV-infected blood samples? Did Richards have a contact at Columbia that mentioned Dan's meetings with Worthington? Maybe Richards had made his partners uncomfortable with the knowledge that Clarence Worthington was the one man left who could shed some light on the nature of Teller's research, and that his insight could lead the police to precisely where he had led Dan. That opened the possibility that Teller, Berger, or even the scientist killed on Chincoteague had alluded to Worthington's background at some point and the conspirators feared he knew more about their work than he really did. Finding Worthington working on limulus blood samples and discovering Snively's journal in his lab would have convinced Richards of the scientist's involvement, possibly on someone else's behalf, such as the police. It's conceivable that it wasn't until Richards saw all this that the decision was made to murder the seventy-year-old enzymologist. Dan realized that had he not asked for Worthington's help, the old man would still be alive. The thought both saddened him and cemented his resolve to close the case successfully.

The more he thought about it, the more it occurred to him that Donna Schulman could have told Norville about Dan's investigation and that Larry

Moretti had given him Teller's journal. Richards would have realized that the police would need Worthington's help to decipher its contents, and that without him around, the notes would have posed no threat to their secrecy.

He thought of a dozen such scenarios and none left him comfortable, most likely because it wasn't his style to label anything as "coincidence." He preferred to think that there was some intricate network involving yet unidentified players that had fed Musto and the doctors every detail of every aspect of the project and the people involved in it. But who else could there be? If he was right, it had to be somebody who knew Worthington. Dan was sure he hadn't told anyone about his visits to Columbia other than Al Wilson, Rasheed, Marilyn...certainly not anyone outside his circle of confidantes, so the leak, if there was one, had to have come from the scientist himself. On the other hand, coincidence did on occasion rear its infrequent head, and though he had taught himself to avoid putting that label on anything, he had to admit that in this instance the possibility existed. Nothing else had gone smoothly in this investigation, so why not chalk up another disappointment to bad luck?

He parked in the fenced lot next to the ristorante that serviced the lords of Brooklyn's underworld and a local clientele wealthy enough to afford the steep prices. You could not find a better meal, particularly if you preferred southern Italian style dishes of veal and seafood on pasta pilafs. On premise they made their own linguine, some as delicate as angel hair, so unique that restaurants as far away as San Fransisco paid five dollars a pound to have it shipped. Without a reservation you couldn't even stand on the sidewalk and inhale the aromas.

The menacing Scarola would have provided enough incentive, but Barracci pressed a twenty into the maitre de's hand when he found a choice corner table and erected a privacy screen around it. Dan was relieved added precaution had been taken. Dabatto's clientele were more than familiar to the police and just to be seen entering there would raise questions. To be reported sharing a table with Barracci and members of his family would be difficult to explain.

They dined on a cold calamari salad laced with garlic and sprinkled with balsamic vinegar, olive oil and basil, followed by an enormous plate of linguine in marinara sauce, covered with langostine and monkfish. Barracci, Nicholas Santucci and Dan took generous servings, but fully two-thirds of the original dish remained. With the slightest motion of his head, Barracci gave sanction to Muzzi and Scarola to share the balance, a license they accepted with ardor. All three marveled at the capacity of the aging soldiers. Later,

Muzzi would try to conceal his whispered instructions to the waiter to package the platter's remains and pass it to him on his way out, only to have the confused fellow deliver it to the table with fanfare. Muzzi's glare terrified him into a prolonged apology. The stoic Scarola never flinched, though Dan wondered if he would later press his claim to a share.

When the espresso and Sambucca had been served, Dan brought everyone up-to-date, at least as to Rinaldi's interrogation, Tataro's arrest and later release, and Worthington's murder.

Santucci volunteered having heard how Dan had leveled Tataro, bringing a barely perceptible nod of approval from Scarola. The Don patted Costa's shoulder proudly.

"So that's where we're at," Dan concluded. "I felt I owed you at least an update."

Turning to Santucci he continued, "Your information was correct, Nick. I have no doubt about their guilt, both with Teller and Berger, but I don't believe Tataro killed Worthington and that's why I asked for this meeting."

Directing his attention back to Barracci, he asked, "Uncle, if you were DePalma, and you knew everything I've told you, and if Musto comes back and asks for your help to silence Worthington, what would you do?"

"I'd have Vito feed Musto to the fishes," the Capo replied evenly. "You don't go behind my back and give a contract to one of my people without asking my permission. Then you got the balls to come to me when things get fucked up? Hey, Musto's not that stupid."

The point was well taken. So Musto probably went straight to Rinaldi, who for whatever reason decided not to bring Tataro. Rinaldi did it himself or recommended someone else. Under any circumstance, George Richards accompanied the shooter in order to identify the victim and to see if there was any evidence that would incriminate the conspirators. Though it didn't explain how they learned of Worthington's involvement, Costa felt comfortable with how it had gone down, meaning he had to confront Rinaldi, a conclusion he shared with Barracci and Santucci. Muzzi and Scarola ignored all the talk. Inspired by a selection of pastries, they had dug in, determined to leave no cannoli unturned. Each ate a half dozen before grunting a consensus that the 'biscotto' should have had more cheese, and the 'baba', more rum.

"What are you going to do to make Rinaldi talk?" the Don asked. "He's already stonewalled you once."

"For one thing, I've got more on him now. The stakes are a lot higher. I'm hoping that by mentioning Richards' name he'll realize I know everything and that it's only a matter of time before I can prove it. With that, he might give up Tataro and the doctors for some leniency."

Santucci shook his head. "I think you're giving him too much credit. You're not dealing with a smart man, Dan. The guy's a '*gavone*' whose gotten his ass kicked by his own people. I don't think he'd clear his head long enough to consider a deal. He probably figures Musto can get him out of anything. Let's face it; mob lawyers are batting close to a thousand."

"Nicholas is right, Daniel," Barracci joined in. "Like Yogi says, 'Rinaldi's too stupid to be smart.' I don't disagree that you should go straight at him, but you either do it hard," and the way he said it left little doubt as to what he meant, "or you trap him. You offer him complete immunity, money, a new life in the old country maybe, but you get it on tape. After that, fuck him."

"I wish it were that simple, Uncle, but we have laws and courts, and neither would permit what you suggest, though I do agree, a lot more criminals would be in jail if we could play the game on their level."

Only after he had said it did he realize to whom he was speaking. Santucci and his godfather exchanged glances without commenting. Dan just wished he had thought before he spoke.

After a long silence the Don observed, "You know, nobody is going to give a good shit if either one of those assholes ends up dead. I know how to get Rinaldi to sing," and he looked across the table. Scarola and Muzzi came to attention, the two old attack-dogs awaiting their master's next command.

"No, I can't ask you to do that even if I wanted to," Dan said, shaking his head, but wondering to what lengths the two would go to complete the assignment. "Thanks anyway, Uncle, I appreciate the offer. I have to do this my way. Everything has to stick, because as Nick says, the D.A.'s office doesn't win many of these."

"What the hell do you think I offered for? You'll bust your ass doin' everything the right way and you'll still wind up losin' because the stupid D.A. will fuck it all up. You wanna' put those doctors away? You let me handle it," the Don repeated, regaining the attention of his enforcers.

Costa had heard enough. "Thanks again, Uncle. I do promise to call you if that's the only way." He hoped that would end the discussion. Apparently it did, for they all sat quietly savoring their sambucca until the Capo announced that it was time to leave for his two o'clock appointment.

Dan shook hands with them all, accepting an embrace and kiss from Barracci. "Just remember, we're family and we're here if you need us," he promised, before following Muzzi and Scarola into the sunlight of a perfect spring day, Santucci a dutiful step behind.

*Maybe his world's not so bad,* Dan thought. *It's a helluva lot more black and white than mine. Good guy gets killed...bad guy who did it gets killed. Eye for an eye.*

He stood on the sidewalk a minute, calculating a route with the fewest lights to the Medici, waving to the darkened windows of the Sedan DeVille as it rolled into the street. He wondered if his father would have approved of how he was handling this case, getting Barracci involved, concealing it from his boss. Was he doing the right thing?

Dan pulled to the curb across the street just as Carlo Rinaldi exited the Medici and headed south. Luck had taken a turn. Costa remembered that Rinaldi lived a few blocks from the club, so he waited until the suspect was well down the street before pulling out and following him, waiting at a corner while Rinaldi turned left onto 165th Street. A short way down Rinaldi climbed the stairs of a well-kept, red brick duplex, entering the one on the left. A minute later Dan rang the doorbell.

Rinaldi's routinely stoic expression changed when he recognized his visitor.

"What do you want, cop? I got nothin' to say to you, so why don't you take a hike."

Calmly, and with his voice lowered, Dan replied, "I can talk to you here, Carlo, or you can come over to Manhattan with me and spend a few hours answering a lot of bullshit questions. Here I can make things brief and to the point. Your choice."

Reluctantly, Rinaldi stepped back and led his caller into a well-furnished front parlor, from which Dan could see a clean, tastefully decorated dining room and kitchen in the rear, nothing like what he expected of the sleazy hood.

"My mother went shopping, but she'll be home soon, so make it quick," Rinaldi ordered, explaining the housekeeping.

"It's nice you live with your mother," Dan said patronizingly.

"Yeah, yeah, I'm a real Boy Scout. Cut the shit and get to it," Rinaldi shot back, his confidence growing in the absence of any hostility.

Dan just shook his head and smiled. "You're going to need all the friends you can get, Carlo, and here you are trying to piss off one of the few that can help you. That's not smart."

Costa began a quick summary of Rinaldi's involvement in the murders, stopping short of implying that he had killed Worthington, but accusing him of responding to Musto's call for help. It wasn't until he mentioned George Richards that the suspect flinched, surprised that Costa had tied the auditor to the conspiracy.

"Who the hell is that? I never heard of him," Rinaldi said. Dan just smiled.

"Look, you got a choice. You can turn state's evidence or you can sweat a few years on death row while some lawyer who really doesn't give a shit about you goes through the motions of trying to get you a stay. Ultimately, you'll get a lethal injection and your mother will lose this house paying the legal bills, if your court case doesn't kill her first." He let it sink in before continuing.

"Hey, Dummy, nobody can be this stupid. Open your goddamn eyes. You're already in DePalma's doghouse, one step short of *bacio de morte.* We're one, maybe two weeks away from an indictment that'll piss your boss off enough that you probably won't live to see your trial. Your mother's going to have to go through a lot. If not for yourself, think about her."

Abe Lincoln was right...*there's so much good in the worst of us....* For everything Carlo Rinaldi was...and that put him at the bottom of the food chain... he cared about his mother.

He began negotiations. "I do time. How does that pay the bills and make her feel any better?"

"Who said anything about time? You give me enough and we relocate you. Because of your mother, we might even be able to arrange something in the old country."

Though he didn't think it would be this easy and despite having learned not to celebrate before the trial's finished and sentences are handed down, Dan Costa began to believe he had won Rinaldi over, the one witness who could make every charge stick. His man lit a second cigarette and paced, moving his lips in a silent debate, only occasionally looking in the detective's direction, never long enough for Dan to read his thoughts.

"You may want more than I know," he said, seating himself and lighting yet another Winston. "I'm not involved in everything. This thing goes way back to some island down in Virginia where they had a guy knocked off because he wanted to bring the government in on everything. I don't know nothin' about that stuff."

"But you do know about Joe Teller and Lewis Berger and what they were working on, and most of us are convinced that you, Tataro and Richards had a hand in Greg Chadwick's and Clarence Worthington's deaths."

"Hey, nobody ever told me why Musto and his friends wanted Teller and Berger hit, so what are you lookin' for me to say?"

"That Musto approached you about a job that DePalma knew nothing about and that Tataro pulled the trigger after you agreed to split the money."

Rinaldi's reaction told Costa he had at least that much right.

"That you were told to leave Berger alone because he was part of the deal, though you were later contacted by Musto and told to drive to the Castle Rock Motel and kill him because he was getting nervous and Musto was afraid he might spill his guts to the cops."

"Albert whacked Berger, too," Carlo added quickly. "I had nothin' to do with it. I just drove 'cause Vinnie was sick. But Berger wasn't goin' to the cops. He was just scared 'cause you told him you wanted to interview him again. He was a sniveling little piece of shit," Rinaldi remembered, "and they were afraid he was gonna' blow their deal, so they had us hit him and take all his papers."

"Was this Vinnie the driver when Albert shot Teller?"

"Yeah. Vinnie Paradiso. We call him Saint Vinnie. You know...'paradise'...Saint Vinnie?"

Dan nodded. *Real geniuses.*

"Then Musto gave you a contract on Greg Chadwick?"

"Yeah, what a fucking mess that was. We wait for the guy to come home from work and convince him we're pickin' up drugs off the coast. We offer him ten big ones to take us out there. The greedy little shit says okay, so he got what he deserved. But fucking Albert, he falls overboard gettin' into a boat Vinnie's drivin'. We had to pull him in. You know what it's like pullin' three hundred pounds, plus all that water? Forget about it. I almost got a hernia. You think that's how Vinnie got sick?"

*I can't believe these morons.*

"Yeah, maybe. Why did you take Chadwick out?"

"Musto gave us twenty big ones."

"No, I mean why did Musto want him dead?"

Rinaldi thought briefly before shaking his head. "I ain't sure...something to do with computers out in Pennsy. Maybe the guy stiffed them, I don't know. Musto didn't tell me everything. I just know he wanted him taken out right away. I think he said we had to do it before that Friday night, something like that...like there was a deadline for some reason"

"Then Musto called about Worthington this week?"

"Yeah. He got me at home and told me that this Worthington guy was on to something, so he wanted me to go with Richards and Albert up to the Bronx and that Richards would tell us what to do, but that there wasn't any time to waste. Albert wasn't home and he wasn't at the club. I found out later he was at the doctor's again, still pisses some blood 'cause of what you did to him. So I called Musto and he said I should just meet Richards by myself 'cause there wasn't any time to find Albert and he didn't want nobody else involved. When we got to this guy Worthington's office, Richards walked in, shook his hand like he knew him pretty good, and then they went over by the desk. The doc opens up this book to show him something and then Richards gives me the signal. I put one right between his eyes. He didn't suffer," Rinaldi reminded Costa, hoping it brought him something his testimony would not. "I ain't killed many guys," he added, "'cause I don't sleep too good afterwards."

"That'll count for something," Dan muttered, pleasing the gullible Rinaldi whom Dan was beginning to believe was the intellectual equal of Tataro.

Still not convinced that Rinaldi was unaware of the reason for the lab and its experiments, he pressed the issue.

"But you can really help yourself, I mean big time, if you'll tell us why Teller had to be killed."

"Who the fuck knows? I don't ask for reasons. Somebody wants to pay me for a hit, I do it, no questions asked. That keeps it simple."

"And you never looked through the papers you took from Berger?"

"Oh, sure, that's the first thing I'm gonna' do after we whack somebody...sit down and read a couple hundred sheets of scientific bullshit. Are you fuckin' nuts?"

The doorbell rang. Rinaldi pointed to the closet beneath the stairs as he headed for the door. Dan heard him speaking to his mother, but waited until they were in the rear of the house before he exited the closet and reached outside to ring the doorbell, bringing Rinaldi back to the parlor.

"I'm going to speak to the D.A. first thing in the morning. You go about your normal business. Don't change your routine. Don't give anyone a reason to think you're acting any differently, because if anyone suspects that you might try to make a deal, they'll have a contract out on you in minutes. Understand?"

Carlo Rinaldi nodded his head.

"I'll get back to you tomorrow, Monday at the latest. In case you have second thoughts, you just think about what's best for you and your mother.

Remember, DePalma and the family don't get hurt by all this unless you haven't told me everything. Musto, Richards, the two doctors, Tataro, and maybe Paradiso, they're the ones we're after. Musto will probably try to make a deal to tighten the noose around the doctors' necks, but none of that hurts the family. You'd piss DePalma off more by having cops link him to Musto. This way, with what you've got to say, we won't even look at him."

Before letting Dan out, Rinaldi parted the drapes to check the streets. Satisfied that no one was watching, he began to open the door when Costa stopped him.

"Before I forget, did the name of Donna Schulman ever come up?"

"I don't think so, but like I said, Musto didn't tell us everything."

"Did he ever mention anything about a woman from the Pennsylvania lab?"

"A blonde piece of ass?" Rinaldi asked, whispering so his mother couldn't hear.

"Yeah."

"Musto mentioned once that there was some broad that was shacked up with one of the doctors, the little one I think, not the one that looks like that James Bond guy. They used her to keep tabs on those two guys before we had to whack 'em. At least that's what Musto said."

"So she knew Teller was going to get hit?"

Rinaldi debated. "I ain't sure. I just know she use to keep the doctors posted because they didn't trust Berger. But that all came from Musto, so I ain't swearin' to any of that."

"Thanks, it's not important anyway. I think we'll keep her name out of it."

As he drove away, Costa began to think that Donna Schulman was nothing more than what Carlo Rinaldi had described, though she had concealed her relationship with Alex Norville, possibly because she suspected his involvement, possibly because she was certain of it, in which case, she was an accessory after-the-fact. Sooner or later he would have to decide about her duplicity and how to handle it officially. Neither appealed to him because of their effect on Jack Shultz, but it went with the job and couldn't be ignored.

It was after four when he called the station to see if Rasheed had returned, which he had not, and to get his messages. Only two interested him. He called his partner first.

"I found the blood disposal firm. They're up in Scranton and they'll check the retention samples by tomorrow, two from each of the four years they were involved. We should know then."

"Good job. Where are you headed now?"

"Home, if you don't mind. I got a splitting headache. I've been doing nothing but looking at tiny little labels all day."

"Alright, alright, that's enough tears. Go home and give Tonya a kiss for me."

Rasheed laughed. "Can't do that no more, man, I'm gettin' serious about her. Must be all this springtime bullshit, you know? Birds and bees?"

"I hear you. Hits all of us. See you tomorrow."

He got back to the precinct as Al Wilson was locking his office. Rather than delay his friend's trip home he advised him that he might have some interesting things to discuss in the morning and that he would shortly begin making a dent in his burgeoning caseload.

Then he called Joe DeLorenzo who surprised him by answering the phone, though his voice reflected sleepless hours and ill temper, both of which he apologized for when he realized who it was.

"I finally have some good news for you. First, Calvin got a mug shot of Jesse Booker out to all the precincts in the five boroughs and Long Island, but we're asking that inquiries be kept low key, so we might not get lucky right away. In addition, Avent's authorized round-the-clock surveillance on the last known address. I got a good feeling about that." Remembering his conversation with Costa earlier in the week, DeLorenzo couldn't help asking, "Did you speak to Wilson? Is that why we got some action?"

"I spoke to Al, but I'd hate to think it took pressure from him to get Avent to authorize a stake-out on a murderer."

"Yeah, well, in the guy's defense, we are stretched kind of thin. Maybe this was all coincidence, me talking to you, you to Wilson and him finally coming up with the resources. Who knows? As long as we get the perp I don't care. In fact, I've given up caring about everything except your dad's case. For the rest of them I'll go through the motions, and if we catch them, okay, and if we don't, that's okay too."

"What's the problem?" Dan asked.

DeLorenzo's reputation as a super-cop was second only to his own. He was as highly regarded for his enthusiasm and commitment as he was for the results he produced and the way he produced them...by the book. Joe D.'s cases stuck. The D.A.'s office knew it and more importantly, the streets knew it. You didn't want Joe DeLorenzo on your ass, because if he was, it was as good as fried.

"The job's become too damn political, Dan. If I call a black perp a piece of shit, Avent wants to know if I'm a racist. If a white cop shoots a black guy waving a gun at him the department has to reassign him because the neighborhood's up in arms. But those same people yell like hell that we're not protecting them, that we're looking the other way because we want to see them kill each other. I don't understand some of them anymore. I can't follow their logic and I'm tired of trying."

"You're thirty-four years old; you've got twelve years on the job. Where the hell you goin'?"

"I've been seriously thinking of asking for reassignment as an instructor at the academy. As long as guys do their job there, they'll let you stay as long as you want. I could last there until I got my twenty in. If they turn that down I might try to get a job in security in a big company. My record's been good. It might count for something, and with all these firms in New York worrying about terrorists, the kind of money they're paying guys like me is double what I make on the force and without all the overtime."

"You might feel differently once Dad's case is behind you and you can get some sleep."

"I used to think that, Dan, but I'm not sure any more."

Costa didn't know what else to say, so he offered to buy his friend dinner despite what that would do to his evening's plans. DeLorenzo begged off, blaming a pile of paperwork and a psyche that cried for some sleep. They closed the conversation promising to stay in touch.

Costa pulled the Teller and Worthington files and began preparing the report the D.A. would need to file for indictments. He would normally have waited until after tomorrow's meeting with the prosecutors, but that would have meant doing the paperwork Friday night into Saturday, and that would mean disappointing both Marilyn Kyme and himself. To wait until Monday to complete the report would not please anyone and could either place Rinaldi in jeopardy or give him too much time to rethink his decision. For all the right reasons he would labor into the night, get a reasonably restful sleep and enjoy the hell out of the weekend, a prospect certain to add fuel to his evening's fire.

Night shift personnel stopped by periodically with some well-intentioned inquiries about his father's case, others simply because Dan Costa was the kind of guy with whom you wanted to be friendly. Despite the interruptions he was making good progress when the phone rang. He chose to let the answering tape come on, hoping that someone had punched in the wrong extension. He picked it up quickly when he recognized Donna Schulman's voice.

"It's me, Donna, how are you?"

"Okay, Dan, I'm glad I caught you. Got a second?"

"Sure," he replied, disappointed that Jack had spoken to her about their call, contrary to his wishes, and wondering now how to handle it without alerting her to his suspicions.

"I've been wanting to talk to you but I needed to do it without Jack," she said, her voice sounding suddenly serious. "It's personal."

Dan still wasn't certain Jack hadn't exposed his concerns, but he was less prepared to believe he had. "Did you speak to Jack? Is that how you got my number?"

"No, in fact, I've been avoiding him. He was just here, knocking on the door, but I didn't answer. After he left I decided I couldn't wait any longer to speak to you."

"This is sounding very mysterious," Dan said, trying to put a light touch on what he supposed would be tantamount to a confession. "How did you get my number?" he asked, still not convinced Jack hadn't persuaded her to voluntarily divulge what she knew.

"I remembered your precinct, so I called information. The desk sergeant told me you probably wouldn't be in, but I thought leaving a message would be a good start."

"A good start to what?"

With some hesitation she finally said, "A good start to being totally honest with you about a few things."

"Sounds like it's very personal, like something between us?"

"I wish," she laughed. "Maybe you'll look at it that way though," her voice reflecting both concern and hope.

"Is it something we can discuss on the phone?"

"No, but I'm willing to come to the city. Are you home this weekend?"

*So you'll be seeing Alex Norville,* Dan thought. "I'm taking a trip, leaving tomorrow, but I'll be back in time to meet with you first thing Monday morning. Can you swing that?"

"Looks like I don't have a choice."

Dan detected genuine disappointment, but wasn't sure of what motivated it. He preferred to believe she wanted to rid herself of the guilt she felt for having withheld information, but he knew that it could just as easily be something of a more designing purpose. Donna had not always taken care to conceal the looks she had given him, looks that had made both Marilyn and him uncomfortable. Though he would have otherwise been flattered, the fact that she did it in Marilyn's presence made him think less of her. Even more incriminating could be an effort on her part and on behalf of Norville to submit misleading and false evidence or to try to determine the status of the investigation. He decided that if either were her purpose, he wouldn't be so lenient when debating if charges should be filed against her.

"Where will you be staying?" he asked.

"How about your apartment?" she teased.

"I told you, I'm going on a trip, won't be home until Sunday night."

She seemed confused. "I don't need a place to stay until Monday night. I'm driving in that morning."

That stopped him. He was certain she had told Jack Shultz a lie in order to meet Alex Norville in Manhattan, but she sounded convincing in her denial.

"Will you be driving in from Nuremberg?"

"Nope, I'll be in Philly; thought I'd sleep at a friend's down there, get up early and meet you at your office, if that's okay."

Confused past caring, he gave her directions from the NJ Turnpike and Lincoln Tunnel, warning that unless she left Philly by six, the traffic would add an hour to the three-hour drive.

"Well," she sighed, "I won't look my alluring best, but I'll take your advice. See you at nine. And thanks, Dan."

She seemed so relieved that he began to wonder how her mood could be explained in light of her affair with Norville, if not her implication in the conspiracy. Nothing would make him happier than to learn that Rinaldi and the doorman were wrong, that she had a hundred relatives and was innocent of all his suspicions, but logic convinced him otherwise.

He completed the case report around midnight, got about five hours sleep and was back in the office by seven-thirty, in time to get an update from Rasheed before Al Wilson's arrival. Martin had documented every delivery of HIV infected blood from the New York area hospitals to the doctors' group practice, over five hundred samples, each from a different donor. He ignored the details of another five hundred non-HIV infected samples, which he assumed were simply sent as part of the practice's routine.

"Good work," Dan said, as he fingered the carefully typed pages of patient numbers, dates and codes representing stages of infection.

"Got something more interesting than that. Take a look at these."

Costa had never seen the forms before. "What are they?"

"Samples of the forms Teller and Berger had to complete for the blood disposal company."

There were about forty pages, all of which looked the same to Dan. After fanning them he studied the one on top, dated two years earlier. Covering both front and back, it listed much of the same information Rasheed's files contained, together with data common to the combined samples.

"Looks like what I'd expect the FDA or NIH to require before the blood could be incinerated, or whatever they do with it."

"Look at the first page and then one from a year later," Rasheed suggested, enjoying the little game. "They're in chronological order."

A minute or so passed and then Costa's eyes widened. "Holy shit," he whispered, turning back to the first three sheets, restudying them carefully before raising his eyes to his partner. "If these mean what I think they do, Teller might have found a cure for AIDS. I'll be a sonofabitch."

On each of the three oldest reports, Joe Teller and Lewis Berger identified the blood as "HIV INFECTED." From the fourth on, the forms were identified simply as "NON-HAZARDOUS CADAVER." Each contained the signature of a technician in the employ of the disposal firm verifying the non-infected status of the cadaver. Sometime over a course of one or two years the samples had changed from HIV infected to non-hazardous. Assuming that all of the starting serum had been infected, the absence of HIV in the retention samples of the past two years meant they had been somehow disinfected.

"Unless these have been dummied or we're missing something, we've got a motive for their murders, maybe not as clear-cut as the D.A. would like, but we're sure as hell on the right track," Costa said. "Now all we have to do is figure out why Teller's discovery of a cure should turn the people who funded his effort against him.

"I've been thinking about that," he heard his partner say, "ever since you first told Wilson and me what you thought, and I've come up with two ideas. Teller was either killed because the doctors wanted to cash in early and he felt there was still more to do, or Teller felt he couldn't do more or do it fast enough and needed to bring in help, which might have cut the pie into too many slices to satisfy the doctors. Either way the motive was greed."

Costa was listening, but his mind was retracing aspects of all the related motive theories he had considered since the investigation began. He swiveled the chair slowly, resting his elbows on its arms, bringing his fingers together, changing expressions as thoughts were massaged and discarded.

Martin studied him with interest.

Dan's expression suddenly fixed as he squinted and stared at the ceiling. "Supposing all the work had been done, or at least all the work that research scientists would have had to do, and it was time to announce the discovery and license companies to begin serum manufacturing. Then suppose Steinberg and Norville decided not to do it because they wanted to make a deal with one particular manufacturer. Wouldn't that put more money in their pockets? Wouldn't a Pfizer or an Abbott Labs pay a hell of a lot more for an exclusivity position than all of them would jointly pay for competitive manufacturing that would knock the hell out of retail pricing and profit margins?"

Rasheed mulled it over. "I don't know enough about the ins and outs of pharmaceutical marketing to decide which strategy would guarantee the biggest profit, but I do have another thought. Maybe Teller wanted to give the discovery away, you know, for virtually nothing. You've made him sound like the kind of guy who would do that. Hell, sharing the Nobel for medicine and a half a mil to live on for the rest of his life would sound pretty good to him. Meanwhile, these doctors are thinking a hundred times that apiece."

"Yeah, that's always a possibility," Dan conceded. "Either way the answer is tied up in how much money the doctors wanted out of all this versus Teller's objective to just get the cure into a vial and onto the market as quickly as possible."

But even as he spoke, his mind struggled uncomfortably with the conclusion, though he couldn't quite put his finger on why. Something was missing. Something didn't quite fit.

"It's also possible that Berger and his partners paid the disposal firm to certify the retentions as non-hazardous when they really weren't."

Rasheed added, "And Teller found out, was going to expose them, so they knocked him off."

Dan nodded without speaking, spun his chair to the side and absentmindedly stared out a window.

"What's next?" his partner finally asked, redirecting his attention.

"What's next for you is another drive to get signed statements from the technicians at the disposal firm swearing they ran their tests properly and that the results were as they certified. We have to have substantiation that the first three months of blood had trace contamination, but that none from the next twenty-one or so did, and we have to tie the non-hazardous retentions back to blood samples that were infected when they arrived in Nuremberg. Also, get them to sign non-disclosures. I want everything kept confidential until we announce the arrests."

Martin passed Wilson on his way out, providing a quick recap of the morning's discussion and promising some exciting details from his partner.

Two assistant prosecuting attorneys arrived on time for their meeting with Wilson and Costa. They listened intently and studied the details in Dan's report, scratching notes in the margins of their copies and only occasionally interrupting him to ask a question. When he had finished, the senior of the two announced that he was very happy with the completeness and clarity of the report and that upon culmination of further review they would be back to him.

Anxious to get back to Rinaldi and concerned that he may not have impressed them with a sense of urgency, Dan asked when that might be.

"There's a lot to absorb here, a lot to consider."

"Agreed, but as I pointed out, if we don't move quickly we're going to lose our informant and I'm not sure I can turn up another. Without him we have nothing but circumstantial evidence to link the doctors to Musto, and Musto to the hit men."

"I understand, Sergeant," the older attorney stated, "and we will try to expedite our review, but we do have other pressing work and this is definitely not an open and shut case. Defense can point to your witnesses' prior record, the fact that he's turning state's evidence for a walk on a murder charge and is, at best, an unsavory character. You haven't exactly given me the Pope to work with."

"Yeah, well, that's because murders have a way of attracting unsavory characters."

Neither detective said much after the lawyers had left, consoling each other in the knowledge that the job had been done well and that it was no fault of theirs that the system would take its time, perhaps at the risk of sacrificing a conviction.

Costa left Wilson's office with the feeling that his approach to the job, if not his life, had taken a turn. Conviction of his father's killers was critically important to him, and somewhat less, the punishment of those who had conspired to murder Joe Teller. On the professional front, nothing else...not his career, not other cases...seemed even remotely important. On a personal note there was Marilyn Kyme, and he hoped to elevate his relationship with her to another level this weekend, a step that could change his life and attitude about everything else.

# CHAPTER 17

Two hours west of Nuremberg in north-central Pennsylvania, Eagles Mere rests atop the Endless Mountains, a finger range of the Appalachians. A nineteenth century hideaway for the wealthy, it features a crystal clear alpine lake, toboggan runs, rich conifer forests and most importantly, peaceful solitude. The old estates, many of which were converted into Bed and Breakfasts, sit on densely wooded acres sheltering them from sightseers, traffic and the distractions of a less privileged world.

It was almost ten when Dan turned off Route 80 onto 42 North, through Buckhorn and its patchwork community of Mennonite farms filling the valley at the base of the mountains.

"Be careful," Marilyn warned as they closed in on a horse drawn buggy, its flashing red tail lights seemingly out-of-place on the black and white carriage of the German plainfolk. A stoic driver sporting a long, gray beard, black dress coat and matching broad-brimmed hat stared straight ahead as Dan maneuvered around him.

"I've never seen the Amish," she admitted, turning in her seat and looking back at the great chestnut gelding trotting effortlessly along the blacktop, its box-like carriage dutifully in tow.

"You still haven't," Dan said smiling. "That's a Mennonite buggy, a little different from the Amish."

"How do you know?" she asked suspiciously.

"I read a lot. Well, I used to read a lot," he corrected himself, remembering the long, lonely nights following Eileen's death, nights he endured by burying himself in books, blocking out memories of a love he feared would never be replaced. Today, this night, he knew differently. The feelings he had for Marilyn Kyme were different than those he had had for Eileen, though the two women were very much alike in many ways. Still, there was little doubt his new love had reserved a place in his heart, filling the void that memories of Eileen never would.

"The Mennonite and Amish are both German communities, sub-groups of a single social-religious sect that refers to itself as plainfolk," he continued. "They dress, speak and act alike, except the Mennonite permit electricity and a few other conveniences in their lives, whereas the Amish restrict themselves to an early nineteenth century lifestyle."

Still skeptical, Marilyn asked, "If they dress alike, how do you know that driver wasn't Amish?"

"The partially gray buggy. Amish buggies are all black."

"Are you sure?" She poked him. "Or are you making all this up?"

"Boy Scout's honor."

"Now I know you're lying," she declared. "The Boy Scouts wouldn't have you."

"You're right about that, but I'm not lying about the Amish. People used to call all the plainfolk the Hook and Eye Dutch. Did you know that?"

"No. Why?"

"Because when buttons and zippers were invented, they stuck to their old ways, using the hook and eye to close everything up. Many Amish still do, though some consider buttons okay now."

"I thought you said they were German?" she asked, her suspicions aroused again.

"They are. Anglos bastardized the German word "Deutsche", or misunderstood the pronunciation. I don't know which."

"I'm impressed," she admitted, turning her attention to the scenery.

Pennsylvania State Route 42 began its circuitous climb up the Endless Mountains through quaint little towns proud enough of their double digit populations to advertise them, though the folks in Picture Rocks didn't seem as certain of the census as their neighbors. The sign that bore its name had been twice altered, first to advertise that its population of sixty-two had been increased by one, only to have that crossed off and a newly scribed "sixty-two" painted at the bottom. Dan pondered the possibilities.

They passed through Loyalsock and Elk Grove and were swinging around a curve to the right when Dan hit the brakes and turned the wheel sharply, spinning the Jeep in circles before it came to rest, pointing against all odds in its original direction. Before she could recover enough to scream, Marilyn saw the reason for Dan's maneuver. A black bear, presumably a female, had exited the woods to the left and was slowly making her way across the road, obediently followed by two gamboling cubs barely the size of tomcats. Enchanted, the young lovers watched them until they disappeared into the night. The excitement over, he restarted the stalled engine while she took a deep breath and recovered from the adrenaline rush.

"Next time, please warn me," she begged, before leaning against him, encircling his arm with hers. "They were adorable, weren't they?"

They passed a cobblestone chapel…St. Francis of Assisi Roman Catholic Church… followed by a hand-carved sign advising that they had just entered the *"Village of Eagles Mere, the Town Where Time Stands Still."* Not a creature was stirring in the mist-filled, turn-of-the-century square, its long, lush bowling green eerily illumined by gas lamps perched atop filigreed cast iron poles. A soft mist floated above, partially obscuring the tops of majestic, century old maples and oaks.

"Where the hell have you brought me?" Dan asked jokingly.

"Oh, hush. You have no sense of adventure," she replied, brimming with anticipation of tomorrow's discoveries, searching her pocketbook for directions to the bed and breakfast.

The Raptor's Aerie, built by a Philadelphia sugar merchant in 1880, sat atop a hillock overlooking Rainbow Lake at the end of a long, twisting, spruce bordered drive. A tail-wagging black Lab greeted them as they climbed the granite steps to the wrap-around porch. The evening breeze had a bite to it, but they stood for a moment before the glass double doors, luxuriating in the strong, fresh scent of mountain air enriched with the aroma of the surrounding forest.

"If you buy a house here I'll come visit you," she promised.

"If I buy a house here, you'll damn well marry me and live in it."

The smell of lilacs filled their room, adding an appropriately nostalgic touch to the canopy-covered bed, dry sink and pine-plank floor.

"I absolutely love it," Marilyn decided as she tested the furniture, a sapling-back rocker with gingham blue padding and a thickly tufted Victorian chaise lounge. Dan watched affectionately while unpacking the suitcases, storing their clothes in a well-preserved maple chest of drawers, laying the toilet articles on a triple-mirrored, mahogany dressing table.

He visited the bathroom. "Hey, come here. Look at this."

"I've already seen it," she replied lazily, "and it's not all that great."

"I didn't mean that, you sex maniac. I mean the bathroom. Come take a look."

The tub and sink were nineteenth century relics supported by gilded bases in the shape of eagles' claws. Elsewhere, from the wooden toilet seat and plank floor to the mosaic window and bronze gaslight fixtures, the décor spoke of a quieter, more serene life far removed from the hectic, sometimes obscene world in which the two survived.

He wrapped her in his arms. "We could live here, you know. No more worries about terrorists, crime or traffic. I could get a job like Jack Shultz's. You could hang out a shingle. Family practice wouldn't be so bad."

She tilted her head back, looking up questioningly. "You could honestly be happy here?"

"With you? Absolutely."

"And you'd never regret leaving the city, the excitement, your friends, your job?"

"You mean the terrorists, pollution, gridlock, escalating taxes and crime?" he asked sarcastically. "My friends and the city we can visit. As for my work, it was my escape hatch until I met you. Now you're my refuge, and as long as I've got you I don't need anything else, least of all a job in a city that may never be safe again," he said, mindful of the two cases that consumed him and the realities of Islamic prejudice and intolerance.

"I don't know that I could walk away from my family and career," she admitted, lowering her eyes. "I've studied and worked hard to get where I'm at and Dante keeps reminding me that he'll step aside in a year or two and the job will be mine." She looked back up at him. "I'll be the New York City Medical Examiner at the age of thirty. Do you know how proud my parents will be?"

"Your parents? What about you?"

Marilyn wished she hadn't mentioned them. "Please, Dan, I'm really tired and you probably are too. It's almost midnight. Why don't we go to bed, and I promise, we will talk about everything before the weekend's up."

After a hearty breakfast they took their host's advise and hired a horse-drawn carriage for an hour's drive along the mountain ridge, down into the valley, around Rainbow Lake and through the town, past narrow streets lined with quaint shops and tiny cafes. If either had a care in the world, they didn't show it. To those who observed them, they were simply a remarkably handsome couple, probably very much in love.

They spent the afternoon walking through the shops, purchasing scented soaps and candles, local crafts and small gifts for each other. They lounged in a used bookstore, marveled at the skill of an itinerant glass blower and casually nursed sodas in an old-fashioned ice cream parlor. A town crier announced the arrival of a chainsaw sculptor who would shortly display his talent in the square, so they finished their drinks and made their way back up the bowling green where thirty or so tourists were milling about, soaking up the sun and sights.

The roar of a chainsaw shattered the idyllic setting, though the artist got right to the task, focusing his audience's attention on his work and away from the noise. Employing a five foot high piece of dark walnut in the shape of a "Y," he chewed the outline of a perched eagle, its wings spread wide in majestic pose. He shifted to a shorter blade to rip detail into the feathers, around the eyes and along the hooked beak, chips and dust flying as the great bird emerged from its wooden shell. Less than a half-hour passed before he flicked the switch and stepped back in critical judgement, nipping fragments here and there with a razor sharp chisel. Finally, amidst a chorus of oohs and ahs, well-dones and polite applause, he announced his task complete. Asking price was three hundred dollars, a bargain considering its beauty and unique genesis, but at six hundred dollars an hour, a more than adequate return on the effort invested.

Arm in arm, they strolled back to their room where the intended showers and changes of clothing were twice interrupted by sexual forays. A third was postponed by Dan's observation that man does not live by sex alone and that he was hungry enough to eat her…literally. She relented only after securing his oath to eclipse all previous performances once dinner and dancing were concluded.

They dined in a lakeside restaurant where the owner boasted that Walt Whitman and other literary notables had once enjoyed robust dishes of elksteak, venison and shepherd's pie, though Dan and Marilyn selected from a more familiar menu, choosing chilled oysters, Caesar salad and sautéed trout.

They opted for another carriage ride around the lake before joining the residents at the traditional Saturday night dance under the stars, an invigorating affair so early in the season. The gazebo in the center of the square overflowed with couples clinging to each other as much for warmth as affection. Dan led Marilyn to a slate patio beneath the trees where a handful of young couples had gathered. They swayed to the big band sounds of a surprisingly gifted quartet, each member as distinct from the other in age and dress as their audience. One fellow deftly alternated between trumpet, sax and trombone, drawing Dan's admiration, while another, clarinet notwithstanding, threatened to fall asleep. "I wonder if that guy will open his eyes?" Dan asked seriously.

"Maybe he has to keep them shut to play well," Marilyn joked.

"I knew a priest like that once. Could rattle on all day as long as he didn't look at his congregation. Soon as he did, he forgot the whole sermon."

Marilyn eyed him suspiciously, soliciting an avowal of honesty. "I still don't believe you," she persisted. "I love you, but I don't believe you. In fact, I'll always love you, but I'll never believe you." She laughed and they kissed. "And I've decided you lied to me about the Amish and the Mennonites."

Dan surveyed the gathering for someone to corroborate his story. He led Marilyn by the hand, across the green and up the gazebo steps, angling his way through the shuffling couples to a comely middle-aged woman dancing with an older, distinguished looking gentleman.

"Hi," he introduced himself. "You're the owner of the bookstore, aren't you?"

"Yes," the still attractive brunette responded. "I believe you were in my shop today."

"Yes, we were. Enjoyed it immensely. I was hoping you could clarify something for me. I've been telling my girlfriend here that the Amish and Mennonites are different, that they're kind of the same sect, but that the Amish cling closer to the old ways."

"That's a pretty fair statement," she said.

"And I think the Amish have black buggies but the Mennonites paint theirs gray and black. Is that true?"

The lady nodded, but it was her escort that answered. "Well, you could be right since the Amish use no colors except black and white. The Mennonite allow a little gray into their lives, though I'm not certain it's written in stone that they have to paint parts of their carriages gray."

"See?" Marilyn chirped.

"See what?"

"The gentleman said a Mennonite doesn't have to paint it gray, only if he wants to."

"Right, but if it is gray, it's Mennonite, not Amish, and that's what I told you."

"He always has to have his way," Marilyn said to the amused couple. "It's getting to be a real problem. We may have to recommit him for a few weeks. Sometimes one treatment doesn't do it."

They left the gazebo with the older couple wondering if they hadn't been at least in part the butt of a younger couple's joke.

"That wasn't nice," Dan said with a smile.

"That'll teach you to drag me up steps and ridicule me in front of strangers."

"I'm going to drag you up the steps tonight, alright, and it won't be to ridicule you."

"Promises, promises."

Sunday passed too quickly, so they promised each other they would return for a week's vacation in the fall when the leaves were changing and the brisk evening air would make sleeping together all the more romantic. During the drive back to Manhattan, Marilyn closed her eyes and slept while Dan rehearsed what he would say when she awoke. As the Jeep maneuvered the series of curves spanning the Delaware Water Gap, she opened her eyes, struggling to recognize the landscape, wondering what time it was.

"We're in New Jersey," Dan said. "You'll be home by midnight."

"No I won't," she moaned, "I'm staying with you."

"Can we talk a little now?"

"Sure. What do you want to talk about?" She seemed less interested than he would have liked.

"We have to talk about us. I love you and I think you love me, and we've got to decide what we're going to do about it."

"What's the matter with the way things are?"

"Nothing, except I can't call you at night, don't know who you live with and why you won't talk about it."

He waited for her to speak, but she turned away and stared out the window, obviously uncomfortable with the whole subject.

"I love you very much and I seriously doubt there is anything you can tell me that will change that. You've got to trust me," he added.

"I do trust you, Dan, and I love you every bit as much as you love me, probably more."

"Then tell me what's bothering you. We'll work it out together. That's what people in love do," he said, reaching over to give her a reassuring touch.

Shifting in the seat, she turned towards him. "My parents are Orthodox," she confessed, as though that presented some permanent impediment to their happiness.

"So what?"

"So they'll never approve of us, don't you see? You're not even Jewish, let alone Orthodox. They'll never accept you."

"Do they really love and care about you?"

"Of course. Jewish parents live for their kids, you know that."

"So they'll want to see you happy?"

"I know where you're going and I can tell you it's not that simple. They'll think I've betrayed them and that will put a guilt trip on them because they'll think they failed me. The very fact that they're Orthodox closes the door on even considering my marriage to an outsider, let alone an Italian Catholic."

"Yeah, we're a real bunch of shits," Dan said, his disappointment tinged with sarcasm. "So where does that leave us?"

"I don't know and that's why I've avoided telling you about them. I have to come up with a solution, Dan, you can't. You're nowhere near close enough to it to understand how black and white they are. Orthodox Judaism is about as close-minded as it gets. They're good people," she reminded him, "just very parochial. To them it's the only true faith, and faith is everything."

He loved her too much to see her agonize over something she had obviously devoted time and thought to, but he needed to understand where he stood.

"I promise to drop the subject if you'll answer just two questions."

"I'll try."

"Do you intend to keep thinking about what we can do to resolve this problem so that we can get married someday? It means a lot to me."

"Of course," she exclaimed, as though the answer should have been obvious.

"And secondly, if I told you this second that you had to make a decision, once and for all, me or your parents' feelings, what would it be?"

"You wouldn't ask me to make that choice right now, Dan. If you did, I'd know you didn't really love me."

That wasn't the answer he wanted to hear, but it was an honest one, so he just pulled her closer and wondered if Marilyn Kyme would indeed be the woman with whom he would spend the rest of his life. He had seemed so certain of it yesterday, but now he was beginning to think it might never happen. They rode in silence the rest of the way, each hoping that they hadn't added to the obstacle that confronted them.

For the first time they shared a bed without making love, though they fell asleep in each other's arms, fearing if they didn't, nothing would ever be the same again.

As he approached his desk the phone rang. It was Joe DeLorenzo.

"Got good news, Dan. Booker's our man. We arrested him last night in his apartment. The last two missing articles, the crucifix and your mom's diamond ring, were in a drawer. I would have called sooner but we didn't wrap up the interrogation until two this morning."

"Did he confess?"

"Nah, he's a cocky hard-ass, the kind you want to smack around. Never looked at me. Directed all his answers to Calvin and Williams. Told them they looked like an Oreo. Jerked his thumb in my direction and said, 'with that guinea honky over there.'"

"Yeah, and all the racists are white," Dan muttered. "What's the next move?"

"I don't think he's going to give it up, particularly now that he's got Jason Muhammed as an attorney."

Muhammed was the poor man's answer to Johnnie Cochran. He had played the race card long before it brought Cochran notoriety and he knew how to use community sentiment, political pressure and the press to influence prosecuting attorneys. By the time he was finished, they begged for a chance to plea bargain.

"So it looks like he might take a rap for receiving stolen property and then have trouble remembering who he bought it from," Dan said. "Muhammed's used that so often law schools include it in their curriculum. Guilt or innocence doesn't mean a damn thing to that sonofabitch. He'll say anything to get a black off the hook, particularly if the victim was white." He paused a moment, reflecting on what he had said. "I hate that kind of talk, Joe, but some of the blacks are no better than the Klan, and Muhammed fits the bill."

"Don't apologize for the truth," his friend said. "Muhammed's responsible for more crime in this city than any one person I know. He preaches racism, fires up the punks and then gets them off, but we only have ourselves to blame. We say we should treat everyone the same, but then we make excuses for some of these shitheads, blame it on their underprivileged backgrounds. On top of that we're afraid to say anything because it's not politically correct. I wish some of them would start taking their hatred out on the politicians. Then we'd see how fast everybody's tune would change."

Dan tired of the conversation. They had had it too often and it had never led to solutions, just more frustration. "So you have the stolen property and the pawnbroker, but nothing to tie Booker to Dad's murder?"

"Right, that's about it. Calvin's due in at nine to take Booker's mug shots over to your dad's neighborhood. If we can put him in or near the apartment building around the time of your dad's murder, he'll have to come up with more than an anonymous seller to explain how your dad's things came to be in his apartment."

"I've been thinking about something, Joe. How far does this Booker live from Dad's?"

"Miles. He's from Bedford-Stuyvesant."

"Then he had to have an accomplice, somebody in Dad's immediate neighborhood, if not in the apartment."

"I agree, and Calvin and I have a suspicion."

"The Turner kid?"

"Yeah. Why do you make him for it?"

Dan didn't bother to relate all he had concluded weeks before. He hadn't wanted to think that the son of one of his father's best friends might be involved, but Mattie Turner's emotions and her husband's conduct upon his arrival home the night of the murder all pointed to their knowledge and subsequent cover-up, if not of the killers' identities, then at least of their suspicions.

"Can you trust Calvin?"

"I trust him as much as any guy in the old neighborhood, and I'd go to bat for him as quickly as I would you. We can trust him."

"Just asking. It might be wise if he didn't let on to Booker being in custody. Muhammed could twist that in court, suggesting people ID'd him only after they knew he was in jail for something."

"Good thought," Joe admitted. "We can't take too many precautions with this case."

The arrival of Al Wilson prompted Dan to close the conversation, but not before reminding his friend to keep him advised of any developments.

"Let's spend a few minutes in my office," Wilson suggested, holding aloft a deli bag containing coffee and Danish. He handed Dan one of each before setting himself down with a grimace.

"Your back again?"

"Spine, to be exact," his friend responded, shifting his weight in search of some relief. "Degenerative spinal arthritis." He spoke the words disdainfully. "Not a lot they can do for it, except that I can lose some weight," he said, followed by a chuckle. "Every goddamn time you have a pain below the neck they tell you to lose weight. I could teach medical school today. Pain above the neck, give 'em aspirin. Pain below the neck, tell 'em to lose weight."

"You forgot 'no salt.'"

"Yeah," he chuckled, "no salt. That cures everything above and below the neck."

"You should try to lose a little," Dan said. "It wouldn't hurt."

Al Wilson ignored the advice. He enjoyed his prune Danish and coffee; wouldn't think of foregoing them. To hell with his spine, to hell with his weight and to hell with his doctor. *'Screw 'em all,'* he thought, as they finished eating in silence.

"Joe D call you yet?"

"Just now. How did you know?"

"Avent phoned this morning. Filled me in on the arrest. Wanted me to know he would stay close to it and keep me advised."

"Nice of him," Dan said cynically.

"Don't be sarcastic. I think his heart's in the right place on this one."

"I hope so, Al, because if it isn't and he gets in the way, he's going to get hurt."

Wilson knew his friend meant what he said. It was no idle threat and that worried him. "I'm your friend and don't forget it. If you suspect anyone is trying to cover up anything, you come to me. I don't want you destroying your life doing something stupid, regardless of how much anyone might deserve it. I'll make things right, I promise."

Dan nodded. "You're a good person, Al, and a better friend. I'll try not to disappoint you. But," he added seriously, "I've had my fill of certain types of people – murderers, hypocrites, politicians – and most of all, those who keep excusing what they do. They're not God's people, Al. He doesn't give two shits about them, and if He doesn't, then I sure as hell don't."

"I hear you, but just remember, they're not worth you losing everything you've worked for. Besides, this city needs men like you, so you just catch the bad guys and let me worry about keeping them where they belong, at least the one or two we're talking about here. And by the way, read your Bible. Even the bad guys are God's people and we're to leave the judging to Him."

Dan left, noting that it was almost nine, time for a job he wished he didn't have to do, but one that might well turn the tide in the Teller case.

He didn't have to wait long as a sudden quiet overcame the usually noisy squad room. Dan turned to see Donna Schulman attired in tight navy blue pants and a matching waist jacket, happily bouncing towards him on three inch heals, looking every bit the fantasy of virile men's dreams. If she had risen before dawn and driven all the way from Philly, her radiant face and smiling red lips belied the ordeal. She seemed oblivious to the attention being paid her, fixing her eyes seductively on Dan. He had to admit, she was some looker and he would have been in hot pursuit if not for Jack Shultz and Marilyn Kyme, not to mention her probable role in the Teller conspiracy.

"Good morning, Sergeant. Sorry I'm a little late," she purred.

*Why,* Dan thought, *does everything this woman says sound so inviting?* He suddenly wished Jack and Marilyn were there.

"Have a seat, Donna," he said, trying to sound official. Over her shoulder he could see the appreciative eyes of his fellow detectives, as well as those of a few uniformed officers who had climbed the stairs for a final look.

She turned in her chair to see what he was glaring at, smiling at her conquests who smiled back appreciatively.

"Proud of yourself?" he asked.

"Shouldn't I be?"

"You shouldn't flaunt it."

"I don't think I do. This isn't exactly a negligee. What am I supposed to wear?"

"Nothing, forget it," Dan replied, disappointed with himself for getting personal with a witness, someone critical to the case, but about whom he had so many questions. He reminded himself of the purpose and importance of their meeting.

"How was the drive up?"

"Good. The traffic wasn't bad at all until I got to the tunnel helix."

"You had some things you wanted to discuss with me?"

Her smile disappeared. "Is there a place we can talk in private?"

"Sure. Let me see what's available. I'll have to check with the Lieutenant," he lied, as he headed towards Wilson's office.

"Man, you didn't do the girl justice," Wilson declared, remembering Dan's summation of his trip to Nuremberg and his description of Donna. "It is definitely going to be difficult to keep that lady out of my dreams," he admitted, stretching to look around his friend.

"You're happily married, cut the shit."

"Yeah, but I'm not dead, and even if I was, I'll bet she could still get me up," he laughed in a way Dan had rarely heard him.

"Well, keep in mind, that lady may be up to her beautiful tits in a murder investigation, and as an accessory to boot. So why don't you do me a favor and put somebody in the viewing room to take notes in case I get her to open up."

"I'll listen in myself," Wilson volunteered, raising Dan's curiosity. "Hey, it's part of the job. Now get out of here and do yours."

Dan poured coffee while making idle talk, trying to get her to relax. She smiled nervously as he recounted stories about the precinct's building, its history, some of the comical episodes it had witnessed and criminals it had housed. Finally, he sat facing her and asked why she had requested the meeting.

She started right in, fixing her eyes on Dan's. He was struck by her intensity. "My real name is Kempler, Donna Kempler. My father was Doctor John Kempler, a contemporary for a short time of Richard Snively, the father of enzyme research in the States. It was my father who taught and worked with Teller and Berger on Chincoteague Island...that is, until he was murdered."

"Pardon me a second, Donna, but my partner spent time on Chincoteague with the police chief, researching Teller's work there. He told me about a Doctor Kempler who died in a car accident...drove off a causeway. Was that your father?"

"My father was murdered," Donna responded angrily, raising her voice and surprising Dan. "Those idiot cops were convinced Dad was drunk because there was an empty bottle in the car. The thought that it could have been planted never crossed their minds. If they had bothered to speak to the bartenders that knew my father, as I did, they would have learned that Dad never left the place drunk. He always knew when he had had enough, and everybody that was familiar with him would have sworn to that. As for the bottle in the car; did you ever know of a scotch drinker who got drunk on vodka?" Her eyes reflected her bitterness and gave Dan cause to rethink the possibilities.

After regaining her composure she continued. "I got word he was killed about a month after it happened. I was doing Peace Corps work at the time in Peru, and by the time I got to Chincoteague after another month had passed, Teller and Berger had left and no one seemed to know where they had gone. I didn't know it at the time, but Berger had made a big deal out of their failure to make any progress, blaming it on my father, telling everyone the project was dead and that Teller had headed home. I returned to Peru, partly because I felt so alone and helpless, partly because I wanted to fulfill my obligation."

Dan was beginning to believe her, in which case, she didn't fit the mold in which he had caste her.

"An acquaintance of my father's, a lady I met when I visited Chincoteague, corresponded with me over the next year or so. She told me that Doctor Teller was doing research in a little town in Pennsylvania. He had apparently been in touch with a guy from the island who had mentioned it to my friend. She got me the name of the town, and when my commitment with the Peace Corps was completed, I decided to move to the Nuremberg area and see what I could learn about my father's death."

"What made you think Teller or Berger knew anything?"

"Dad never trusted the medical doctors that funded the research work on the island. They promised him a lot more than they ever delivered. He became particularly upset when they told him to hire Berger because Dad didn't feel he was qualified. Aside from that, he neither liked nor trusted him. Dr. Teller had to play mediator and it was only because of him that Dad remained with the program. They needed each other. Dad was a renowned virologist, maybe tops in his field. Dr. Teller held similar stature in enzymology. Together they formed a hell of a pair."

She paused briefly, reflecting fondly on some memorable moment she had shared with her father.

"Anyway," she continued, "Dad kept telling me how he didn't care for the medical doctors and how he was going to have it out with them as soon as he completed phase one of the study."

"Phase one?" Dan asked.

"I'm not sure what that meant, except that Dad was to be paid a bonus of some kind once phase one, whatever that was, was completed. He kept promising me a long vacation and money for my doctorate, so I guess he felt completing phase one was not a problem. Then, he claimed, he had an opportunity to renegotiate compensation before initiating phase two, which if it were completed successfully, would make him millions. Those where his words."

"So you thought Teller knew about all this and that's why you tried to find him?"

"I knew that my Dad trusted Joe Teller, for whatever reasons. What I also knew was that my father never trusted the doctors or Berger, that he was going to eventually confront them and that money was involved. All that was enough to arouse my suspicions about how he had died, and since Dr. Teller was key to the project's success, following him might lead me to the truth. By the time I found him, I was so paranoid that I didn't trust anyone, so I changed my name and concealed my identity from everyone, including Jack."

"Does he know you came to see me?"

"No. I trust him now, but I've decided what I want to do with the rest of my life and Jack doesn't fit in."

"He's a helluva' good man," Dan said earnestly, "and I know he cares deeply about you."

"Not enough to do what I intend."

"And what is that?"

"That's got nothing to do with what I'm here for, so let's skip it."

"It has everything to do with our conversation if revenge is what's on your mind. You can't just take the law into your own hands without paying a price and I'd hate to see that."

"Don't be melodramatic, Dan. I want to see whoever killed my father get what's coming to them, but I'll let the law do its job and then I'll be out of here. I'm not in love with this country. I just want to find out who killed my father and let heroes like you take it from there."

She was winning him over. "Okay, I'm on your side and we'll see this thing through together, right to the end, provided you answer one personal question."

"Shoot."

"If you believed those doctors were involved in your father's murder, how could you have an affair with one of them? We know you visited Norville on weekends and that you stayed overnight in his Manhattan condo."

"Is that what you think I did? You think I slept with him?"

"I jumped to that conclusion, yes. Did you?"

"No, I didn't. Not once, not ever. He met Greg Chadwick in Nuremberg on two occasions to oversee installation of the computers. He drooled all over me each time so I led him on in hopes of getting to the bottom of everything. He was easy to manipulate. I think I would have eventually gotten him to tell me everything."

"But you stayed with him overnight. What the hell did you do?"

"Are you just curious, Sergeant, or is this part of the investigation?"

"I need to know you're not lying to me, Donna. If we're going to help each other then you're going to eventually learn everything we know, and that could seriously jeopardize our case. Everything we have here is circumstantial. If you were to tell Norville and Steinberg what we have, they could cover every one of their tracks."

Donna looked at the two-way mirror that separated the viewing and interrogation rooms. "Who's in there?" she asked, pointing to it.

Dan stood and headed for the door. "I'll be right back. Pour yourself some more coffee."

"What do you think, Al?"

"I want to believe that she's telling you the truth," Wilson replied as he watched Donna walk to the cabinet and refill her cup. "I want to believe her because it's a helluva' story, and if it's true, she's a helluva' girl."

"We think alike, Al…with our hearts. Care to join me? I don't want to lie to her and she may not say anything too personal if she thinks someone's in here."

"Nah, I'm satisfied. Do what you think will get us some convictions."

When Dan reentered the interrogation room, Donna was standing in front of the window, her hair sparkling in the midday sun. He couldn't help but think how beautiful she was.

"My boss was alone in there, but he's gone back to his office. He's satisfied with your story. Can we continue?"

"Why not. I think you wanted to know how and why I spent some weekends with Alex Norville. You already know why. The how is less obvious, I guess." She looked at Dan. It was a confident, yet somehow reluctant stare, one that spoke of self-assurance others might not understand.

"Alex Norville is a masochist. He likes to be dominated by a woman, particularly one that looks as good in leather as I do. So I oblige him. I even find some twisted sense of satisfaction in doing it, and you'll never know how many times I've been tempted to really put a hurting on him, or worse. But we never had sex. I've never let him touch me, though I've promised him all kinds of stuff. I don't know how long I can keep him happy this way, but I think I'm getting him to the point where he'll do just about anything I want."

Dan said nothing, though he looked at her in a way that said he understood and that everything was all right between them.

"So maybe I lied, maybe it was sex in some twisted kind of way, but not to me. To me it was getting one tiny step closer to the truth the only way I could."

"You don't have to make excuses. You did what you thought was right and not too many women would have had the guts to do it."

They sat quietly for a while, sipping coffee. Dan debated about whether he wanted to involve Donna further, knowing that if he was wrong, if she was there as an accomplice to determine what he knew, he shouldn't say another word. On the other hand, if she was everything she professed to be, it would be difficult to take advantage of her position with Norville if he didn't tell her more. He needed time to think.

"What are your plans for today?"

"I'm having lunch with a sorority sister who works for CBS. Then I'll get a hotel room because we're going to try to get tickets for a show tonight. In between I thought I'd do some shopping."

"That means you're free tomorrow morning?"

"Yes. Why?"

"Here's my home phone number. Leave a message where you're staying and I'll pick you up there tomorrow morning for breakfast. That will give me time to put a plan together."

"You mean you need that much time to decide whether or not you can trust me, and I don't blame you. Before today very little of what I said was the truth."

Dan respected her honesty and admired her power of deduction.

"Yeah, well, maybe there's some of that, too, but I really do have to think about how we can take advantage of what we each know. We're too close to screw it up now."

Donna Kempler broke out in a big smile.

He noticed. "What's so funny?"

"We're not, you know."

"Not what?"

"Too close to screw," and she blushed, laughing to conceal it.

"You have a one track mind. Just don't forget to call me tonight," he reminded her as he led her out of the room and down the corridor to the stairs.

"Don't loiter down there," he warned, "unless you want a dozen offers."

"God! Do I really look that cheap?"

"No," he admitted, "just downright gorgeous."

She smiled and reached out her hand to touch his cheek. Somehow neither of them thought it inappropriate.

He waited until she turned right at the bottom of the stairs and disappeared into the suddenly quiet main-room of the Thirty-fourth Precinct, the normally deafening, raucous chamber where protesting suspects competed with dispirited patrolmen and frustrated desk-sergeants. In about the time it took Donna to walk to the door and through the vestibule, the bedlam resumed.

Costa was staring off into space, accomplishing little in his effort to sort out the conflicting evidence of the Teller case, while his heart and mind kept bringing him back to his father's. Al Wilson's voice seemed a welcome relief.

"Need to talk?"

"Yeah, might do some good," Dan conceded.

He rattled off all the facts and conclusions he had collected to date, holding back on the identity of the informers who had fingered Albert Tataro and Carlo Rinaldi and emphasizing his certainty that their attorney, James Musto, had been the middleman in their dealings with the doctors. He expressed concern that with client privilege on their side, little if any of the circumstantial evidence he had on the doctors would lead to anything sustainable in court. The same applied to Dave Richards, the FDA auditor whom Dan was certain had played a key role in the identification and murder of Clarence Worthington. Together with the Berger homicide, Musto and the doctors had very efficiently severed any ties to witnesses who had either direct knowledge of their motives or of their roles in the conspiracy.

"Short of Donna getting a full confession from Alex Norville, I'm not sure we have anything they can't refute in court, or at least enough to confuse a jury"

"I hate to admit it, but I think you may be right," Wilson agreed, "but you did a helluva' job figuring it all out."

"A lot of good that will do. I'd rather trip over my own feet and get a conviction."

"I'm gonna' think on it a bit," Wilson promised as he stood and stretched his back. "Some of this evidence ought to be able to stand on its own, particularly if that Rinaldi character substantiates it."

"You know, Al, it's times like this I wish the courts would recognize the difference between suspects and criminals and let us sweat some confessions out of these creeps. Sometimes I wonder how many fewer people would be killed if we had more leeway."

"The problem is that not everyone would use more power for the right purpose. Look at Jenkins. Would you want to give someone like him more authority? It's a fine line the law has to walk and I think it does a pretty damn good job under the circumstances. If it makes our work a little more difficult, well, that's why they pay us the big bucks," he said smiling. "Don't get yourself sick over this. Sooner or later we'll hit on an idea and these doctors, Musto, that FDA rep...all of 'em, they'll get what they deserve."

"What they deserve is what they gave Teller," Dan said flatly.

Wilson could only offer unspoken agreement before heading back to his office, leaving his friend as he had found him, deep in thought, searching for an answer.

# CHAPTER 18

The solution was inspired by a mounting concern that his father's case could easily go the same route Teller's appeared to be headed. Given that, he knew what he would do and he began to understand that the Teller case justified similar action. So he started formulating the steps that had to be taken, the people he would need and the roles they would play. By noon he had devised a plan, surprised that he was neither concerned about its possible failure nor the affect it would have on the rest of his life. If a less drastic alternative could be found he would use it, but failing that, he was committed to seeing this new scheme through to the end.

He was preparing to leave when Rasheed Martin dropped himself heavily into a chair. "Man, I'm exhausted."

Dan ignored him as he gathered his notes, stacked and stapled them, sealing them in a manila envelope.

"Heading out?" Martin asked.

"Yeah. Got a lunch appointment. Need me?"

"No, that's alright," his partner replied unconvincingly.

Dan felt guilty. "Sorry, I'm a little preoccupied. What have you got?"

"Nothing, really. Just wanted you to know I canvassed the Fourth Avenue neighborhood where that drug killing went down and we got what sounds like corroboration from three different people on a description of the shooter. They're downstairs looking at mugshots now and I've arranged for them to meet with the artist if they don't pick anybody out."

"Good work, Rasheed. I mean it. You've been handling a lot of these on your own and I'll see you get full credit."

"No need. You'd do the same for me."

"Better not be so accomodating. I'll start to think you're white," Dan joked.

Martin screwed up his face. "You really know how to hurt a guy."

Massimo Barracci, Muzzi and Vito Scarola were seated in the corner of a tiny restaurant in Bay Ridge, shoveling cold antipasto onto their plates. A wickered bottle of Chianti and two sesame-crusted loaves of Italian bread completed the fare.

As they ate Dan spelled out his idea, at times surprising Barracci with some of the more sordid details and levels of risk. Neither Muzzi nor Scarola heard anything startling enough to distract them from their food, though they did glance up once or twice without skipping a bite. By the time the last crumb had been used to sponge the last drop of balsamic, Dan had laid out his entire plan, together with the one or two contingencies he thought necessary. The Don was impressed.

"You would have made a hell of a consigliere." He looked to his soldiers for confirmation, which they gave with grunts and slow nods of their heads, though they both wished for more important roles in the scheme. Dan sensed their disappointment.

"Uncle Massimo has been more than kind to me," he told them, "and it would be disrespectful of me to ask for his help before I tried to resolve this problem myself. I only ask him for your help if I fail because I know he would not refuse me and you would never fail me."

Their pride restored, they turned their attention to espresso and lemon biscotto, ignoring an inferior Sambucca.

Dan finished his business, slightly regretting the full disclosure he had made. Now Barracci knew all the players, including the details of Donna's previous involvement as well as her future role, but he felt it was necessary in light of the commitment he was asking the Don to make. Besides, he wasn't worried that Barracci might intentionally divulge the scheme, only what might accidentally be uncovered should he be unsuccessful. Since disclosing some of the more sensitive information couldn't be avoided, he decided to ignore the risks, confident he had devised a plan that could work, had provided for contingencies, and that no better option existed. His only alternatives were to round file the investigation, wait for the D.A.'s office to move with what they had, which he knew they were unlikely to do, or turn everything over to the Barracci family, a not altogether inappropriate conclusion given the treachery of the conspirators and the finality the *capo* and his people would bring to the affair. Whatever ingenuity Scarola and Muzzi might employ in disposing of Steinberg, Norville and Musto could be justified by what they had done to Teller, Worthington and Donna's father. Dan would feel no remorse if it had to come down to that.

As he drove along the BQE towards Bobby Avent's Canarsie headquarters, the knowledge that his life had taken some dramatic turns in the past few months weighed heavily on him. His growing dissatisfaction with the job and life in the city was understandable. There were too many politically correct influences and too few resources available to do an adequate job. He knew good cops were needed more than ever and that he could cope with the distractions if he chose to ignore them, but he seemed to welcome them as excuses for his feelings. His father's murder, the bombings and political diatribe over civil rights versus the war on terror…they were all closing in on him, making it increasingly difficult to separate issues in his life. He was obsessed with the negatives to the exclusion of anything positive, including his relationship with Marilyn. Even that was no longer a reprieve from his anxiety, not since she had disclosed her parents prejudice and her concern for their feelings, putting her own happiness at risk. He was beginning to think he needed a new start, a different life, away from New York, far from the circumstances that were contributing to his mood. Without a change he wondered what he might become, or if he could ever be really happy again, the way he was when Eileen was alive. The thoughts were beginning to depress him, so he decided to put them out of his mind for now, to concentrate on closing the Teller case and ensuring his father's killers got what they deserved. After that he could give serious thought to the rest of his life.

DeLorenzo was out on another call, but Bobby Avent was in, so Dan knocked on his door in the hope of getting some good news about his father's case.

"Hi, Dan, come on in," Avent greeted him warmly. "How are you doing?"

"Not bad, Lieutenant, considering its been a couple of months."

Avent gave him an apologetic look. "Have a seat. Joe's out on a call."

"Yeah, I know, the desk sergeant told me. Calvin with him?"

"Are you kidding? Those two are bonded. Funny pair, but they're good. Head and shoulders over anybody else I got."

They both felt a bit uneasy, Avent doing a better job of concealing it. "Get you some coffee?" he offered.

"No, no thanks. I just stopped in to see if you had made any progress with this Booker guy."

"We have until tomorrow to press charges. When Joe gets back we're scheduled to meet with the D.A. to make a final decision. Joe and Calvin are pushing to arrest him for murder so there would be little chance of bail. I think we should just press right now for possession because that will stick. We caught him with the goods, as you know."

"But the judge will set a low enough bail for possession that he'll post it. He'll run for sure."

"I'm not sure of that," Avent said, giving it serious consideration. "It's stolen property related to a murder case. The judge will have to take that into account. Besides, no one puts Booker at the scene at the time of your dad's murder so we can't put him in a line-up. That doesn't leave us with a lot of choices."

"What does the D.A.'s office think?"

"I really don't know. That's why we're meeting later on. The weekend has given us some time so we don't have to rush any decisions. I want this guy as much as anybody because I think he's guilty, but that doesn't mean jack-shit in court. You know that. Whatever label we put on him has to stick and right now possession will stick. If he makes bail we put a tail on him and hope he screws up. If he stays in we try to sweat him."

Avent waited to see if Dan had any insightful opinions, apparently willing to try anything that made sense. For whatever reason, and Avent wasn't comfortable with it, Dan Costa chose to just thank him for the update, asking him to have Joe D call once the meeting with the D.A. had been concluded.

From there it was a short ride to his father's apartment and a chore he had been putting off for weeks, one that might confirm his initial instincts about his father's case.

The aroma in the halls was familiar, evoking further memories of his childhood, good times and his father's contentment. That he should have been murdered in a place that had brought him years of comfort seemed the cruelest of ironies. No one should have had the right to desecrate the memories. The thought changed his apprehension to controlled anger as he climbed the stairs and knocked on the door.

Someone lowered the volume on a radio and walked across the squeaking floor towards the door, standing before it, blocking the light from the eyehole. The person he had come to visit froze, prompting Dan to knock a second time. He waited nervously, hoping he was doing the right thing, searching for a reason to rethink the mission.

He heard the deadbolt turn, followed by the sound of a sliding latch. Slowly, the knob turned and a tearful Mattie Turner opened the door. She looked older and tired, in sharp contrast to the animated, happy face that had greeted neighbors for as long as Dan could remember. She and her husband had been the first blacks in the building and Frank Costa had seen to it that they were teated no differently than anyone else. They were respected and admired as the good people they were, and when the cultural transition was completed and his father had replaced them as the exception, they repaid him for his thoughfulness by treating him in kind. Now it was their turn to shield him from the bigots, though he seemed to need it less, for his neighbors were amongst the kindest, most sincere people Dan had ever known.

Never once had his father thought about moving, nor had his son ever found a reason to encourage him. They enjoyed the people and the relationship they shared with them, at least until that fateful day.

"Come in, Daniel," Mattie whispered, lowering her eyes as she wiped them with her apron.

"How you doing, Miz Turner?"

"Not too well, Daniel," she replied, struggling to control her emotions. "I miss your father terribly."

"I'm sure you do," he responded softly.

"Would you like some coffee?"

"No, no thank you. I just stopped by to see if there was anything you wanted to say to me, or anything that you had thought of during the last couple of months that would help put everything to rest." Dan Costa had chosen his words carefully.

Her tortured expression made him wish he hadn't come. He didn't really need to see her reaction to know that her son was involved and that she and her husband had known it from the beginning. Still, he hoped she would persuade him to come forward and bring finality to the investigation, in which case the courts would have reason to consider leniency.

With as much kindness and understanding as he could summon, he offered the only advice his position would allow.

"I'm not sure what I would do if I were a parent. I also know that I can never forget the generosity you extended to my father all those years. So I guess all I can say is what my father always taught me and what I think he would want me to say under the circumstances. Do the right thing, Miz Turner."

As he turned and opened the door he heard her begin to cry. As he closed it and descended the stairs her weeping became louder and followed him out the small vestibule. He stood for a moment at the top of the stoop, wondering if he had done and said what his father would have wanted, wondering too, if this would bring a quick resolution to the case.

Across the street three little girls skipped rope, their skirts and pigtails flying as they jumped with youthful energy. He watched as they stopped to permit an old lady to pass, respectfully wishing her a good day.

A few stoops down, a handful of young men traded cash for reefers and pills, exchanging obscenity-laced insults. An anxious, elderly couple gave them a wide berth, stepping into the street to avoid confrontation. Down on the corner, a short distance away, a blue and white patrol car pulled to the curb and a uniformed stuck his head out to engage a pair of garishly dressed young ladies in heady conversation.

Dan wondered if this was the way it had always been. Somehow he remembered it differently. When he was growing up kids respected their elders. Their parents made sure of it. All the cops were tough but fair and all the old people smiled contentedly. That was what he wanted to remember whether he had a right to or not.

Though barely past four, the commuters leaving Manhattan for their homes in Brooklyn and Long Island were already snarled in eastbound traffic. Dan couldn't understand why people who thought of themselves as being so intelligent would put up with the stress and aggravation, not to mention the sacrifice of a quarter of their waking hours. Cramped quarters, unreliable schedules and equipment failures made mass transit less than perfect, but it seemed a far better option, even with the threat from terrorists. Once you make a decision to live near the city you might as well make it as easy on yourself as possible, and driving in stop-and-go traffic was surely not the better choice. You could sleep, read or converse without the pressure of having to watch for lunatic drivers or pedestrians with their heads up their butts.

Except for some teenagers transfixed on the beat of blaring rap, the faces he passed were sullen, reflecting their attitudes and temperament. *They brought all this shit on themselves and they're too damn stupid to realize it. Screw them.*

He spent the rest of the trip to his apartment contemplating the realities of urban life. It just didn't make sense for him any longer, or for many others, for that matter. That there would be more acts of terrorism was certain; only when and where were in doubt. To stick it out in a place that included so many other inconveniences betrayed logic. He began to realize that he was mentally ready to get away from it all, and if that meant leaving his job and his friends, Marilyn included, he was prepared to do it. How much of his melancholy was due to his father's murder and the Teller case was debatable, though he had to concede they were contributing factors. Still, life was too short, there were too many other things to do and too many places to see to waste it in a city that had more than its share of crime, congestion, greed and danger. It would be lunacy to tolerate it for a lifetime.

The messages on his phone included one each from Marilyn and Donna, the latter advising him of her hotel and room number. He surprised himself by calling her without first trying Marilyn's office where she had promised to be working well into the evening.

"Enjoying the Big Apple?" he asked.

"Your Big Apple sucks as always," she responded without hesitation. "Your men may wear expensive suits but they haven't any more class than the worst rednecks."

"What were you wearing?"

"The same blue outfit I had on this morning."

"There's your answer."

"That's no excuse for some of the stuff I heard today or for the looks they give you, either. They must be hard up as hell. Besides," she countered, raising her voice, "what's wrong with the blue outfit? I happen to like it."

"You should. You look great in it."

"Well, I'm not going to apologize for how I look, particularly not when I'm wearing something appropriate, and I'm sure as hell not responsible for the adolescent behavior of insensitive morons, which your precious Big Apple is loaded with. Egotistical, ugly assholes...pardon the expression."

Costa laughed. "Boy, they really got to you, didn't they?"

"Nope. I've always thought New York men were boorish egotists who didn't begin to deserve the lofty opinions they had of themselves. Today just confirmed it."

"I'm a New Yorker. Am I like that?"

She hesitated. "I'm not sure. You've got this macho thing about you, but I suspect it's not an act, in which case you're probably okay. Besides, I'm talking more about the suits you see walking around."

"Well, that's nice to hear. How about some dinner to make up for all that boorish behavior?" Even before finishing the question, he wondered if he had made a mistake.

"Well, that's a pleasant surprise," Donna admitted. "Are you sure you want to? It's not your fault. You didn't do anything."

"Yeah, I'm sure," he conceded, knowing he couldn't rescind the invitation. Suddenly he remembered that Donna had made plans for the theater.

"Oh, I forgot. You and your friend are going to a play."

"Sorry, pal, you don't get off that easily. We couldn't get the tickets we wanted, so you're stuck with me."

"Being stuck with you isn't so bad. I'll pick you up in an hour."

"Great. I have a plain black dress I can wear with a white jacket. If that's too dressy, I have a pink outfit like the blue one. It's kind of sporty."

"The dress and jacket will do fine," Dan said, fearing another tight pants and pullover might lead him down paths he'd regret.

"Okay. I'll be waiting outside so you won't have to park."

He dialed Marilyn's private number. He tried to figure out why he felt disappointed when she answered.

"You sound depressed," she said.

"Sorry, didn't mean to," he said honestly, already wondering how she would react to his dinner plans.

"It's alright. Ever since Sunday night I've been down in the dumps myself and I haven't snapped out of it yet. Even Dante asked what was wrong, and normally he couldn't care less."

Marilyn's admission made him feel worse, so he decided not to mention Donna. "If our discussion Sunday upset you, put it out of your mind for a while. In time you'll reenergize."

"Thanks for the advice, but the problem's not going to go away. I love you too much to stick my head in the sand knowing that won't solve anything."

"I know, but if you're thinking with a clear head you'll have a better chance of coming up with a solution and you can't do that if you're tired."

She laughed lightly. "Okay, Doctor, you're probably right."

She waited for Dan to respond but he remained quiet, raising her suspicions. "Are you sure you're alright? You're certainly not your warm, bubbly self."

"Yeah, I'm okay, just a little beat up over my father's case, and I've hit a dead-end on the Teller one. That doesn't help. I have to come up with something that will push the doctors' panic buttons," he lied, confident that his recently devised plan had a good chance of working.

After some more small talk he convinced her to finish her work and get home for a good night's sleep, deceiving her into thinking that he intended to do the same. When they hung up, the realization that he had lied to her tempted him to call again and tell her the truth. He rationalized his way out of it, opting instead for a quick shower, shave and change of clothing. As he drove downtown towards the hotel he wondered if he would ever be inclined to tell Marilyn the truth about this evening and whether Sunday night's conversation had changed his whole attitude towards her and their future together.

His thoughts evaporated as he caught sight of Donna Kempler. Flanked by two well-dressed businessmen, she was wearing an above the knee, form fitting, black dress stylishly offset by a collarless white jacket. Black nylons and patent leather spiked heels only added to the vision lustfully shared by more than a few pedestrians. Dan pulled to the curb, got out and peered over the top.

"Got anything planned for the evening, lady?" he asked mischievously.

She bit her lower lip and squinted seductively. "What have you got in mind, big boy?"

The eyes of her two acquaintances widened.

"Get in and I'll show you."

"Don't mind if I do," she said in her best Mae West, dropping the young men's jaws. Their eyes followed her as she slid into the Jeep, her hemline rising to new heights as she swiveled her legs, briefly exposing ebony garter snaps pressed tightly against milky smooth thighs.

"They will either suffer coronaries on the spot or enjoy the hell out of tonight's dreams," Dan predicted, observing their gaping, frozen faces in the rearview mirror. "Don't you feel guilty?"

"You started it, so don't blame me."

"I noticed how quickly you picked up on it. I think you enjoy being a tease."

"You think so?" she said in a way that told Dan Costa he would have to swim like hell or stay out of the water. He decided to change the subject.

"What kind of food would you like?"

"The food doesn't matter. I'd like to go someplace where your people go."

"My people? You mean cops?"

"No, Italians, the kind with reputations."

Dan knew what she meant. "Reputations? What are you talking about? I come from a family of nobodies."

She laughed. "Okay, you win. I want to go where we might see mobsters…you know, Mafia."

"Mafia? What the hell's the Mafia?"

She laughed again. "You stinker, you know what I mean."

He smiled. "Yeah, I know what you mean. Do you have to be back early?"

"Nope. Checkout time is eleven. I'm just driving back to Nuremberg."

"Okay. Then we'll go to a little place in Jersey, in Newark's North Ward.

That will give me time to explain what I'd like you to do if you still want to help me nail Steinberg and Norville."

"I told you I'd help in any way I can and I meant it," she said seriously.

Jersey commuters share the same frustrations as New Yorkers, leaning hopelessly on their horns, cutting carelessly across lanes and cursing anonymous deities responsible for the mayhem. That they endure the traffic for reasons solely their own escapes them. Distracted at times by the chaos, Dan finished his description of the plan only minutes before arriving at Vittorio's on the corner of Bloomfield Avenue and Tenth Street in a still predominantly Italian section of Newark.

He had expected Donna to ask a lot of questions, but throughout his explanation she just listened, prompting him to believe his design had frightened her into rethinking her commitment.

"You don't have to go through with this," he said sympathetically, "and I wouldn't think less of you if you backed out."

"That's funny, because actually I was wondering what you thought of me for promising to go through with it."

"I think you're a brave and resourceful girl, in addition to being tantalizingly beautiful and remarkably intelligent."

"You forgot generous, sensuous and desireable," she laughed.

"Those too," he said earnestly.

"We'd better get out of this car or talk about something else before we do something you'll regret," she said.

Vittorio's usual weeknight crowd of lawyers, doctors and wise-guys gave long, approving looks as Donna made her way through narrow passages, brushing chairs to the delight of their male occupants. Only the imposing figure of her escort restrained their enthusiasm. In a ristorante infamous for shapely young mistresses Donna Kempler had managed to attract the fancy of the most discerning connoisseurs, many still staring as she sat facing her admirers. She leaned over the table. "I feel like I'm on display."

"You are. Half the men in here envy the hell out of me and the other half are trying to figure out how to get rid of me."

A waiter brought them menus and water with lemon wedges. "The gentlemen in the corner table," and he motioned lightly over his left shoulder, "would like to buy you and your lady cocktails or wine, whichever you prefer."

Dan glanced at the table and four middle-aged men in expensive looking suits raised their glasses. He nodded his appreciation and turned back to see Donna smiling broadly at them, her water glass raised in turn.

"Flirt," he accused her.

"Jealous," she shot back.

"Jealous of what? I'm the one that has you."

"Has me?" she asked coyly. "You wish."

*You're right,* Dan Costa realized, as he laughed and joked away the evening with the one woman whose charm and beauty matched Marilyn Kyme's, but whose life was her own.

As they neared her hotel he looked for a place to park. "I just want to spend a minute or two discussing when we'll make our move."

"You could come up for a nightcap," she suggested, not really expecting him to accept.

"I'm afraid I wouldn't control myself," he admitted, as he turned toward her and backed the car against the curb. "I thought you were attractive as hell the first time I saw you, but I never really appreciated everything else until today. As much as I'm committed to someone else, I'm not sure being alone with you is something I could handle."

"There's a compliment there somewhere, I'll bet." Her mood was light, but she wasn't teasing. She knew she couldn't feel the way she did unless Dan Costa felt the same.

Dan wanted to say more, to somehow vindicate his conduct while reassuring her, but he sensed it wasn't needed. She knew how he felt about Marilyn, about her, and what he was asking of her. To elaborate wasn't necessary.

They agreed to meet next week on Friday afternoon in his office, affording her time to pack and store her things, say goodbye to those she would miss and make arrangements for her trip later that month. With less apprehension than he anticipated, he told her she could stay at his apartment next weekend. "That's the only way I won't worry about you," he insisted. She didn't argue.

He walked her to the hotel lobby and watched her get on the elevator, waiting until the door slid shut before turning outside. He walked to his car picturing Donna Kempler slipping out of the short, tight, black dress, standing on spiked heels in black hose and panties. He wondered what she would do if he knocked on the door, no longer doubting what he would do if she opened it.

The following morning Dan was at work earlier than usual. Anxious to help Rasheed complete the paperwork on some unsolved drug related shootings, he arrived at seven and was reacquainting himself with the details when the phone rang. It was Joe DeLorenzo.

"I was beginning to think you had died."

"Sorry, buddy, it's been a bitch. Never had so much work or so little time to do it. I know you're anxious about the D.A.'s decision." He continued without waiting for his friend to answer. "We decided late last night to charge Booker with burglary and murder. The D.A.'s meeting this morning with Jason Muhammed at eight-thirty to try to appease the bastard, and then he'll announce it at a press conference at nine.

"What do you mean by appease him?"

"Muhammed's already working the minority community and religious leaders, telling them our case is weak, that the only thing his client is guilty of is buying some stuff off the street and being black."

"Do you think he's guilty, Joe?"

"It's all gut feel based on experience, Dan, but, yeah, I'm convinced he's our man. I don't know if he struck the blows, but he was there when it happened."

"Do you think he had an accomplice?"

"Hard to say. He's a wise-ass, tries to come off tough, but he's also into himself, the type that would give everyone else up if he thought it would help him manipulate a deal. The problem is, we may never get another crack at him. Muhammed got him to clam up pretty good."

"What about the Turner kid?" Dan asked uneasily, his feelings for his parents, particularly his mother, weighing heavily on him.

"Calvin and I are going to his apartment this morning on the premise that he was seen in Booker's company once or twice and that we need to know if he was there the day your dad was killed."

"Is that true?"

"Yeah. A couple of people from your dad's apartment house have ID'd Booker from mug shots as being in the neighborhood a few months back. None of them could recall any specific days, but two of them volunteered that Booker was definitely in the company of John Turner on more than one occasion. Booker's a loudmouth who uses a lot of profanity and the witnesses spoke to Mattie Turner about it because they didn't think her son was that kind of boy. They were surprised he hung out with Booker."

"I've got a feeling, Joe, that if you handle it right, you can get the Turner kid to come forward. It wouldn't surprise me if his parents have already entertained the idea."

Bobby Avent was motioning for DeLorenzo to come into his office so he said goodbye to his friend, promising to keep him advised of developments.

As he hung up, Dan saw the large frame of Al Wilson emerge from the stairwell and move slowly towards him. The clock on the wall read seven fifty-nine. His friend's record remained intact.

Wilson stopped by Dan's desk and surveyed the orderly piles of forms and typed reports. "The Teller case?"

"No, the drug and gang shootings on the westside that I dumped on Rasheed. We're getting nowhere with them. I thought we'd put them in the inactive file and wait for some payback. It's gotta' happen sooner or later," he stated confidently.

"Okay." Wilson shrugged with the look of a man resigned to the realities of big city police work. You picked and chose where you put your effort and it certainly wasn't in the direction of cases involving bad guys on both sides.

Rasheed arrived a few minutes later, delighted to hear of his partner's decision, even happier to see him engulfed in the required paperwork.

Dan reminded him that they weren't round-filing the cases, simply postponing active investigation until new evidence surfaced, a condition that didn't diminish Martin's relief. He pitched in and before noon both desks were cleared, all the forms and reports neatly typed, signed and filed.

Rasheed surveyed the uncluttered desktop.

"That's the way I like it. Too bad we can't dismiss all the cases this way."

His partner gave a disapproving look, long enough for Martin to see it, and hit Joe DeLorenzo's automatic dial-up, leaving a message when a recording came on. Then he phoned Marilyn Kyme, hoping she would agree to meet him for lunch. He had decided to tell her about his dinner with Donna, and without disclosing the details, of his plan to use her in the Teller investigation.

"Hi, I miss you," he said when she answered.

"Me too, but I can't talk. Dante and I have a couple of deadlines neither of us can possibly make, but we want to at least try."

"I guess there's no point in asking you out to lunch."

"Lunch? What's that?" She breathed a tired sigh. He felt sorry for her and disappointed in himself for last night's deception.

"Go back to work. I'll call you later this afternoon."

"Don't forget. I need to hear your voice. I need to know you care."

"Ditto," he replied and hung up.
"Watcha' doin' for lunch?" Wilson asked.
"Spending my money on it for you. Let's go."
"Where?"
"Corner deli, unless you want me to bring it back."
"That's a good idea," Wilson said. "It'll give me time to make some calls so we can eat in peace. Bring me back a hot pastrami on rye, kosher dill, hot mustard and orange soda. That oughta' hold me until this evening."

He arched his back in the pain relieving way that had become familiar and shuffled back to his office.

"I wish you'd learn to eat salad and lose some weight so your back would get a break," Costa called after him.

Without stopping or turning his friend shouted, "And I wish you'd learn to mind your own damned business and get me my pastrami."

They made small talk as they ate, Dan asking about the kids, Al Wilson about Marilyn. Dan confided that as much as he wanted her, he wasn't certain they would end up together, relating in summary fashion the discussions they had had over the weekend.

"It's like John Wooden used to say," Wilson reminisced between bites, "It's never as bad as it seems when you lose."

Dan frowned. "What the hell are you talking about?"

"You know what I mean. You're lookin' at it negatively now because she said some things that didn't fit your little world so perfectly, but that doesn't mean everything wouldn't work out. Things and people have a way of accommodating themselves eventually, provided they get enough nourishment, which in your case is love. Nurture with love and you two will be fine."

His advice concluded, he tackled the second half of the sandwich, regretting that he had ordered only one pickle. Neither spoke again until they had finished eating and drained their sodas.

"I'm glad we have a few minutes to talk," Wilson started. "We never seem to have time anymore, not like when you first joined the squad. You used to drive me nuts with questions," he laughed. "Remember?"

"Yeah, and you were a good teacher," Dan acknowledged gratefully.

"Well, I never minded taking the time because I always believed you would turn out this way. You're a good cop, Dan, and that's all I ever expected."

Costa knew there was a purpose to this little session, but he suspected some reluctance on his friend's part. "Don't hesitate to say something you think needs saying," he reminded him, using an expression he had learned from him.

Wilson smiled. "Okay, what I want to say is, I'm worried about you because you're changing and I'm not sure it's for the best."

"What do you mean?" Dan asked, remembering that days before he had entertained thoughts about changing his life when the smoke cleared, but unaware that he had been acting differently.

"You have this absorbed look about you, like, *Leave me alone, I got my own problems.* I know you don't mean it, but that's how it comes across. You're so occupied with your thoughts people are reluctant to approach you anymore. Rememeber how everybody would bring you their problems, run to you for advice. You were like a damn magnet for everybody's troubles. Am I right?" he asked rhetorically. "Now they keep their distance, maybe because they want to respect your privacy, maybe because they don't think you give a shit anymore. But whatever the reason, you have changed, my friend, and I just want to make sure you can handle it, that it won't get the best of you."

"You've got nothing to worry about, Al, I'm fine. I've got nothing on my mind except the Teller case."

"You know that's not true. You're concerned about your relationship with Marilyn and you're worried your dad's killers may not get what they deserve. Most of all, you're concerned about how you'd react to that."

"This is getting too deep for me," Dan confessed, but with a smile to assure his friend he was not offended.

"Look," Wilson continued, "you're a cop, not a lawyer, or businessman or any ordinary Joe. You're a detective, probably the best in this city, maybe as good as ever was. And you know why?" he asked, without intending to wait for an answer. "Because you think like and wanna' be like a knight in shining armor. You're Lancelot or Galahad, one of those noble dudes you read about. You charge up hills at bad guys and protect people who can't take care of themselves. That's how you're made, that's what you do and nothing's going to change you…not logic, not money, certainly not anything I'm smart enough to say. And that's all fine and good unless you let it destroy you."

Wilson leaned over his desk, as if getting closer would make his message clearer or drive it deeper. "God didn't make this world perfect, Dan. It's filled with injustice. And He didn't make you to set it all straight. Neither God, nor me, nor anyone else expects you to kill yourself making everything right because that's not the nature of things. That's not the way it's supposed to be.

All anyone expects is that you do your best, make as many people as happy as you can and get on with your life."

"So you think I can't handle the issues in my life?"

"You wouldn't be the first strong person to bang his head against a wall. Good men have a limit too. Your problem is you see things black and white, moreso than most, and that's why you have to see Teller's and your father's murderers punished. That's why with Marilyn it has to be you or her parents. You can't accommodate compromise once your mind is fixed on what you feel is right. Except in our world, my friend, what's obvious isn't always true or right, and gray always outweighs black and white. Once we accept that, we can accomplish a lot more because we don't drive ourselves nuts over the one percent that's left undone or the one time we felt unsatisfied. Learning to accept something between our opinion and the middle road allows us the freedom and time to explore more worlds, to accomplish more things; in your case, to do more good, both for yourself and the people around you."

They sat awhile reflecting on Wilson's argument. He was dissatisfied, uncertain that he had articulated what he felt, what he knew Dan had to hear.

For his part, Dan accepted the obvious wisdom and appreciated his friend's interest, but he also believed in principles, and as they applied to the men that had murdered his father and Joe Teller, there was no gray. He could accept compromise in his relationship with Marilyn and had in fact already convinced himself to back off and give her all the time she would need, but not in his dad's and Teller's cases. He left Al Wilson's office still feeling comfortable with both positions.

Just before five Joe DeLorenzo called to say they had questioned the Turner kid in the presence of his parents and that both he and Calvin Washington had concluded the kid was involved with Booker. Whether John Turner had participated in the bludgeoning or had even been in the apartment at the time it occurred wasn't certain, but his reaction to virtually every question had convinced the detectives that the kid knew Booker was involved in the break-in and murder.

"A meeting with the D.A. is scheduled for the morning. We would be having it right now, but Avent wants to be in on it and he's tied up."

"Did you tell Avent enough for him to draw a conclusion about the Turner kid's probable involvement?"

"We told him what I just told you."

"Then Jason Muhammed and our beloved police commissioner will probably know it too."

Dan had always suspected Avent's intentions, but out of respect for their mutual friend, Al Wilson, he had kept his opinion to himself, at least until his father's murder. Jason Muhammed had been an outspoken critic of former white mayors and senior police officers for as long as he had practiced law, but had been publicly supportive of every black official and cop, even when their actions had been criticized by other minority leaders. He had publicly announced that his purpose was to see a wholesale changing of the guard, the only means in his opinion by which the black community could be assured of justice, a position which Avent had supported, sometimes publically. Avent wasn't dirty, but he was decidedly prejudiced and more than a little self-serving.

DeLorenzo was all too familiar with his friend's opinion of Avent and certain other activists in the Black Officers' Association so he didn't want to seem confrontational, but he felt obliged to at least disclose what he knew.

"I'm not sure Avent postponed things for the reason you think, Dan. Before Calvin and I left for the Turner's apartment he told us he had a counseling session to attend, something involving a youth group he's working with, and that if he had to leave before we returned, to page him. It's possible that's all there is to the story."

"It won't take long to find out, will it?" Dan muttered, making no attempt to conceal his suspicions.

"No, it won't. I guess we can both be a little patient before passing judgement," Joe D replied before hanging up.

Costa sat at his desk tapping a pencil, swiveling slowly in his chair, while his mind meandered amongst the subjects and people that had occupied his thoughts during the recent months. He tried to analyze his feelings about each, but maintaining objectivity in his present mood was difficult. Sometime during the process he picked up the phone and punched in a number, not certain why, perhaps not fully aware that he had, but it felt good to hear her voice.

"Hi, Donna, it's me. Just thought I'd call to see if you made it home okay."

"Who's me?" she teased.

"Me is I."

"No, you can't be I. I is me," she giggled.

"Please, you're giving me a headache."

"I'm sorry," she said. "It was thoughtful of you to call and I'm being a wise-ass. I apologize. How are you doing?"

"I've been better. In a long streak of shitty days this one's filled the crapper."

"Less than poetic, but I get the point. You're not worrying about me, are you? Please don't. I have no problem going through with this and I'm sure I'll find some perverted satisfaction doing it, and once it's over I'll sleep well. My conscience is clear. Besides, I'll have you to protect me."

He marveled at how sensuous she could sound, even when she wasn't trying to be, if in fact she wasn't at the moment. With Donna it was difficult to tell. He delighted in her intemperance, trying to imagine living with a woman who was a constant turn-on.

They talked a while longer. He pretended to review aspects of the plan he had omitted, but she could tell he just needed someone to talk to, while wondering why it wasn't Marilyn Kyme.

"Well, I guess that covers everything," he concluded, still unwilling to hang up, hoping she would find something to talk about. "Anything you want to discuss? Any questions?"

She saw through Dan Costa without trying. "Yes," she whispered seductively, "why didn't you come up to my room last night?"

The question caught him off-guard. For long seconds neither spoke. Finally she asked, "Cat got your tongue?"

"Uh, no," he laughed, unable to come up with any reasonable response other than the truth. "I guess I can't answer because I don't have one. The closest I can come is, I felt guilty."

"I understand," Donna responded in a less provocative tone. "I just needed to hear that it wasn't because you didn't want to."

"You needn't have worried about that," he confessed.

"Too bad you're not up here tonight. You'd have a chance to reconsider."

"You are absolutely, flat-out cruel. You know that?"

"Uh-huh," she breathed lustily into the phone, "and on that thought I'll wish you sweet dreams."

The following morning he arrived at work early again, anxiously awaiting Joe DeLorenzo's call and the bad news he was certain it would bring. Convinced that Booker and the Turner boy had broken into the apartment and that Booker had murdered his father when he walked in on them, it was difficult for him to focus on anything except what it would take to see them brought to justice. But he knew Muhammed would offer the stiffest defense possible and that a Commissioner overly sympathetic to almost any minority cause would be less than supportive of aggressive police tactics. Neither the investigators nor the D.A.'s office would catch any breaks on this one. Any attempt to shortcut due process, intimidate the suspects or play one against the other would likely bring the politicians and black activists down on everyone and jeopardize any chance of a conviction. He had been telling himself to be patient, to not expect too much too soon, but his emotions kept getting in the way of logic. It was wearing him down and he knew it. He wished it were next week so he could be occupying his time with Donna Kempler and the plan that would get the confessions he needed to secure warrants for the arrests of the conspirators in Joe Teller's murder. After that he would take care of whoever contributed to his father's death.

The phone rang and he answered it anxiously.

"Thirty-fourth Precinct homicide, Sergeant Costa speaking."

It was Joe DeLorenzo, and by the sound of his voice he was using a speaker phone. "Calvin and me are on our way over to the Turner's to bring the kid in for questioning. I thought you'd appreciate the update."

"How does it look?"

"The D.A.'s comfortable with bringing the kid in again for questioning, particularly because of your dad's neighbors having linked him with Booker. But he's worried that without something meaningful from him, our case against Booker may be too circumstantial to secure a conviction."

"Do you think he might drop the charges?"

"I don't know, Dan, I can't read his mind. What do you think, Cal?"

The older detective responded in his normally deliberate manner, taking time to consider every word.

"You can't ignore the racial overtones of the case, Dan, and I'm sure that's weighing heavily on the D.A.'s mind. He knows he'll stir up a hornet's nest if he can't support an arrest with all the publicity it's sure to get. So he's moving cautiously and I guess none of us should blame him for that."

"I understand the D.A.'s position, Calvin. I'm just afraid of what the Commissioner's influence and Muhammed's bullshit might lead to. There were hundreds of felonies committed during the Brooklyn Heights riots, but only a handful of arrests with even fewer convictions. There was a black mayor then and this Commissioner seems to have the same sense of selective justice. I don't want to see them bury my father's case like that."

"Many of us share your concern, Dan," Washington replied. "Maybe that's why we're working so hard on it, so there's no way anyone can weasel out of this. I think we can see justice done here if we just remember what our jobs are and how we were taught to do them."

It was difficult to not like Calvin Washington or to mistrust his intentions.

"I couldn't ask for better men on this, Calvin, and I have all the faith in the world in you. All I expect is that you do your best. If you don't mind, Joe, give me a call later today or tonight and let me know how things are going. I'd hate to get any bad news over the radio."

"You got it, buddy. Rest easy. We'll get 'em."

Dan stayed up reading until after midnight but his friend never called, heightening his concerns over the handling of his father's case. It bothered him from the time he awoke until he arrived at the Stationhouse a little after seven. There he was greeted by Rasheed Martin's smiling face, a rare sight at so early an hour, his partner having become infamous for his last second arrivals.

"Good morning," Martin said happily.

"Good morning, Rasheed," Dan replied, though less enthusiastically. "I'd like you to bring me up to date on the cases you've been handling by yourself. I've been thinking how some other work has really dominated my time and I've got to begin managing everything better. It's not fair to dump as much on you as I have."

"Hey, it's understandable, not that I don't welcome the help."

Over coffee and donuts the two shared thoughts on the NBA playoffs, eventually settling on a wager, Dan offering odds that the Nets would beat the Knicks.

"Foolish bet, my man," Martin chided him.

"Just have your money ready," Costa said dryly, "and I don't expect checks, particularly not from bachelor cops who make stupid bets."

Martin disposed of the empty cups. "Where do you want to start? Crime is alive and well in New York City despite what the Commissioner would have us believe."

As they spoke, dividing the work that each agreed had to be done, Dan's mind occasionally drifted, wondering why Joe DeLorenzo hadn't called with an update, what Donna was doing and where his relationship with Marilyn was headed.

By now the Turner kid would have been interviewed, most likely in the presence of Jason Muhammed and the D.A. The absence of a call could mean only one thing: Turner had said nothing substantial to implicate either himself or Booker in the break-in and murder, so the D.A. had acquiesced into releasing him. In the absence of any other new evidence, that could necessitate dropping the charges against Booker, particularly in light of the notoriety the cops had been receiving. Anything short of eyewitnesses or overwhelming circumstantial evidence would make it difficult for the D.A. to defend his original position. With the increasing frequency of burglaries, possession of stolen goods had become commonplace, and often enough the holder had not been the original perpetrator, so Booker's claim to have bought the items off the street would seem reasonably acceptable to a jury, particularly one dominated by minorities. Regrettably, the pursuit of convictions too often depended upon community opinion, press coverage and the D.A.'s workload, which during the past year or so had escalated beyond manageable proportions. Though the feds were responsible for pursuit of terrorists, the City's resources allocated to support them left too little time to resolve the spate of everyday crime. Perpetrators were falling between widening cracks and few in law enforcement saw any relief on the horizon.

His preoccupation aside, the two communicated well and were about halfway through when the phone rang. Dan anxiously grabbed it. It was Marilyn Kyme.

"You sounded strange yesterday. I was worried, and when you didn't call this morning I thought I'd better check to see if everything is okay."

"Everything is fine. We just have a lot of work to do and not enough time to do it," Dan replied.

"Sounds like our place. We're all working twelve hour days but the backlog keeps getting bigger."

"You need more sawbones."

She laughed. "Fat chance. Yesterday we got a lecture from somebody in the Controller's office that we're over budget and he wants a cutback on overtime. I think he really does expect us to work for nothing."

Dan couldn't resist. "And you find this preferable to a place like Eagle's Mere?"

"This will all pass. It always does. Besides, New York has everything."

"Yeah, you're right about that. It's got more terrorists than the rest of the country put together, more than its share of greedy bastards, pollution, a racist police commissioner, rampant taxes, pedophiles...what else do you want to hear? When are you going to wake up to the reality of this place, Marilyn?"

The change in his attitude during the last few days deeply concerned her, but she found it difficult to believe that it all emanated from the discussion in the car about her parents.

"Dan, please don't personalize this?"

"How can I not when you refuse to see all the bullshit in this city? At least be honest about it and I'll be able to deal with it."

"Alright, but don't blame me for everything. I know that what I said about my parents upset you, but it's only one issue and I did promise to address it and find a way to deal with it."

"Look, my father's been murdered, I'm tired, I have a ton of work and there's not much going right in my life right now. If you don't understand why I can't be in the best of moods, then maybe you don't love me as much as you think. Maybe our relationship has to be all about you, in which case, we're both going to wind up being very disappointed, because right now I have other things on my mind than just trying to make you happy every minute. For once take my feelings into account and maybe you can find something to help me through all this."

He had never spoken to her so bluntly before and she wasn't sure if he was as serious as he sounded or what she could do about it, but she knew that to discuss it over the phone would only add to his frustration.

"Are you going to try and see me this weekend?"

"Of course," he replied. "How about dinner? I may work late Friday, but that doesn't mean we can't get together."

"I've been looking forward to it. I'll plan to stay over, though I do have to get up early and work Saturday."

"Sounds good," he said, trying to inject some enthusiasm. "I'll call you tomorrow and arrange a time. Now I've got to get back to work, and by the way it sounds, you do too."

Rasheed had been sitting quietly, pretending not to listen. Dan knew otherwise.

"Sooner or later this city will change you," he said, "and it probably won't be for the better."

"If it starts to, I'll know enough to get out," Martin replied confidently.

They ordered sandwiches through the desk sergeant and ate a leisurely lunch in Al Wilson's office, updating him on their cases as they downed an assortment of corned beef, smoked turkey and pastrami specials. Wilson campaigned for and received the dill pickles, in turn surrendering the coleslaw, which nobody wanted.

When Rasheed had gathered the garbage and left to dispose of it, Wilson asked his friend if he had heard from Joe D.

Dan shook his head.

"Let's give them a call," Wilson said, punching in the numbers and hitting the speaker button.

Avent answered.

"Dan's with me, Bobby. Can you give us an update on his dad's case?"

"It's not real good news," Avent apologized, "but we're not dead yet. The Turner kid gave us nothing, but his whole demeanor says he knows everything. All of us here agree that at least he and Booker were involved. You can read it on their faces, their body language, everything, but getting them to admit to it is another thing. Muhammed's tutored them real well, but we're not giving up."

"Are you still holding Booker?" Dan asked.

"Yes, we are. The D.A. was for dropping the murder and forced entry charges but we held him off until the Grand Jury hearing next week. With what we've got none of us feels like we'll get an indictment, but it at least gives us time to work the Turner kid."

"Were his parents there?" Dan asked.

"Yeah, nice people too. It's one of the things that make us think we're right for putting the Turner kid at the scene. His mother just cried through the whole interview and neither of them looked any of us in the eye. You could see that Muhammed was annoyed.

"That sonofabitch will be more than annoyed before this is over," Dan said to no one in particular.

"What do you mean by that?" Avent asked. When no one answered he said, "Give us a chance to do our job, Dan, and please don't do anything that will make it any harder than it already is."

Sensing that Costa had nothing more to say, Wilson finished by stating that they understood and wished Avent good luck. Then he turned to his friend.

"You and I aren't the only good cops in this city, Dan. Give them a chance. They deserve at least that. If they fail, you'll still have an opportunity to do something stupid, though I pray to God you'll smarten up."

Dan stood. "Don't preach, Al. You have no idea how it feels."

He returned to his desk and a waiting Rasheed Martin. Before resuming work he called Massimo Barracci to arrange a supper meeting, avoiding the use of names in case his partner was listening.

It was almost five by the time they finished, each convinced that at least two months of hard work faced them, and then only if no new cases were added. Dan provided Wilson with a final summary of their schedules, appearing to accept his boss's advise to be patient, to trust Avent and to find something other than work to occupy his mind for a while. But as he watched his friend hurry from his office, Al Wilson suspected that Dan Costa had already devised a means to see justice done, and failing a more conventional closure he was certain he would use it, regardless of the consequence.

## CHAPTER 19

Barracci, Muzzi and Scarola were slurping spicy fish chowder when Dan arrived at the waterfront cafe in Sheepshead Bay, a fifteen-mile drive that took well over an hour because of the traffic. Anxious to discuss his concerns, he declined the waiter's offer of soup and waited for the grilled Chilean seabass smothered in roasted peppers, mushrooms, onion and garlic. Over thick, steaming espresso spiked with Sambucca Dan told them of the telephone call to Avent and the status of his father's case.

"What do you want us to do?" Barracci asked.

Dan recounted Paulie Ippolito's story of the two men that had stolen from St. Anthony's Poor Box. "You made inquiries and came up with the right names. Booker has a long record and a reputation, no different than the two you found. Could you do it again?"

"Of course," Barracci replied, "but then what?"

"We get your informants to come forward, to say they heard Booker bragging or trying to sell what he stole, whatever they can repeat that puts him at the scene."

Barracci hesitated, weighing the possibilities. "To be honest with you, Dan, you're asking for a lot. It's one thing for them to point the finger, another to go to the cops and give testimony. I can tell you now; they won't do it. They would put a bullet in Booker's head if I asked, but I couldn't make them get involved with the cops, no matter what."

"It may come down to that if the bastard gets off. But I would prefer to do it by the book."

"We can work on the Turner kid," the Don suggested. The prospect got Scarola's attention. Muzzi's mind functioned less quickly

Dan shook his head. "His lawyer would have a field day," he said, picturing how Muhammed would turn the press and public. "Within a month no one would even remember that Frank Costa had been murdered, much less care who had done it."

Barracci's response sounded more like an order than a suggestion. "Then give me some time to think. You said we should know in a week or two which way the case will go. That buys us time to make inquiries. We'll see if anybody knows anything we can use."

Dan drove to his apartment feeling less optimistic than when the day had started, realizing that there might not be anything else he could do, at least for the present. So he would leave things in Joe D.'s hands with the hope that his friend could convince the Turners to come forward.

As it seemed to whenever he had a long drive, his thoughts shifted to how his attitude and priorities were changing, and not necessarily for the better. It was becoming increasingly easy to excuse the accomodations, particularly those involving his father's and Teller's cases, with the conviction that the end justified the means. A year ago he wouldn't have considered asking for Barracci's help with anything, much less two murder investigations, or designed a scheme to extract a confession from Alex Norville that had so much downside. He realized his whole outlook on life was being affected, diverted by circumstances he couldn't control unless he compromised his moral convictions. Though he maintained an untroubled ability to distinguish right from wrong and a commitment to pursue an honorable course, he was finding it convenient to dismiss those instincts in the interest of justice. How he would survive all this, what kind of a person he would become and what he would do with his life were issues he chose to ignore until Booker and Teller's conspirators were dead or convicted. He realized how these cases obsessed him, but he also knew there was no way he could distance himself from them. To even think about that was foreign to his personality and to everything he had been taught. You simply didn't walk away from injustice, not if you were Dan Costa.

The eleven o'clock news came on as he pulled to the curb. He sat listening to Donald Jenkins refute a New York Times article about the increase in crime and the failing morale of the police force. The Commissioner railed against what he called racist journalism that twisted the facts about his performance and the statistics that supported their allegations. The rhetoric convinced Dan he was right to pull up stakes, get out of New York and never look back, precisely what he intended just as soon as his father's and the Teller cases were closed.

That was followed by a report that another bomb suspected of containing a fatal and fast-acting form of anthrax had been released in a crowded Queens subway station, the fourth since the original Radio City Music Hall incident. All told, about sixteen hundred had been exposed to the bacterium. Short of a nuclear detonation, this unknown and untreatable form of anthrax represented the greatest threat to Manhattan's civilian population. Compact and difficult to detect, easy to transport and detonate, and with no immediate prospects for a medical breakthrough, the "dirty bomb" had become the number one target of NIH, the research community and the federal task force on terrorism.

The report did nothing to lift his spirits. He ignored requests from Joe D and Al Wilson to return their calls, opting instead for large doses of brandy and a British film about World War II on Cinema Classics. Both helped him get the best night's sleep he had had in weeks.

That Friday he arrived at work late, stopping on the way for a leisurely breakfast. Wilson and Martin had already called his apartment, both concerned that something might have happened. The coolness with which he dismissed their questions added to Wilson's conviction that his friend was not handling the pressure well, but he didn't know what else to do. He had said all he could. Repeating it didn't seem worth the effort, but he made the attempt anyway, suggesting as well that he take a few days off, adding that Marilyn might help in refocusing his priorities.

Dan remained apathetic, though he thanked his friend and reiterated his contention that he was in control of his emotions. "My only problem is not having enough time to give all my cases the attention they deserve," he said.

Around seven, Dan picked Marilyn up at work and drove back towards his apartment, stopping a few blocks away for dinner at a small café on West Fifty-sixth Street. His reticence worried her though she avoided bringing it up. She talked about her work and the growing rumor that priorities might be changed to permit more time to help with the anthrax autopsies, previously the sole responsibility of federal agencies now stretched well beyond their capabilities. He nodded a few times, acknowledging her concerns, but responded to her questions indifferently.

As they walked back towards the car she asked, "Are you sure you want me to stay with you this evening?"

"Sure. What makes you think I don't?"

"You seem so pre-occupied. I think you're angry with me, or worse."

"I'm not angry with you."

She believed him and that bothered her most. "Then are you tired of me?"

"Tired of you? We've only known each other about three months. Why do you think I'd be tired of you?"

They walked another block to where the car was parked before she spoke again. "Dan, do you still love me? Please tell me the truth. I know something's wrong and I need you to be honest with me. Do you still love me?"

He turned towards her, taking her hands in his.

"Yes, I still love you, and yes, something has changed. I realize now that nothing can ever be perfect and I'm beginning to believe that our worlds may be too different for us to find happiness together. That's where my head is at right now. I don't want you to be disappointed or hurt, but I'm not going to pretend I'm happy when I'm not, and that's all I'm going to say about it. I'll understand if you want me to take you home."

She leaned against him, resting her head on his chest, indifferent to the people passing. "No. I just want you to hold me."

She awoke early Saturday morning and took a cab to work, leaving Dan in bed to reflect on everything transpiring in his life. Though he still loved Marilyn it was no longer in the wildly romantic, hopefully optimistic way he remembered, for he associated her with the city and the kind of indifference towards its problems that he couldn't accept. With frustration heightened by his father's murder, he couldn't understand why the woman he loved didn't share his anger. She seemed to ignore the crime and terror as though they were some abstract subjects that didn't touch their lives. While wondering if she would react the same if it had happened to her father, the phone rang, breaking his concentration.

"Hi. Are you alone?" It was Donna.

"Yeah. What's the matter?" he asked, surprised by the call.

"Nothing. I just felt like talking about what we have to do." Her mood seemed cheerful.

"You want to talk about that at eight-thirty on a Saturday morning?"

"Well, we could talk about where I am and what I'm wearing, but that might upset you." She breathed the words more than spoke them.

"I don't think so," he said bravely, forgetting all that had just seconds before occupied his mind. "But while we're at it, what are you wearing that might get me all hot and bothered?"

"Hot and bothered?" she giggled. "You do have a one track mind, Sergeant Costa. I happen to be wearing a Philadelphia Eagles teeshirt. Knowing how devoted you are to the Giants I was sure that would upset you." She delighted in small victories. "But if you like," she confided, lowering her voice, "I could tell you I was wearing a see-through black teddy and G-string panties."

"Knock it off. You are absolutely over-sexed; either that, or the world's biggest tease."

"I could be both."

"Yeah, you probably could," he admitted. "Are you serious about wanting to talk about Norville?"

"Yep, and I know what you want me to do, but I've been thinking about some of the things you said and I'm just not sure I know how far you want me to go."

"It's not something we should discuss over the phone. Can't we talk about it on Friday like we planned?"

"I want some time to think after we talk and I won't have it if we meet Friday afternoon. Why don't I drive in on Thursday? We can meet when you finish work and then I'll stay at my girlfriend's apartment until Friday night."

He conceded that that might be a better plan, so they agreed to meet at his apartment at six on Thursday evening. He gave her directions and promised to have a nice dinner waiting.

"Okay, but I don't want you spiking the food and trying to take advantage of me."

"Don't you ever stop?"

"Only when you can't take it anymore," she whispered before hanging up.

Donna Kempler was getting to him. What he would do about it was becoming an enticing question, one that he happily permitted to occupy his leisurely thoughts that weekend.

By the time he arrived at his office on Monday, he had resolved to concentrate on his work and put aside speculation about the women in his life until both the Teller case and his father's had been resolved. He felt comfortable with the decision and confident that he would abide by it.

It was mid-afternoon when Joe DeLorenzo called. He was well into explaining a break in his father's case when Al Wilson approached to relay the same story from Bobby Avent. A petty thief whom the cops in Bedford-Stuyvesant had arrested as he was leaving an apartment with stolen goods had volunteered to give the police something big if he could walk on the burglary charge, promising to clear up a widely publicized murder case. After the usual conditions and assurances had been exchanged in the presence of a public defender and an assistant D.A., the informant identified Jesse Booker as Frank Costa's killer. He fingered John Turner as an accomplice, noting that Turner had not taken part in the bludgeoning, but had been in the apartment and witnessed it. Pressed for details, he explained that Booker had approached him the evening of the murder and offered him a gold and silver watch for twenty dollars, bragging that he had taken it off an old man he had just beaten with an iron pipe. Booker had also shown him a diamond ring and a diamond studded tie clasp that he could have had for a hundred dollars, but he declined, fearing that everything was too hot. He was willing to testify that Booker had given details of the apartment, Turner's involvement and where he had found and later disposed of the murder weapon.

Following up the lead, Joe and Calvin had gone to a condemned apartment building a few blocks from the murder scene and found a rusted window weight amongst some old mattresses and rubble in a crack room, exactly where Booker had reportedly left it. It was at forensics being analyzed for traces of blood. DeLorenzo concluded the call by saying they were preparing to pick up the Turner boy, but not before confiding that the Public Defender had updated Jason Muhammed and that the activist attorney had reminded him that he was representing John Turner, so any interrogation of the young man had to be conducted in his presence.

Dan said, "I wouldn't wait another second to arrest Turner, Joe. You can't give Muhammed time to concoct a story."

"I know. We're leaving now."

Al Wilson had taken a seat and heard the conversation. "That's just about what Avent told me. He feels the witness is reliable and should hold his own in court. This nightmare might be coming to an end."

"Yeah, it might be," Dan said hopefully, "but I don't trust Muhammed. That sonofabitch would take an oath and lie to protect any killer, as long as he was black."

"Don't' get yourself worked up before you have reason to," Wilson advised his friend, before returning to his office.

Dan waited for another call from Joe D that afternoon and evening, finally phoning his apartment at midnight and leaving a message. He chose not to call early the following morning, expecting that his friend had had a late night and could use the sleep, so he was surprised when the desk sergeant advised him that Joe had called at seven that morning just minutes after Dan had left his own apartment. He ran upstairs and phoned Brooklyn. Calvin Washington answered.

"He's taking a shower, Dan. We were up all night."

"Why? What happened, Cal?"

"I think Joe should explain it," the older detective said. "I'll have him call you the second he comes down."

Washington's reluctance to discuss the Turner interview had Dan expecting the worst, so he sat anxiously by the phone. Barely five minutes passed before it rang.

"Dan, it's Al. Have you spoken to anyone in Brooklyn this morning?"

"Calvin, but he wouldn't tell me anything. I'm waiting for Joe to return my call," he replied. "Avent speak to you?"

"Yeah, just now. I'm tied up in traffic. Whatever Joe has to say, you wait for me to get in. Understand?"

"Give me the bad news now, Al. I'm tired of playing kid's games."

"You wait for me right there and that's an order," Wilson repeated, before cursing the congestion and hanging up.

A half-hour passed before the phone rang again.

"Dan, it's Joe."

"Yeah," he replied anxiously. "What's going on, Joe, and give me a straight answer."

"It's all bullshit, Dan."

Costa started to lose his patience. "If you don't tell me what the hell's going on, I'm coming over there and finding out for myself, and nobody will appreciate the mood I'll be in."

"Alright, alright, just calm down." Joe D took a deep breath, still wondering if he was doing the right thing. Bobby Avent had recommended that he wait for Al Wilson to arrive and tell Dan, but he knew their friendship was strong and counted for something.

"We picked up the Turner kid. By the time we brought him in Jason Muhammed was here along with Turner's father. Muhammed said the boy was traumatized so he read a statement that was supposedly the kid's story. In it Turner claims that your father had sexually abused him on and off for a couple years. The statement says he told his friend, Booker, and that the two went to confront your father and do worse if he didn't move out of the neighborhood. He claims a couple younger kids were molested but that they don't live in the neighborhood any longer so he doesn't want to name them.

Anyway, Turner's statement says your father attacked them and that Booker hit back in self-defense. They were afraid he would get violent. That's the excuse for bringing the pipe. They took the rings, watch and other stuff to make it look like a burglary, supposedly because Turner didn't want his parents to find out what had been going on."

There was a long silence. DeLorenzo didn't know what else to say, fearing that any advice or assurance would push his friend over the edge. Dan Costa had rarely lost his temper, but on the few occasions he had, there had been hell to pay.

"Where's the Turner kid now?" Dan asked coolly, surprising his friend.

"In jail. We charged him with burglary for now."

"What's your next move?"

Joe was stunned by his friend's apparent composure. There was no hint of rage, no sign of a man about to lose it. "We all know it's bullshit. Avent wants me, Calvin and another team for a strategy session in his office at nine. We're supposed to come in with what we think we should do."

"What are you going to recommend?"

"First, I want to interview Booker again to see how many inconsistencies there are between his story and Turner's. Second, we interview every kid your father ever came in contact with, the boxing team, church, the neighborhood…all of them. Then we hit the neighbors again. We prove these are the only two punks in the world with this story and that it's nothing more than a cover-up for a burglary and murder. And when that's all over, we get a statement from the Turners that Muhammed put the kid up to all this bullshit and we go to the press and the Bar Association and nail his lying ass."

"Yeah? Just like the D.A. tried to do in the Tawana Brawley case? The bastards that tried to frame those cops really got theirs, didn't they? They're a bunch of fuckin' celebrities now."

"The world's not perfect, Dan."

"The hell with that shit, Joe, I don't want to hear it. If you got something I should know, call me, but keep the psychological bullshit to yourself."

Joe D wanted to apologize, to say he understood, but his friend didn't give him a chance. Dan Costa slammed down the phone and within seconds was down the stairs, through the garage and headed for Brooklyn.

It was a bright, clear day, the sun shimmering low on the horizon. He adjusted his sunglasses, lowered the visor and began weaving his way eastward, taking scant notice of the traffic crawling across the bridges into the city, trying to focus on what he would say, struggling to ignore a voice that told him to turn around. Reason battled frustration as he alternated between the wisdom of what he was doing and the need to do something...anything. As he turned down side streets to avoid traffic, he asked himself if his father would approve. His instincts, perhaps self-serving, told him that he would, that it was the right thing to do and that it would resolve everything before lawyers and an apologetic press distorted the issues. This was all black and white. There was no gray and no one had the right to suggest otherwise.

He pulled to the curb alongside the old brownstone and sat behind the wheel, permitting himself a few minutes of final reflection, suspecting that he would not be deterred, but allowing that it was reasonable to be certain. The face of his father's old friend, Mr. Gadsden, appeared in the passenger side window.

Dan got out and walked around the car to shake his hand. Somehow he sensed that the old man knew everything and his eyes confirmed it. He grasped the young detective's hand firmly, though for long seconds he said nothing. Finally, barely above a whisper, he fought back tears and said, "Your father was the finest gentleman I ever knew. Those who are saying otherwise will soon be proven the lying scum they are and your father's reputation will survive. Don't you worry about that and don't you do anything to shame him. That would be his greatest disgrace."

Mr. Gadsden held on as if to ensure his message had been received. Dan nodded his understanding and placed his arms around him, drawing him close. He heard him say, "Go home, Daniel. Your father is with the Good Lord. He knows best how to handle these things."

The old man shuffled up the steps, reaching as he did for a handkerchief to wipe away his tears. At the top, he turned and repeated, "Go home, son," before pushing the big door open and disappearing into the vestibule.

The traffic that engulfed him on his return to Manhattan seemed detached, a long way from his thoughts and even further from his emotions. He talked to his father, asking him for guidance, explaining his feelings, debating his intentions. An hour and a half later he pulled into the precinct garage, confident that Mr. Gadsden had been put there to stop him. For whatever reasons, Dan Costa felt that by turning around he had done the right thing and that he would always know what the right thing would be. Whether or not he would choose it seemed less of a certainty.

As he approached his desk, Al Wilson motioned for him to come to his office where a half-dozen detectives from the night shift were seated. He spoke in a controlled, serious tone, careful to say nothing that might trigger his friend's emotion.

"The men have volunteered their off-hours to interview all the young people your dad coached," Wilson explained. "We're waiting for Bobby Avent to get back to us. There's been an outcry from the parish and the neighborhood. Phone calls are coming in by the hundreds and people are volunteering to come in and sign statements, so we may not be needed."

Dan thanked the men for the gesture. He knew how much overtime they had all been working, and to volunteer their few off-hours to drive to Brooklyn and go door-to-door was a real sacrifice. "I'm hoping it won't be needed," he told them. "Nobody but a sick bastard could believe my father would do anything like what they're accusing him of." He thanked them again and returned to his desk to call Massimo Barracci. Al Wilson watched him walk away, knowing Dan Costa had his own plans for seeing justice done.

"Muzzi and Vito are waiting for instructions," the Don advised him. "The lawyer gets it first, the only question is where." Barracci shared Dan's appreciation for keeping things simple, and much the same as the young detective, saw things as black or white.

"Don't do anything yet, Uncle, please. I have my own plan and I may need you to convince a couple of guys of the wisdom of it, but otherwise everything is under control."

"You're a better man than me, kid. I'd be on the streets killing every black I saw."

"This isn't a racial thing, Uncle. It's one or two sick sons-of-bitches. You gotta' remember, some of my father's best friends are black. This bullshit is hurting them as much as it hurts us. I called to make sure you weren't planning any trips because I'm going to need to talk to you sometime this weekend about a job I have in mind for Muzzi and Vito."

Barracci promised he would be available whenever needed. "You should be with your own people right now," he added. "Meet me and Pam at Severino's for dinner. Bring the Jewish girl."

"Thanks, Uncle, but I've got a lot to do this week. I appreciate the offer and I appreciate that you're willing to help me, too."

"Hey, that's what the hell I'm here for. Make sure you call the second you need me. *Capisce?*"

## CHAPTER 20

There were more than a dozen messages on his desk, three from Marilyn, the rest from Father Boland and members of St. Anthony's parish. He really didn't want to speak to her, but he felt guilty, so he reluctantly punched in Marilyn's number.

"Hi. Got your messages. Sorry, I couldn't call sooner."

"Are you alright?" She sounded really worried.

"That depends upon your definition of alright."

"Yeah. Stupid question. Are they letting you get involved in the investigation?"

"They'd prefer I stay out of it, so I'm giving them time, but I think they know there's a limit. Al's worried to hell I'll do something stupid."

"So am I. Promise me you won't."

"Won't what?"

"Do something stupid."

"That depends on your definition of stupid."

"Dan, please don't play games with me. I love you terribly and I couldn't bear to see you hurt."

He felt like telling her that if she loved him she would leave with him, but that had nothing to do with what was on his mind right now, much less what she wanted to hear.

"I'll be okay, but I gotta' get going. I'll call you later."

"By five?"

"Sure, by five. How can I forget that I'm not allowed to call you at home."

He hung up, mostly because he knew nothing Marilyn Kyme had to say could help right now, but partly because he didn't mind making her feel guilty. He didn't know why and didn't feel good about it, but he didn't intend to think about it either. Other calls had to be made that were more important.

He called the ordinance and supplies clerk to requisition recording equipment for a Thursday night checkout. No one bothered questioning Dan Costa when he signed for surveillance equipment or special arms. It was assumed he had higher authority approval for whatever he wanted.

He phoned Forensics and Bill Mason confirmed that traces of blood found on the rusted window weight were the same type as his father's. Unless the young thief turned state witness was lying about who told him where the murder weapon was, Jesse Booker would never be able to change his story.

Before he could execute his plan to nail Alex Norville and Bruce Steinberg for the murders of Joe Teller, Lewis Berger and Clarence Worthington, he had to place a call to the Peace Corps' Headquarters in Washington D.C. He had decided to forego the inclusion of a charge for the murder of Donna's father, fearing that it would delay the trial and muddy what would otherwise be a clear and convincing case. Uncertain of how Donna would receive his decision, he would rely on his powers of persuasion, certain that she would accept their conviction as payment enough.

The Peace Corps's personnel section verified Donna's story, including her assignment in Peru and the dates of her sabbaticals. A faxed photo confirmed her identity. Donna Kempler was precisely who she claimed to be and that was the best news Dan Costa had had in weeks.

He was preparing to leave when Al Wilson called to him. "Heading out?"

"Yeah. I've got a ton of work and if I don't get going I'll never catch up to Rasheed. He's trying like hell to do a good job and deserves more of my support. Someday he'll be a hell of a detective"

"I hope you're around to see it, but I'm beginning to suspect you've got other plans."

"Yeah, well, you can't tell one day to the next what life has to offer. A couple months ago my father was alive and doing a lot of good. Now he's dead and some piece of shit is accusing him of the worst kind of things. Everybody but stupid assholes know he would never harm a kid, but because some black activist that everybody's afraid of shoots his mouth off we gotta' walk on eggs. Don't dare call him a lying, racist sonofabitch. That might upset the Commissioner." He stared hard at Al Wilson. "Well the fucking Commissioner and his black activist friends can all go to hell and when they do they'll find Jason Muhammed and his white liberal apologists waiting for them. That scumbag is going to wish he was never born."

Wilson had never seen his friend this angry, and at the risk of making things worse, he felt compelled to say something.

"Please, Dan, listen to me for a second. I don't want you walking out of here like this. Avent and Joe D can handle your dad's case and they'll do a good job of it. Jenkins is staying out of it and the case against Booker is getting stronger. Bobby just called to tell me that they picked up two more witnesses that will swear Booker frequented that crack house and bragged about taking your father down. Nobody's going to buy Muhammed's story."

"Just like nobody would buy OJ's? How many idiots still think he's innocent? Don't be naïve, Al. Somewhere there's a jury of minorities that will look the evidence and justice in the eye and say 'fuck them both.' I don't half care anymore if justice is done or not. I can take care of that with one phone call. What's getting to me is that scum like Booker and Muhammed can even accuse my father without getting their balls cut off."

"That's Klan talk. Your father would be ashamed to hear you say something like that."

"Klan, my ass," Dan replied angrily, raising his voice. "Don't turn this on me, Al. I'm not the only one fed up with seeing the laws twisted by self-serving bastards like Jenkins and Muhammed. Good people get killed and bad guys walk, partly because we have a lying bastard for a Commissioner, who because he's a minority, can say and do just about any goddamn thing he wants and get away with it. And that's why garbage like Muhammed think they can lie about anything and never have to answer for it. Well that shit's got to stop, and if the system can't do it, there's alternatives that can."

Wilson shook his head slowly. "Dan, you're tired, you're angry and you're just not thinking straight. I can understand all that, but I can't believe you're talking about taking the law into your own hands. Christ, son, it runs against everything your father taught you, everything you've studied and worked for. I know this whole thing sucks, but that's what life is about sometimes. Millions of people in this world are starving, children right here in the U.S. are getting killed and innocent people get shit handed to them every day of their lives. It's up to people like us to stop it, but in a way that helps prevent it from happening again. That's why we have to do it the right way, the way your father would have wanted. We gotta' prove that the law works and that it works for everybody, regardless of who's Commissioner, who's accused or who the victim is. Deep down you know I'm right. Just go home and get some sleep. Tomorrow you'll still be hurting, but you'll be thinking straight. We both know your father would give you the same advice."

Wilson felt he had made his point and that his friend knew he was right, though they sat uneasily for a minute without speaking. Finally, Dan stood, picked up some folders, and without looking at Wilson, walked past him towards the stairs. "I'll see you in the morning."

As he rounded the corner at the bottom landing he heard a commotion coming from the room they used to fingerprint and photograph suspects. A disheveled, wild-eyed young man burst through the door, discarding cops like flies. High on drugs and oblivious to pain he set a course for the main entrance where a muscular, club wielding officer blocked his escape. Just before impact the suspect lowered his head and shoulders, taking a glancing blow across his back, driving the stunned patrolman to the floor. He yanked the nightstick from the cop's hand and raised it high, intending to smash his skull, when a powerful grip encircled his wrist. He stood to confront his next challenge, straining through bloodshot eyes to locate his target. He never saw the fist that flattened the cartilage in his nose and drove his teeth in directions they were never intended to travel. Nor did he see the one that burrowed deeply into his stomach, doubling him over, before a third crashed angrily down across his neck, blackening his world.

Dan Costa washed some blood from his hand, cleaned it with peroxide and applied a bandage before leaving through a side door, ignoring the desk sergeant's advice to go to the hospital and have the cut cleaned properly.

At home he ignored another series of phone messages, including one from Marilyn, to enjoy more than a few ounces of wild turkey and a steaming hot bath, before dialing Donna Kempler's number in Pennsylvania. She didn't answer. He went to bed wondering where she was and what she was doing, ultimately deciding that Jack Shultz was one lucky sonofabitch.

The phone rang, jolting him upright. He fumbled for it, fighting the cobwebs that snarled his brain.

"Good morning," he yawned.

"Hi, Dan, how are you feeling?" Marilyn's voice seemed anxious.

"I'm fine. What time is it?" he asked, struggling to focus on the nightstand clock.

"A little after seven. I didn't think you'd still be there. Are you okay?"

"Just ducky," he lied, only now conceding that he had consumed more bourbon than he could handle.

"Are you going to work today?"

"Sure, why wouldn't I?"

"You're usually out of there by now."

"Yeah, well, today I'll just take my time and get there whenever." He sounded detached, mentally and otherwise. "Where are you calling from?"

"I'm at work."

"Stupid question."

"I love you," she said, "and I'm desperately worried about you."

"Why? Because you know I don't want to live in this pigsty of a city you find so marvelous and convenient?" He not only knew he was hurting her, but that he was doing it intentionally.

"Please, Dan, neither of us needs that right now. I just want you to know that I'm here for you, that I love you and that I'll do anything I can to help you get through all this."

He knew he had no reason to blame her for anything, but he didn't feel like apologizing. None of that mattered. He knew the futures each of them envisioned were growing apart more each day, as were their attitudes about life, particularly their willingness to accept change. He needed it, while she refused to think about it. Both knew compromise was unlikely and accommodation, impossible. Yet Marilyn Kyme believed beyond hope that somehow it would all work out, that she would share her life with Dan Costa, that they would love each other always and that he would remain the strong, sincere man who had so completely won her heart.

"I'll come over tonight and every night until all this mess is behind us," she promised.

He didn't want to hurt her more than he already had, but sleeping with her now would be hypocritical and he couldn't afford the guilt trip. Besides, he needed to focus on what had to be done that week and being with Marilyn at night would provide him little time to plan the details. Even if he still loved her, sleeping with her now would be a mistake.

"I appreciate the offer and I know that holding you every evening would help, but it won't eliminate the problems. For that I need time to focus...to concentrate. There are ways to close both my father's case and Teller's, and I've got to make sure that's what happens, whether I have to get involved or not. Until then, nothing else matters. So for now, just give me my space. That will help more than anything else you can do."

"Are you sure?"

"Yeah, that's the way it has to be. I'm no good to anyone, most of all to you, until things are set right."

"Do you think you'll feel differently about your job and living here once we're through this mess?" she asked hopefully.

"Let's hope so." It was the quickest way he knew of ending the conversation. "I've got to get going. I don't mind being a few minutes late, but if we keep talking they'll be sending someone over to check on me."

"Okay, but please make time to call me this afternoon. I can't stand not hearing your voice at least once a day."

"Sure. You know I feel the same." The deception made him feel worse.

He showered, shaved and dressed quickly, but the rush hour was well underway, so he didn't get to his desk until eight-thirty. Rasheed Martin had already checked in and out, intent on pursuing the investigation schedules he and Dan had agreed on.

Al Wilson stopped by to assure himself Dan was reasonably together. "Rough night?"

"No, rough morning," Dan replied. "Had to address some personal problems. Took longer than I thought. I'll leave Guttierrez a chit for personal time."

Wilson frowned. "You know that's not necessary. Besides, you'll need all the comp time you can get when you resign." He looked for a reaction.

"What makes you think I'm going to resign?" Dan asked indifferently.

"It's better to say nothing than to lie to a friend," Wilson remarked, as he returned to his office.

Wilson knew his friend all too well and Dan realized that could cause some problems. The steps he would take over the next few weeks required that no one suspect anything out of the ordinary. For things to go smoothly, everyone had to believe that he had rested the outcome of his father's case in the capable hands of Bobby Avent's people and the D.A.'s office and that his full attention was now being paid to a long list of neglected cases. He made up his mind to get out of the office, pursue the investigations and make sure everyone knew that that was precisely what he was doing. The next three days he interviewed dozens of witnesses, wrote reports and conferred with Rasheed at the beginning and end of each shift, as he should have been doing all along. To everyone but Al Wilson, Dan Costa appeared to have focused on his work with renewed energy and to somehow have controlled the anger that the allegations against his father had raised. It brought increased admiration for his dedication to the job, which he reasonably explained as the best way for him to keep his mind occupied and his temper in check. As the end of Thursday's shift approached, he had convinced those around him that whatever crisis had developed over his father's case, it had been successfully overcome and all was back to normal. Only Al Wilson and Marilyn Kyme knew differently.

The phone rang.

"I thought you were going to call me," he heard Marilyn say as the second shift detectives filed in, preparing for their four-thirty start.

"It's been a long, busy day and I'm still not finished," he responded, feigning exhaustion.

"You've used that excuse all week."

"Maybe because it's the truth. You know I had to try to catch up with all the work I had ignored. Rasheed and I are going to be busy for weeks. I told you that."

"Too busy to call me even once in three days? Please, Dan, don't insult me."

"I intended to call you before leaving," he said honestly, knowing that he couldn't risk her calling his apartment that evening or showing up unannounced, not with Donna Kempler due to arrive.

"What time will you be home this evening?"

He hesitated. "If I had to guess I'd say after eleven, but I can't be certain." By establishing so late a time he hoped she would be at home, unable to call.

"Make it ten and we can be together for a while. We both need that."

"Not tonight we don't, at least not me. I've got deadlines to meet for the D.A. tomorrow, and regardless of how late I work tonight I'll be in here by seven. I've got no choice."

He knew she was hurt and he didn't like doing it, but the other issues in his life were more important than his failing romance.

"Well, I guess that tells me something. Call me when you can spare the time." Her voice wavered as she hung up.

A strange sense of relief came over him, quickly followed by one of guilt, for he had always been sensitive to people's feelings. To hurt someone who didn't deserve it, physically or emotionally, ran against his grain. He thought about everything influencing him...the Teller case, his father's murder, Donna Kempler, his workload... none by itself could have changed his feelings for Marilyn, but collectively they had managed to caste her in a new light, a less essential part of his life. A month ago he could not have imagined feeling this way, but a month ago his father wasn't being accused of the lowest kind of depravity and Marilyn hadn't placed conditions on their relationship. As he thought more about it, he had to admit that Donna Kempler was also playing a role in all this, but to what degree and what end he still hadn't decided.

Donna was feminine to a fault, yet spartan in her commitment to avenging her father's murder. Despite the serious nature of her mission, she approached it as she did the rest of her life, with a carefree enthusiasm Dan envied. Well-educated, altruistic and brimming with self-confidence, she could challenge a man intellectually, delight him with her exuberance, or simply drive him crazy with her sensuality. Since the morning she had exposed her true identity, not an hour had passed in which he hadn't thought about her, often to the detriment of other issues and people in his life. Though he wished otherwise because of the potential danger, she had assumed an increasingly important role in his immediate plans, while becoming a frequent and welcome subject of his casual thoughts. Whether one led to the other or not, it was difficult as hell to concentrate on anything else, and now was not the time for distraction. Each moment's effort had to be dedicated to the subject at hand. As he locked his desk and prepared to leave he vowed to refocus his attention and to ensure Donna Kempler did not become an unwelcome diversion, at least not until the problems in his life had been resolved.

On the way home he bought fresh haddock fillets, potatoes, the ingredients for a salad and his favorite California Chardonnay.

It wasn't quite six when the doorbell rang. She didn't disappoint. Her hair seemed longer than he remembered, and even in the dim light of the hallway, cast a golden glow around her remarkably beautiful face. Her bright blue eyes laughed mischievously as she swung the overnight case in his direction.

"Yes, you can take my bag," she joked, as it slammed into his stomach. He just stood there admiring her.

"Am I going to get to stay out here all night or do I have to come in?" she asked without changing her smile.

"Oh, sorry," he said, stepping aside and motioning her in.

As she passed him, he couldn't resist focusing on the inviting outline of her buttocks, tightly wrapped in a lightweight black skirt. Nothing was left to the imagination as each step seductively shifted her weight, accentuating her well-defined derriere. The girl knew what she had and how to use it.

"What's in here?" he asked, lifting the bag and gathering himself, aware that she had turned in time to see him staring at her backside.

"Just some things to wear if we decide to celebrate," she said, folding a clothes bag across the back of a chair. No one would have guessed that in twenty-four hours Donna Kempler would expose herself to serious danger, undertaking a seamy, difficult assignment few women would consider.

"You're casual as hell about all this," Dan noted. "I hope you're just whistling in the graveyard. To treat this as anything other than a deadly game would be a huge mistake, one that could easily get you killed."

"Your concern is touching and I'm happy that you care." In a more serious tone she confided, "But don't worry, I know exactly what I have to do and how to do it. If that sniveling little shit tries anything, I'll beat the hell out of him. I might even do it if he's a good little boy," she joked.

Dan Costa had known and seen his share of tough people, but none displayed more self-confidence than Donna Kempler. Though still not certain she was aware of the danger, he allowed himself to relax, feeling that she at least seemed up to the task and certainly not intimidated by it.

"The potatoes are just about finished. It'll only take ten minutes for the fish to bake, so why don't you put your feet up and relax with a glass of wine?"

"Thanks. Mind if I change into something more comfortable?"

"Not at all. Bedroom's back there. If you want to call your friend there's a telephone on the nightstand."

"She's not home," Donna said. "Death in the family...an aunt from Baltimore. She drove her parents down there last night."

"Sorry to hear that. Do you have a key to her apartment?"

"Nope. Guess I'll get a hotel room close by," she stated evenly, as she took the valise into the bathroom. After a few minutes she returned wearing a knee length, royal blue, silk nightshirt. The black hose and pumps had been removed, and judging by the way the shirt clung to her body, he suspected that everything else had as well.

"Or maybe I can sleep on the couch?" she said innocently enough, eyeing the overstuffed sofa, a not uninviting prospect.

"You have to be perfectly rested for tomorrow," he reminded her. "Take the bedroom. I've slept on the couch a hundred times. I'm used to it."

"I wouldn't think of putting you out, and I sure as hell don't want you thinking I set everything up just to be able to stay here overnight."

"I don't think that, so don't worry about it. Just put your stuff in the bedroom. I'll be fine out here."

"Get unexpected guests that often?"

"No, just fall asleep watching TV. It's as comfortable as a bed."

Their minds were worlds away from Joe Teller's murder, the involved doctors or their plans for the following evening as they enjoyed the food, wine and each other's company. They traded secrets about comments Jack Shultz and Marilyn had made about them, what their first impressions had been and what they thought about each other now. The wine loosened their tongues, releasing their inhibitions and exposing their feelings. Dan repeated his concern for her safety. Almost as often, she laughed it off, though never failing to mention how it touched her. He opened a second bottle that they brought to the couch. She curled her legs up and snuggled next to him, as naturally as if they were lovers. He didn't think anything of it.

"You're not sleeping on the sofa tonight," she said softly.

"I told you, you need a good night's sleep."

"I'm not sleeping out here either," she replied, as their eyes met and she placed a hand behind his head, raising her lips to his.

As he wrapped her in his arms, felt the warmth of her body and the touch of her other hand upon his chest, he wondered how big a role the Chardonnay had played in all this. The thought disappeared as his hand slipped beneath the silky blue shirt to caress the smooth, soft body that until now only his imagination had been permitted to explore.

Hours passed as they kissed and stroked, sometimes gently, more often with lustful abandon. They moved to the bedroom where inhibitions were lost in the mad rush to satisfy the longing that had been slowly building since the first day they met.

Finally, shortly after midnight, they lay beside each other, still naked, sweating and exhausted. She turned towards him, curling a leg over his and resting her head on his shoulder, her youthful, flowering scent covering them both.

"Why did you make me wait so long?" she asked.

"Stupidity," he answered.

"What will you tell Marilyn?"

"That I'm going away. She won't want to come."

Donna rolled over on top of him and gently rubbed the sides of his head. "Where are you going?"

"Wherever you want, as long as it's not to a city."

She raised herself up, staring at him incredulously. "Are you serious? You really want to leave with me, go anywhere I want?"

"That's what I said, as long as it's far from here and nothing like this."

A smile spread across her face. "I can't believe this is happening, much less that you're willing to run away with me. What brought all this on, and so suddenly?"

"Not so suddenly; I've been thinking about you damn near every second since the night we went to that little restaurant in Newark. Actually, you've been on my mind a lot since the day we met, but with Jack and Marilyn in the picture, I never let myself think seriously about what it would be like to be with you. I didn't know if you felt about Jack the way I know he feels about you, and I certainly wasn't going to do anything to hurt him. As for Marilyn…" and he hesitated before continuing, "well, let's just say she and I both know we'd have to compromise too much to be together. Neither one of us would be happy doing that." He paused again, as if to weigh what he had said, reflecting a final time to be sure he was right. He looked back at Donna. "But you, you gorgeous piece of ass," he said playfully, "you're confident, free to do what you want and willing to try anything. Most of all, you're great in bed," he joked, gently squeezing her buttocks. "Just don't change," he added, "because for me you're perfect, just the way you are."

"I think I could fall in love with you, Dan Costa," Donna said seriously. "I know I love how you make love to me and that I've never, ever, thought of someone as often as I thought about you. I even began to wonder how I was going to get over you."

"That's good, because being with you like this, I can't imagine ever wanting to give it all up, to not want to love the hell out of you every night." He rolled her over gently, pulled up the covers and said, "Now go to sleep. We have a lot to do tomorrow."

The alarm went off at six but he didn't get out of bed until seven. It only took a kiss on the neck and a wandering hand before he was devouring her, delighting in her moaning and pleasuring in the feel and scent of her body. Once inside her he controlled himself, maintaining a slow, gentle rhythm that brought her to one squealing climax after another. She marveled at his restraint, reveling in every thrust, luxuriating in every shudder, before turning him on his back and grinding him to an exhausting finish.

"God, am I going to love messing around with you," he groaned, "every night, every morning, every second. I might just make you walk around naked so we don't waste any time."

"I hereby resolve to never wear anything underneath," she announced solemnly, "so no matter what's on the outside, a quick lift and you're home free."

"Suppose you're wearing slacks?" he asked, conjuring a serious obstacle.

"Quick lift, quick drop, no difference," she winked. "Whenever you're ready, it'll be there waiting, just like it is right now," she promised, lowering her voice and writhing seductively.

"I'd better get out of this bed right now or I never will," he decided, his recovering appendage responding noticeably to her touch.

As soon as Rasheed left to interview some witnesses to a drug related homicide, Dan dialed his apartment. Donna waited until she heard his voice on the tape before lifting the receiver, just as he had instructed.

"Whatcha' doin'?" he asked.

"Lying here thinking about you. Why don't you come back for a quickie. I'm ready."

"You're wicked," he complained. "Are you wearing anything?"

"Unh-unh. I'm just as you left me, only wetter."

"Don't you ever stop?" He couldn't avoid wishing he were with her. "You'll be happy to know that I miss you. Been thinking about you all morning."

"Good. It makes me feel secure."

"I'll be home by three. We'll go over everything one final time. Don't forget to call Norville from the corner phone booth."

"Yes, dear. Anything else, dear?"

"Yes. Get serious when it comes to this. Now we have another reason to make sure it all comes off right."

"What's that?"

"A lifetime together."

"I've been dreaming about that from the beginning," she said before hanging up.

A quick call to Massimo Barracci confirmed that Muzzi and Vito Scarola would be stationed in a car outside Alex Norville's condo by four. Another to Joe DeLorenzo verified a news report that Jesse Booker and John Turner were being held in custody under charges of robbery and manslaughter, neither being able to post the required bail. Joe D added that every neighborhood kid and boxing team member had testified as expected, that Frank Costa had never said or done anything to suggest that he harbored any thoughts related to homosexuality or child abuse.

"Some of the boxers threatened to kick the shit out of Turner and Booker if they got off, and three of them went to the Turners' apartment, threatened the parents and told them their son was going to end up in the hospital if he didn't recant his statement. Avent wanted us to get their descriptions and bring them in, but the Turners wouldn't cooperate," Joe informed him.

"That's because they know their kid is guilty and they're ashamed of what's been said in his defense. If you could keep working on them you'd probably get them to come around."

"No dice, buddy. The D.A.'s office has told us to steer clear of the Turners. When I said I thought we could crack them, Avent said we had our orders and that was that. I'm starting to think the D.A. feels he has enough to make the manslaughter charge stick and he's satisfied with that."

"The hell with the manslaughter charge, Joe. That doesn't prove my father never touched that kid or that Muhammed fabricated the defense. We gotta' get the Turners to come forward."

"I've told Avent that three times and three times he's said the D.A. won't allow it. What do you want me to do?"

"Nothing. In a week or two I'll take care of it myself."

It was almost two by the time he finished what he had set out to do. Al Wilson was in his office, engulfed in some coroner's photos and what were probably related detectives' reports.

"Got a second, Al?"

"Sure, come on in," he answered without looking up. "How are you and Rasheed doing with your cases?"

"You stuck me with all the drug hits. You know how long they take. But we have gotten around to all the statements and follow-ups, so it's getting there. Next week I'll start comparing the testimonies and figure out who's lying. Then we'll turn up the heat."

"Can you take on two more?" he asked uneasily, knowing his caseload was already past managing.

"I can take on whatever you give me, but that doesn't mean I have the time to handle them properly. I've got nine now and that's counting the whole Teller case as one."

"That scientist, Worthington, he's Morningside Heights' problem, not ours."

"His death's tied to Teller's, Al, I can't ignore anything they uncover. We have to work the two together, you know that."

"Yeah," Wilson said despondently. "Well, I got no choice. I've gotta' give you two more and neither one's easy. They're both about four months old, but the bodies were just found. Do the best you can, when you can."

He handed over two stacks, each with a photo of a decomposed body on top, the clothing suggesting the victims were young women. Dan just shook his head sadly.

"Yeah, I know," Wilson said, "but wait until you read the reports. They'll really make you sick. The M.A. thinks gang rape and mutilation. Drugs had to be involved, either that or the killers are getting sicker."

Dan thought about his father. "Why not? Lawyers can get anybody off and they're the sickest of all."

Wilson chose not to comment, partly because he was beginning to think that maybe Dan Costa was right and partly because he knew it wouldn't do any good to preach; not anymore. He only worried about what Dan intended to do and what might happen to his friend if he went through with it.

As he started to leave, Wilson said, "I'm not going to put anymore of my two cents into your life, Dan, but I want to remind you of something your father taught you. You said he told you to always do the right thing. I think it goes without saying that he wouldn't consider doing something outside the law."

Dan thought for a moment. "You know, Al, there's so many laws that aren't fair and there's so many lawyers out there twisting the law, that I don't know what's inside or outside the law anymore. Pornography used to be outside the law; now the First Amendment protects it. Perjury is outside the law, but Clinton made it a habit. I think I'd waste a lot of time trying to figure out which law was still worth enforcing and which law didn't matter anymore. The best thing for me to do is just trust my instincts, get the bad guys any way I can and then worry if God agrees with me or not, because His opinion is a lot more important to me than the law. The law and the lawyers can all go to hell."

"How long do you think you can last that way?"

"Long enough to get the bad guys I want."

"And then?"

Dan Costa smiled and shrugged. "After that it won't matter. See you Monday, Al. Give my love to Camille."

## CHAPTER 21

Donna unlatched the door and threw her arms around him, planting a long, wet kiss on his lips, pressing her body against his.

"It's almost three. Why aren't you dressed?" he asked.

She pulled open the nightshirt, exposing a black patent leather corset with half cups to support her naked breasts. A matching garter belt framed a thick patch of blond hair and stretched a pair of ebony fishnet stockings over shapely, alabaster white legs. The contrasting shades were eyecatching.

He grinned in appreciation. "The sonofabitch doesn't deserve the sight."

"Oh, but what a price he's going to pay," she smiled back, pointing to a leather riding crop on the chair.

"Too bad we don't have time for a quickie," he said, still admiring her body.

"It'll give you something to look forward to."

"Yeah, I'm sure it'll keep me thinking. Now let's get you wired."

A state-of-the-art transmitter, barely the size of a shirt button, was secured inside the corset's top with velcro, its jet black color blending well with the garment.

"Don't even think about the transmitter. It's powerful enough at twenty feet to pick up any sound above ten decibels and it doesn't really matter where you're facing."

He pulled a Velcro lined video camera no bigger than the palm of his hand from a box. It had just three buttons.

"To set the mood and help conceal this, remember to turn just one light on, this one," he said, pointing to a small square on the sketch she had drawn of the living room. "You press this button here when you want to begin recording. It triggers a low light sensitivity that will give us daytime quality images. You could be five feet from this and not hear it, so don't be concerned if he drifts towards it."

"He'll drift wherever I want him to," she smirked.

"I'm sure he will," Dan agreed, permitting himself another admiring look at the buxom Miss Kempler.

"I'll bet I know what's on your mind," she murmured.

"You win."

"And I intend to collect as soon as I get back."

"You do drive me crazy, woman, but I think we better get our minds back to this," he said, holding up the camera. "I want you to place it here, on top of the rod holding these drapes," he said, pointing to a spot on the sketch directly opposite the door. "Remember, we don't need shots in the bedroom. The audio tape will be enough to nail him once we establish his presence in the apartment and his voice on the video. So when you get there, shoot the whole apartment using the lighting we discussed. Then set it up in the drapes and turn it off until he arrives."

"Okay, I lock the door from the inside using the deadbolt and latch. That will give me time to start the camera before letting him in."

"You got it. Now for the tough part. He's in the room. He sees you in this outfit, probably approaches you. What's your next move?"

"I lead him into the bedroom, get him to strip and tie him to the bed."

"Then what?"

"Then I get him to tell me why they had to kill Joe Teller and Berger and close the lab, because if he doesn't, it means he doesn't love me and he'll never see me again. But if he does let me in on everything, I'll move into the condo and be his sexy, dominant bitch forever and ever."

"This isn't a child's game," he reminded her. Placing his hands on her warm, bare shoulders he said affectionately, "This will work, Donna, believe me. You have no idea how far a woman can lead a weak-willed asshole like Alex Norville, but you have to play him right. You have to be patient, teasing him for hours if you have to, until he's ready to explode. Show him everything but give him nothing, and I do mean nothing."

"Is that the jealous green monster I hear, or are you speaking professionally?"

"Maybe a little of both. We're never going to get a second chance to make this work and I don't want to risk you getting hurt. The best shot at both is to take your time and drive him to the brink. Then make him believe you're the sadistic, wild bitch he wants and he'll say anything to keep you."

"I understand…really! Don't worry. I won't get hurt and I'll get everything we need."

"You will if you do what I've told you," he assured her, and just to be safe, decided to go over everything one final time. "Okay, you start by telling him that you know he, Steinberg and Berger conspired to have Teller murdered because he wanted to go public with their cure for AIDS and that they had an attorney named Musto hire a couple of Mafia goons to do it. Then you tell him you know they had Chadwick and a scientist from Columbia named Worthington killed. He probably won't ask how you know all this, but if he does, tell him that Berger was afraid they'd kill him too, so he made a tape all about the research project, the cover-up involving an FDA inspector and Teller's murder. You can say that you found the cassette taped to the inside of a file cabinet in the lab that you began cleaning out when Jack told you Berger had been murdered. Tell him that Berger expected them to have a guy named Richards murdered as well because he was getting greedy, maybe even blackmailing them. Adding that ought to convince him that you already know everything, so there's no harm in his admitting it, especially considering the reward."

"What about Dr. Worthington?"

"Tell him that I questioned you in Nuremberg this past week, asking if you had ever heard Teller or Berger mention a Clarence Worthington and that you asked me about him. When I told you who he was, what he did and how he'd been killed, you put two and two together and figured that he was murdered because he knew the real purpose of the Nuremberg lab, that it was there that the trials were being conducted using AIDS infected blood."

Dan let everything sink in before asking, "Do you have any questions? Do you feel comfortable with the story?"

"Absolutely. You're a genius," she said without a hint of apprehension.

"I don't know what to think of you," he admitted. "You're either the most fearless woman I've ever known or a completely naïve dummy."

"Is that any way to speak to the woman you love? Maybe you're the one that deserves a whipping." She pretended to snarl but couldn't help laughing. "Stop worrying, Darling. You have no idea what a groveling little worm Norville is. I'll have him eating out of my hand and autographing a confession."

"Don't get cute, Donna. Get what I told you, grab the video camera and get out of there. I'll be parked near the entrance. If anything goes wrong, if he gets free, someone comes in on you, whatever, you just yell 'Muzzi.' Can you remember that?"

"Yep, 'Muzzi.' Got it, but what the heck does it mean?"

"It's somebody's name. I'd have you yell something else, but I'm afraid it might go over their heads. I'd rather rely on your memory than theirs."

"Will it take long for you to get to me if there's a problem? I can take care of myself if I have to."

"Do whatever you have to until my guys get there. Once they do, you just get out fast."

"Then you won't be coming to my rescue?" she asked, pretending to be disappointed.

"It's better I make sure nobody sees me. But trust me, once my friends bust in, you are definitely rescued."

"Where will you be?"

"Parked right outside the entrance, waiting for you to come out."

"You'd better be, or it's going to be a long, cold night when you get back here," she joked.

"I wish you'd concentrate on something besides sex until this is over."

She threw open the nightshirt again. "Sure about that?"

"Give me a break, woman, please," he begged.

"Okay, I'll be serious."

"Once you're set up in the apartment, two of my people will go in and hide in the service room down the hall. They'll be seconds away and monitoring every word. So will I. Just do what I've said and everything will be fine. Okay?"

"Yep, got it. But suppose he won't confess. How far can I go?"

"Just be patient. String him out until he can't take it anymore. He'll tell you anything you want after that."

"If I go through all that and he doesn't, I might beat a confession out of him."

"Don't adlib. Just do as I say and you'll be fine."

Satisfied that she understood and was comfortable with the instructions, he recounted everything in his mind as she slipped on a designer sweatsuit and tennis shoes.

"You might want to tell him you want ten thousand dollars a month spending money in addition to living in the condo. That will show you've given this a lot of thought and are serious about being his mistress."

"Sounds good. Maybe I'll ask for twenty thousand and destroy the tapes. I can always get a real man on the side."

"You never stop, do you?"

"You wouldn't love me if I did and then I wouldn't have you to love the rest of my life," she replied, planting rapid fire little kisses on his face.

"Knock it off," he pleaded, holding her at arms' length. "But you do look great," he confessed. "Ready?"

"Ready and able. Let's do it."

As they approached Norville's condo on the East Side, Dan passed Vito Scarola's black Sedan deVille parked a block away. Muzzi sat beside him drinking coffee. Neither seemed to recognize the Jeep as he drove past and turned the corner before stopping to let Donna out. She gave him a quick kiss, grabbed her overnight bag and jumped out as if she were going for a walk in the park.

Dan circled the block and pulled to the curb a hundred feet or so from Scarola. They watched him approach but said nothing, even as he slid into the back seat and closed the door.

"We'll wait here until she gets in the room and tests the transmitter. If it works out here you won't have any trouble with it inside."

Dan saw Scarola's eyes shift to the rearview mirror.

"What's a transmitter?" he asked.

"It's like a radio. That's how we'll know what's going on."

"I knew that," Muzzi grunted, still staring ahead.

"Bullshit," his partner whispered.

Neither spoke again. Only Muzzi's comical slurping and heavy breathing from one too many fractured noses broke the quiet.

"One, two, I love you; three, four, I'm a little whore."

Dan rolled his eyes. "Okay, let's go."

"Was that her?" Scarola asked as they exited the car.

"Yes, you could hear her good?" Dan asked to be sure, not altogether certain that one or both weren't at least partially deaf.

"Yeah, what was she saying?" Scarola looked confused.

Muzzi said, "It was like a code; right Danny?"

"Yeah, right, Muzz."

Muzzi smiled triumphantly. Scarola flipped him the finger.

While Dan showed his badge to the doorman, occupying him with a series of questions related to some fictitious drug hit, the Barracci soldiers slipped into the building and took the elevator to the seventh floor. They walked to the end of the hall where they found the service room, forced the lock and made themselves comfortable.

"If she calls my name, we go down the hall to number seventy-two," Muzzi reminded his partner.

Scarola stared indifferently before re-exercising his finger. "I don't need you to tell me what to do."

"Yeah? Well you might forget."

"Who the hell are you all of a sudden, Albert Einstein?"

Muzzi winced. He had heard the name. He just couldn't place the face.

Scarola smiled triumphantly.

Muzzi flipped him the finger.

Dan bought coffee and a hot dog from a street vendor before moving the car closer to the building and settling in for what he knew would be a long, anxious evening. Occasionally, he could hear Donna move about, but as he had instructed, she said nothing.

Shortly before five he heard the doorbell ring, followed by a whisper well magnified by the sophisticated transmitter.

"That's him. We're on."

The sounds of a deadbolt turning and latch sliding seemed inches away.

"Jesus, you're magnificent," he heard Norville exclaim.

"Get in here and shut up. I'm not in the mood to listen to any of your bullshit tonight. You're here to amuse me, and if and when I get my fill, maybe you'll get yours."

Dan knew Donna was a strong, confident woman with an obvious hold on Norville, but the stakes were high. The doctors and their associates were conspirators in multiple homicides, so even if everything went well this evening, her life remained in danger. He believed that what they were doing was the best and perhaps only way to bring closure, that he had planned everything well and that if they followed the plan there would be no opportunity for any of the suspects to get to Donna. The tapes and other evidence should secure indictments. Whether or not they led to convictions depended upon a legal system in which he had decreasing faith. Naïve or incompetent juries and suspect judges were easy prey for defense lawyers who placed wealth and ego above justice. Even that was beginning to matter less, at least as far as his father's and Teller's cases were concerned. If the courts failed, there were back-up plans to see that justice was served.

Every now and then his thoughts were interrupted by some lurid remark or resounding slap of the riding crop. Though he wanted her out of there he prayed for patience. "Take your time, string him out," he whispered. As though she heard, Donna frequently left the room, frustrating the bound Norville, but fueling his passion and the need to release it.

She varied the length of time she would take to return, sometimes a matter of minutes...once, a half-hour. Occasionally, she would return in a foul mood, wielding the crop, jabbing and slashing, screaming insults, until Dan wondered if she had lost her patience. Other times she would come back laughing, teasing and promising years of deviantly delicious sex. He listened, picturing her in the black leather, reliving her scent, until the windows fogged. He rolled them down, grateful for the air, despite the fumes from passing traffic. The closer he listened, the less he relied on his imagination and the hotter it got. Donna Kempler was one erotic woman.

With each passing hour Donna became more aggressive, her speech nastier, blows harder, promises more tantalizing. Dan began to wonder if they had underestimated the doctor's fortitude. Donna's antics were bordering on torture when suddenly Norville began admitting his and Steinberg's roles as financial backers in a history making research project, alluding to a series of problems with the involved scientists that necessitated their elimination. But his thoughts were scattered and disjointed, almost incoherent at times, offering no clear picture of the roles each character played and the series of events that led to the murders. He seemed obsessed by the sexual satisfaction he received from this act of ultimate submission. Donna slapped his face two, three, four times, each successively harder, demanding he calm down, lashing his backside with the riding crop until he began whimpering like a baby. Wisely she changed tactics, offering him a cold drink, wiping perspiration from his face. She had complete control of his mind and will.

"Now stop crying or I'll just have to punish you again. Just look at me and tell me everything, nice and slow. The slower you tell me, the hotter I'm going to get and the better I'm going to taste."

As Norville regained his composure, he focused on the events, recounting them chronologically and clearly, both of which were important if the tapes were to be used as evidence. The story he told paralleled Dan's suspicions, indicating that Norville believed that Berger had indeed disclosed everything on a tape.

At one point Donna pressed for the names of the hit men, raising the doctor's suspicion, but a few erotic threats followed by another whack from the riding crop and he gave up both Carlo Rinaldi and Albert Tataro, though he denied ever having met or spoken to them. Getting a full report on Dave Richards' role in the lab conspiracy and Clarence Worthington's murder took less persuasion. *In for a penny, in for a pound.*

What Dan didn't know was that Teller hadn't been murdered simply because he wanted to accelerate delivery of an AIDS cure to the public at the risk of sacrificing millions in profit. His work with Donna's father on Chincoteague Island, under-written by an investment group headed by Steinberg, Norville and Musto, had begun as research for an antidote to a hybrid bacterium called Anthrax 35, a U.S. biological weapon developed and stored at the Aberdeen, Maryland laboratories at which Teller had worked in the late eighties. As part of the project, John Kempler experimented with limulus cell separation, accidentally discovering a process that isolated an anti-viral cell. It was Kempler's insistence on publishing his findings that got him killed. Any announcement before patents could be established would have deprived Steinberg and Norville of the millions that could be theirs. In accepting Kempler's death as a coincidence, Joe Teller simply displayed his naivety.

A small vial of Anthrax 35, or X-35 as it was called, was secreted out in 2000 and sold to a Middle East country sympathetic to Islamic terrorists. There it was cloned, stabilized and packaged for transport back to the U.S. where it had been successfully released at least five times, claiming over four hundred lives and threatening the loss of thousands more.

In isolating the lysate to combat the AIDS virus, Teller had to separate it from a second cell, which he soon discovered provided the crab with immunity from virtually any form of life threatening bacteria, a cell that he used repeatedly to neutralize traces of X-35 from blood samples taken from Radio City Music Hall victims. That was the purpose of the light-blue-stickered blood samples delivered to Nuremberg that originally showed no trace of the AIDS virus. Getting them transferred from NIH's custody to the care of the doctors under the guise of analysis verification was a service easily provided by FDA Agent Dave Richards.

Teller knew that scientists in companies such as Pfizer, Sandoz and a score of others, could pick up the anti-viral project and have an AIDS cure on the market within a year, so he argued for its immediate publication. The simultaneous sale of manufacturing rights to qualified pharmaceutical firms would generate more than enough money for him to accelerate the anti-bacteria program and package an X-35 antidote within weeks. Steinberg, Norville and their associates had, of course, other plans.

The longer an announcement of an AIDS cure was delayed, the greater the return. That thousands would die in the meantime was of no concern to the conspirators. Properly documenting all the research steps, test validations and manufacturing protocols would take time, but once completed, would provide a total packge for awarding to the highest bidder, and generate a return to the investors a hundred times what Teller had in mind. The X-35 cure would be handled much the same, guaranteeing even greater profit since there were no alternative drugs on the market and no hope of survival once exposed. A few more bombings in the interim would only increase the value of the serum.

It was past eleven. Norville had given up more than they could have hoped for, resolving the few loose ends Dan had had before the night began. Now if she would just do as he had asked and get out of there.

"You've been a good little boy, so I'm going to loosen these knots while I freshen up. And if you can get free by the time I come back, you'll get a very special treat that I've been storing for you in a very special place."

"Will you please stop and get the hell out of there," Dan muttered.

A few minutes later Donna Kempler exited the building, spotted the Jeep and ran to it.

She dropped herself on the seat, let out a big breath and smiled.

"Hi, lover, how did I do?"

*Just a walk in the park.*

"You did great. Glad it's over?" Dan asked as he pulled out into traffic and headed cross-town towards his apartment.

"Yep, but I was kind of getting into it…you know, warming up for you tonight." She kissed him on the cheek, then ran her tongue along his neck while her hand moved down his shirt, past his belt. "Mmm, it's nice to know you've missed me."

Inside the apartment Donna headed straight for the bathroom. "I need a shower."

"Take your time. I want to run the video to make sure it's okay."

He could hear the water running as he inserted the tape and pressed the PLAY button.

It opened with Donna, her bare ass outlined by the garter belt and stockings, approaching the door to unlock it. The lighting and angle were perfect. Alex Norville entered; a short, trim, well-dressed man in his fifties, not bad looking for a spineless wimp.

It would have taken the world's best actor to duplicate his expression. As Donna dragged him in it never changed. Only his eyes moved from one delectable body part to another.

The tape ran for another ten minutes, until she had securely bound and left him for the first time. As she reached to turn off the camera she licked her lips and mouthed the words, "I love you."

He removed the tape and was placing it in a case when the bathroom door opened. Donna stood there, arms stretched wide, wearing nothing but a smile.

"See anything you like, sailor?"

Except for two half-hour breaks she insisted on, they spent all day Saturday editing and reproducing the audiotapes. Besides the one original and three full-length copies, they made three shorter versions, each carefully edited for Dave Richards, Carlo Rinaldi and James Musto. By the time they finished, no one could have suspected the circumstances under which Alex Norville had rendered his confession.

"You were fantastic and these tapes are absolutely perfect," Dan admitted, surveying the stacks and drawing Donna towards him. "How about celebrating?"

"Okay, last one in bed has to make dinner," she shouted, racing ahead, her victory assured by a head first dive. He dropped on top of her, wrestling her jeans down.

"No fair, I can't see you."

"If I have to buy dinner," he said nibbling her ear, "I get you any way I want."

After an hour he showered and was preparing to leave for an Italian takeout on Eighth Avenue when she told him, "I'll clean up while you're gone, so don't rush. I'm going to shower and have another surprise waiting for you."

"Save it until we're sixty. I don't need anything except one look at you."

As soon as the door closed Donna hurried to the shower. Within minutes she was dressed and down the stairs with an audiotape and player tucked in her sweatsuit. A light drizzle fell as she raced to a phone booth. Inside she fumbled with a handful of quarters before dialing a familiar number. She anxiously waited for someone to answer, aware that she had to hurry back and change into dry clothes before Dan returned. Donna hadn't counted on the rain. She told herself to relax, that the worst was over, but the phone just rang…five, six times. She was about to hang up when she heard his voice. She put the phone next to the tape-player and pressed the PLAY button.

Unable to fathom why his lover had made a tape without first telling him, a flustered John Norville stumbled through half finished questions, mumbling incoherently, until the reality of his indiscretions and Donna Kempler's purpose struck him.

He leveled a threatening, obscenity laced tirade until she said, "Keep it up, you sick sonofabitch, and the tape will be in the cops' hands in ten minutes, and you better believe I mean it."

The implication of the cops' learning of the tape's contents was immediately clear.

What do you want?" he asked contritely.

"Ten million dollars. I don't care what you have to do to get it, but I want it by ten o'clock Tuesday morning. If not, I give the tape to the cops, together with my statement, which thanks to you, will include all kinds of incriminating details I didn't know about until tonight." By the time I'm done, there won't be a lawyer in the country who'll want your case. You, Steinberg, Musto...all of you... you'll all go away for the rest of your lives."

"How do I know you won't do that anyway, or that there aren't other copies?"

"You don't, asshole, that's the price you pay for murdering my father. You're just lucky the money means more to me than seeing you fry. Besides, I don't feel like going to jail for blackmail."

There was a long pause. "Alright, we'll do it but we need more time. I can sell stocks on Monday, but the checks won't clear until Wednesday."

"Bullshit. Turn the stocks over to the broker and you'll have your money the same day. And if you try anything my partner will have this tape in the cops' hands within minutes."

Mention of an accomplice would dissuade them from trying anything, or so Donna hoped.

"Bring the money in a white suitcase to the Holiday Inn on Eighth Avenue. Give it to Ramon at the courtesy desk and tell him it's for Miss Stevenson. Then drive to Grand Central Station. Walk in the Park Avenue South entrance and wait five minutes for a messenger to deliver the tape. Do that and you'll never hear from us again. Do anything else and the cops get the tape. Oh, by the way, there's a video version your wife would enjoy. You'll get that, too, if you cooperate. We didn't really need it except to show how pathetic you are. Remember; Tuesday, ten sharp."

A half-hour later Dan returned, a large brown bag cradled in his arms and a bottle of red wine protruding from his jacket.

"Mussels marinara, veal parmigiana, garlic bread and salad. Come and get it while it's still hot," he announced.

"That's funny, I was about to say the same thing." She stood in the bedroom doorway, the light from behind silhouetting her in a transparent red teddy.

"You are unnatural," he laughed. "Can't we wait until we've eaten?"

"Sure, but you can always heat up the veal and mussels. What do you really want first?".

## CHAPTER 22

A little before nine on Sunday they rolled out of bed, exhausted, but more than a little relieved that everything had gone so well. Before leaving for a restaurant in Jersey, Dan called Massimo Barracci to thank him and inquire about Muzzi and Scarola.

"Are they okay?" Dan asked.

"Yeah, but that Donna must be some piece of ass. I waited at the club all Friday night for them, but they never showed. They finally came in around noon yesterday. They said you guys didn't get out of the hotel until almost midnight and that they went right over to Sylvia's. Those two haven't gotten laid in two, three years. So I asked them what the hell's goin' on and the best I can figure out is your girl made them both nuts, whatever she was doin'. They banged a couple of Sylvia's broads over an hour apiece. Lucky it didn't kill them."

"Good for them, and by the way, Uncle, I owe you one. Having them there took a load off my mind."

"Hey, kid, that's what I'm here for. Just remember, I wanna' meet your new lady."

"You got it. I'll call you later this week."

"Do that. By the way, anything new on your old man's case? Heard anything from DeLorenzo?"

"Not much. The two that did it are in custody, charged with manslaughter. It may stay that way until somebody can prove what they're saying about Dad is bullshit."

"Hey, give me the fuckin' word. By the time we're done that Turner kid's old man will beg to tell the truth."

"Thanks, Uncle, but we have to do this thing by the book. Otherwise, their lawyers will turn everything around. Those two little bastards could even walk."

"The day they do, they're dead; them, their parents, that piece of shit lawyer and anybody else stupid enough to get in the way."

"Let's hope it doesn't come to that."

A bright sun and cool breeze greeted them as they exited the car in Pine Brook, a small, affluent town in Passaic County off Route 46. Having skipped breakfast, they gorged themselves on Graffino's renowned Sunday brunch, a smorgasbord of Belgian waffles, steamship roast and countless side dishes. As Dan expected, men's heads turned whenever Donna got up. A few even jumped back into line to get a closer look, ignoring protesting wives and giggling offspring. With matching cream-colored slacks and a bust-enhancing turtleneck, she was impossible to ignore.

Understandably proud, Dan appreciated everyone's reaction, but couldn't resist some good-natured ribbing. "I am the single most unpopular person in this restaurant and it's your fault."

"Here we go again. What did I do now?"

He tried to appear serious. "All these men envy me and their wives hate me for bringing you here. Even the kids notice you."

"Stop worrying about it. I won't leave you until I find somebody younger and better in bed. But since you mentioned kids," she started, taking a seductive bite from a plump strawberry, slowly licking the juice from her lips.

"Oh, you are going to get yours."

Donna laughed. "Stop complaining. You love it. But I do want to be serious for a minute. Dan, what do you think about having children?"

"Sure, how many do you want?"

"Really? You wouldn't mind having a couple?"

"Of course not," he said honestly, draining the last of his coffee. "It's all fun for me. If you don't mind nine months of hell, why should I complain?"

"I would think you'd be a bit more romantic about it. After all, it's a child, your own flesh and blood."

"Hey, it's just my way of saying I love you. Sure, I'd like to have some kids, but if we didn't, that wouldn't change my plans for us because you, all by yourself, you're the reason for everything in my life now."

"That's nice to know," she said, reaching for his hand. "I hope you'll always feel that way."

At six A.M. the alarm clock rescued Dan from a troublesome dream involving Marilyn Kyme. If he had any faults, and he believed he had more than his share, his liaisons with scores of women were probably his biggest. When Eileen died, a number of Manhattan's most accomodating women had been all too willing to help him forget, and to a degree, their efforts worked wonders. There were weeks during which he had companionship every evening, and he frequently had to turn down offers on weekends because of a full schedule. After a while, he became more selective, but no less active, parlaying one night stands into weekend get-aways. During three consecutive summers he even managed to share vacations with as many different women, all of whom were professionals, wealthy and insistent enough to pay for rented cottages, and in one instance, a two-week stay in Hawaii. He had his choice of the loveliest, and at times, the most socially prominent of Manhattan's ladies, and he took full advantage of the opportunities. He never felt as though he was using them, since he was always open and forthright about his dedication to the job and the memory of his wife. He even went so far as to tell those whose intentions were not obvious to him that he was in it for a good time and that they couldn't expect more. To women who had to suffer the same old come-ons night after night his honesty was refreshing and they didn't hesitate to express their gratitude or extend the relationship according to Dan's rules. The fact that he had movie star looks, a body-builder's physique and knew how to satisfy a woman's sexual appetite made him the talk of the city's single set, not to mention a few married women whose interest he had managed to dissuade. Perhaps because he had been so up-front about his intentions, or maybe because the women had always gotten what they wanted out of the relationship, however brief, Dan had never felt guilty when the affairs ended.

But Marilyn Kyme was different and his treatment of her was weighing heavily on his mind. He had honestly thought she would be the one to replace Eileen in his heart and in his life, and probably would have been, had she been able to divorce herself from her career, family and New York. Now, particularly because of Donna, that was all behind him. He regretted the lies he had told her, the secrets he had withheld from her and the pain he had caused her, but his greatest anguish lay in the knowledge that it wasn't finished. She had to be told the truth...all of it...and that was going to hurt more than anything she had already endured. As uncomfortable as it would be for both of them, he had to tell her everything. He owed her at least that much.

He showered, shaved, dressed, and before leaving for work wrote a quick note to Donna, who lay sleeping soundly.

The phone rang as he reached his desk.

"Sergeant Costa. May I help you?" he answered, as he slipped a small manila envelope into a drawer and locked it.

It was Marilyn. "Good morning, Dan, I was hoping you would try to reach me this weekend and when you didn't I began worrying about you. Are you alright?"

He felt worse. "Yeah, as good as can be expected. Look, I know we have to talk and I'm going to try and call today and let you know when. But I can't say right now because of some pressing issues at work. Hopefully, I can call by the end of the day; if not, definitely tomorrow." He felt stupid for beating around the bush but the call had taken him off-guard.

"That's fine. I just wanted to hear that you're okay. Call me when you can."

*Why does she have to be so damn understanding?*

She was really a good person in addition to everything else. There was just too much big city in her and much too little in him. Yet, he cared deeply for her and regretted that they had been intimate. If he had known how things would work out, he never would have pursued her. Still, at the time he had no idea she would be so dedicated to her job and family that they would come between them.

Minutes later the phone rang again. It was Donna.

"Hi. Why didn't you wake me?"

"You looked so comfortable sleeping there, I didn't have the heart. Besides, I was afraid we'd get into it again and I'd be late."

"Hmm, we'll just have to make up for it when you get home."

"Sounds good to me. Just do me a favor. Curl up with some books, work out, watch TV, do whatever you want, but don't leave the appartment. There's no reason for them to suspect you'd still be in the city, but you never can tell. Keep the door bolted and don't even think about going out. There's plenty of food in the fridge."

"Don't worry, I'll be good, but we do have to decide where we go from here. I don't want to stay cooped up forever."

"I'll decide by tonight exactly how to handle the tapes. That will give us a timetable so we can decide what we're going to do and when. We're only talking two, three days at the most, so just be patient."

"Okay. Love you, and don't worry about me. Just get home on time. I can't stand being away from you."

As they said goodbye, Dan saw Al Wilson, a briefcase in one hand and deli bag in the other, walking towards him. It was seven forty-five.

"Got you some breakfast," Wilson announced. "Wanna' join me?"

The coffee was hot and the prune Danish was fresh, as it always was on Monday mornings. You took your chances later in the week. As he wiped his mouth and deposited the empty cups, Wilson asked, "Did you have a good weekend? Manage to relax?"

"A bit. You?"

"Yeah. Did a little yard work with the boys. Actually, did very little. Mainly supervised them."

"You're lucky, you know...a beautiful wife, terrific kids. Not many men are so fortunate."

"Yeah, you're right, I am." He looked at his friend, remembering Eileen and how much he loved her. "You'll have a second chance someday, and next time it will work out for you. How are things between you and Marilyn?"

Dan shook his head. "We're too different."

"Sorry to hear that, she could have been good for you. Still, marriage is one thing you gotta' be sure about, 'cause there's nothing so depressing in the world like a bad one."

"Now how the hell would you know that? Your marriage is about as perfect as it gets."

"Yeah, that's true, but more than half the guys under me are either divorced, in the process, or wishing they were. You can see how unhappy they are. I think half the ones that aren't divorced hold on because of some guilt trip they're on, but that's not the healthiest thing. No one wins, not even the kids, unless the parents are awfully good actors. Facing the facts would be better, at least in the long run."

"You're philosophical as hell this morning; any reason for it?"

"Nah, we just never get a chance to sit and shoot the shit anymore. I'm just letting you know what's on my mind, nothin' else. So, back to you. Anything intelligent to say? What's goin' on in your worrisome little life that you haven't told me about?"

Dan debated telling his friend how his life had changed so dramatically, but as with Marilyn Kyme, it had to be said and now was as good a time as ever. Still, he hesitated, wondering how much he should disclose about his plans and what had prompted his decision.

"Al, how much notice will you need if I decide to pack it in?"

Wilson's reaction was a mix of surprise and disappointment, despite having suspected the possibility for some time. "Are you serious?"

His friend nodded. "Very serious. I'm close to wrapping up the Teller case and it looks like Dad's is coming to a head. I'd like to see both of them through to the end and then get out of here, but I don't want to leave you holding the bag either, so maybe we should talk about how we can make things as easy as possible."

Wilson hadn't deceived himself into thinking this couldn't happen, but the timing did surprise him since Dan had seemed to refocus his attention on his work the past two weeks. He had also harbored the hope that when Frank Costa's case was favorably resolved, his friend would realize how attached he was to the job, something that seemed to give his life purpose.

"You sure about this, Dan?" he asked again.

"Yes, very sure, Al. I'm tired of the greed and hypocrisy, of politically correct bullshit and everything else that's wrong about this city. And most of all I'm tired of listening to all the excuses. I'm beginning to feel that if I don't get out of here my emotions are going to get the best of me and that could hurt some good people…their feelings, if nothing else. I've already done more of that than I want," he reminded himself.

Wilson wasn't sure of what to say. "Give me a day or two to think. If you're that unhappy, I won't ask you to drag things out. Are you okay with that?"

"Like I said, I hate to leave you holding the bag, but I've given this a lot of thought, more than three months worth, so another a few days won't hurt. Until then I won't mention it to anyone else and I'll keep working like nothing's happened."

Donna waited at the bottom of the stoop until she could hail a cab. It was eight-thirty. "Holiday Inn on Eighth Avenue," she told the turbaned driver who returned a toothy smile. With sunglasses and a cheap black wig she sat confidently, enjoying the ride while rehearsing her next move. The cab pulled smartly to the curb where she exited and paid the fare before entering the main lobby. The courtesy desk was to the left. An overweight Hispanic gentleman with thinning hair combed straight back stood behind it, indifferently surveying a circle of chattering Oriental tourists.

"Pardon me, are you Ramon?" she asked.

"Si, yes, Madam," he responded, straightening up.

"I called you earlier. I'm Miss Stevenson," she said formally, extending a small white envelope that he accepted and placed in his jacket pocket, peering about to see if anyone was watching. "I'll return tomorrow for my suitcase. You will take good care of it, won't you?"

"Absolutely, Madam," and he bowed slightly.

## LIMULUS

The doorman flagged a cab and minutes later Donna Kempler was climbing the stoop of Dan Costa's apartment house, reaching in her pocketbook for the key. As the lock turned and she pushed against the outer door, a thin, coarse looking man in a black suit extended his arm, helping her open it. She walked quickly ahead, unaware that another man had followed them in. At the end of the hall she slowed to get the apartment key from her bag. It was then that she heard footsteps behind her, but she turned too late to see the fist that smashed the side of her face, sending her hard against the wall and knocking her out. The smaller man opened the apartment door and stepped aside while his friend carried her in.

Dan studied the teenager as she flipped through the mug shots, admiring her willingness to identify the shooter in a drug hit, if in fact his photo was included in the mounting criminal file. She wasn't more than sixteen, but Maria Ramos had chosen to take a stand instead of looking the other way, as a lot of witnesses would have. The victim, a twenty-year-old with a long rap sheet, was the brother of a friend, and she was determined to help if she could.

Dan wondered what kind of life she had. Physically mature, decently dressed and made up, she could easily pass for twenty-one, drawing more than a passing interest from the pimps and pushers.

"Want to take a break?" he asked, as she blinked her eyes and stretched.

She smiled back, flattered by the handsome detective's interest. "No, I'm okay," she said softly.

"How about some soda or juice?"

"That would be nice. Coke, if you have it."

He glanced at his watch as he strode towards the break room. It was almost noon. He brought back two sodas and buzzed the desk sergeant.

"It's lunch time, Maria. What kind of sandwich would you like?"

Her dark eyes lit up. "Really? I get lunch, too?"

"Sure, you must be hungry. What do you want?"

"Whatever you're having," she replied, blushing with intimacy.

"Hey, Sarge, it's Costa. Can you get us two turkeys on toast with lettuce, tomato, and mayonnaise? And throw in some French fries. We're starving up here," he winked at Maria, "so put a rush on it."

"I've gotta' make a phone call. If you feel okay, keep flipping," he advised the young girl as he punched his number. It rang and the tape came on but Donna didn't pick up.

"Hi, it's me. I guess you're indisposed. I'll call back in fifteen minutes."

A disconsolate Rasheed Martin returned from a morning round of interviews, none successful.

"Man, nobody sees nothin' in this city," he griped as he approached his desk. Maria looked up and smiled. Rasheed couldn't help but return it. "Hey, who are you? My replacement?"

She giggled.

"Maria Ramos, this less than cheerful officer is Rasheed Martin, and unhappily for me, my partner."

"Hi," Maria said a bit more comfortably.

"Hi yourself. What are you doing there, looking for a boyfriend?"

"No, the man that killed my friend's brother," she replied seriously.

Rasheed felt stupid. "Ahh, shit, I didn't mean that. Sorry."

Maria dismissed it. "I knew you were making a joke." She returned to her flipping.

Rasheed turned down half of Dan's sandwich, rummaging through files before selecting some papers and announcing that he would be back by four. "I'll be over on the West Side if you need me."

His mouth full, Dan gave a thumbs-up as he re-dialed his number. It was almost twelve-thirty.

The phone rang and the tape came on again. *Still no answer.* "Maria, I have to leave," he said with a worried look.

"Is everything alright?" the girl asked.

"Sure," he said unconvincingly, "I'll be back in an hour. If you want to leave, just slip a paper into where you left off, and if you think you see the shooter, write his number on the sheet and clip it to the page. Okay?"

"Okay. Will I see you again?"

He tried to smile. "Oh yeah, you can't get rid of me that easily. I'll call you to follow up if I don't get back early."

Dan Costa didn't believe in things like ESP. He preferred to think that sometimes there were circumstances to justify a person's anxiety, that most often it was unfounded and that man was simply an insecure animal prone to worry. As the Jeep sped up Ninth Avenue he tried to convince himself that Donna was fine, that he would find her asleep or pacing the hall or doing any of a dozen things that might keep her from the phone. Still, his heartbeat quickened as he scaled the steps two at a time and hurried down the hall. He knocked and called to her before unlocking the door. When it swung open and he saw the chain hanging motionless from the frame, he braced himself.

Taking a deep breath, he stepped into the living room. His head pounded and his throat tightened as he struggled to focus. The couch and chair seemed to move with his eyes. He closed them tightly, telling himself to breath slowly, reminding himself that he was a professional, that he had to control his emotions. As he tried to think about something else, anything other than Donna, his blood pressure gradually receded and his heartbeat slackened.

The room looked untouched, much the same as when he had left that morning. Only the coffee table in front of the couch appeared different. All the tapes except the ones he had taken to the office had been laying on it when he left. Now there were none. He stared at it for long seconds, hoping his eyes were deceiving him, that suddenly the tapes would appear and she would call to him from another room or rush playfully to his side. The ache in his temples slowly spread across his eyes as he made his way towards the bedroom door and gently pushed it open. She lay on the bed staring at him, the strange dark hair framing her incredibly beautiful face. He tried to avoid looking at the thin white rope that encircled her neck, as if ignoring it would make it go away. Before he could reach her, tears filled his eyes and he dropped to his knees beside the bed. Days later he would recall that his emotions raced from despair to anger, back and forth, time and again, until he no longer knew where he was or what he was thinking. But he would remember that he prayed, though he would never be certain of why or to whom, for it was hatred and revenge that filled his heart.

Just before calling Dante Fiore, he decided who was going to pay and that nothing in the world would matter until they did. After phoning Al Wilson, he stood beside the bed and told her that he loved her and would miss her always. Then he covered her with a sheet and sat in the living room. A patrol car with two uniformed officers arrived first, followed by Wilson and Martin. Wilson told them to stay outside and keep everyone except the M.E. from entering.

"I don't know what to say, Dan." It was the first words he had heard. He was glad his friend was there, but he didn't know why that mattered.

Rasheed started to say something but Wilson put his finger to his lips. No one spoke again until the M.E.'s showed up

Dante Fiore shuffled in, steps ahead of Marilyn Kyme. They walked quietly past Dan who was still sitting on the couch, his head back and eyes closed. A minute later someone sat beside him, crying, taking his hand. Marilyn's head was down and her eyes were closed, but he heard her whisper softly, "I'm so very sorry, Dan."

After they had removed the body and everyone had left, Al Wilson said, "We have to talk, Dan; not now if you feel you can't, but soon."

Dan nodded.

"Will you be in later?"

He shook his head. "I'll see you tomorrow."

There was a good deal more Wilson wanted to discuss. Why was Donna Kempler in Dan's apartment? What role was she playing in the Teller investigation that Dan hadn't told him about? Who did he suspect killed her and why? But he would wait until tomorrow. His friend had suffered more than most men could handle and pressuring him now served no good purpose. The investigation could wait a day. He deserved at least that.

Shortly after everyone left, Dan phoned Father Boland to tell him what had happened. "I need a favor, Father. She wasn't Catholic, but I'd like to have her buried at Gate of Heaven next to Eileen. She hasn't got any family. I'm closer to her than anyone."

"I don't think God will mind," the priest said, more concerned about Dan Costa than church tradition. "Can I come over and sit with you a while?"

"Thanks for the offer, Father, but I'll be alright. I'm getting immune to all this. I need to call Paulie and make arrangements. I'll speak to you tomorrow."

"*Madonna*," a disbelieving Paul Ippolito said when Dan told him what had happened, but without disclosing why Donna had been there or how close they had become.

"You know, kid, they say God never gives us more than we can handle. Keep the faith. Things have to get better for you."

"It doesn't matter, Paulie. He can lay all the shit on me He wants because it doesn't hurt anymore. I don't feel anything. I'm empty inside."

"Give me an hour and I'll pick you up. We'll go somewhere," Paulie said, aware that his friend had hit a wall and worried that even a person as strong as Dan Costa had his limits.

"No, you don't have to. Besides, I've got things to do. You just call Fiore and let him know you'll handle the pick-up and that I've made arrangements with Father Boland. Just remember to leave me a message whenever Fiore releases the body."

"You going to have a showing?"

"No, just pick out a nice coffin. Then you, me, a couple of your guys...we'll take her to the cemetery." He thought about how he would want to be alone with her then to say goodbye.

"Whatever you want, kid. I'll call you."

When Paulie had hung up, Dan phoned Massimo Barracci, told him what had happened and made arrangements to meet at five.

"Good, we'll have dinner before we talk. Don't worry, kid, we'll make everything right," a somber Barracci promised.

"Thank you, Uncle, but I don't think I can eat right now. Just have Muzzi and Scarola there."

He spent the next two hours making notes, scratching out some, rewriting others. He was getting ready to leave for his appointment when the phone rang. When he heard Marilyn's voice he regretted picking it up.

"Are you alright?"

"Of course not," he snapped, before realizing how much she must have been hurt. "I didn't mean that. Thanks for calling." He took a deep breath. "If there was any point to it, I'd explain everything, but it doesn't matter anymore. Sometimes things happen in our lives that we don't have anything to do with, that we don't even understand, like my father's murder. But they change our lives because they destroy so much of it. Then nothing else matters." He spoke the words as though she weren't there, as if to himself, trying to understand what had happened and why he felt as he did.

"I almost feel as if it were my fault," he heard her say.

"Don't ever feel that way. None of this is your fault."

"If I had followed my heart she wouldn't have been a part of your life. She wouldn't have come to New York and stayed with you, and she'd still be alive and you would be in love with me." Marilyn began to cry.

"What happened between us had nothing to do with why Donna was murdered."

"No, but it did bring you together and it was my fault. I was selfish and I couldn't see how that would destroy any chance we could ever have of being happy. Oh, Dan, I loved you so much, I still do. How could I have been so blind?"

Reminiscing was the last thing he wanted to do and thoughts about what might have been were the furthest from his mind. "I have to go. People are waiting for me. I promise to call within a day or so. In the meantime, don't beat yourself up over this. None of us had any control over what happened. None of us did anything wrong. We're all victims."

What he would say to Massimo Barracci occupied Dan's mind as he crossed the Brooklyn Bridge and headed south on the Belt Parkway. There was no longer any point to withholding information from the Don, particularly if full disclosure would help bring finality to the Teller case and ensure that every conspirator paid for what they had done to Donna. So he would tell Barracci everything about Donna's relationship with Norville, the circumstances of her death and what he intended to do about it. For topics such as those, he could think of no better counsel. Then his thoughts shifted to his father's case, to what Jason Muhammed had convinced Jesse Booker and John Turner to offer as a defense. How he would address that would be next on his list.

## CHAPTER 23

The three men sat studying their drinks in a small private room in the rear of Visconti's, a men's club and restaurant in East Brooklyn, minutes from Long Island. They stood as Dan approached and wrapped their arms around him, offering their condolences.

"They'll all pay," Barracci promised. Muzzi and Scarola nodded assurances.

"*Gratia,*" Dan acknowledged, "but it has to be done a certain way or more innocent people will be hurt."

"Tell us what you want," the Don said, voluntarily foregoing his position.

Before disclosing the details of what he intended, Dan gave an account of what he thought had happened after leaving for work that morning.

Disguising herself as a precaution, Donna had left the apartment, probably to say good-bye to her girlfriend, since the plan was for her to fly to Peru where he would eventually join her. He could think of no other reason for her to ignore his repeated warnings to stay put.

"But Norville knew of this girlfriend and maybe figured Donna was staying with her, so he told Musto, who in turn had Rinaldi and Tataro watch the apartment, hoping Donna would show."

"But why would Norville suspect anything?" Barracci asked.

"He had just spilled his guts to this girl who's supposed to become his live-in mistress. Suddenly she disappears leaving him tied up, doesn't show up that evening or the next morning. She leaves nothing in his condo. There's no way he would believe she intended to come back. He probably figured she was going to blackmail them or go to the cops."

Barracci admitted it made sense if Norville knew where the girlfriend lived and if Donna did in fact go there. "So Rinaldi and Tataro follow her, not knowing she's going back to your apartment, and they kill her there."

"Right, and they find most of the tapes, maybe even thinking they've got them all."

"So now what do we do?" the Don asked, anxious to stick it to Musto and the two goons, none of whom were connected in any way to him or his family.

It took less than five minutes for Dan to explain his plan, emphasizing the importance of its timing. "If we don't do it exactly this way, we come out with half the heads and I want them all."

Barracci warned Muzzi and Scarola, telling them in Italian that they were to keep their mouths shut until he gave them their orders. They gave their customary nods, anxious to get on with the more serious business of dining. Taking out some marks, particularly ones they disliked, was routine, nothing to get excited about, particularly not when there was food in the offing.

Dan saw them open the menus and knew he had lost their attention, but felt comfortable that they would perform well when called on. "I have things to do, so I'll be leaving, Uncle," he said, standing and extending his hand. Barracci grasped it firmly.

"You've been through a lot, kid. We need to get this shit done so you can get the hell out of here and take a long vacation. When it's finished, I want you to take the keys to my place in Florida and go down there for as long as you want. No matter what we do, you won't forget, but it'll hurt less each day."

Sound advice, but nothing Dan Costa wanted to hear, nor did he care one way or the other about how much it would hurt or what the rest of his life held. The only people in his life that mattered now were the ones he wanted dead.

He was crossing the bridge into Manhattan when the phone rang. It was Rasheed.

"We got a lead. Al had me contact all the cab companies. Donna took one to the Holiday Inn on Eighth Avenue at noon and returned to your apartment in another one twenty minutes later. Figuring the driving time, she couldn't have been there more than a minute or two. Maybe she met somebody in the lobby."

"Or forgot something at the apartment and went back to get it," Dan added, not certain he wanted anyone investigating as thoroughly as he knew Rasheed would. His plan would be more easily accomplished without interference, particularly from his boss and partner. The less they dug, the better chance he had of exacting his revenge and covering the trail.

"I'm headed for my apartment now. I'll stop at the hotel and ask if anyone remembers seeing Donna."

"I'll meet you there."

"Don't bother, I can handle it. We have too much on our plates right now to duplicate effort. I'll call you later and let you know how I make out."

The hotel manager, Ms. Martinez, was an attractive, well-groomed woman in her mid to late forties with Spanish eyes and a Titian figure. She showed Dan into her office, a small room off the lobby decorated with photographs of chubby-faced children. "My grandchildren," she beamed with pride. "There's only two now, but another is coming shortly."

Dan envied her. "You look good for a grandmother."

"Thank you, Sergeant," she responded with a knowing smile. "Now, what can I do for you?"

Dan described Donna, her clothes and the black wig. "She would have come in around noon and left almost immediately. Sometime after that she returned home and was murdered. We're trying to trace her steps...where she went, who she spoke to, who might have followed her. The cabbie who drove her home gave us your hotel."

"I won't be much help because I spend very little time in the lobby, but we can talk to the people who should have seen her."

She pressed a button and summoned whoever answered. A handsome young man with thick, jet-black hair and a desk clerk's smile entered. The name-tag on his jacket lapel identified him as, "Javier, Asst. Mngr." The manager introduced Dan, who repeated his description of Donna.

"Oh, yes, I remember her," he admitted a bit sheepishly. "She was quite attractive. She was only here in the lobby for a minute, spoke to Ramon, our bell captain, handed him something, an envelope maybe...I'm not sure...and then left."

"She left right away?" Dan asked. "Are you sure she didn't talk to anyone else?"

"I'm sure. Like I said, she was very attractive. I didn't take my eyes off her until she was outside."

"Ask Ramon to come in and return to your station," the manager instructed him.

As Dan recited his description of Donna for the third time, Ramon frowned and shifted uneasily, neither of which escaped his notice.

"I am not sure I remember the lady," he said, directing the comment to his manager.

"How many attractive, well-dressed women do you converse with each day?" Dan asked.

"Many more than you might think, Sergeant, so I really can't say that I remember one like you described."

*Macho asshole,* Dan thought.

His arrogance did not sit well with the manager. "This officer is on official business, Ramon, and we will all cooperate," she said sternly.

Dan stood. "I think we'd be better off discussing this downtown, Ma'am." Turning his attention to Ramon he said, "You're involved in a murder investigation whether you like it or not, and if you choose to be uncooperative the D.A. is going to want it on record in front of other police officials." He made a move to take Ramon by the arm.

"Wait a minute," Ramon pleaded. "I haven't said I won't cooperate, I just said I'm not sure I remember the lady. Can you describe her again?" Little beads of perspiration were forming on the bell captain's balding pate.

Dan didn't reply. He just stared at Ramon.

"I suggest you tell the sergeant what you know," the manager said impatiently. "I won't have anyone reflect poorly on this hotel."

Ramon thought a second more. "You might be talking about a lady who asked if anyone had delivered a suitcase for her," he started, looking away as if trying to remember. Dan felt like slapping him.

"What exactly did she say?" he asked, trying to appear calm.

"I think she said, 'My name is Miss Stevenson. Did anyone leave a suitcase here for me?' Yes, that's it. I remember now," Ramon exclaimed, turning a still anxious eye in Dan's direction.

"And had anyone?"

"No. I told her that and she thanked me and said she would be back later because someone was going to drop off her suitcase with me."

"Did anyone ever show?"

"No, no one with a suitcase. Nobody except you has asked about the lady either."

"What was in the envelope she gave you?"

Ramon's eyes widened. He looked back briefly towards his manager. "She gave me no envelope," he said nervously, before lowering his eyes.

A police academy cadet wouldn't have been fooled, but since Dan was certain Donna would have given the bell captain a tip, the envelope's contents were no mystery. Still, he didn't like liars, even petty ones, so he left Ramon with a warning, one he hoped would keep him awake for a few nights at least.

"The case I'm investigating has a lot of consequences for a lot of people whose names and reputations you would recognize. If I find out you've told anybody anything other than what you've told me, or that you're holding anything from me, I'll come back here and escort you downtown. So you've got one last chance to think about whether or not you've told me everything you can about this woman."

Ramon swallowed hard and appeared to make an honest attempt to recall the incident. After twenty seconds or so he said, "I've told you everything, Sir. She wasn't here that long. What else is there to tell?"

"Just don't forget what I said," Dan reminded the bell captain as he returned to his station.

The manager's dark eyes flirted with Dan as they shook hands and he thanked her for her help. "Please remind Ramon that we have to keep all of this quiet," he asked her. "Until the investigation is completed I want no one to know that we spoke or that the lady who was here today was murdered."

He was preparing a dinner of hotdogs, sauerkraut and baked beans when the phone rang. He recognized the monotone voice of Dante Fiore.

"I'm not finished, but I did a cursory exam and I thought you'd want to know that she hadn't been molested in any way. From what I can see right now she was already unconscious when she was strangled. She's got a hematoma on the right side of her head and a bruise on her left jaw…tells me she got whacked pretty hard, probably enough to comatize her. I know it doesn't help, but I don't believe she suffered."

"Thanks, Doc, it does help to know that and I appreciate your calling."

"Uh," Dante started, hesitated, and finally said, "not for nothin', Dan, but Marilyn's taking all this pretty hard. Maybe you could give her a call?"

"Sure. I'll speak to her tomorrow."

"Yeah, okay. Just don't let her know I said anything. It's hard enough working with these women. I don't need any of them pissed off at me." Dante Fiore had a bigger heart than he was willing to admit.

That night he lay in bed trying to decide if Donna had really intended to return to the Andes, to the people for whom she had labored in the Peace Corps, as she had told him. In that case there was some noble purpose to her blackmailing Norville and Steinberg, the only conclusion he could reach from the evidence. Still, he couldn't eliminate the possibility that everything had been a hoax, including her avowed love for him, and that her sole purpose was to escape along with the money to some far-off hideaway. The thought saddened him because he had fallen in love with her, and to be deceived by someone with whom he had intended to share everything cut deeply, scarring the memories, the only things he had left. He preferred the first scenario and eventually fell asleep imagining what life in the high mountains with Donna Kempler would have been like. She came to him in his dreams, playfully teasing, as warm and real as if she were there beside him.

That morning he drove to work convinced that they had meant too much to each other for Donna to have betrayed him and that made him even more determined to do what he intended. What life held for him after that was unimportant.
 Wilson and Martin were talking near his desk when he arrived.
 "You look like you slept some," his friend said.
 "Yeah, surprisingly well. I guess I was pretty drained."
 There was an awkward silence until Rasheed asked, "Anyone at the hotel remember seeing Donna?"
 "Yeah, but I don't think it's going to help," Dan replied casually, opening a drawer, pretending to search for papers. "She had asked if a Miss Stevenson had checked in, but then she left as soon as the desk clerk told her she hadn't. He also remembered her saying, 'Well, I guess I'll call back later.' That was it. I kind of remember her mentioning a Miss Stevenson, but I'm not sure she ever mentioned where she lived or what she did."
 "Why didn't she phone the hotel to check?" Rasheed wondered.
 "Good point," Dan said, wishing he had rehearsed his story. "Maybe they had already made an appointment to meet at a certain time and Stevenson just hadn't shown up yet."
 "No one saw her talk to anyone else?" Wilson asked.
 "No, apparently she was in and out in a minute or so, just as Rasheed had thought."
 "Then why didn't she wait a few minutes to see if her friend would show up?" Rasheed wondered.
 Wilson arched his back and stared at the ceiling as he often did when considering a problem. "She disguises herself because she doesn't want to be recognized, maybe because she's in some danger. Yet, she goes out to see a person in a hotel, a person who hadn't even checked in yet, and a person whom she could have spoken to over the phone. So why expose herself to danger? Why not use the phone?" he asked, turning towards Dan as if he had the answer.
 "Maybe she just had to get out of the apartment," Dan said, trying to

appear pensive. "She had tremendous energy. I can picture her going nuts, wanting to just go out, anywhere."

Wilson wasn't buying it. "If she wanted to burn nervous energy she would take a walk, not a cab. I still think anyone would use a phone to see if someone had checked into a hotel. Either that desk clerk is lying or Donna saw someone else there," he concluded, leaving the subject open for debate.

"I don't know, Al," Dan interjected, trying to steer the conversation, aware that a follow-up would expose his story. "I can usually read people pretty well and I'm sure the desk clerk was telling the truth. As for the possibility of a third party being there, the desk clerk is positive Donna left immediately after speaking to him. He said he couldn't help following her with his eyes."

Wilson considered the argument before walking away, shaking his head and mumbling, "Still doesn't make any goddamn sense."

"I'll follow up just to be sure," Dan called after him.

Certain that his story couldn't be defended, Dan had to ensure Rasheed would be too busy to drop by Eighth Avenue. "Give me your updates on our cases. We gotta' get off Donna's for now, at least until the M.E.'s report comes in, or everything else is going to start slipping again. We've got jobs to do whether we like it or not."

Rasheed respected his partner's commitment, but wondered how he could distance his emotions so quickly. The man had suffered the loss of his father and a woman he was at least close to, both tragically and without warning, and here he was one day later, coldly talking business without the slightest hint of emotion or stress.

While Dan's focus was drawing Rasheed's admiration, it raised Al Wilson's suspicions, for there was still a lot about Donna Kempler and her relationship with his friend that he didn't know. Had she come to the city merely to spend the weekend with Dan, or had they intended to take one more step towards closing the Teller case? Dan had interviewed her in his presence and concluded that she was telling the truth. He trusted her and even voiced the opinion that she could play a role in nailing the suspects. Was it that role that had gotten her killed? Had Dan exposed her, and would guilt over that drive him to get even?

He reviewed the facts, and using simple logic and experience, concluded that neither Donna's actions just prior to her murder, nor Dan's at present, made any sense. There were missing pieces to the puzzle and he knew Dan Costa too well to suspect that he believed differently. He asked him to step into the office.

"Close the door," he said, gingerly seating himself and straightening in the chair. Dan sat across the desk, facing his friend, suspecting why he had summoned him.

"You need to tell me everything you know and don't bother repeating anything you've told me. There's nothing wrong with my memory. I want to hear what you haven't told me."

"Like what?"

"Like how Donna was going to help you nail those two doctors."

"I hadn't exactly decided," he lied. "I was only going to involve her directly if everything else failed."

"And what exactly was everything else?"

"Interrogation, beginning with what I knew and how it could be used to get convictions. I thought it might convince one or two of them to give the others up for a shot at a reduced sentence."

"Then why was she in the city?"

"Because we loved each other and she came to spend the weekend with me."

The admission surprised Wilson, and though he believed they could have been in love, he didn't believe that was the only reason for her trip to the City. "Why the disguise when she went out?"

"I told her that the doctors would be more than a little suspicious if they knew she had come to Manhattan without telling them, so I didn't want her going out where someone might spot her."

"How do you explain the trip to the hotel?"

"I can't, but I do believe she was going there to meet a friend. It was all probably innocent as hell."

"Yeah, so innocent it got her killed. Look, Dan, I won't lie to you. I think you know a helluva' lot more than you're letting on and that's a damn insult. I'm your superior officer and your friend, two damn good reasons why you should be opening up to me."

He waited, hoping for an honest response, trusting that his friend would give him an opportunity to help.

Costa looked him in the eye and calmly replied, "I told you everything I know, Al, everything except that I'm sure Norville is involved in her murder. How he found her, who he hired and why he had her killed are questions I can't answer right now, but give me time and I promise you'll get everything you want."

They sat staring at each other until Wilson said, "Give me your word you won't embarrass this department or yourself."

"I give you my word that whatever I do will be the right thing, that no innocent people will be hurt and that the people who murdered Joe Teller, Clarence Worthington, Donna and her father will be brought to justice."

"Yeah," a worried Al Wilson murmured, "but whose justice? Get out of here and pray you know what you're doing."

A message from Joe DeLorenzo indicated that there was nothing new in his father's case and that a Grand Jury hearing was scheduled for next week. Dan thought about it briefly before deciding to put it out of his mind as he had cautioned himself to do, at least until Norville and his conspirators had been dealt with. He decided to return to his apartment and search Donna's bags carefully, hoping to find something that might tell him what she had intended to do.

A red light on Eighth Avenue made him hit the breaks at the crosswalk, where he sat patiently observing commuters on their hurried way to the Port Authority Bus Terminal. A frail little woman in a soiled black dress and kerchief, a baby in one arm and a small child tethered to the other, tried to keep up. As the tiny family plodded across, a mindless pedestrian bumped the little boy, sending him stumbling to the ground. The mother bent to help him and she was knocked to the pavement as well, though she clutched the infant tightly, sparing it injury. As they struggled to rise, Dan could not escape the fact that no one stopped to help. Some took the time to cast curious glances, while the most charitable gingerly stepped around, possibly hoping for divine intervention.

When they were about to free themselves, two teenage boys lugging boom boxes, ignoring the traffic and close quarters carelessly bumped into them, separating mother and child, sending them both to their knees. They looked at the hapless family, laughed and high-fived before continuing on their way.

Dan leaped from the car and grabbed the punks by their necks as they neared the sidewalk. They felt the mounting pressure as he clamped tighter, digging his fingers deep into flesh and muscle. They dropped the boxes and screamed in pain a second before he threw them to the ground. Neither thought about getting up as he stood menacingly over them.

When he turned, he faced a stunned crowd and the backs of the mother and boy, now on their feet, their tedious journey resumed. Pedestrians wisely cleared a path as he made his way towards them. The light turned green. He ignored a chorus of horns and obscenities to bring himself to face the woman, whose tired red eyes said all he had to know. He lifted the little boy in one arm, and gently placing his hand behind the woman, guided her to the Jeep where he opened the door and helped them in.

The motorist in line behind Dan's Jeep shouted a threat, which under other circumstances he would have ignored, but not today, not in the mood he was in. He approached the still ranting driver who would have been wise to roll up the windows or run like hell, but out of bravado or stupidity, sat motionless.

Dan didn't bother to extend a warning or offer the man a chance to apologize. He simply opened the door, dragged him out, straightened him against the car and brought his fist hard into his stomach, doubling him over. He walked back to the Jeep, gave his frightened passenger a reassuring smile and drove off.

The adrenalin rush gradually wore off and his blood pressure subsided as he thought about what he had done and whether he could have chosen a less volatile option. *Screw it,* he concluded, *and screw every other shithead from now on.* He knew he had had his fill of people who didn't give a damn about anyone except themselves, and he knew he no longer cared about the fall-out from his actions. He wondered if he had done the right thing, eventually concluding that under any circumstance the man would think twice before threatening anyone again.

As they drove towards his apartment the exhausted woman struggled to answer Dan's questions. Beyond fear or the strength to resist, she had resigned herself to whatever fate held in store, silently praying for delivery from the demons in her life.

Alone, starving and destitute, she had been walking the streets for days, unaware of the soup kitchens and shelters that assured survival and reasonable safety. Widowed at twenty and abandoned by a boyfriend, she had no one except her children.

Dan carried the infant and little boy up the stoop. The baby, six months old, barely moved, and not until he had felt its pulse was he certain it was alive. The other child, whom he guessed was about three, gazed sadly at him through distant, glassy eyes. Dan wondered when he had eaten last.

"The bathroom is there," he pointed out to the mother. "You can wash while I prepare some food. Do you have a bottle for the little one?"

She opened the cloth bag draped across her shoulder and extracted a plastic baby bottle encrusted with dry milk. He watched the woman drag herself to the bathroom as he boiled water and contemplated a menu.

He prepared a tuna salad and elbow macaroni with peas for the mother and little boy and sanitized the bottle, filled it with milk and warmed it. When everything was ready he knocked on the bathroom door and advised the mother, who shortly returned to the living room, cleaner, but looking even thinner in a black slip. Her battered sandals removed, she stood barely five feet tall. For the first time Dan took note of her features and coloring.

"*Espanol?*" he asked, as he poured milk and handed the boy a small glass. She shook her head. "Native American."

"Tribe?"

"Navajo."

"New Mexico?"

"Arizona."

"How did you get here?"

Tears welled in her eyes and she slowly shook her head.

"It's okay," he said, "we can talk later."

The little boy finished the milk and held the empty glass out. Dan Costa was as tough as the city streets but he felt his throat tighten. He lifted the boy and took him to the bathroom where he washed his hands and face. "You can take a nice warm bath in there," he said, motioning towards the tub, "as soon as you eat dinner."

He offered to bathe the baby but the mother said she would do it as soon as she had eaten. While they ate, Dan phoned Marilyn Kyme.

"Are you okay?" she asked, happy to hear his voice but still concerned about how he was handling everything.

"Yeah, I'm fine, but I need your help with something."

Without mentioning the confrontations, he related the story of the little family before asking, "Can you come by and look the children over? They may need more than milk and sleep."

"Of course. Do you need any food? I can pick it up on the way."

"No, just get over here as soon as you can. The baby is already asleep and the little boy is exhausted."

"Be right there."

By the time Marilyn knocked on the door the mother had bathed the infant, a little girl, and dressed her in a couple of Dan's cotton undershirts, one of which she fashioned into a diaper, the other into a sleeping gown.

"Start with the infant," Dan told Marilyn as he lifted the three-year-old from the tub and began drying him.

A half-hour later Dan and Marilyn sat across from each other, picking at the tuna fish salad, sipping iced tea. In his bed a young Navajo mother slept with her children.

"How did they come to this, Dan?"

"I'm still not sure I have the whole story, but while we were washing the kids, she said she had left the reservation when she was fifteen with an over-the-road truckdriver. Two years later they had the little boy. That's when he married her. She traveled with him coast-to-coast until he got killed in a fight outside San Jose. She and the boy were all alone, no money, no family, so she hooked up with a driver she knew, a guy who had been a drinking buddy of her husband's. She traveled with him and I guess it was okay in the beginning, but then she got pregnant again and he wasn't too happy about it. Anyway, a week ago he pulled into the Hunt's Point produce market with a load, and when she was out getting milk for the baby he took off. What few clothes they had were on the truck. She's been walking the streets ever since, scared to death and so depressed she couldn't think straight. As a last resort she begged to buy milk for the kids, at least enough to keep them alive."

"And then you came along," Marilyn said admiringly.

"A lot of guys would've done the same," he mumbled.

"What are you going to do now?"

"Keep them here until I'm sure I can get her somewhere safe."

"How about St. Catherine's?"

He considered the overcrowded mid-town shelter before shaking his head. "I'll think of something."

She reached across to take his hand and Dan didn't draw it back, though he felt awkward. There was nothing she could ever do or say that would make everything right between them again.

After Marilyn left, Dan stood in the doorway to the bedroom, studying the sleeping mother and her babies, trying to figure out why they had come into his life. He had been raised to believe that everything had a purpose. As his mind searched for answers, the little boy opened his eyes and reached out as he had done earlier that evening. Dan remembered something a Marine buddy, a Nez Perce Indian, had told him. He stretched his arm and held out his hand, palm facing the boy, fingers extended and separated. The little boy smiled, withdrew his arm and closed his eyes.

Suddenly Dan Costa knew what he would do, and for the first time in a very long time, neither anger nor revenge motivated him.

## LIMULUS

At six he rolled off the couch, showered and dressed without waking his guests. He drove north on Ninth Avenue to an all-night food store where he purchased diapers, feminine care products, fresh fruit and produce.

He brought it all home and left a note describing where everything was, that he would be back before noon and that under no circumstances were they to leave the apartment.

By eight he was at his desk reviewing with Rasheed each other's progress on the investigative work and follow-up interviews they had agreed to. Dan fabricated reports, something he wouldn't have considered doing a month ago, but that he now found convenient, rationalizing that he would eventually make things right. For his part Rasheed dutifully reported his successes and failures, documented them as the SOP's required and closed with an itinerary for the balance of the week.

"Good job," Dan told him. "Let's hit the streets. We'll meet here at four. I've got to cover something with Al, so you get going. This is liable to take a while," he said, motioning over his shoulder towards Wilson's office.

With his partner gone, he extracted the remaining Norville tapes from his desk and went downstairs to the equipment room where he duplicated them. He put a copy of each back in their hiding place, the others in the inside pocket of his jacket and slipped out unnoticed. He checked his watch as he started the engine; ten-thirty, right on schedule.

By eleven he was in the private backroom of Visconti's where he found Massimo Barracci sipping an espresso.

"Where are Muzzi and Vito?" he asked.

"I sent them on a mission," the Don answered.

"Something I should know about?"

"You don't want to know."

Dan was more than curious. "Uncle, if it has anything to do with what I've asked for your help on, please tell me. We have to be careful how we handle this."

"It has nothing to do with any of your police work," was all Barracci would say. "Now let's get on with this call."

Dan had chosen the club's phone in case Alex Norville's office had caller ID. He didn't think Donna would have been stupid enough to call him from the apartment, but the possibility did exist, and if Rinaldi and Tataro hadn't followed her from the Holiday Inn, then it would explain how they knew where to find her.

A receptionist answered.

"I need to speak to Dr. Norville. Just tell him it's a friend of Donna's," he said, lowering his voice.

Norville picked up and Dan started the tape, permitting it to run for about fifteen seconds before stopping it. "Now, you fucking piece of shit, you're going to do exactly what I say or this tape will be in the hands of every radio and television station by the end of the day, not to mention the D.A.'s office. Did you get the money she asked for?"

Dan could think of no reason besides blackmail for Donna to have inquired about a suitcase, and although Ramon may not have disclosed everything, the part about the suitcase was probably true.

"Half of it," a trembling voice responded.

"Yeah? Precisely how much?"

"Five million."

Dan was surprised, so was Barracci. Donna didn't mess around.

"You got exactly twenty-four hours to get the other five mil. Be at this number at eleven tomorrow morning or the tapes are distributed by noon."

Dan cradled the phone before Norville could say anything.

"*Bene,*" Barracci exclaimed, "now we enjoy some antipasto."

"Can't, Uncle, gotta' run. I'll meet you at that office you have at the old Navy pier tomorrow before eleven. Okay?"

"Sure," Barracci mumbled, waving Dan away, noticeably offended that his offer to break bread had been refused.

Dan felt badly. The Don had made himself and his men available without hesitation and had yet to ask for anything in return. "I promised a priest something and I'm running late. That's the only reason," he said. Lying was becoming easier.

"Yeah, yeah, get outta' here," the Don said, only slightly mollified.

It was a warm, sunny day, the kind that kids expect and older people pray for. As he drove back across the bridge into Manhattan, he thought of how much he and Donna would have enjoyed days like this up in the mountains. It still hurt to realize they would never share either.

He stopped at a women's discount outlet and a children's store before reaching the apartment a little after two. He had to make three trips to unload the Jeep. The boy and his mother watched quietly as he stacked boxes and piled bags on the couch, each hoping but not really expecting that any held surprises for them.

"The baby asleep?" he asked when the last packages had been dropped.

She nodded with a smile, the first one Dan had seen. It was faint, but a smile nonetheless, and it made him feel good.

"Did you make lunch?"

"Yes," she answered softly, "would you like some?"

"No, I'd rather watch you open these," he said, motioning towards the couch.

"What are they?"

"Clothes for you and the little ones. I hope they all fit. If not, I'll take them back and exchange them. Oh yeah, there's toys for the kids, too, and some personal things for you."

His eyes were fixed on the little boy so he didn't notice her tears, not until he heard her cry.

"Hey, hey, what's all this? Things are turning around for you. Everything's going to be okay."

He wanted to put his arms around her to comfort her, but suspected he shouldn't. "Here," he said, offering her a handkerchief.

She took it and after a few seconds looked up at him through sad, yet beautifully dark eyes and said, "Thank you for everything. You are very special," and she began crying again.

The little boy stepped to her side and wrapped his arms around her leg. A small tear drifted down his face.

"Hey," Dan said softly, "you're making the little one cry. Come on, let's let him open some presents, and you do the same. It'll make you feel better."

"You never did tell me your name," he said, as he sipped some iced tea, watching her hold shirts and pants up to the boy, checking for size.

She smiled at him. "Elena. Elena Guttierez, and this is my Antonio. My daughter is Maria."

"Nice names. I like them," he said, walking over to the couch and pulling a particularly large bag from the pile. "Let's see what we got here for Antonio."

He pulled out a stuffed Mickey Mouse easily the size of the little boy and held it out to him. Antonio looked to his mother for approval before taking a step and pulling it to him.

"Oops, I think there's more in here," Dan exclaimed, easing a Bugs Bunny out by its ears.

Antonio smiled, looked up at his mother and with sanction in hand somehow managed to secure both in his little arms.

There had been occasions in Dan Costa's life when he had experienced that special feeling, the one that comes from doing something for someone that they could neither do for themselves nor expect another to do for them. Some he had rescued from drugs, others from abusive fathers and husbands, still others from the filth and violence of the streets. But never had any touched his heart as this young, mistreated mother and her two defenseless children. As he continued showering gifts on the little boy, he knew that somehow he would see to it that no one would ever hurt them again.

"I'm going to move you to another place today," he told her as he gathered the empty bags and boxes. "It may not be safe here."

He saw Elena Guttierez shake her head, fear crossing her face. To be abandoned again when hope had barely settled in terrified her.

Dan sat beside her, taking her hands in his. "I promise I will not leave you until you are safe and happy, wherever you want to be. I need a few days to finish my work and then we will leave together. In the meantime, I'm going to bring you someplace where you will be able to rest and be safe, and I promise to come every night and visit."

He said it in a way that reassured her, that left no doubt that Dan Costa would keep his word.

"And you will be safe?"

"Don't ever worry about me. I'm doomed to die a lonely old man."

She looked at him questioningly, as he began cleaning up the living room before phoning Father Boland at St. Anthony's.

As they drove towards Brooklyn, Dan called the station and left a message for Rasheed to phone him. It was almost three. He knew he couldn't make the four o'clock meeting and he didn't want his partner to suspect anything, not now that he was so close to setting things straight.

When they arrived at Saint Anthony's Convent, Father Boland was there to meet them, together with the Mother Superior and two other nuns. Dan deposited Elena and the children with the good sisters, assuring everyone that it would only be a few days before he would make arrangements for their relocation.

"You look well, Dan," the priest said as he walked him back to the Jeep. "God give you something to take your mind off your problems?"

"Maybe, Father. At least I know there's a tomorrow."

As he drove off, the priest's eyes followed him, not certain of what he had meant, but satisfied that it held promise.

# CHAPTER 24

The phone rang as he slowed down to pay the toll for the Midtown Tunnnel. It was Al Wilson.

"Are you on your way in?" he asked gruffly.

"Yeah, I'll be there in fifteen. Problem?"

"We'll talk about it," he said before hanging up.

His voice sounded ominous. Had the two teenagers or motorist he roughed up filed a complaint? Or worse yet, had someone checked his story about Ramon at the Holiday Inn? He began formulating a defense. A few days were needed and then he'd be out of there. He could confuse the issues that long. His record and reputation would help. Confidence restored, he pulled into the garage and headed for the office. As he ascended the stairs he met Rasheed, both arms stuffed with files.

"Leaving for the day?" Dan asked.

"Yeah. Anything happen?"

"No. Why?"

"Well, you didn't show at four and you're normally punctual as hell. Then Al comes out breathing fire, lookin' for you. I thought maybe something had happened."

"Not that I know of," Dan said nonchalantly. "See you tomorrow."

"Yeah. We'll catch up then."

Martin is a good man and a good cop, Dan thought, the kind the city needed. He wondered how long it would last.

He tried to appear calm as he entered Al Wilson's office. "What's up, Boss?"

"Shut the door and have a seat," his friend replied in a dead-serious tone, but reflecting none of the fire and brimstone for which Rasheed had prepared him.

"The Police Commissioner called me from the Mayor's office. That was right after the Chief called me and that was about two seconds after Bobby Avent phoned. Thanks, friend, I really needed their heat."

"Sorry, Al, but I really don't have any idea what you're talking about," he said, relieved to hear Avent's name, which meant it had nothing to do with Elena Guttierez or Donna's case.

"Don't bullshit me, Dan. I've told you before, I don't deserve it."

"I'm telling you, Al, I haven't done anything that any of those people should be coming down on you for."

"So you don't know nothin' about your *goomba* uncle sendin' a coupla' gorillas over to Arthur Turner's and threatening to kill him?"

*So that's why Muzzi and Scarola hadn't been with Barracci.*

"What the hell are you talking about?" he asked, doing a good job of pretending.

"Two wise guys showed up at Turner's apartment. Luckily the old lady was out, but the husband had just gotten up. They told him that if his son didn't tell the truth, he and his wife would pay."

"Anybody else see these two alleged people?"

"What? Are you saying you don't believe me?"

"No, I'm saying I don't necessarily believe Turner. And why should I? For that matter, why do you? You're the one who believes he lied about the door to my father's apartment being open and that he was probably covering for his son. Or maybe now you believe the Turners. Maybe you think my father was a child molester."

"Stop right there, Dan. Don't say another goddamn word, because we both know where you're heading and I don't want to hear it. You can be as hurt and pissed off at this city and the system as you want, but don't make this personal, not with me. You're in that chair right now for one reason and one reason only. I know you've made calls to Barracci from here and I know you've been convinced the Turners are lying. It's not a stretch for me to believe you knew some of his people might try something like this."

"And it's not a stretch to believe that Jason Muhammed concocted another lie to swing black sentiment, or that it might even have your black racist commissioner's blessing."

"Knock it off. I don't like Jenkins any more than you do, but I have reason to suspect you might know something about all this and it's my job to find out. If you say you know nothing about it, I'll believe you."

"Thanks, can I go now?" Dan asked coldly.

"Don't let anger and frustration destroy twelve years of friendship. I'm on your side and you know it, but I want things done legally, and for that matter, so would your father."

Dan appreciated the sentiment, but as he reached the doorway he turned. "I'll talk to some people, and if Turner's telling the truth I can take care of it…keep his lying ass safe. But if I ever hear anybody in this building refer to my family or my friends as goombas or anything like it again, I'll bring charges. That seems to work for the minorities, guilty or not."

Al Wilson could feel the tie that bound him and his young friend stretch and he cursed the people and events that threatened it. But mostly he chastised himself, because the things that were wrong with the city, the things he told others to ignore, were beginning to get to him.

As soon as he got to his apartment, Dan called Massimo Barracci, ignoring two calls from Marilyn Kyme and one from Bobby Avent.

"Uncle, you never should have sent Muzzi and Vito to the Turners. It brought a lot of heat down on some good people and will probably play right into Jason Muhammed's hands."

"Yeah? Well tell me what you goddamn cops are doin'. I'll tell you…nothing!"

This had not been a good time to call. The Don was renowned for his temper and Dan had clearly ignited it.

"Your father's murderers are sittin' in protective custody at Riker's. It's like a goddamn hotel, probably better than they're used to. A coupla' bucks here, a coupla' bucks there, and they probably got all the crack they want. Meanwhile, your old man's in a grave and no one gives a rat's ass that they're destroying his name. So don't give me any of your shit, kid. You don't like what I'm doin'? Call the fuckin' cops. That'll really scare the shit out of me," he sneered before slamming the phone down.

*Nice going,* Dan told himself. *That call accomplished a lot.*

He made dinner, watched some TV and read a book. At precisely two a.m. he called Switzerland. Five minutes later he was in bed recalling the day's events, believing that as bad as it had been, more had gone right than wrong.

Camille Wilson rubbed her eyes and searched for the nightstand clock. Gradually, the hands came into focus; three a.m.

"Are you alright?" she asked, as her husband shuffled back to bed.

"I'll be fine. Go to sleep."

"What's the matter?"

"Nothing retirement a long way from here wouldn't fix."

"It's late, but we can talk about it if you like."

"Nah, I already know what you would say," he told her, kissing her on the forehead before rolling over. "But I appreciate the offer. We'll talk soon."

The phone rang as Dan was exiting the shower.

"Dan, it's Al. Pick up." It was six-thirty.

"Morning, Al."

"How about we have breakfast? I'll meet you at the diner on Forty-sixth and Ninth in an hour."

"Okay, see you then."

As he shaved, Dan began regretting the things he had said and the crazy ideas his anger had spawned. There wasn't a bad bone in Al Wilson's body and Dan Costa would see to it that he apologized for yesterday, but without admitting to the closeness of his relationship with Barracci or that he knew who had visited Arthur Turner. He would simply let his friend know that he trusted him implicitly, would do anything for him and that he knew he could rely on him to do the same.

Whether it was Wilson's call or the realization that within a few hours the most difficult part of his ordeal would be over, Dan Costa's outlook took a turn for the better, so he phoned Marilyn Kyme and left a message inviting her to dinner.

Before leaving for the diner, he placed a call to St. Anthony's Convent where a nun answered, advising that Elena was at Mass.

"Please let her know I called to see how she and the children were doing and that I'll call again after lunch."

It was seven forty-five before an annoyed Al Wilson slid his expanding frame into the booth. "Damn traffic's getting worse," he muttered, while opening the menu.

"And good morning to you, Lieutenant," Dan said, smiling.

"Sorry. Good morning, but this damn traffic can put anybody off," he defended himself.

"I seem to recall someone telling me that half the complaints people have with Manhattan wouldn't be problems if they had more patience."

"Yeah," his friend grinned, "I guess I did lay that on you a few times, didn't I?"

"A few dozen, maybe."

"Don't get carried away. Nobody's perfect."

They ordered three-egg omelets, bacon, toast, home fries and coffee, while promising they would atone by skipping lunch.

"That'll be the day," Dan remarked, "when you skip lunch."

Over breakfast, while casually exchanging opinions about the Yankees' chances of winning the pennant, they prepared apologies, both concerned about how close they had come to destroying their friendship. As they enjoyed their second cups of coffee, Al Wilson started.

"I guess we thought and said some things yesterday that I'm sure we regret and I want to apologize for my part."

Dan started to speak but Wilson cut him off.

"Ten years ago I saw something special in you, something this city needed. You had a rare gift, what the knights used to call 'noblesse oblige,' a commitment to do the right thing. Over the years there were times you made me forget you were human. I came to expect too much of you and that wasn't fair. So I just want to say today, that you are and always will be my friend, and that even though I hold you to a higher standard, I'll try to remember you've got your faults like everybody else and that I'll be there when you need me."

"Thanks, Al. You've been the only constant in my life the last few months. I could always rely on you to remind me of what I was taught, and even though that's been put to the test with everything that's happened, you've still been able to keep my head on straight and I'll never forget you for it."

Dan despised his hypocrisy, but he couldn't hurt his friend. Besides, until the last few days, everything he said had been true. "Someday I might do something that will make you wonder about me and whether it was a mistake thinking of me as your friend. But if that ever happens, I want you to know that whatever I do, I'll do because I firmly believe it's the right thing and that there was no better option."

Wilson looked deeply into his friend's eyes and sensed that in a very short time he would never see him again, and that he would indeed question whatever it was that would separate them. He felt he should say something, but he knew somehow it wouldn't change anything.

"There is absolutely nothing I've done that you wouldn't agree with, Al, and I hope I'll be able to say that years from now. But if you ever doubt me, just remind yourself that I am human and that you had a big part to play in everything that was right about me."

Wilson understood. "Thanks for that, Dan. I promise not to forget."

They finished their coffee, paid the bill and left. As they climbed the stairs to the second floor of the Thirty-fourth Street Precinct House, Wilson couldn't help but feel that it was the last time they would do it together.

Marilyn's voice on the tape sounded tired but hopeful. "I'd love to have dinner tonight. As soon as I'm sure what time I can get out of here, I'll call you."

Dan wondered what she might be thinking, reminding himself that he had to prepare something to say that would let her down easily. His only alternative was to write to her after he had left. Even considering it seemed cowardly, but not without merit. He decided to do both without disclosing his ultimate decision over dinner.

He checked his watch before calling Barracci and asking again to use the phone in the pier office. Still angry over yesterday's call, the Don told him he could do whatever he wanted.

"Can I still rely on your support if I need it?"

"What the hell do you need me for?" he replied angrily. "You got your goddamn cops. Get them to help."

"I apologize for yesterday," Dan said, knowing he could well need Barracci's influence before this was over. "You couldn't know the problems you were creating for people who are trying to help just as hard as you, but in a different way. Maybe it's my fault for not having told you more, letting you know everything that was going on behind the scenes. I'm sorry, Uncle."

"Yeah, alright," Barracci finally relented. "Call me if anything goes wrong. Right now, I gotta' run."

Ominously dark clouds were rolling in from Jersey as Dan turned the Jeep onto Thirty-fifth Street heading east. Summer was late coming, not that he minded. He could do without the hot and humid days that suffocated the city, but he was tiring of the rain. The newscasts had promised more of it, particularly today when heavy showers were expected. As he crossed the Brooklyn Bridge and glanced in the rearview mirror, he could see a blackened sky behind him, one he would shortly have to revisit.

Barracci's offices on the pier were vacant except for a busty, well-dressed redhead and a truckdriver on the make. When Dan walked in the secretary's eyes flashed a welcome.

"Good morning, Detective," she cooed.

Her name escaped him. "Hi, nice to see you again. Did Mr. Barracci call to let you know I was coming?"

"No, but that's okay. Handsome visitors are always welcome."

Dan smiled back. "I have some calls to make and he told me to use his office. I won't be offended if you call and check."

"I trust you," she flirted, further ignoring the driver still perched on her desk.

The lady made no attempt to conceal her interest or purpose. Dan wondered how often and in how many ways the Don had had her.

His opportunity lost, the disappointed driver shuffled off leaving Dan alone with the redhead. Actually, she wasn't bad looking…late thirties, a bit hippy but well-stacked, pretty face and gorgeous hair. She saw Dan taking it all in.

"See something you like?"

"Any other time but now," he said, biting his lower lip. He winked and headed for Barracci's private office, permitting the encouraged redhead time to consider another approach.

His watch read ten fifty-five. Close enough. He dialed Alex Norville's number. A nurse answered and forwarded the call.

"Dr. Norville here."

Dan recognized the voice, and following it, the faint sound of a click. Someone had picked up an extension.

"Do you have all the money?" he asked gruffly, trying to imitate Vito Scarola's voice.

"Yes."

"Wire it to Account Number 22-60971-44, Bank of Geneva, 5709." He repeated it. "You have fifteen minutes and it should only take ten. I'll call you back at 11:15." He hung up.

There was a knock on the door. It could only be the anonymous redhead. He told her to come in.

She looked taller and not as heavy as when she was seated. She had seen better years, but still had more than enough to turn men's heads, even younger ones like Dan Costa's. She sensed his curiosity.

"Coffee, tea, me?" she teased.

"Like I said, bad timing."

"You don't seem to be doing anything right now," she said just above a whisper as she came around the desk.

His heart picked up a beat.

"It gets terribly lonely here," she said, lowering her voice.

He could smell her perfume, a nice heady choice. He wished he could remember her name.

Now inches away, she slowly raised the bottom of her dress, a light cotton pastel, well suited to the weather and the room's rising temperature. He didn't say stop, so she didn't. He followed the rising hemline past soft, creamy thighs to the tiny pink patch of an overmatched G-string. He wondered if she dressed like this all the time. She tucked her thumbs within each side of the panties and began a slow, sensuous strip when the phone rang.

"I don't believe it," she cried, reaching across the desk to answer it. He ran his hand across her ass, concluding that it would have been infinitely enjoyable.

"It's Mr. Barracci," she said with a pained expression, handing him the phone, exchanging it for a gentle squeeze of his privates and a parting sigh of disappointment.

"Everything okay?" the Don asked.

"Everything's fine," Dan replied, swallowing hard as the redhead reached the door, looked over her shoulder and raised her dress a final time, revealing a perfectly shaped, if slightly oversized, derriere. He cleared his throat.

"You sure you're okay? Rachel hittin' on you?" he asked suspiciously.

"Hitting on me? Of course not. I'm just getting ready to call Switzerland."

"Alright. Call me when it's all over and tell that bitch to keep her clothes on."

The Bank of Geneva confirmed the transfer at 11:12 AM, Brooklyn time. The transaction couldn't be rescinded unless Dan Costa gave written authorization. Alex Norville and Bruce Steinberg had each coughed up five million dollars for tapes they would never receive; tapes that would put them, Richard Musto, David Richards, and possibly Rinaldi and Tataro, in prison for the rest of their lives. He wanted to celebrate, but that would have desecrated the memory of those whose lives had paid for the victory. He began to think about them...Joe Teller, Clarence Worthington, Donna, her father...until he remembered the call he had to make before returning to Manhattan.

"Norville here."

"You did good, shithead. The original and copies of the tapes will be delivered to your office within forty-eight hours by messenger service."

"How do I know you won't screw us?"

"You don't, but I have what I want, so there's no point in my hanging around." *Just long enough to stick it to you, asshole,* he thought, as he cradled the phone.

Dan Costa leaned back in Massimo Barracci's overstuffed chair and stared at the ceiling as his mind raced through the last six months, past the call from Al Wilson, his father's funeral, Marilyn Kyme and Donna Kempler. He had paid a terrible price, but one more job remained before he could put it all behind him and start over someplace else. He allowed himself to think about the freedom the money would bring and all the good he could do for people who had no reason to suspect that there was someone out there who really cared. As he walked towards the door, he sensed a renewed energy, nothing to replace the sobering thoughts he had, or the realization that Donna was just a memory…they would always be there…but a feeling of hope, of anticipation, that would at least replace his depression. His life could never be what he had hoped, but he could still do some good and that might be enough to buy him some happiness. He took a couple of deep breaths, telling himself, *Today is the first day of the rest of your life. Don't fuck it up.*

Rachel the Redhead looked up from her desk as he opened the door.

"All finished?" she asked, smiling.

"Nope. Just gettin' started. Now where were we when we were so rudely interrupted?"

## CHAPTER 25

An hour later Dan Costa ran through a summer rainstorm to his Jeep. Soaked and sweating, he shifted uneasily in the seat, debating about using the heater to dry off. He wiped the side window and looked over to see Rachel standing in the doorway, waving. She had given him her number and he had promised to call, which he fully intended to do, though he knew they would never see each other again. His plans included neither Rachel nor New York, but he smiled and waved as he drove past, grateful for her talents and willingness to share them.

He called St. Anthony's Convent to reassure Elena that within days he would take her and the children someplace out West. She hadn't seemed overjoyed with the prospect of returning to the reservation, though the only family she had still lived there. Wherever she chose, he would see to it that she would be safe and well taken care of, thanks to the donations from Drs. Steinberg and Norville.

The next call was to Joe DeLorenzo. His friend sounded tired and disheartened.

"Nothin' new, Dan. Neither the Turners nor their kid will talk without Muhammed's approval and he refuses to agree to any more interrogations unless we come up with new evidence. The D.A. is considering a plea bargain for second degree manslaughter."

"Both kids will be out in two years, three at the most," Dan guessed, probably accurately.

"Yeah, I agree, but the D.A. is worried that they could get off altogether, particularly if they get a minority jury that doesn't know the kind of person your dad was. They'll accept the sexual assault shit as gospel and let them off on self-defense when Muhammed turns the race screw."

"Then why would Muhammed even consider a plea bargain?"

"That's a good question," Joe D. admitted. "Avent heard that Missus Turner doesn't want a trial, something to do with her son taking an oath and with dragging your father's name through the mud. On the other hand, all of us here believe the Turners knew their son was involved right from the start and they've been protecting him, so we're not expecting any favors either."

Dan could imagine the conflicting pressures that were squeezing Mattie Turner, but it did little to soften his anger or dissuade his purpose.

"Her son's a killer, or at least a witness who won't come forward. If he won't tell the truth and if she won't make him, then neither of them deserves my sympathy. I gave up caring what happens to them the day they let that goddamn racist lie about my father. To hell with them."

"I know how you feel, buddy, and I'm sorry I've let you down, but I can't find a way short of the Turner kid's testimony to refute their story. Unless he comes forward, the D.A.'s offer just might be our best bet."

"It's may be, Joe, but it's not what I want."

"And I don't blame you. I'm not sure I could have held back as long as you have if it had happened to my father."

Neither spoke for a few seconds, each recognizing that justice for Frank Costa wasn't going to be served by due process. A frustrated Joe D switched subjects. "By the way, a couple weeks back, didn't you ask me about a wise guy named Rinaldi? He had something to do with that scientist's case?"

"What about him?"

"Well, they just found a guy named Carlo Rinaldi floating in the East River with a .38 size hole in the back of his head. Same guy?"

"Yeah, same guy," Dan replied, wondering what Rinaldi had said or done to have warranted the hit. He didn't think anyone had seen him enter or leave Rinaldi's house. How could they have suspected that Carlo was considering a plea bargain?

"Any idea how long he's been dead?"

"According to the news report he was shot within the past twenty-four hours."

"Last week that bit of news would have pissed me off. Now it doesn't matter. Just one less piece of shit to worry about."

An accident on 34th Street forced him a few blocks uptown so he decided to call the office instead of driving there. It was a little past one. Rasheed was still in the field, Al Wilson hadn't returned from lunch and none of his messages were urgent, so he decided to go to the apartment and begin packing the few things he would take West, write a few checks and figure out how and where to transfer some of the money for easy access. He had already devised a scheme to move the bulk of the money under fictitious names from Geneva to a series of international banks, just in case all the facts came out, including his involvement in the extortion of money from Steinberg and Norville.

It was raining even harder, adding to the conditions that routinely brought midtown traffic to a crawl. He found himself drawn to the news of Rinaldi's death and the fortuitous murders of Berger, Worthington and Donna, all seemingly a day or two removed from major roles in exposing everything about the Teller case. If it weren't for the tapes, each of those murders would have provided a timely relief for the conspirators. But there was something else about them that nagged him, though he couldn't quite put his finger on it. As the rain increased he was forced to pay attention to his driving, promising himself to rethink the coincidental timings of the murders when he got home.

With his wipers at full speed he finally pulled in front of his westside apartment just before two. Cars were parked illegally on both sides so he was grateful for the hydrant at the bottom of his stoop and the "Police on Duty" placard he stuck in the windshield.

Rain danced off the steps as he took them two at a time. Something reminded him to lock the car, and as he turned at the top and pointed the remote he saw the two men, their arms raised, squinting in the rain, guns in hand. Instinctively, he dove to his right while reaching inside his jacket for his thirty-eight. He heard bullets crack above him and burrow into the brown fieldstone before one found its mark, driving into his left side, cracking ribs, searing flesh. He screamed, less in pain than fury, and rolled back to the left for a clear shot at the large target closest to him. With both hands steadying the revolver, he squeezed off three shots before he felt something slam deep into his right shoulder, sending a shock down his arm, loosening his hold on the .38. He closed his left hand tightly on the grip and rolled again further to the left as rain filled his eyes, blurring everything before him. Another hit, more burning, this time on the side of his leg. Raindrops bounced before his eyes, shielding a second shooter. Only a bright red flash to his right front hinted at the source of the pain that raked his leg a second time. Steadying the gun in his left hand he fired three times, praying as he did that the bullets would find their mark. Twice more he squeezed the trigger before realizing the chambers were empty.

For long seconds he lay on his stomach expecting the worst, watching small rivulets of red cascade slowly down the brownstone steps, spilling over the last onto a great, motionless heap on the sidewalk. He was wondering what or who it was when another red flame leaped towards him and he felt two sharp objects scrape his face, one lodging somewhere beneath his eye. He closed his eyes, trying to clear them, hoping to make sense out of what was happening when he saw the black shoes sliding, inch-by-inch, through the puddles. He watched as they struggled slowly up each step, stopping frequently, summoning strength to continue, until they stopped inches before him. Dan lifted his head, straining to bring the face that went with the shoes into focus, but the rain blinded him.

"So long, hotshot," were the last words he heard before a loud noise, something like gunfire, exploded around him.

A door behind him slowly opened and shadowy figures moved before him…running, motioning. And the rain kept falling as the large black, or was it dark blue, sedan pulled away.

Al Wilson got the call at two-thirty and raced to the hospital, arriving a few minutes before Father Boland and some detectives from the Fifty-eight Street Precinct. They told Wilson that both shooters were at the morgue.

"He's been shot four times, once each in the side and shoulder, twice in the leg," the emergency resident explained. "Vital organs seem to be intact, but we won't know for certain until the operations are completed." Glancing at his watch, he added, "Should be starting now. I don't think we should assume a favorable prognosis. We'll do our best, but he lost too much blood for us to be optimistic."

He glanced at the priest. "Prayers are certainly in order, Father. They may accomplish more than anything we can do."

He couldn't hear their voices, but Dan could see the doctors and nurses in their green scrubs…six, maybe eight of them…some standing around a table, others carrying cloths and arranging instruments. They all seemed intensely occupied. He wondered why they had left him alone in such a curious place, a room above another. And what or who was attracting their attention? The whole room seemed to rotate as he tried to move closer, positioning him directly above the doctors and the mysterious object on which they were working. Everyone had seemed blurred in the beginning, but they were slowly coming into focus along with the details of the room. There were lights and machines, trays and cabinets, and in the center of it all, a long table around which the doctors were huddled, working furiously. As he became more alert he realized he was looking at an operating room, though he wondered who had brought him there and why.

He seemed to be directly above the table, and when one of the doctors moved, Dan caught a glimpse of a body, then a face. It was a muscular young man, one who looked remarkably like him. Then he realized that it was him and that he was floating, suspended above it all, looking down on himself and on the doctors working on his nude, blood-soaked body. Two looked at a clock on the wall and then at each other before returning to their labors.

Confused at first, Dan convinced himself he was dreaming, but why this dream, why in this place? As he tried to make sense of it all he began moving upwards from the room, slowly at first, but increasingly faster until he could no longer see the faces of the doctors or the body he was certain was his own.

Away from it all there was a comforting light, brilliantly white, yet somehow softly warm and inviting. He seemed more drawn to it by some distant energy than by choice. Only now did he begin to realize that he had left his body, that he had observed the doctors vainly trying to revive it. Now he was separated from it, ascending by an unknown force to some unfamiliar place, though strangely, he was neither sad nor frightened. It was as if he had always known it would be like this.

As the light became brighter and his upward passage slowed to a stop, he looked out across a great meadow, or what seemed like a meadow, even though there were no greens or yellows, just brilliant tones of blue and white, gently rolling hills and a sparkling stream that rippled with sunlight. Across it he could see shining figures, brighter even than the light, though so distant he could not make them out. As he moved towards them they did the same until they were at the water's edge. Then he could see that they were Eileen, Donna and his parents. They smiled and he knew they were happy. But how could they be? He had just died and he wasn't yet with them. He tried to speak but couldn't. The stream seemed shallow and the thought occurred to him to cross it, but his father raised his hand.

"*It isn't your time,*" he seemed to say. "*You still have much to do and more to learn. You will know when it is time, but not now.*"

They drifted from him until they blended into and became one with the light. Though he tried to follow he could not, for a force as strong as the one that brought him there began to draw him back, back to the light away from the meadow.

He sensed their love and he knew they would always be with him, waiting, until he could join them. But other thoughts filled him as well...knowledge and wisdom he had not known and a sense of inner peace he had never felt. Their purpose became clear, without doubt or question, and a great confidence overcame him. This time all would be right.

# CHAPTER 26

The pain below his left eye was the first he felt, followed soon by those in his shoulder, side and leg. For the briefest of seconds he wondered where he was. Then it all came to him, the shootings, the ambulance, and most clearly, what he would come to know as his near-death experience. He remembered seeing the meadow and stream and the four people that meant everything to him and he could still feel the warm glow of the light that had guided him. He knew that he had experienced something else, something that made him feel confident about himself and his future. He struggled to remember, and though it all seemed familiar, he couldn't recall what it was. In the deep recesses of his mind and heart there remained a conviction that it would all come back to him when the time was right

Curtains barred the light, though he could feel someone in the room, someone sitting in the chair to his left. He turned to see who it was but bandages sealed his sight. As he tried to turn further his shoulder screamed with pain, so he rolled his head back on the pillow, content to lie in quiet peace.

He reflected on all that had happened, wondering how much time had passed, but mostly he thought of his father's words and their meaning. He accepted that he had much work to do, but that he had much to learn intrigued him. Was he to learn that he really was not the good person he had always tried to be? Was he to learn more about life, what made people the way they were, what caused them to do what they did, particularly to each other? Or was he to learn what the universe and the spirit were all about, as a Jesuit teacher once advised him to contemplate, for the answers he had promised, would bring wisdom and then the path to eternal love.

Days, even hours ago, such thoughts would have seemed ludicrous. Now he welcomed the solitude to dwell on them. A smile crossed his lips as he envisioned his future, one afforded the time and circumstance to study and learn, to acquire the wisdom which he would use to the advantage of others. How and where would be made known to him. For now he knew only that it would begin far from New York, away from the life he had known, the life that had brought him anger and regret, hatred at worst, indifference at best. Surely his father would not object, for he had said he must learn and he could learn nothing more here.

The door opened and a solitary figure entered, holding in each hand a large vase of flowers. Their scent filled the room.

"Hi, how are you today?" he asked softly.

Startled, a woman's voice responded, "Well, look who finally woke up."

Light poured into the room as his visitor opened the curtains. He turned towards them until his shoulder hurt, enough to see a shapely, blond nurse walking towards him, a happy smile filling her face. Then another figure appeared, the one he sensed had been sitting to his left.

"Elena," he said, surprised to see her.

"Hello, Daniel," she answered, tears emerging from her dark, sad eyes.

"I thought you'd be happy to see me," he joked.

"I am," she said, embarrassed. "Two days ago none of us ever thought we would see you open your eyes again."

"Yeah, I know," he said earnestly.

She looked puzzled. "Father Boland said your heart had stopped beating, that you had died, but that four bullets weren't enough to keep you down."

He smiled. "Oh, they kept me down alright. You said two days?"

She nodded. "How do you feel?"

The question drew the nurse's attention as she reached past Elena, pressing buttons, checking monitors.

"Except for what I guess are four bullet wounds, not that bad. My face hurts a little though, under the left eye," he complained, directing the comment to the nurse.

"We had to dig some stones out. I can't tell you how they got there or what they looked like. One of the operating room nurses told me. That's why your eye is bandaged. There was some hemorrhaging and a lot of swelling, but your sight is fine and the scars won't be too bad. They'll be kind of sexy, if you don't mind my saying so."

Dan smiled. "I don't mind."

The nurse went about her duties, taking Dan's pulse and checking the monitors.

A sixty-something doctor with wavy gray hair and Paul Newman eyes entered. His smile seemed genuine. "Well, Sergeant, it certainly is nice to see you awake and alert. You are alert, I assume."

"Enough to know that it's good to be alive."

Doctor Adams, as Dan learned from his i.d. badge, grinned. "For a man who was seconds from being pronounced dead, that's surprisingly good progress in two days. How do you feel?" he asked, as he began repeating the blond nurse's routine.

"Like a range target."

"Understandable."

"One-ten over sixty-eight," the nurse announced.

"More good news," Dr. Adams replied.

Elena Guttierez had stepped back, her frail figure dwarfed by the six-foot doctor and shapely nurse. She looked lonely, out-of-place. Dan opened his left hand and reached as far as his aching shoulder would allow.

"Come here and hold my hand," he told her. "These people scare the hell out of me."

Dr. Adams smiled knowingly.

Elena stepped happily forward and took his hand, barely wrapping both of hers around it.

"If you'll pardon the pun," the doctor said, "it looks like you're in good hands. It's almost eight and I'm hungry, so I'm going to have some breakfast, order some liquids for you and bring something back for your friend. Then I'll fill you in on everything we did to you and what your future looks like, providing of course you don't stand in the way of any bullets again."

"Thanks, Doc, and thanks for thinking about Elena. She could probably use some food."

"Yes, and some sleep," he said, scolding her with a wag of the finger as he left with the nurse.

"What did he mean by that? You been here long?"

"The sisters are taking care of the children. I wanted to be here when you woke up. I knew you would. I prayed to Our Lady."

"Of Guadalupe?"

She nodded. "She always takes care of people who take care of others."

Dan wanted to say something appropriate, about how he appreciated her vigil, her prayers and how she need never worry again, but he felt drowsy and he knew sleep would help his strength return.

"Make sure you eat whatever they bring you. I'm going to try and sleep a little," he said, before closing his eyes and drifting off.

Later that morning Father Boland arrived carrying Elena's son. Little Antonio stared at Dan, finally recognizing him despite the bandages covering a portion of his face and the tubes protruding from each arm.

"Elena, I'd like to talk to Dan. Would you mind taking Antonio for a walk before we leave? It'll only be a few minutes."

She took Dan's hand again. "I'll come back as often as they let me," she promised, "but if I'm not here, I will still be praying for you."

"Good, but don't worry about coming here. I'd rather have you take care of your children. In a few days I'll be well enough to travel and we'll head out west."

When the door closed the priest stood beside the bed, looking down at his friend's son, uncertain of how to begin, but aware of what had to be said.

"Carmine Pecora was one of the two men killed in front of your apartment. The other was a two-bit hit man named Albert Tataro. Until they talked to witnesses and dug two bullets from Pecora's gun out of you, the police suspected that the mob had hit both you and Pecora. Witnesses said a late model black Cadillac pulled up about the time Pecora was planning to finish you off. Someone rolled down the window and blew the back of Pecora's head off with a .44 magnum. Apparently no one bothered to get a look at the license plate, but the police think the Barracci family is involved. They figure Tataro and Pecora are connected to Donna Kempler's murder and others you were investigating and that they came after you because you were getting too close. But they also think you've been concealing something and they brought Massimo and some of his people in for questioning."

"Why them? Tataro isn't part of the Barracci family and Pecora certainly wasn't on his payroll. If anything, Massimo would have burned them himself."

"You and I know that, but the police aren't so close to the situation."

"That's nuts. Al Wilson will straighten it out."

"You shouldn't expect too much from him. Neither the attempt on you nor the people who did it are in his precinct. I only told you all this because Al and I spoke and he was worried that if you recovered, you'd have to answer a lot of questions and you might not be in the mood to cooperate. So do all of us a favor and control your temper. If you did nothing wrong, there's no reason not to cooperate."

"Thanks, Father. I'll keep it in mind."

"I'll take Elena back with me now. She's been here since just after they brought you in. She must be exhausted."

Dan nodded. "Don't worry about her, Father. She's in good hands. Will be from here on."

"She may think it's more than friendship."

"I know, but I can handle it without her getting hurt. If I can help it, nothing will ever hurt her again."

"You will keep bearing people's burdens, won't you?" the priest sighed, shaking his head as he opened the door to leave. "You're a lot more like your father than you think."

Dan was about to stop him, to tell him about his near-death experience, when he heard a familiar voice.

It was Joe DeLorenzo, and peering around him, Calvin Washington. The pretty blond nurse smiled as she followed them into the room and began adjusting more dials, pushing more buttons.

"A sick man shouldn't have to look at such ugly kissers," Dan joked.

"Nice to see you, too. How you feelin'?" Joe D asked.

"I'm two days removed from four bullets tearing into me. Got any other stupid questions?"

"Yeah. Feel like goin' out tonight?"

"We sure are glad to see that you've come out of it," Calvin said warmly. "A lot of your dad's friends have been praying long and hard."

"Mattie Turner, too?" Dan asked sarcastically.

Washington glanced at his partner. "Called me twice since it happened."

"Guilty conscience," Dan scoffed.

"We weren't going to say anything, but..." Joe D hesitated.

"Tell him," Calvin said. "The hell with procedure."

Dan looked from one to the other. "Tell me what?"

"On the way over we got a call. The Turners want to meet with me and Calvin in their apartment."

"They say why?"

"No, just that Calvin and me are to come alone; no other cops, no D.A., no press."

"Sounds like they've talked something important out," Washington suggested.

"I hope so," Dan said softly.

"We'd better be going if we're going to get there by one," Joe said, shaking his friend's hand.

Calvin Washington did the same.

"I owe you both an apology," Costa said as they began to leave. "I said some things I never meant and I'm sorry as hell for them. You're two decent guys. Lousy cops," he joked, " but damn good guys."

He passed a few minutes thinking of all the hurtful things he had said to his friends, promising himself he would never let his emotions get the best of him again. Logic told him it would be a difficult promise to keep, but one worth the effort. He was trying to think about everything he would do to change his life when he saw the door slowly open and Camille Wilson's face slowly emerge from behind it.

"Look who's awake and kicking," she proclaimed happily.

Al Wilson followed, his smile widening as he approached the bed. "Damn, boy, you don't look that bad. A helluva lot better than last night, that's for sure."

"You here last night?"

"For a bit."

"More than a bit," Camille reminded him. "He came rolling home at midnight, two nights in a row. I wonder if he'll worry as much about me."

"Thanks, Al," was all Dan could find to say.

"Hell, there were all kinds of people here. That little Guttierez girl wouldn't ever leave. Slept right there in that chair, so damned tired she didn't know guys were in and out all night... Kennedy and his crew, Zimmerman, Rasheed! The boy was here round the clock that first day, but I made him leave with me last night. Pissed him off, I think. He's on his way over now. Oh, yeah, and Marilyn, too. I understand she stayed until two or three each morning." With a look that suggested disapproval, or at least concern, he added, "Barracci and two of the biggest, meanest lookin' guys I've ever seen were here a coupla' times, but they behaved themselves."

Dan smiled. "They're not as bad as you think, Al."

He struggled for the right words. Since his father's murder he had begun to distance himself from everyone on the force, from Al Wilson on down to the beat cops, guys whom he had befriended and had always taken the time to talk to. He had lied to Rasheed to cover his actions and avoided his duty by shoving work unfairly onto him. Yet no one had complained. Unlike what he had done to Joe D, Calvin and others, including his best friend, they had understood.

"Al, I want you to know that I'm very sorry for how I acted over the past few months. I have no excuses. My dad's murder, Donna's, and everything else were all things I should have handled without taking it out on everyone around me, particularly on you. Please accept my apology, because I can't take back the things I said and did."

"No need to apologize. If I needed to hear that I'd be no friend. Besides, even on your worst day you're a better person than most."

They talked a while longer, preparing to leave when Doctor Adams returned, but promising to visit again tomorrow.

"Please don't' make the trip, Camille, I'll be fine. Just give me a call. We can have a nice long talk."

"Not on your life. I make Al buy me dinner when I come into the city. It's the only chance we get to go out without the kids. But I'll call you anyway," she promised as they left.

"Nice people," Adams said.

"The nicest."

After checking each wound, his blood pressure and some charts at the foot of the bed Adams declared him on a tentative road to recovery. "You won't be running any marathons for a while, but your body's recovering remarkably well from all the trauma and that's a very encouraging sign. In a week or two you'll be out of here and probably back to duty in a month, though you may have to ride a desk for awhile"

"I won't be going back, Doc. I'm leaving, going out west, not sure exactly where just yet."

"Really? From what I've heard you'll be sorely missed. Sure you don't want more time to think about it?"

"It has nothing to do with this. It's been a long time coming. I just need to start over someplace else."

Adams nodded. There was something very likeable about him, even comforting. Dan felt at ease talking to him.

"Doctor, have you ever had a patient tell you they had seen their own operation from somewhere above the room?"

"A couple." The question kindled Adams' curiosity. "Did you have a near-death experience?"

Dan nodded. "I saw my family as clearly as I see you. They were bathed in white light but I'm sure it was them. And my dad communicated. I'm sure I understood what he wanted me to know and a lot of other information that I've kind of forgotten, but I have this feeling that I'll remember it when I have to."

Adams listened, smiling as though he understood.

"You do believe me, don't you?"

"I've listened to and studied too many similar experiences to dismiss them as products of our imagination. What I don't know is if you actually communicated knowingly with your father or if your subconscious is convincing you that you did. We store a lifetime of memories in our subconscious, even those of previous lifetimes, if we're to believe some spiritualists. What you think was a near-death experience could also be the recall of a lifetime or more of memories, of the things and people closest to your heart and therefore to your mind and memory."

Dan shook his head. "I don't think this was my memory or imagination. I saw and communicated with my dad and I saw my mother, my wife and girlfriend. I'm sure of it."

"Then follow your heart and believe in whatever wisdom they impart. I'm sure they've learned far more than we can possibly know down here."

Later that day Rasheed stopped in and they had a long talk, with Dan recounting his early years on the force, the commitment he had to making the streets safe, the promises he made to himself to be the best cop in the city.

He spoke of how his enthusiasm eroded, as much because of his own loss of commitment as any of a score of outside influences.

"There's only one reason this city needs you," he said. "All kinds of bad guys are out there. It's your job to nail their asses and you can't ever let them get you down. Just take it for granted that every hour of every day you're going to face another one, and you'll just go about your job of finding them and putting them away. Don't ever expect it to get any better because it never will. And if you don't like it, get out and let someone who can handle it do the job."

Early in the evening Marilyn Kyme came. She sat by the bed and held his hand, though she knew there wasn't enough left to hold him, not there in the city he could no longer accept and she could never leave. But they cherished the memories of their love, reliving the nights they shared, embracing the hours they had stolen from the city that would keep them apart, that wouldn't allow them to live their dreams.

"When will you leave?" she finally asked.

"As soon as they let me out of here…a week maybe. There's only one thing left to do."

"Please don't, Dan. Let it go. Let Al and Joe take care of it. You have so much to share. Don't throw your life away."

He put his fingers to her lips.

"It's nothing like that," he lied.

She wanted to believe him, but when she pressed the issue Dan told her he was tired and that he needed to sleep.

"You're worrying about nothing," he said as she got up to leave. "Put it out of your mind."

She kissed him gently on the lips. "I'll always love you, Dan. Someday I'll marry and have another man's child and I'll be a good wife and a very good mother, but I'll think of you often, because you're the man I wanted to share my life with."

As she kissed him a final time he saw her tears and he wished it could have been different for both of them.

Shortly after she left, Massimo Barracci walked in, dutifully followed by Muzzi, Scarola and Nicholas Santucci.

"Hey, look at this. It's a freakin' miracle. I oughta' slap ya' for gettin' us all worried," the Don bellowed as he leaned over and kissed Dan on both cheeks.

Dan could only shake his head lightly and smile. "I have a feeling I owe my life to somebody in this room, and it's a favor I'm never going to be able to repay, so I'll just say that I'll never forget any of you and that I'm very, very grateful that one of you was there when I needed you most."

He couldn't be certain but he thought both Muzzi and Scarola glanced at Santucci for the briefest second.

"Yeah, well, if you want to be grateful to somebody you'd have to thank Musto, the lawyer. He's the one that told us about Pecora bein' on the payroll and that the hit was out on you. That fat slob Pecora's the one that fingered them all. He kept on top of who you were talkin' to. That's how they knew who to take out."

"I can't believe Musto gave everything up. Why did he do it?"

"You don't wanna' know, kid, believe me."

This time it was Santucci's eyes that seemed to shift ever so slightly. But Dan didn't have to see that to know the Don had given an order, and like so many times in the past, it had been dutifully carried out by the two ruthless but efficient warriors that stood silently at the side of his bed. Dan nodded his appreciation, but neither Muzzi nor Vito Scarola gave any indication they deserved it.

Weeks would pass before James Musto's battered remains would be found in a shallow grave near Sheepshead Bay. By then he would be implicated in a conspiracy involving multiple murders, a good enough reason for the cops to round-file an investigation into his death.

# EPILOGUE

"Dan, wake up. It's Joe."

His eyes burned as he forced them open.

"What time is it?"

"A little after midnight. Are you awake?"

"No, I'm talkin' in my sleep. Jeez, Joe, it's late. What are you doin' here?"

"I wanted to tell you in person. The Turners gave everything up, including their lawyer. Everything their kid had said was Muhammed's idea…you know, about your dad being a pervert."

"Did Booker kill Dad?"

"Yeah. The Turner kid was there, in the bedroom, when it happened. They came in through the fire escape. Dad walked in on them and Booker hit him. That shit, Muhammed, he made everything up, but Missus Turner couldn't live with it. Hearing about you getting shot was the last straw. Her kid didn't argue. I think it kind of occurred to the whole family to come forward. The D.A. is going to go as light as possible on him, but he's really going after Booker and Muhammed. At least that's what he's saying to the press. Want to see if it's on TV?"

"No. No, Joe, it's over for me, but I do need a small favor."

The next morning, as Costa had asked, Joe DeLorenzo called Massimo Barracci and repeated exactly what he had been told. The Don said he understood.

Before supper Rasheed and Al Wilson stopped in to see how he was getting along.

"I'm fine, stop worrying about me. I'll be outa' here in a week or two, guaranteed."

"That's what the doctors tell me. I thought maybe we could talk about your future," Wilson said.

"My mind is made up, Al, has been for awhile. It's time for me to move on. It's not easy for me to leave my friends behind, and knowing how much work you've got makes it that much tougher, but my future is someplace else."

"You may want to reconsider when you hear that I'm getting my Captain's bars."

"You're kidding. No shit? Man, that's great, Al, not that you haven't deserved it for a while. I couldn't be happier for you and Camille."

"And one more thing. I think we'll all be calling you Lieutenant by year's end. Whether it's recognition of just how damn good a detective you are, or how you've handled your dad's murder or what you just went through...I don't know...but City Hall seems hell bent on getting you promoted. There's a test next month that they're clearing the way for you to take. The smart money says you'll get promoted if you sign your name properly."

Dan thanked his friend but repeated his decision to move on. "I really believe I'm supposed to be someplace else, to take on a new phase of my life...what, I don't know. I guess I'll recognize it when I see it."

Wilson shrugged. "I kinda' thought you'd say something like that. I just wanted to be sure."

"You gonna' make some changes?"

"Yeah, don't really have a choice, not with half the city's detectives working with one federal task force or other. I thought I'd pair up Rasheed with Zimmerman."

"Not a bad idea. They're both damn good cops. They'll make a good team."

Two weeks passed during which Dan Costa saw his friends frequently, though each time they had less to say and less to laugh and feel good about. They all knew he would leave soon and that they would probably never see him again.

Friday, September 1, began as a cool, brisk, overcast morning, the kind that reminds us another summer has passed and colder days are coming. The wounds in his leg still hurt, but he would let Elena drive once they were out of the city, and everything would be fine when he could stretch out, lie back and enjoy the ride.

It was a little before seven when Dan Costa recovered a video tape he had secured behind the bottom drawer of his desk, placed it in a small brown-paper wrapped box and delivered it to the desk sergeant at the Thirty-fourth Street Precinct House. "See that Lieutenant Wilson gets this when he comes in."

NBC had received a copy a day earlier, about the same time the AMA had gotten theirs. But it was the one that soon-to be-Captain Albert Wilson would shortly open that would seal the convictions of two of New York's more noted physicians and a not-so-famous FDA Inspector.

As he drove towards Brooklyn and St. Anthony's Convent, Dan Costa noticed a tiny break in the clouds. It didn't last long, just a few seconds, but long enough for the sun to shine through, like a beacon to light his way. He said a prayer. He asked for wisdom to recognize the truth and strength to do what was right. The rest he would handle himself.